STRIKE FROM THE SEA

Ainslie made to wipe the spray from the gyro compass and felt the bile rise in his throat. In the flashing lights his hand looked black, but he knew it was the dying seaman's blood.

'Steer one-three-zero!'

He heard Quinton call, 'I've got her, sir!'

Ainslie wiped his face with his wrist, seeing the land swinging across the bows and the way the guns pivoted on their mounting, still tracking their target.

Then he saw the patrol vessel properly for the first time, swinging away, her role changing from hunter to hunted as the surfaced submarine turned to meet her.

'Shift target! Patrol vessel at red one-five!'

Douglas Reeman

STRIKE FROM
THE SEA

ARROW BOOKS

Arrow Books Limited

62-65 Chandos Place, London WC2N 4NW

An imprint of Century Hutchinson Limited

London Melbourne Sydney Auckland
Johannesburg and agencies throughout
the world

First published by Hutchinson 1978
Arrow edition 1978
Reprinted 1979 (twice), 1980, 1982, 1983, 1984 and 1986

© Bolitho Maritime Productions Ltd 1978

Printed and bound in Great Britain by
Anchor Brendon Limited, Tiptree, Essex

ISBN 0 09 918780 9

To my friend Myron J. Smith Jr.
who gave me the idea

Contents

Away from It All

COMMANDER ROBERT AINSLIE sat very still in a cane-backed chair and surveyed the waiting-room without enthusiasm. It was painted white and almost completely bare but for a couple of chairs and a portrait of the King on the opposite wall. An on-looker, had there been one, would have imagined Ainslie to be listening, or crouching on the chair ready to leap up. In fact, he was trying to keep his spine away from the chair back, for despite the revolving fans above his head the room was stuffy and humid, and any sort of contact increased the discomfort and made his shirt cling to his skin like a damp rag.

He looked at the shuttered window through which the harsh sunlight sliced across the room with silver bars. It seemed incredible that people could breathe out there, let alone use so much energy.

Booted feet stamped lustily across some sort of square, and he heard a Royal Marine sergeant's voice from a great distance away, controlling the marching men, manoeuvring them like a ring-master at a circus.

'At the *halt*, on the *right*, f . . o . . r . . m *squad*!'

The sudden silence was almost worse.

Ainslie tried not to look at his watch, knowing it would only rouse his anger again. He could feel the weariness closing in on him and had to fight it back like something physical. Hold on a bit longer until he had 'settled in', as someone had remarked upon his arrival.

It was hard to compare this place with Britain, he thought. November 1941 and the London he had left four days back had been a far cry from the naval base on Singapore Island. Four days of flying in various aircraft, watching the changing scenery at each touch-down, meeting the mixed bunch of passengers on their way to join service units, to replace dead or wounded, to set up headquarters, and all the countless other missions of a nation at war.

As he had climbed stiffly from the aircraft on Singapore Island five hours ago he had sensed the difference immediately. Ainslie was thirty years old, and a professional naval officer to his fingertips. He had visited Singapore several times during his career and that made it all the more surprising, for apart from a lot more uniforms wandering about the airport, or thronging the streets through which he had been whisked in a staff car, nothing appeared to have altered.

He thought again of Britain, and London in particular. Nightly air raids, rationing, blackout, and the grim knowledge that only the English Channel stood between liberty and the might of the German Army. Every ally had fallen to the seemingly invincible Axis war machine, and London's streets were as full of those uniforms as Britain's and her Commonwealth's. Dutch and Danish, Norwegian and Free French, Belgian and Polish, Czechs and all the rest. They helped to remind everyone of the Germans' successes almost as much as the sad defiance of their old allies.

Only in the air above Britain and along the North African shores where the newly formed Eighth Army had somehow managed to hold the German advances had there been actual victories. The Battle of the Atlantic, which had mounted to an increasing ferocity with each bloody convoy, had long outpaced the margin of winning or losing. It had become a matter of survival. Daily the toll of ships lost to torpedo and bomb rose higher, and the Navy's demands for more and more men increased accordingly. Officers were given commands normally offered to men of greater experience and service, trained ratings were spread thinly over the growing mass of recruits and volunteers to share their skills as best they could.

Robert Ainslie had been a submariner for almost half of his service and had left his last command, the *Tigress*, just three months earlier after an unbroken commission in the embattled Mediterranean.

Three months with the underground world of intelligence in the Admiralty's bomb-proof bunkers or visiting the submarine base at Gosport where he had done his original underwater training. And now, after all that, and the arduous flight from England, Ainslie had been sitting in this waiting-room like a new boy at school.

He could tell from the way he had been greeted by the base

staff that they knew something of his work, if not his actual mission, which was supposed to be top secret – if anything could be kept secret when more than two people knew about it.

Ainslie had tried to think that they felt out of things here in Singapore. The island, like the Malayan peninsula to the north, was untouched by war, and apparently clung rigidly to an almost colonial existence.

But he was beginning to think differently. They actually resented him because he reminded them of that 'other war'. He touched his reefer jacket with his fingers, the small effort making the sweat trickle down his armpit. He was still wearing the blue uniform he had donned in London. It was to be hoped his tropical gear had arrived safely, he thought wearily. His fingers moved along the ribbons on the left breast. Distinguished Service Cross and Bar. He had got used to them, and at home decorations were commonplace. But out here he was different, or so it appeared. An odd man out.

A door opened and a small, wiry man in a very crumpled grey suit came in and sat down in the other chair.

Ainslie watched him, recalling their first meeting, and how his affection for the little man had grown. He looked like a badly paid schoolteacher, or a clerk from a City office. In fact, he was Commander Gregory Critchley of naval intelligence.

Critchley took out a cigarette and lit it unhurriedly. He glanced round for an ashtray and, finding none, threw the match on the brightly polished floor.

'Inhospitable bastards!' He smiled at Ainslie, dropping his tired lines like another skin. 'Not long now. I've spoken to someone.' He chuckled. 'I think we are about to be received.'

Ainslie stood up carefully and walked to the window. The marines were drilling again, and he remembered hearing there was to be a big parade in the city in a few weeks' time. A Christmas celebration apparently.

It made him suddenly angry. He thought of the crowded air-raid shelters in London, a pub with its windows blasted out, a double-decker bus on its side amongst the rubble. Tired, brave, often pathetic people. How long would they hold out if they knew about this sort of red tape? he wondered.

Critchley watched him through his cigarette smoke, reading his thoughts. He had come to like Ainslie very much. He even *looked* the part. Tall, with a clean-cut, youthful face, fair hair and bright blue eyes, he had an air of confidence about him which Critchley now knew to be deceptive. Despite the medals, the stories of Ainslie's considerable courage and ability, he knew him to be very critical of himself, and conscious of the men who from choice or compulsion were made to follow him.

Ainslie asked, 'Don't they *want* to win the bloody war? What's the matter with everyone?'

'Self-preservation, old son. They think they're doing their job merely by standing firm in this "invincible fortress", as they call it.'

Ainslie turned back to the window again. 'All the ships lost, all those men killed. You'd have thought they would have learned something, surely?'

Critchley stood up, his head cocked to the sound of footsteps. 'Keep your Scottish temper under its lid, Bob. They'll come round. I'll do the explaining, and you impress them with your splendid calm!' He dug him in the ribs. 'They are in our Navy, you know!'

Ainslie picked up his new cap with its bright peak of oak leaves. 'I was beginning to wonder!'

A poker-faced flag-lieutenant ushered them into a large office where the chief of staff was standing beside his desk waiting to greet them. Ainslie had the impression he had arranged himself for their entrance. He was a full captain, and his white uniform, like his desk, was as neat as a pin.

Critchley announced, 'This is Captain Armytage.' He glanced calmly at the senior officer. 'The commodore is away at Keppel Harbour, and the admiral's apparently up country on an inspection.'

Ainslie caught his tone, the merest hint of sarcasm.

But the chief of staff shook their hands and offered them chairs.

He said, 'Sorry to keep you waiting. You know how it is. Lot to do just now.'

Critchley asked mildly, 'The war, sir?'

'Well, yes. In a manner of speaking. There's the regatta coming off, too. All part and parcel of morale, what?'

He picked up a manilla folder and put it in the OUT tray. Then he said, 'All a bit of a mystery. Your mission, that is. The admiral takes the view that Whitehall is getting too much steam up when they ought to be putting their minds to better things.

Ainslie said, 'Does he?'

Critchley said quickly, 'I think Commander Ainslie could put you in the picture better than I, sir. He is, after all, a professional at this kind of thing.'

The captain's brows came together in a frown. 'I *know* why you're here. I'm not a fool.' He calmed himself with an effort and looked at Ainslie. 'Tell me about it then.'

Ainslie stared across the office, the neatness, the timeless order of things.

'At the start of the war, sir, we and France had the two finest navies in the world. When France fell, it was imperative that all her ships which failed to join our fleet and the Free French under de Gaulle, or refused to intern themselves in neutral ports, must be put out of action.'

Ainslie relived his own feelings as he spoke. It must have been a cruel decision for someone, he thought. The Royal Navy's heaviest units had been forced to fire on their old ally, to sink her ships in the protected bases at Oran and Dakar and other anchorages outside occupied France. Many fine vessels had been sunk or severely damaged, and a lot of men killed. Men who had fought beside the British against the common enemy had shared the same fate as many a German and Italian. It would be a long time before the bitterness and the hurt was forgotten, let alone forgiven.

Had those same ships fallen into enemy hands the war would be over right now. With supply routes cut, and her own forces crippled by lack of fuel and war materials, Britain's capital would have fared no better than Paris or Warsaw.

Ainslie heard himself say, 'I have spent all my recent years in submarines.'

Captain Armytage said crisply, 'I am aware of your record, Commander.' He fell silent as Ainslie's eyes levelled on him.

Ainslie said, 'The French Navy built a submarine well ahead of her time, the *Surcouf*, something along the lines of our old M-class, but far more sophisticated, and successful. I went aboard her once when she came to England. A giant, with two big turret guns like a cruiser, and her own aircraft for spotting. She was built around 1931, and for three years she was the biggest submarine in the world.'

He let his eyes rest on the chief of staff's face, feeling the man's sudden discomfort, sensing, too, Critchley's rapt attention.

'Then came the improved *Surcouf* boat, larger still, over four thousand tons submerged.' He waited, thinking of her, of all the planning and the hazy ideas which had suddenly cleared like a prismatic gunsight. 'The *Soufrière*.'

The captain shifted in his chair. 'Yes. Of course.'

Of course. Ainslie added quietly, 'Two eight-inch guns, extremely powerful and rapid firing, plus ten torpedo tubes, her own seaplane, and a range of twelve thousand miles. If she chose to cut loose, she could rip our ocean supply routes to bits, from the East Indies to the Cape of Good Hope. It would take a fleet, a fleet which we do not possess, to hunt her down.'

The room was very still and, apart from the gentle hum of fans and a far-off bark of commands, completely silent.

Then Critchley said, '*Soufrière* was in Madagascar when France fell, sir. Then when feelings went this way and that about the Free French versus Petain's Vichy impotence she slipped out and made for Indo-China, to their base at Saigon. We know she was there almost to the day when the Japs marched in and completed their occupation of the colony. It was said she was damaged, by the Japanese, by sabotage or accident, we don't know. Yet. But our instructions are to seize her, before she falls into the enemy's hands, or her own company decide to hand her over in exchange for some kind of reward. Patriotism is not just a British thing. The French Navy has its brand of honour, too.'

Captain Armytage glanced at the clock. 'I still don't see the need. We could have her bombed if she tried to act against us.' He discarded his own suggestion and added, 'If we could find her in time, that is.'

Critchley took out a fresh cigarette and looked at it. '*Soufrière* must be taken, sir. We believe that the Japanese will continue their expansion in the China Sea and Pacific, for unless the Americans choose to come into the war alongside us there is nothing to stop them.' He looked meaningly at the wall map behind the desk. 'They could even come here.'

'Now that *is* rubbish.' The captain seemed to recover slightly. 'You may know all about missing subs and cloak and dagger escapades, but you obviously don't know much about the defences here and in Malaya.'

Critchley eyed him coolly. 'Let us hope, sir, that the Japanese are also in ignorance.'

The captain's fingers drummed busily on the desk. 'I'm still not convinced.'

Critchley stood up abruptly. 'Fortunately, it is not our choice, is it, sir?'

'What the hell d'you mean? Just because –'

Ainslie stepped forward without even realizing he was on his feet. 'Commander Critchley means the decision has been made, sir. By the Admiralty, by the Cabinet, and obviously with the Prime Minister's fullest support. Nobody wants to upset the French again, but neither do we want the Germans eating at Claridges!'

The chief of staff flushed. 'I am fully aware that in wartime some officers get promotion advanced more swiftly than in normal processes! I am equally conscious that others get an inflated sense of their own importance!'

Ainslie shrugged. 'I obey orders, sir. If *Soufrière* falls into enemy hands, for *whatever* reason, I shall go back to sea again in another submarine.' He glanced around the office. 'I will be the fortunate one.'

The chief of staff looked away. 'I'll do what I can.'

Critchley stubbed out his cigarette and brushed some ash from his crumpled suit.

'Fine, sir. We'll begin tomorrow.' He seemed not to see the captain's anger. 'Maybe the admiral will be here by then, too.'

They left the office and Critchley said, 'Not bad for openers, Bob. Now a bath and a nice big drink are indicated.' He peered round for the staff car. 'They've put us aboard a commandeered motor yacht. All the luxuries. Also, it'll keep us from reminding everyone there's a war on!'

Later as they stood on a jetty, their faces searing in the afternoon glare, Critchley said, 'Captain Armytage is probably right, *of course*. *Soufrière*'s quite likely out of commission for good. Maybe one of her people felt as we do, that no French vessel should help the Jerries.'

Ainslie nodded, watching the launch which was coming to collect them sweeping around the lines of moored warships in a shower of fine spray. Beyond the ships, sweltering beneath taut awnings and limp flags, he could see the Malayan coastline, hazily green, shimmering above the water of the Johore Strait. He thought of his companion's words to Armytage, spoken as much out of frustration as anything. But if the Japanese did declare war, could Britain withstand an even greater weight in the balance? If Critchley was right, and Armytage was deluding himself, it was not difficult to picture the Japanese Army swarming across this narrow strip of placid water. Singapore's defences were famous and respected. But so, too, was the Maginot Line.

He sighed. 'But if she's not, then the problem is still there.'

Critchley turned to study his profile, the level stare, the small crow's feet at the corners of his eyes, evidence of watchkeeping, of hunting the enemy.

A few more like Ainslie and there'd be room for optimism, he thought. As it was . . .

The commandeered yacht must have been a beautiful vessel in her day, Ainslie thought. In spite of being stripped of many of her old owner's refinements she retained an air of elegance and grace, from the clipper bow and figurehead to her fat yellow funnel. As a young sub-lieutenant in a destroyer, Ainslie had come across many such yachts, probably even her, in the peacetime days of service with the Mediterranean fleet. Malta, Naples, Piraeus. Soft nights, music, girls with tanned shoulders and bold stares for the young officers. Another world, probably gone forever.

Lady Jane was the yacht's original name, and there was a builder's crest and plate in the spacious saloon. Now she was labelled as *Tender to Terror II*, the title of Singapore's naval base.

The day after Ainslie's arrival was another scorcher, but aboard the old yacht, moored apart from the warships and harbour craft, it seemed cooler, while the perfect service provided by two Chinese messboys added to a sense of unreality and detachment.

While Critchley was ashore on one of his secret missions, Ainslie waded through the pile of correspondence, instructions and orders which had awaited his attention.

He found he could forget the chief of staff's unhelpful attitude as he studied the carefully collected details of his giant prize. Perhaps because all the uncertainty had become less so, or maybe, as he suspected, it was due to the first good night's sleep and leisurely breakfast he could remember for a long while.

Secrecy was vital. To stay out of the limelight with every security man working to that end was one thing. To hide a complete prize crew for the massive *Soufrière* was another entirely. A real headache for Critchley and his colleagues, Ainslie thought.

Ainslie knew most of the men who would make up his new company, some very well indeed. Like John Quinton, who had been his first lieutenant in *Tigress*, and who by rights should have a command of his own. An Australian with a rugged and cheerfully unorthodox attitude to his British companions, he had said more than once, 'If they'd had subs in *our* navy I'd have stayed put.' They had been in some very tight corners together. Ainslie hoped he would be the same and not embittered by being appointed as his Number One again.

He knew the senior engineer officer, too, Lieutenant Andrew Halliday. They had served together in another submarine at the outbreak of war.

There were others, too, like Bill Gosling, the coxswain; Dugald Menzies, the yeoman of signals; and a torpedoman named Sawle who had acted as wardroom messman aboard the *Tigress*, and had volunteered for this mission without even asking what it entailed.

Ainslie had met the others at HMS *Dolphin*, the submarine base in Hampshire. It was to be a mixed company indeed, which would include four Free French officers, two of whom had served in *Soufrière*'s forerunner *Surcouf*. They would be invaluable.

At the Admiralty, just before he had left for Singapore, Ainslie had completed a final briefing with the head of naval operations.

Brushing aside Ainslie's doubts he had said cheerfully, 'Well, if nothing comes of it, it'll be damned good experience anyway.'

For what, Ainslie had wondered?

He stood up and walked to a polished brass scuttle as he heard a motor boat chugging alongside. He saw Critchley, strangely changed in white shirt and shorts, followed by two other officers, clambering up the accommodation ladder. The second officer he did not recognize, but the last one, with two gold stripes on his shoulder straps, was John Quinton.

Ainslie turned away and looked across the saloon, examining his feelings. If Quinton had been brought here it meant one thing. The operation was going ahead.

Critchley hurried through the door, mopping his face and hurling his cap on to a chair as he exclaimed, 'I need a drink!'

Ainslie smiled. 'At this hour?' He turned as the tall Australian lieutenant crossed the worn carpet and grasped his hand firmly. 'Hello, John. It's good to see you.'

Quinton was as dark as Ainslie was fair. He had deep-set brown eyes, and skin so tanned he looked like a buccaneer from the Spanish Main. Although he was only twenty-seven he looked older than his commander.

He let his glance rest on Ainslie's new shoulder straps and said, 'Congratulations, sir. You earned it.' He looked over at Critchley. 'A beer if you've got one handy.'

Ainslie watched him thoughtfully. Quinton seemed unchanged, except for the 'sir'.

Critchley introduced the other officer as Commander Melrose, the senior operations officer.

Then as one of the Chinese messboys busied himself with glasses and, mercifully, ice, Critchley said quietly, 'We've *found* her, Bob.' He nodded to the messboy who left as noiselessly as he had entered, and then unrolled a chart on the table. 'Here. About three hundred miles north-east of this table.' His finger rested on a scattered line of islands of all shapes and sizes about two hundred miles off the coast of Borneo at a guess. Critchley continued calmly, 'This one, Datuk Besar, part of the archipelago, but under French control. Up to a point anyway. There is a local ruler, but he does what the French tell him. Well, he did.'

Ainslie was not deceived by Critchley's calm. He was bursting with excitement. Maybe the *Soufrière* operation had found life in his brain. It seemed very likely.

Quinton said, 'From here it looks as if the Japs are about the same distance from the place as ourselves.' He rubbed his dark chin. 'Interesting.'

The operations officer regarded him curiously and said, 'Our agents stumbled on the information by accident. Even the RAF hadn't spotted anything on their recce flights. There's some sort of lagoon at Datuk Besar, not much room, but plenty of depth. Just the place to hide the beast.'

Ainslie glanced at Quinton. *The beast.* They were already creating a personality.

Quinton said, 'I still don't see we've a chance of surprise. All that way.' He shook his head. 'Reckon we'll have to go in with guns popping!'

Melrose smiled. 'The agents are right down south, in Java, Surabaja to be precise. They discovered that someone had chartered an old tramp steamer for passage to Datuk Besar. Closer investigation showed she was filled to the hatch covers with drums of diesel. It shows carelessness on someone's part. Nobody in his right mind would need that much oil in a place that size. But it does show urgency, too. Otherwise they'd have sent the ship a longer way round to allay suspicion.' He smiled broadly, pleased with himself and his department. 'The old tub's steaming up the Java Sea right now.'

Ainslie looked at Critchley. 'All right?'

He nodded. 'With any sort of luck we'll bag her without raising a squeak.' He frowned. 'Then it'll be up to you, Bob.'

Quinton spread his arms. 'As it used to say in my mother's cook book: first, catch your fish. . . .'

Melrose said, 'The ship left Surabaja two days ago. It's only just been confirmed by W/T. At her speed, say six knots, she'll be suitably placed in five days' time.' He raised his glass, his part done. 'Cheers.'

Ainslie could almost see it happening, as if it had already been. Some clapped-out old freighter eking out her days with any cargo she could get. Trying to avoid the war at all costs, yet unable to resist the temptation which with luck might lead them to the French submarine in her hiding place. Urgency, Melrose had mentioned. Perhaps the French commander had heard something, or expected the Japs to mop up this last tiny fragment of empire with *Soufrière* still at her moorings.

He knew so much about the *Soufrière* from his investigation and instruction that he even remembered the French captain's name. Capitaine de Frégate Michel Poulain. A good officer to all accounts, and no traitor. But a sailor first and foremost, unwilling to destroy his boat or hand her to another power without protest. If he had wished to do so he would have acted earlier.

Critchley said, 'I'm off ashore, Bob. Get things moving. The others had better be mustered tomorrow, just to be sure. The admiral has been informed, and *he*'s going to add his weight.'

Ainslie gave a grim smile. The very mention of Winston Churchill's interest in the operation could change higher minds than the admiral's.

When Critchley and Melrose had departed Quinton said, 'I'm glad it's started. It was getting on my bloody nerves.' He grinned. 'The old firm, eh?'

Ainslie poured two glasses of whisky. There still seemed to be a plentiful supply out here. 'Thank you for that.' He looked at him. 'You had a raw deal, and I'd not want you to think I'd blocked your command for selfish reasons.'

Quinton thrust out his legs and stared up at the deckhead. 'Fact is, you couldn't manage without me.' He laughed. 'True?'

Ainslie relaxed. 'True.'

Quinton was serious again. 'I wonder how the old *Tigress* is managing. After the last battering we took from those Eye-tie depth-charges, I reckon she needed a longer refit than a month, poor old girl.'

They lapsed into silence. Ainslie had often thought of the *Tigress*. A new company, her skipper with his first command. It was too much. They had all been very close in *Tigress*. They had endured attack from air and sea while they had fought to prevent enemy supplies crossing to North Africa.

There were plenty of music-hall jokes about the Italian lack of zeal when it came to fighting, but it had been hard to raise a laugh when their depth-charges had come thundering around the submarine's hull.

Quinton remarked, 'I think I'll have a last run ashore. Make a real night of it.' He chuckled. 'Can you imagine all those stuffed shirts in the Long Bar at Raffles if I gave them a few verses of "Eskimo Nell"?'

Ainslie smiled. 'No chance, John. You're staying put. There's a security blanket on this one.'

'Careless talk costs lives.' Quinton sighed. 'I know.'

He raised another glass and nodded approvingly at it. 'Watch out, guts, here comes the flood!'

Ainslie watched him. It was one of Quinton's favourite expressions. Nothing had changed.

At the end of the week, true to his promise, the operations officer passed the word that everything was ready.

The night that Ainslie and his party left Singapore was perfect, no moon, good weather and as black as a boot. As the commander of the destroyer which was to carry the prize crew to the rendezvous point had said, 'If we lose this one, my head will be on the block!'

It was a curious feeling, Ainslie thought. Watching his men hurrying up the destroyer's brow like fugitives, to be guided below with a minimum of delay.

Critchley came to see them off. With just a few minutes to go he said simply, 'No more risk than necessary, Bob. You've done enough for ten men. Wish to God I was coming with you. I'll have to sit here, waiting for the reports to come in.'

A sub-lieutenant came out of the darkness. 'Ready when you are, sir.'

Critchley touched Ainslie's arm. 'They've probably picked up some news aboard the destroyer already.' He sounded at a loss. 'I'd like you to hear it from me.'

'What news?'

'Your old command, the *Tigress*. She's done for. I just heard it at HQ. Bombed returning to base. No survivors.'

Ainslie turned away. It happened every day. It was not even as if he knew her last company, and yet . . . Did submarines really have personality?

'Thank you. I'm glad you told me. She was a good boat.'

He could picture it. Returning to base, the lookouts relaxed after the patrol, probably their first in earnest. Then out of the clouds, no warning, no chance.

Without thinking he said, 'I'll miss her.'

Then with a quick glance at the lights of the base he strode up the brow of the ship.

He met Quinton below the bridge and guessed that he also knew.

'You heard?'

The Australian nodded slowly. 'Makes this job that bit more important, Bob.' He nodded again. 'Too right.'

Like a grey ghost the destroyer backed clear of the jetty, her screws churning the darkness into white froth. In an hour she was out in the Strait, heading eastwards to the rendezvous.

Ainslie stood on the destroyer's bridge and watched the land sliding away into a deeper darkness. They were all committed now. The hunt had begun.

2

The Team

LIEUTENANT (E) ANDREW HALLIDAY sat in a corner of the destroyer's wardroom and glanced at the other officers near him. He tried not to listen to the ship's pounding screws and the steady whirr of fans, to calculate and consider what her performance was like. It only made him feel more out of things, a passenger.

Opposite him, leaning over a small table, his features set in a frown of concentration, was Lieutenant David Forster, who, if the operation proved to be successful, would be the submarine's navigating officer. A typical Dartmouth product, Halliday thought. Usually ready with some witty comment at exactly the right moment, and nearly always right about something or other.

Halliday looked down at his hands. They rested in his lap like extensions of his brain, his tools. Strong, bony fingers, with a few scars as souvenirs of his trade.

He hated this kind of operation, although he kept his doubts to himself. It was not his sort of work. His was the world of machinery, he was used to it, as he was used to being depended upon. Unlike the debonair Forster, Halliday had come up through the ranks, the hard way. A Scot by birth, his home was in London, about ten minutes' walk from Tower Bridge. He thought of the skipper, Robert Ainslie, how they had first met in the small, élite circle of submariners. Halliday had been the chief engineroom artificer of the little S-boat *Seamist*, and Ainslie, then a lieutenant, had been in command.

North Sea patrols, dodging dive bombers and seaplanes, E-boats and anti-submarine trawlers, feeling their way as the war exploded across Europe and Scandinavia in an unstoppable onslaught.

It had been rough going, relearning all the peacetime lessons, rewriting the rules and then breaking them, too. They had done well, better than several other boats which had failed to return from their patrol areas. He had learned to work closely with Ainslie, skipper and chief thinking as one. Halliday was the first to admit that he was a withdrawn, self-sufficient person, and his feelings for Ainslie had remained professional rather than personal. Until that day off the Norwegian coast. Despite the humid, oily warmth of the destroyer's crowded wardroom he felt a shiver on his spine.

They had been at sea for days, waiting and hoping for a chance to have a crack at a German heavy cruiser which had been reported nearby shelling a Norwegian town. The cruiser had not come, but two destroyers had arrived instead. For days they had played cat and mouse across the mouth of a fjord, twisting and turning to avoid a seemingly endless bombardment of depth-charges. Their sealed, dripping world had gone berserk around them. Lights shattered, the hull reeling to the thunder of explosions, each threatening to burst them open like a sardine tin. Sometimes they had been hard put to hold the boat at the right depth, other times she had gone mad as she had plunged through an outflow of fresh water from the great fjord.

The destroyers eventually gave up and left. Gingerly *Seamist* had surfaced, examined her wounds and turned tail for home.

In all those miles of sea, after all the hours of manoeuvring and changing course, they had hit a drifting mine. A small submarine and a tiny pinprick of a mine, somehow they had been drawn together. Halliday still could not remember much more. He had been going to the bridge to report to the skipper about leaks. It should have been safe enough. They had been well within range of fighter cover for the last miles. He could vaguely remember climbing through the conning tower, feeling the air pumping past him as the diesels sucked it down through the hatch. The unshaven lookouts, muffled to the eyes, their binoculars covering the grey sea. Ainslie turning towards the hatch to greet him even as a lookout yelled, 'Mine, sir! Dead ahead!' Then the bang, the excruciating pain in his ears as he had fallen half down the ladder. The boat going into a dive, men screaming, their cries smothered by the icy inrush of water.

Then, what seemed a long, long time later, coming to, half choked by salt and oil, and realizing that Ainslie was supporting him in that bitter, bloody sea. There had been seven of them, gasping and cursing, trying to help one another, but losing to the grip of freezing water.

Halliday had wanted to die, but Ainslie's voice had refused him even that.

Eventually, a hundred years later, an RAF rescue launch had found them. Two officers and two seamen. The others had died.

After that, if Halliday felt anything for Ainslie it was as near to love as a man could feel for another.

When Ainslie had picked up his half-stripe and been given the *Tigress*, Halliday had asked to go with him. Ainslie had given him that quiet, grave smile which he knew so well and had said, 'No, Chief. The next time you come with me I want to see some gold lace on your sleeve.' He had known that in the larger submarine Halliday would have been under an engineer officer. He was the sort of man who thought about things like that.

Halliday looked down at his hands again. Well, he had two stripes now, and Ainslie had been promoted ahead of time, too. He smiled grimly. Two plants forced up by glass.

He thought about the *Soufrière*. It would make a change working with the French officers. But just let them make a mess of it and he would show them.

David Forster, the navigating officer, closed his notebook and leaned back in the chair. He was twenty-six years old, with all the confidence of youth honed by war. Forster had felt Halliday watching him and had made a point of not showing it. For despite his normal air of casual optimism, Forster was worried. On the face of it, and provided he could stay in one piece, he had the world at his feet. He came from a respected naval family with a pedigree which went back to the Armada. He was the oldest son, and heir to a considerable estate in Sussex, and he had already gained a DSC for bravery under fire.

He looked upon his appointment as navigation officer as the final stepping-stone to a command of his own. Then he would get out of submarines and use his experience and the considerable dash which being a submariner always gave to find something better. Forster planned well in advance and thought things out for himself. A good command, something which might offer him more chances of advancement ahead of the pack and with luck allow him some time for leisure. He was an all-round sportsman, as much at home on the rugger field as he was carrying a gun on the moors.

But he had one flaw, a real weakness which had given him a frown to cloud his good looks. Forster, above all else, enjoyed

24

the company of attractive women. Like the sports field, he went all out, as far as he could, then discarded them, being content to shelve them in memory like trophies.

At the submarine base in Hampshire, while they had been preparing for this operation without any real hope that it might come off, Forster had met Daphne. He had known her at a distance for a year or so, the wife of another submariner. It had started after a party, perhaps too many drinks. In wartime you cut corners, made the prospect of death a ready excuse for almost anything.

Forster had never gone to bed with a married woman before. It was not that he held any scruples on the matter, it was just that it had never happened. It had been like being reborn, driven mad in a frenzy of love so primitive that he could still not believe it. If only he had kept to his previous arrangements. If only Daphne's husband had been at the base instead of the Mediterranean.

But whatever else had happened, he knew Daphne was not a liar. And when she had told him she was pregnant, just hours before he had been ordered to leave for Singapore, he had been stunned. He had not even been able to tell her. The secret orders left nothing to chance. Perhaps even then he had expected the operation to be called off, another false alarm. They were common in wartime.

He listened to the drumming engines, the swish of water along the destroyer's hull. This was real enough. And she was back there, worried sick. She might do something stupid. He swallowed hard, wondering if he was thinking of her or himself. Maybe the job would soon be over. There was still time. He rubbed his chin desperately. So what? The problem was still there.

He looked at Halliday, his face deep in thought. He would have no such troubles. Set in his ways, the 'little woman' back in Blighty knitting balaclavas for sailors. A picture of dad on the mantelpiece.

Forster stood up, feeling sick. *Christ.*

Halliday watched him leave and relaxed in the chair. Soon now. Those fine engines and electric motors were out there, waiting for him and his assistant engineer, Sub-Lieutenant Arthur Deacon. He smiled gravely. *And* the Frenchies, of course.

Further along the hull, in the destroyer's chief and petty

officers' mess, Bill Gosling, a submarine torpedo coxswain of long standing, sighed with relief as the tannoy called the company to action stations. It was no clamouring, mind-stopping klaxon, just a mild request to stand to. They'd have to act a bit livelier if they were in Western Approaches, he thought grimly.

His friend and drinking partner, a yeoman of signals, Petty Officer Dugald Menzies, looked at him and said, 'Good thing to get rid of that lot. Bit more room for us now.'

The coxswain grinned. He was a large, battered looking man, running to overweight, and old for his years. He had been in the Service since he was a boy. It was his life, his reason for being.

He replied, 'Probably they'll say the same about us, Jock.'

The yeoman said, 'Not like being at war, is it, Bill? Out here, I mean. D'you reckon the Japs will come in against us?'

Gosling shrugged. 'Can't tell. Maybe they'll stay out of it like the Yanks. To see who's going to win.' It seemed to amuse him. 'Went to Japan once. Lots of tiny little women.'

The yeoman of signals waited for his friend to elaborate, but he did not. Poor old Bill Gosling was getting past it, he thought worriedly. The best coxswain in the submarine service, everyone knew that. But a surface ship or a nice little billet ashore handing out leave passes and ration cards to green hostilities-only seamen would be more like it.

He asked, 'Ever thought of putting in for a shore job?' It just slipped out.

Gosling had had two large tots of rum and was feeling ready for a nap. But the casual question stirred something all the same.

'Me? A sodding barrack stanchion? When that happens I'll really know I'm done for!'

But he had thought about it. He had been in submarines since he had been a leading hand. It was demanding work, always with the nagging thought something might go wrong, even in peacetime. Like the poor *Thetis*, which had taken her crew to the bottom while on trials in sight of land. One error, that was all it needed. So why had he volunteered for the *Soufrière* job?

Bob Ainslie, the skipper, had offered him the chance to get ashore and wait for something quieter. He smiled. Ainslie would. One of the best. Together they had made the *Tigress* a happy ship. Now she was on the bottom. Had someone forgotten the drill at the last moment? A lever pushed instead of pulled, a vent open instead of shut? Men under fire were never what you expected them to be. He glanced down at the brand new ribbon of the Distinguished Service Medal on his jacket. Ainslie had done that for him. He'd see the drafting officer in bloody hell before he quit on Ainslie. Now of all times.

Then he fell asleep, his heavy frame rocking to the ship's plunging motion in time with the drawn curtains on the tiered bunks where others of the raiding party were enjoying some rest.

It was the same throughout the ship. While the destroyer's company were at action stations for the last miles to the rendezvous the secretly gathered prize crew dozed, wrote letters or thought of the prospects of success. The bulk of the party were aboard, although others, like the RNVR pilot who was to take over the *Soufrière*'s seaplane, the cook and a few seamen were still back in Singapore waiting to see what would happen.

Up on the destroyer's open bridge, Ainslie stood beside the commanding officer and watched the sea changing colour as a low, filmy haze drifted to meet them. Strange how naked you felt up here, he thought. Too long in submarines probably. But the war seemed far away and only the trimmings were in view.

The destroyer's CO turned and said, 'Pilot's told me that we should make contact in two hours, sir. My people know what to do. One peep on the old freighter's morse and we'll drop a shell over her bows.' He walked across the well-scrubbed gratings and looked down at the iron deck where the motor boat was already swung out on the davits. 'My chaps have a machine-gun mounted in the boat. Should be all right.'

Ainslie put on his dark glasses. 'Good.' He thinks we're all potty, round the bend. Either that or he believes the job should be his instead of a lot of roughnecks from Britain.

He heard footsteps and knew it was Quinton.

The Australian said, 'I've done my rounds. The lads seem okay. Glad to get on with it, I expect.'

'D'you want to talk about it, John?'

Quinton shook his head. 'I think if I try to remember any more I'll forget everything!' He grinned. 'First we get aboard.' He ticked off the points on his fingers. 'The crew will probably be native, so we'll put 'em below under guard. Up to the bridge, tell the master we're on to him and order him to proceed.'

27

Ainslie nodded, only his lips showing any expression below the dark glasses.

'If he makes trouble, shoot him.' How easily it came out. But it was not so strange when you thought about Norway and Holland, Greece and Crete. Not strange at all.

He added, 'The remainder will come across immediately so that the destroyer can push off.'

'The rest? You'll be with them surely?' Quinton sounded anxious. 'That was the way it was planned.'

Ainslie clapped him on the shoulder, feeling the strength of the man. 'If I make a mess of it, John, so be it. If you do, I'll not forgive myself. I want you to have a command of your own, right?' He walked to the bridge ladder. 'I'm going to have an hour's shut-eye.'

The destroyer's commanding officer crossed the gratings. 'He's a cool customer.'

Quinton nodded. 'Sure. A real beaut.'

'I'd not be able to sleep until it was all over!'

Quinton smiled to himself. And neither will he. It's an act, all of it. For our sakes, and for his own. God, have you got some lessons to learn, chum. But aloud he said, 'He's had plenty of practice.' He saw the shutters drop behind the other man's eyes and added calmly, 'Sir.'

Two hours later, almost to the minute, Ainslie was called to the bridge. The other ship was in sight. Phase two was about to start.

He nodded to the destroyer's commanding officer and trained his binoculars over the screen. At first he imagined the old tramp steamer was painted bright red and orange, but as she hardened in the lens, hull down in the lingering haze, he saw she was covered with rust and daubs of red lead from stem to stern.

She was really old, with a long trail of black smoke hanging motionless above her small wake.

The destroyer seemed to come alive as the orders rattled through voice-pipes like pebbles.

'Yeoman, make a signal to her now: This is a British warship. Stop instantly. Do not use your wireless.'

Ainslie kept his glasses levelled, hearing the clatter of the signal lamp's shutter, the impatient movement of feet on the bridge gratings.

He could just make out her name on the rounded, dented

stern. *Kalistra*. If she ever turned up in a convoy her slow speed and dense smoke trail would drive the escort commander mad, he thought.

He stiffened. Someone had appeared on the *Kalistra*'s outdated bridge.

A rating said tersely, 'She's not transmitting, sir.'

Another said cheerfully, 'Don't look like she's got a bloody thing to transmit with, mate!'

Then the commanding officer's voice. 'Silence on the bridge!'

Ainslie glanced over, sorry for him. He was afraid he was going to make a hash of it. A lot of people, important ones, were now involved. The accuracy of the intelligence reports and the punctuality of this ancient tramp steamer proved that.

He said, 'She's stopping.'

Then he turned as he felt someone fastening a webbing belt around his waist. It was Forster; he too was wearing a belt and heavy pistol.

He said, 'All right, sir? Just in case.'

Ainslie nodded, smiling. He liked Forster, in spite of his energetic appetites. He did his job well, even to remembering to help the gunnery officer issue side-arms.

Quinton would be down with the first boarding party, each man keyed up, raring to go.

Two of the destroyer's guns had trained to starboard, following the other ship, as if they were sniffing at her. Even the voices below the bridge were hushed.

'Slow ahead together.' The destroyer's commander crossed and re-crossed his bridge. 'Stand by to drop the motor boat.'

Men were already climbing into the boat while a hoarse voice bellowed, 'Turns for lowering!' And as the commander waved his hand. 'Lower away!'

Ainslie nodded to his opposite number and touched his cap. 'Thanks for the lift. I'll be off.'

It seemed like only seconds when he was bundled up with the others in the motor boat and bouncing across the small wavelets towards the motionless ship.

He removed his cap and laid it on the deck. To Quinton's curious glance he said, 'If they see a brass hat coming aboard they'll know there's more than a routine check-up afoot. They could still give us a bad time if they wanted to. The destroyer wouldn't like to blaze away with us halfway up the side!'

Some of the armed seamen near him chuckled, as if it were all a huge joke.

Ainslie watched the *Kalistra*'s worn-out hull looming towards him, marvelling at the way men could laugh and joke at times like these.

A crude rope ladder had been lowered, and Quinton said, 'I'll go first, sir.' He met Ainslie's gaze firmly. 'This time.'

As he reached out for the ladder he said, 'Sawle, bring the skipper's cap! Remember who we are!'

There were more laughs in the boat, and Ainslie thanked the fates which had brought him and Quinton together.

As the boarding party clambered over the bulwark, and a frightened-looking Javanese seaman pointed towards the bridge to show the way, the motor boat swung away to collect the next party. It would have been far quicker to lay the destroyer along-side, no matter what the contact did to her paintwork, but if there was an unseen watcher nearby this would appear more natural.

Ainslie looked at the sea. Bright blue. Like silk. Another scorcher.

Sawle, the torpedoman cum wardroom messman, hurried be-side him, and as Quinton ran up the bridge ladder and into the wheelhouse he handed Ainslie his cap with something like reverence.

'Just like old times, sir.'

Hardly that, Ainslie thought.

He joined Quinton in the wheelhouse, taking in the disorder, the flaking paintwork, the ragged, half-naked helmsman made more pathetic by his seamen with their levelled weapons.

The ship's master was Dutch, probably a half-caste, and as dirty as his ship.

Ainslie took out his pipe and filled it very slowly, the action giving him time and his men an opportunity to cover the most vital parts of the deck and engineroom.

'I am ordered to take control of your ship, Captain. By the authority entrusted in me I intend to proceed with her to . . .' He watched the man's features, the way his mouth was hanging half open. Poor devil. He looked terrified. '. . . to her destination, Datuk Besar.'

The man stammered, 'I poor man, *Kapitein*. I know nothing of war.'

Quinton said quietly, 'Holland is overrun. It is forbidden, nevertheless, for her old colonies to aid the enemy.'

More feet clattered on the bridge ladder and Petty Officer Voysey, second coxswain, shouted, 'It's 'ere, right enough, sir. Enough oil for a bloody fleet!'

The ship's master dropped his head. 'I only do what I am told, *Kapitein.*'

Ainslie put a match to his pipe. 'Good. Then we will get along very well.'

He looked across at the destroyer. The motor boat was coming back, but this time she was towing the whaler, equally loaded down with men and weapons.

'Signal *Arielle* and tell her all's well.'

Quinton looked at him for a moment. '*Arielle?* I never even saw her name!'

Ainslie trained his glasses on the two boats. Halliday was with this lot. Just as well, he thought. Otherwise the old tub might never make it to Datuk Besar.

Half an hour later, with her signal lamp flashing like a diamond-bright eye, the destroyer swung away in a steep turn.

Petty Officer Menzies said, 'From *Arielle*, sir. Good hunting.' He looked round the dirty bridge with obvious distaste. 'Och, what a potmess!'

Ainslie smiled. 'Thank you, Yeo. I hope you'll not have to put up with it for long.'

Forster was in the small chartroom, his hands spread on the stained chart.

'Just as well we took over, sir.' He jabbed his dividers on the chart. 'This joker had a course laid through the outer reef!'

Ainslie looked at the wheelhouse as the telegraph clanged and the old screw started to thrash at the sea again. It was a joke to Forster, to most of them. They were used to seeing pain and suffering, and had been made to shield themselves against it.

He watched the *Kalistra*'s master as he stood near the wheel. Beaten, one more bit of wartime flotsam paying the price.

It was no joke to him.

Ainslie felt someone shaking his shoulder and was instantly awake.

'Dawn's coming up, sir.' It was Forster, looking surprisingly wide awake.

Ainslie eased himself from the battered wicker chair which had been brought to the freighter's bridge for him, and stretched. Then he walked out on to the starboard wing and peered ahead. The dawn came up quickly here, and there was already a definite glow along the horizon's edge. Not long now. He yawned and stretched his arms, mentally comparing the shabby, makeshift surroundings with his more usual mechanical world.

Quinton came out of the gloom, like a ghost against the wooden screens.

'I've called the rest of the hands, sir, and sent the native crew below. Also I told the Chief to keep a weather eye on the engine-room people.' He walked to the rail and gripped it with both hands, sucking in several deep breaths.

Ainslie said, 'The master still persists that there is no recognition signal for the delivery of his cargo. I'm not sure if I trust him or not. We'll head straight into the lagoon and anchor, that's apparently the drill. Then we'll take it from there. If we get no co-operation from the local people I shall try to explain the advantages of helping us.' He hesitated. 'At worst, we'll have to blow up the submarine.'

Quinton was watching him intently. 'Suppose the Japs are there already?'

'Unlikely, John. But if they are I'll have to speak with them. After all, we've no quarrel with them. Yet.'

A shaft of light spilled over the horizon like pale gold liquid. It was broken in one place by a shadow, a long hump of land.

Forster said, 'There it is, sir. Our little island. Right on the button.'

'Fetch the gunnery officer.' He thought he heard Quinton groan, and added, 'His part is pretty important, John.'

They fell silent, watching the land rising in the warm glow like a surfacing whale.

Ainslie knew that Quinton did not like the gunnery officer very much, and that seemed to go for almost everyone else. Lieutenant Peter Farrant had been in submarines at the very start of his service but had transferred to general service at his own request. He was everyone's conception of the stiff-backed, efficient gunnery officer, the product of Whale Island, but aboard a submarine he would stand out like a cactus in a rose garden.

He did not need to be popular, Ainslie told himself; he just had to be good.

Aboard even the largest submarine the gunnery officer's work was limited. He was usually required to do several other jobs as well, from watchkeeping to taking boarding parties aboard suspicious-looking merchantmen. *Tigress*'s deck gun, for instance, had been a small four-inch weapon. *Soufrière*'s massive twin turret was little different from that of a heavy cruiser where Farrant would be much more at home.

He came on to the bridge, a pistol at his hip, his cap tilted across his eyes as if it were already broad daylight. He was thin and tall, with a narrow face which rarely smiled.

Farrant said, 'You wanted me, sir?'

'Yes, Guns. You've got your people ready?'

Farrant looked at him, his eyes hidden. 'Yes, sir.' It sounded like 'of course'. 'Two Brens, the rest with sub machine-guns.'

More light grew and spread across the dawn sky, with tiny, fleecy clouds here and there reflecting the greater darkness of the sea. It was a damn good spot to complete some makeshift repairs, Ainslie thought. In half an hour the old *Kalistra*'s slow approach would have been sighted and reported.

He said, 'It's possible that the French skipper may have set scuttling charges.'

He waited for some comment from Farrant, whose life, after all, would be at the greatest risk if that happened.

When he said nothing Ainslie added, 'Use your own judgement, but I want no unnecessary shooting.'

'Aye, aye, sir.' Farrant's mouth opened and closed with the precision of a rifle bolt. 'Is that all, sir?'

'Yes. Go and join your men.'

He glanced past Quinton and Forster into the wheelhouse. It was strange to see British sailors where the native hands had been. Gosling, the coxswain, was at the wheel, his belly against the brass boss as if for support. Menzies, the yeoman, on the opposite wing, a telescope trained towards the island. On the untidy foredeck, dotted along the bulwarks and behind the windlass, other kneeling and crouching figures revealed themselves in the growing light.

The ancient tramp steamer was not what they were used to, but even in the savagery of the Atlantic many British sailors were putting up with ships long due for the scrapyard.

Forster said, 'There's a village on the southern side of the anchorage, sir. But there are two marks on the chart which could mean something.'

'Thank you, Pilot.'

Ainslie listened to the screw's thrashing motion and tried to put himself in the submarine commander's position. If Britain and not France had fallen, and he had found himself in a damaged sub on this tiny, useless island, would he have scuttled and left his company marooned and open to possible capture?

He shook himself angrily. It was no good thinking like that. No bloody use at all.

The sense of isolation and unreality set against the war he had so recently left behind became even more evident in the last few miles of the approach. Past a line of submerged reefs where the water looked like that in a Japanese painting, on towards some small fishing boats with batlike sails, motionless above their own reflections.

The sun had risen to lay bare the ship and the island, pinning the men down in its grip behind their hiding places.

Ainslie trained his glasses on the entrance and heard Forster say, 'Port ten. Midships. Steady.' And Gosling's gruff acknowledgement as he eased over the wheel.

The opening was still difficult to make out, the dipping headlands so close to one another that it appeared as if the ship was steaming for the beach.

There were more craft in sight now, very small, for local fishing, or whatever they did to earn an existence.

A voice-pipe whistled, and Menzies called, 'Masthead lookout reports there are several boats moored in the entrance, sir.'

Quinton breathed out slowly. 'Now we know. They're expecting us all right, but taking no chances.'

Ainslie walked to the engineroom voice-pipe and blew down it. At any other time it would be comical to think of Halliday down there in the ancient, single-shaft engineroom. He was more used to thousands of horsepower and all that went with it to drive a modern submarine.

'Chief? This is the captain.'

Halliday answered, 'Aye, sir. Everything all right up there?'

'May be a spot of bother in about thirty minutes. Boats moored across the entrance. I might want full speed. Fast as she'll go. Never mind the gauges.'

He heard Halliday give a dry chuckle as he said, 'Full speed. Aye, sir. Eight knots at a guess, and I'll mebbe blow the bloody boilers doing *that*!'

'Fair enough.'

Ainslie closed the pipe and raised his glasses again.

'Put some hands up forrard, Number One. Have them stripped off, like a lot of waterfront layabouts. I want it to look as if we are going to anchor.'

As Quinton hurried away Ainslie said to Voysey, the second coxswain, 'Pass the word, PO, I'll need the starboard anchor let out ready to drop.'

The next few minutes were alive with preparations, as steam was raised on the capstan, and with a protesting clink of cable one anchor was lowered from its hawse-pipe. Occasionally, as the ship rolled, it boomed against the hull like a giant hammer on an oil drum.

Gosling remarked dourly, 'One good thump and the hook'll come right through the bloody bows!'

Ainslie made up his mind. A quick glance at his watch and a further one towards the island.

'Slow ahead. Steer straight for the entrance, Swain.'

The telegraph clanged, and Gosling pressed his belly harder against the wheel while he peered through the glass screen towards the gap and its small barrier of boats.

Ainslie hurried down the ladder, the sun searing his shoulders like heat from a furnace door. Across the blistered deck and then up the iron ladder which mounted the foremast to the podlike crow's nest above the derricks.

Leading Seaman Calver, a gunlayer, was acting as lookout. Quinton would choose him. He had been one of the best in *Tigress*. Even his eyes, like pieces of pale glass, gave an appearance of alert watchfulness.

'Here, Calver, lend me your glasses.'

They were big, heavy ones, Calver's trophy from a captured Italian torpedo boat. Ainslie trained them on the ledge of the crow's nest and studied the entrance. It looked almost up to the bows through the powerful lens. He saw the boats, tiny like the others, some people standing up in two of them to watch the approaching ship.

Calver said, 'Don't look like much, sir.'

Ainslie bit back his disappointment. Once he had never believed it would work. Now, right on the doorstep, it all seemed wasted, a great big sham. He moved the glasses carefully, knowing they would soon need him back on the bridge. Clusters of huts, *Forster's village*, swam into view, a few trees, more boats tied up to a pier. There were no beached boats, a sure sign that the water was deep inside the lagoon.

But equally there was no sign of a submarine, of anything. Perhaps they submerged the boat during daylight? He dismissed the idea at once. The chart, and the two intelligence folios, were insistent that the bottom was too rocky. A submarine's hull was tough, but not enough for that.

Then he held his breath. There was a long building near the pier. Like a communal dwelling you often saw in Borneo. But it seemed wrong. Out of place.

He thrust the glasses into Calver's hands. 'Keep watching. Don't hesitate to call me if you sight anything.' He met the man's bright stare as he climbed on to the ladder. '*Any* damned thing!'

The sun was so hot on his head and shoulders that he could barely keep up with his racing thoughts. As he clambered down the ladder he kept thinking of the strange longhouse. Natural enough in some places, but far too large for a small outpost like this.

They would be watching the old *Kalistra*'s approach, waiting to see what she would do.

He reached the bridge, gasping for breath.

'Fetch the master! Chop, chop!'

Kalistra's captain was under guard in the galley, and appeared between two seamen within a minute.

Ainslie seized his arm and pushed him to the screen. 'See those boats?' He could feel the man's fear, and hated himself for adding to his despair. 'What do they want us to do?'

The small man said brokenly, 'Anchor, *Kapitein*! They will send someone – '

Ainslie snapped, 'Like hell they will. Get the Chief on the voice-pipe. Now.'

The lookout on the port screen shouted suddenly, 'Submarine surfacing, sir! Port quarter!' He sounded as if he disbelieved what he saw.

Quinton raised his glasses and exclaimed, 'The crafty bastard! He must have been outside the whole time, stalking *us*!'

Ainslie walked from the wheelhouse, ignoring the glare, the sudden anxiety all around him.

Very deliberately he trained his glasses on the low, glistening fore-casing and the first hump of a conning tower as the submarine continued to flounder to the surface.

Forster called. 'Chief's on the line, sir!'

Ainslie watched the submarine, amazed he felt so calm. 'Tell him I want full speed. He knows what to do.' He lowered the glasses and looked at Quinton. 'It's not the *Soufrière*. It's a Jap sub.' He saw the swift understanding on Quinton's dark features.

Gosling reported, 'Engine full ahead, sir.'

Even the bridge was beginning to quiver as the old shaft worked faster and faster in response to Halliday's efforts.

Ainslie looked once again at the submarine, fully surfaced now. Tiny, white figures were flitting down from the conning tower towards a deck gun, and the ensign with its red rising sun insignia was floating above the periscope standards.

'Steer for the moored boats, Swain. Pass the word forrard. *Stand by to ram.*'

He looked across at Menzies. 'What have you got there, Yeo?'

Menzies showed his teeth in a fierce grin. 'Thought you might need it, sir.' He unrolled a new white ensign and looked at Ainslie with the same expression as a good gun-dog waiting for the order to retrieve.

Voices echoed along the foredeck, and Ainslie saw Farrant and his men scurrying to their positions, weapons at the ready.

It was too late now for any more surprises. The Japanese submarine had put paid to that.

In the same level voice he said, 'Very well. Run up the colours.'

Then he walked to the forward screen and watched the entrance which appeared to be reaching out to embrace the ship like arms. The boats were still moored there, and the occupants seemed too stricken by the change of events to move.

Quinton looked from the newly hoisted flag to the submarine and said, 'I'll bet that shook the bastards!'

Then, like a great, rusting battering-ram the *Kalistra*'s stem smashed through the first two boats and hurled the others aside like empty crates.

They were through.

3

Two Flags

Down in the *Kalistra's* engineroom it felt as if the ship was shaking herself to pieces, plate at a time.

On one of the quivering catwalks, worn to a treacherous smoothness by many years and countless feet, Lieutenant Auguste Lucas, once an experienced engineer officer in the French Navy, watched the scene beneath him with rapt attention. He was a slightly built Breton of twenty-six, with a mobile, humorous face which set him completely apart from the grave-featured Halliday who was leaning on the shuddering throttle wheel, or his squat assistant, Sub-Lieutenant (E) Arthur Deacon. Lucas not only was French, he *looked* it. He could be nothing else.

He still could not believe all that had happened to him. The sudden, chilling disbelief at the news that France had fallen. His first instinct had been to make for his home in Nantes to be with his parents and sister when the Boche marched in. Had he been in a French anchorage at the time he might well have done so, he was still not certain. But he had been in a British port, serving in a small coastal submarine employed on the North Sea patrol. That same night he had gone ashore to a mass meeting, more like a trade union gathering than anything to do with the Navy. It had been pitiful. The married men demanding to go home, the younger ones unsure, left naked by the abrupt surrender.

A senior British naval officer had come to address them. Needless to say, he spoke no French, and the whole laborious appeal for loyalty, for the old *esprit de corps*, was mostly lost through an interpreter.

Lucas had felt his hand waving in the air with the rest. Stay and fight. Stand together and join de Gaulle's Free French.

From then on he had been kept very busy, shutting his ears whenever possible to tales of the British taking over French vessels by force when their crews had demanded otherwise than to fight.

Now, he was glad of his decision, although he felt he had still learned very little about his British counterparts. They were so mixed, often so unsure of themselves. They had courage, but were embarrassed if you told them so, and were likely to deride their own efforts at almost everything. But should an outsider dare to criticize, that was different. *Bloody foreigners! What do they know?*

He peered down at the bottom of the engineroom. The bare light bulbs danced above their reflections on a swilling surface of scum and bilge water. Or, as was quite likely, he thought, they had already started to sink.

Halliday shouted, 'Stand by to ram!' He glared through the steamy mist. 'That means, bloody well hang on!'

Lucas shrugged and gestured to some native stokers to stand clear of the clattering machinery. Ram? The *Soufrière* perhaps? He thought of Ainslie when he had first met the Free French officers who were to assist in this crazy task. Lucas had been prepared to dislike him. Ainslie must have had a good instinct for people, he thought. He had said, 'Relax, gentlemen, I am a Scot. The Admiralty is taking no chances with you lot!'

Lucas forgot England with its green fields and vapour trails high overhead where the young pilots fought their daily duels, as with the shuddering force of running aground the *Kalistra* smashed through the barrier of boats. Stokers yelled up through the steam like souls in hell, but the great shining shaft was still in motion, and as far as Lucas could tell, they were not foundering.

Halliday bellowed, 'Up on deck! They want you at the double!' He gripped his arm as he dashed past, his hand leaving a black outline on the sleeve. 'Watch yourself! I'll need you later on!'

Lucas grinned. He never really knew about Halliday. If he cared for his safety, or merely for his experience.

The sunlight which greeted him was blinding, and as he was knocked sideways by a running party of armed seamen he was astonished to see the land right alongside.

He saw the gunnery lieutenant, Farrant, hands on hips, one foot theatrically placed on a bollard, watching the land and some bobbing pieces of timber which must once have been boats.

Farrant he did not like. The fact he was British had nothing to do with it. There were Farrants in every navy.

Farrant looked at him, his eyes cold. 'About time.'

Lucas mopped his face. 'So?'

More running feet, this time the first lieutenant's. He shouted, 'We're going alongside, starboard side to.' He swung Lucas round and pointed at the gaunt pier, the longhouse beyond. 'The skipper thinks the sub's in there.'

There were shouts of alarm as the deck gave a violent lurch before coming upright again. An uncharted rock, a wreck, nobody knew, and it was too late anyway.

Quinton turned to run back to the bridge. 'By the way, fellows, there's a Jap sub astern of us!' Then he was gone.

Lucas watched his companions as they gathered along the bulwark and guardrail, their faces set, and no longer cheerful. They were all looking at the land, the village and the groups of people who were stampeding away from it.

Crudely, without warning, the war, not of their making, was amongst them.

Farrant was saying to his petty officer, 'Now, Osborn, I want you to take the covering party. Have some grenades ready. You know the drill.'

Somewhere through the drifting funnel smoke and above the din of fans and racing machinery came a shot.

Farrant stared at the petty officer with astonishment. Osborn's expression matched his, as with a gasp he dropped to his knees, a great pattern of blood spilling from his stomach and covering his webbing belt and weapons like paint.

Lucas ran to help him, but a seaman yelled hoarsely, 'No good, sir! 'E's done for!'

Lucas could scarcely believe it. A man had just died.

He turned as Farrant said harshly, 'From your people, I should think. Better hide your rank markings. They might not take kindly to de Gaulle's warriors.'

Lucas swung away, knowing that if he said anything to Farrant it would lead to far worse. He felt like killing him.

From his vibrating viewpoint on the bridge Ainslie had seen some of it and had guessed the rest. He would make Farrant's ears burn later, but right now . . .

Forster shouted, 'There she is, sir!' He ducked as some bullets smacked into the wheelhouse or shrieked over the water like demons. 'Look!'

The *Kalistra*'s failure to anchor, and then her dramatic entrance plus the additional appearance of the Japanese submarine must have caught everyone off guard.

As Ainslie ordered the wheel hard over, and the old ship staggered round towards the pier, he saw the giant *Soufrière* for the first time. Beneath a framework of matting and bamboo, her hull trimmed as high as possible, she looked even larger in the confined space.

There was froth along one of her saddle tanks, and for an instant Ainslie imagined she was moving and began trying to plan how he would stop the freighter's charge and turn her in time to prevent escape. But it was probably a generator or a pump, for when he saw the mooring lines to the pier he knew she was in no state to slip free.

He ran to the wing. 'Guns! They may try to scuttle!'

He saw the lieutenant nod before urging some of his men towards the forecastle and the point of impact.

A few more shots cracked against the *Kalistra* and Menzies growled, 'Why don't we give *them* a basinful?'

Ainslie took his cap from the flag locker and jammed it over his unruly hair. Then he walked out into the sunlight, clearly visible to anyone on the shore or the submarine as he raised his megaphone and shouted. 'This is the Royal Navy! I have orders to take control of your vessel immediately!'

From the deck below he heard his words being repeated in French. That was Lieutenant Cottier, Lucas's companion.

Ainslie felt the sweat pouring down his chest and spine in a hot flood. Yet his blood was like ice as he waited for the sickening impact. The light going out as a bullet found its mark. Like poor Osborn.

Then across the water came the reply, sharp and metallic. 'If you attempt to board my ship I will destroy her.'

Ainslie's eyes narrowed. They were at least talking. That must be her captain, Poulain. He measured the distance as the *Kalistra* pounded towards the pier.

'Half speed ahead.' He felt the response, and seemed to sense the bows dropping with relief. Less than half a cable to go. 'Wait for the order, Swain.' He lifted the megaphone again. 'There is a Japanese submarine about to enter the lagoon! Be in no doubt as to what will happen to you and your people if I withdraw now.' From one corner of his mouth he whispered, 'Ease her a bit to starboard, Swain. *Easy.*'

Somewhere below him he heard a man cough, another humming fiercely between his teeth. Osborn lay where he had fallen, arms and legs outflung in his blood, his eyes fixed on some point above the masthead.

Everything depended on *Soufrière*'s company as much as her captain. What news that had slipped out of Indo-China had been terrifying. Japanese atrocities had been reported against men, women and children alike. Their own fate, should they deny their submarine to such a ruthless attacker, would be a terrible one.

He heard a seaman grunt with alarm as the submarine's great gun turret, which stood as high as the freighter's bridge, suddenly began to swing towards them, the two barrels moving until they were depressed and sighted on the *Kalistra*'s hull.

Ainslie looked straight along the nearest gun, feeling nothing, yet wanting to understand. He was about to die. It was bound to happen one day. But not like this.

He realized the gun was no longer in his line of sight. The turret had stopped turning, and he saw some white-clad sailors climbing through an upper hatch, their arms at their sides, their dejection like something physical.

The metallic voice called again, 'Do you guarantee our safety?'

Ainslie wanted to measure the last yards, but dare not move now. He heard Quinton taking over the con. He must have guessed, understood his anxiety.

'Yes. We are not at war with Japan. If that submarine interferes with us, we will be.'

Quinton said sharply, 'Hard astarboard. Stop engine.' The hull was already swinging heavily towards the pier. 'Midships.'

The tension was unbearable, and all the while the *Soufrière* seemed to be growing larger as the freighter thrust over the last strip of water.

'*Full astern!*' Quinton ran to Ainslie's side as the telegraph jangled noisily. Then as Gosling yelled, 'No response on telegraph, sir!' Quinton exclaimed, 'Jesus! We'll ram it.'

But Forster had managed to get through to Halliday on the voice-pipe, and within five yards of the narrowest part of the pier the *Kalistra* shuddered to dead slow, until with a great sigh she came alongside, bringing down a small hut and a pile of empty oil drums.

Ainslie hurried from the bridge, Quinton on his heels. Seamen were already across the pier and groping for handholds on the submarine's casing or around her big conning tower. Others were trying to make fast the freighter's lines, urged on by threats and curses from Petty Officer Voysey.

As Ainslie reached a small brow which was the only connection with the *Soufrière*'s hull, he saw a group of French seamen being held at gunpoint by some of their companions.

He said quietly, 'Take charge here, Number One. Be easy with them. There'll be bitterness enough later.' To Farrant and Lucas he added, 'You come with me.'

Then he walked between his men and stood on the *Soufrière*'s grey deck. For a moment longer he looked at the tricolour which hung from the conning-tower staff, then he raised his hand to his cap in salute.

A tanned French lieutenant strode to meet him, his face grim.

He said, 'This way, sir.' He glanced questioningly at Lucas and shrugged. It could have meant anything.

Ainslie turned to question him, but Lucas was staring up at the flag, his eyes blurred with emotion, his hands balled into fists at his sides.

Ainslie reached out and touched his arm, seeing Halliday's trade-mark on his sleeve.

'One day, Lucas. *One* day you will be back.'

Then with a nod to the watching sailors, British and French, he followed the lieutenant through a massive watertight door and into the conning tower.

If it were possible, the *Soufrière*'s interior was even more impressive than her upper deck. The control room seemed twice as big as any Ainslie had seen, and the equipment, dials and torpedo firing controls shone like those of a newly commissioned boat. What was strange was the small number of her company in view. Just a handful here and there, staring at Ainslie and his companions as if they had landed from the moon.

The sounds of generators and fans were muted and remote, adding to the impression that this great submarine was sealed rather than enclosed.

The French officer stopped in a passageway by a curtained cabin and said, 'The *capitaine* is waiting for you inside.'

Ainslie glanced at his companions. 'Wait here.'

He had to force himself to speak calmly, to prevent any kind of urgency transmitting itself through them to the others and maybe spark off serious trouble. They could all be taken prisoner, or shot down like the petty officer. Everything depended on the next minutes, even seconds. He must shut out the need for action, the mental picture of that other submarine. Everything.

He stepped over the coaming and removed his cap, allowing the curtain to swing behind him. Again the cabin, a rare luxury for any submarine commander, was dramatic and impressive, a modern version of Jules Verne. Well-made bookcases, a curtained bunk and, bolted to the deck itself, a desk which would not look out of place in an office.

But his attention was immediately locked on the *Soufrière*'s captain. Michel Poulain was small and very neat, with a dark beard, greying at the edges, and intensely penetrating eyes. He stood up slowly, his eyes moving to indicate a vacant chair.

It was impossible, of course, but Ainslie had the notion that Poulain had been waiting and planning for this very meeting for months. Dreading it, but at the same time hoping for somebody to take away his self-made responsibility.

Poulain sat down again, very carefully. 'I am sorry about your sailor who was shot.' His English, like the man, was even, well modulated. 'These things can happen.'

Ainslie leaned forward, feeling the silence pressing in on him, the great hull surrounding them like a shell.

'What I said, Captain, was the truth. With the war as it is, we cannot afford to strengthen our enemy's resources. Your submarine must be prevented from falling into enemy hands.' He let the words hang in the air. 'One way or the other.'

Poulain looked around the cabin as if he had not heard. '*Soufrière* is no longer a mere *sous-marin*. She is part of France. While she is in being there is something to hold on to, to believe in. Soon the war will end.' For the first time he smiled, but it made him look incredibly sad. 'You British delude yourselves. At worst you will be invaded and made to suffer all the horrors of occupation. At best you can hope for stalemate and some

44

kind of ignominious armistice which will leave you alone in helpless isolation.'

'That is much how we are today.' Ainslie tried not to listen to muffled footsteps overhead, his men or Poulain's he had no way of knowing. 'But we will not give in. It is not our way.' He opened his hands as if to contain the cabin. 'But your ship, I find it hard to call her a boat, could bring havoc to us, and so indirectly to France.'

Poulain sighed. 'I had intended to take her nearer home. To North Africa perhaps. You will have seen that I am short-handed, less than half the proper complement.' He gave an eloquent shrug. 'They had their reasons for leaving me. I did not try to prevent them.'

Feet came pounding along the passageway, and then after a muttered conversation with Farrant, Quinton thrust his way past the curtain.

He nodded formally to Poulain and then said, 'I'm sorry to bother you, sir, but the Jap boat is coming into the lagoon now.' He glanced at the Frenchman and added coldly, 'I think we'd better get weaving.'

Poulain said quietly, 'I respect your attitudes. You must do me the same favour.' He stood up and moved about the cabin. 'We cannot dive. We had trouble with the forward hydroplanes, an inspired madman tried to put them out of use for ever!' His tone hardened. 'I buried him at sea. I have had some repairs carried out, but not enough. However, with the extra oil I had intended to run on the surface by another, less troublesome route.'

Ainslie did not know how he knew, but he was sure the moment had arrived. Perhaps it was what Poulain wanted now that his original plan had been stopped dead. Either way, Ainslie had more than the *Soufrière* to worry about now, he had his men and the French sailors to contend with.

He stood up. 'Number One, carry on with the plan. Lucas and his assistant will help the Chief, the rest is up to you.' He hesitated. 'Tell Menzies to hoist another ensign – '

'*Non!*' Just one word, but it sounded as if it had been torn from Poulain's throat. He recovered slightly and picked up his cap. 'I will lower my flag first.'

Ainslie followed him out and towards the gleaming control room.

Farrant said in a sharp whisper, 'What are we waiting for, Number One? We're sitting ducks!'

Quinton glared at him. 'Stow it! D'you imagine for one bloody minute the skipper doesn't know that? Get up top and prepare to cast off, to cut the moorings if so ordered!' He watched the lieutenant stride away, his neck red above his shirt. 'Stupid sod!'

Lucas said, 'I'll go aft. I must stick the labels over the controls for your men to read.'

Quinton clapped him on the shoulder. 'Too bloody right! Who speaks French anyway?'

On deck once more Ainslie could feel the change. Most of the French sailors had vanished below, where they would be watched but not harassed. It had been that easy.

He heard Voysey yell, 'Attention on deck!'

Very slowly the tricolour came down, to be replaced instantly by Menzies's second white ensign.

There ought to have been a ceremony, Ainslie thought, later there probably would be. But then it would be too late. Meaningless. Here, a man was losing his ship, his own visible sign of hope. And he was doing it with dignity. The British seamen watched impassively, a French mechanic was sobbing uncontrollably, as Poulain gathered up the flag and in turn saluted Ainslie's.

Ainslie said, 'I am getting under way, Captain, I will understand your feelings if you wish to go to your quarters, but . . .'

Poulain looked at him across the folded flag and said proudly, 'She is ready to move. She has always been so, since the day she was built.' He turned to look around once more. 'I will stay with you until you have the same satisfaction as myself. Then . . .' He did not go on.

How strange it was to stand on the bridge and look down past a pair of long guns. The transition was almost complete. Ainslie's own men were moving about the fore-casing while others ran along the pier, slackening mooring lines and releasing the brow.

Ainslie looked at the voice-pipes and handsets below the bridge screen, recalling all the photographs and plans he had studied of this same array back in England.

Taking his hesitation as uncertainty, Poulain said, 'This one.' He tapped a speaking tube.

'Control room, this is the captain.'

He heard Quinton's voice immediately. Very sure and unruffled. 'Ready, sir.'

'Lookouts to the bridge. Clear away main armament. Fast as you like.'

Men were clambering up through the conning tower hatch, and on either side a powerful machine-gun was mounted, the belts trailing down through the hatch like brass snakes.

The bridge gave a sudden tremble, and from aft Ainslie saw a cloud of blue smoke rising above the longhouse as the diesels coughed throatily into life.

'Take in the springs!'

Ainslie stood on the steel gratings watching his men as they struggled with unfamiliar lashings and wires. In spite of the responsibility, and the possible danger that the Japanese boat might try to stop him from leaving, Ainslie could feel the excitement rising within him like a drug.

'Main armament closed up, sir. Cox'n on the wheel. Ship's head two-three-zero.'

Ainslie glanced at the gyro repeater by the screen and took a quick bearing of the nearest headland. Across one side of his vision he could see the other submarine, standing quite still like a basking shark.

'When we get under way, Number One, tell Guns to train his turret on the other sub and load with semi-armour-piercing. She'll be at about green four-five.' A war of nerves. One torpedo from the Japanese boat would put paid to everything. The sight of these big guns would have to do the trick.

Quinton came back again. 'Captain, sir? Guns says he can't manage it, for Christ's sake!'

Ainslie licked his lips. It was all too fast. But for the Jap they would have had time for Farrant to get the hang of it.

He made himself reply calmly, 'Not to worry, we'll manage.'

Voysey was yelling up from the fore-casing, 'Singled up to 'ead and stern ropes, sir!'

Poulain stood at his elbow, watching everything. He said suddenly, 'The men in the turret will obey me. I could have them brought up to instruct your gunners, yes?'

Ainslie smiled at him gravely. 'Too late, I'm afraid.'

He shouted, 'Let go aft!' He saw the other ensign above the listing *Kalistra* suddenly vanish and wondered how she would fare now. Probably better under the Japanese than her original owners. A few more years, a few more weary passages. 'Let go forrard!'

He heard Voysey acknowledge and then yell, 'All clear, sir!'

Ainslie took a quick breath. 'Slow ahead, both engines.' He listened to the water foaming around the screws, and then saw the rickety pier begin to slide astern. *They were moving.*

Very slowly the *Soufrière*'s blunt bows slid from beneath the makeshift longhouse, her periscope standards tearing away the matting and allowing the new ensign to flap in the hot breeze.

'Clear the upper deck.' Ainslie raised his glasses and studied the outlet channel. 'Close all watertight doors.' Men bustled past, glancing at him, or staring quickly at the sky as if expecting to see neither again. 'Steer two-three-five.'

Gosling's familiar rumble. 'Course two-three-five, sir.'

Ainslie could picture him, his fat bulk hanging over the steel chair as he had seen it a million times.

Menzies said abruptly, 'The Jap sub's signalling, sir!'

Ainslie raised his glasses again as the yeoman read the winking light. 'Request we heave to, sir. To parley.'

It came to Ainslie like a cold shower. *The Japs dare not fire.* Not because of international law, but simply for self-preservation. If they fired a torpedo into *Soufrière* at this reduced range it would be like igniting one gigantic bomb. *Soufrière*'s tubes were all loaded, and Quinton had already said that she carried forty spare torpedoes. All that, plus ammunition, fuel and probably the exploding oil from the *Kalistra* would reduce the whole lagoon to one devastating furnace.

'Make to the Japanese, Yeo. Request refused. His Majesty's Submarine *Soufrière* is leaving harbour.'

Menzies sucked his teeth and then trained his lamp, well pleased with Ainslie's signal.

Ainslie turned to see how Poulain had taken his remarks, but the little Frenchman had disappeared below. He stepped from the gratings and crossed to the after part of the bridge. The pier was already well astern, but there was no sign of anyone in the village or anywhere else.

He heard a slight squeak and saw the turret begin to turn, the right and then the left gun moving up and down to emphasize their readiness. It might be a lie, but it would have a great effect on the Japanese, whose deck gun was no more than a three-inch. He returned to the fore part of the bridge and took another bearing from the gyro.

There was the open sea, held between the twin headlands like blue glass.

He touched the screen, feeling the strength beneath him. He smiled. *The beast*.

Menzies said, 'The Jap's not following, sir.'

Ainslie leaned over the voice-pipe. 'Number One. Tell Chief to increase to full revolutions. Just until we get clear. It will give them something to remember us by.'

Moments later, with a bow wave creaming away on either side to wash over the rocks and the flotsam left from *Kalistra's* ramming, the big submarine pushed her way out into the open water, her wake ruler-straight like a long white tail.

Only when he was certain the other submarine was not following did Ainslie fall out his men from their action stations.

He added for Quinton's benefit, 'See if you can get some food and drink going round. It will break the tension. Then put our people to work. Back to school. When we get back to Singapore I want us to be halfway to being a going concern.'

Up the voice-pipe he heard Quinton chuckle and say, 'The catch of the season, eh?'

If the *Soufrière* resented the sudden change of ownership and command she did not show it. But her previous commander, *Capitaine de Frégate* Michel Poulain, a man who had needed to believe that some day, all on its own, things would be as before, could not accept it. After leaving Ainslie on the bridge he went quietly to his cabin and shot himself through the head.

As darkness closed around the surfaced submarine, Poulain, wrapped in his own flag, and Petty Officer Osborn, draped in his, were buried at sea.

Ainslie closed the prayer book and replaced his cap. Perhaps the simple burial was an omen. Or, better still, a symbol.

4

The Real Thing

COMMANDER GREGORY CRITCHLEY followed Ainslie into the *Soufrière*'s spacious cabin and said, 'Better shut the door, Bob. I don't want the whole boat to hear.'

Ainslie unslung the binoculars from around his neck and placed them beside his cap on the desk. Outside the pressure hull it was early morning and, as ordered, he had entered Singapore's naval anchorage at dawn, to be met by a solitary tug and a watchful guardboat.

It had been an exciting passage from the little island, and Ainslie was proud of the way his company had got down to work to put their training and skills into operation. There had been several mistakes, but nothing really bad, and certainly nothing Lieutenant Lucas and his companions could not put right with a swift translation from French to English, or by taking over the offending instruments themselves.

Now, tied up to a high-sided depot ship, all but hidden from the base and the rest of the world, it was like an anticlimax, a slap in the face.

Critchley had been aboard the old depot ship, waiting, watching them as they had made fast alongside. He had said little so far, but Ainslie knew him well enough to recognize the signs. Frustration, anger, despair. He even managed to look his old crumpled self in his white shirt and shorts. There was a smudge of grease on his cap cover like a mark of defiance.

Ainslie said quietly, 'She's a fine boat, Greg. With a bit of work and a few spares I could get her on top line again. She was built when yards had time and money for good results. And to think that all we wanted to do was get her away from the wrong hands.'

Critchley watched fixedly as Ainslie poured two large Scotches, then almost snatched his glass as he exclaimed. 'They're all raving, bloody mad here!' He put the glass down empty and stared at Ainslie. 'When we got the signal that you'd pulled it off, I went straight to the chief of staff. I thought he'd be jumping up and down like me. Not a bit of it. Everything's changed again, that is, if it ever did change originally as we thought! You saw the new arrivals, did you?'

Ainslie nodded. It had been impressive in the dawn glow. While they had picked their way through the buoys and anchored vessels, he had seen the two great warships towering above all else like grey cities. The new battleship *Prince of Wales* and the battle cruiser *Repulse*, the most powerful units Singapore had welcomed for a long while. They might give heart to anyone who feared the Japanese would lose interest in their conquest of Indo-China and turn their attention nearer home. On the other hand, the people Ainslie had met so far on the island might see the show of force as further proof of their own invincibility.

Critchley exploded, 'The fool said that the Navy is going to operate this new squadron much as the Germans are using their *Tirpitz* in Norway. A reminder, a warning if you like, to tie down enemy forces.' He shook his head despairingly. 'So I went to see the admiral, no less. But he was well genned up already if you ask me. He even suggested that the fact there was no protest from Tokyo or the Japanese Navy about your seizure of the *Soufrière* from under their noses proves their disinterest in us, and that they have no evil intentions towards Britain.' He downed another whisky. 'I ask you, Bob, what can you do?'

Ainslie watched him, picturing him darting from one office to another. 'Well, we've got what we came for. *Soufrière* is still the biggest sub in the world. Put to proper use she will make a fine addition when we most need her. She could even run stores and ammunition to Malta, she's big enough.'

Critchley said abruptly, 'I've made a signal to the Admiralty. We'll see who they back up. In the meantime I'll do what I can about your spare parts, you know that.'

He looked around the cabin, seeing it for the first time since his outburst.

'What a boat! I see what you mean. She's different. Like something alive and breathing.' His glance fell on the strip of carpet by the desk. 'All the comforts.'

Ainslie also looked at the carpet. There was a bright patch on it where Sawle had cleaned away the bloodstain. Poulain had appeared even smaller, lying on his side, his eyes tightly shut at the moment of the pistol shot.

Critchley stood up and groped for a cigarette. 'Word to the wise, Bob. If you want to keep this command, I suggest you get started right away.' He watched the smoke being dragged into a deckhead fan. 'The admiral and most of the top brass from miles around will be visiting the *Prince of Wales*. There's a big party arranged for tonight, by the way. Nobody senior will be available to see you, or give you the praise you deserve for what you've just achieved. So put out your feelers, and do what you can to carry out the repairs. A vessel ready for sea is always a better argument than a dockyard job!' He laughed shortly. 'You're still on the secret list. So far as the outside world is concerned, you are living aboard the tender, *Lady Jane*.'

He cocked his head as a speaker intoned, 'Hands to breakfast and clean. Ordinary Seamen Booth report to the cox'n immediately.'

Then he said, 'It should have been said with a French accent. She even *sounds* like one of ours now!'

Ainslie led the way through the control room and the ladder to the upper deck. Quinton was there, cap on the back of his head, while he chatted with a handful of petty officers and leading hands. It was his own special way of doing things. Informal, even casual, but the steel was always there when he needed it.

'A word, Number One.' Ainslie waited below the conning tower and said, 'We'll have a meeting after they've eaten. As soon as the French hands have been escorted ashore I want the wardroom to start on Operation Scrounge. We need those hydroplanes stripped and the motors disengaged. Until we can use them again we're only a surface boat. Tell the Chief to begin taking on fuel. I'll get the go-ahead from the base captain and the BEO. Check everything. If we need something, send an officer to get it. Beg, borrow or *requisition for the duration*, got it?'

Quinton grinned broadly. 'Too right.'

Critchley pulled himself up the ladder towards the oval of bright sunlight.

'I can see that you've done this sort of thing before.'

Ainslie nodded grimly. 'A few times.'

For a while longer they stood together on the bridge gratings, protected from the glare by the depot ship's tall side. Apart from

52

the quartermaster and sentry at the brow, the deck and casing were deserted.

Ainslie touched his chin and realized he still had to shave. There was a lot to do yet, a hell of a lot. At first it had been just another doubtful operation, a calculated risk. Now the thought of losing the submarine because she was larger than the minds of those who were supposed to control her destiny was hard to accept. *Soufrière*'s presence here was much like his own. An embarrassment. Something which would go away if suitably ignored.

Feet clattered on the ladder and Vernon, the bearded petty officer telegraphist, climbed nimbly on to the bridge. He saluted and said, 'Beg pardon, sir, but the first lieutenant sent me.' He had a round Devonian dialect, a homely sound so far from England. He added quietly, 'He said you'd want to deal with it, sir.' Vernon held out a signal pad. 'Able Seaman Booth. Signal just in. His parents were killed in an air raid.'

'Thank you.'

Ainslie took the pad and looked at Vernon's pencilled writing. Round like his voice. But he saw only the pathetic pile of bricks, the gap in a line of houses like a missing tooth.

'Yes, I'll see him now in my cabin.'

Critchley was already making his way down to the casing. 'I don't need seeing over the side, Bob.' He paused on the ladder and their eyes met as he said, 'The war has a long arm, doesn't it?' Then he was gone.

Ainslie made his way below, wondering why he had never got used to it. *I have to tell you some bad news.* Or those dreadful letters he had written to parents of men killed in action. *He died bravely.* To a young widow. *You would have been proud of him.* But would they have understood? Could anyone see past loss and grief? That was why it *mattered*.

He saw the seaman named Booth standing outside his cabin with the fat coxswain nearby. Set against Gosling he looked like a child.

The door closed and Ainslie laid his cap on the desk. *God, look at him. He's guessed already.*

'I have to tell you some bad news.'

When Ainslie, accompanied by the tireless Critchley, was eventually summoned to the naval headquarters building, he found the chief of staff in an almost jovial mood compared with their first meeting.

It had been two busy days since their return to Singapore, during which time Ainslie's Operation Scrounge had worked wonders. Spares, fuel, electrical gear, even ammunition for the French-made automatic weapons had mysteriously appeared on the jetty and had been whisked into the *Soufrière*'s hull with a minimum of delay.

It was so like the Navy, Ainslie thought. If you asked permission to do something the answer was usually no. If you went ahead on your own steam you always seemed to get away with it.

Perhaps the additional work had done more to weld the new company into a team than any routine training. They had worked all hours with little complaint, and the hull had echoed to the tune of drills, pumps and generators well into the night, until the depot ship's people had complained about the din spoiling the film shows in their canteen.

Halliday and his French assistant, Lucas, had stripped the faulty hydroplanes and replaced them, and were eager to put them to a proper test. Lieutenant Ridgway, the torpedo officer, and his men had gone through the fore-ends and torpedo storage until they could operate the tubes and reloading tackle blindfolded. Even Farrant, stiff-backed and severe as the moment he had stepped aboard, had admitted a grudging satisfaction with his gun crews.

But perhaps the most contented man of all was Lieutenant Jack Christie, RNVR, the naval pilot who had been chosen to operate the *Soufrière*'s neat little seaplane.

Christie had been a stunt pilot before the war, reduced to doing five-shilling trips at seaside resorts when things had been bad. When things had been good, he had risked life and limb to give the spectators their money's worth. He had been a misfit aboard a fleet carrier, and not much better ashore. He simply could not adapt to the Navy's ways, and Ainslie suspected the *Soufrière* had been his last appointment merely to get him out of some senior officer's hair.

The seaplane was in excellent order, although it had not been launched from its catapult for many months. With his equally dedicated observer, Sub-Lieutenant Jones, also RNVR, Christie had taken the aircraft apart.

Ainslie had heard Quinton telling him on one occasion, 'God, Jack, if you bust that kite, remember it's the only one we've got, right?'

Christie had given him his lazy grin. 'She'll go like a bird. You see.'

All in all, Ainslie was pleased with his company. It was certainly the largest he had yet commanded. Twelve officers, including himself, and one hundred and twenty ratings, many of whom had seen active service in other boats. The others, like the wretched Booth who had just lost his parents, would have to learn as they went along.

It seemed likely they would have more time than most, Ainslie thought. For although Singapore, like the forces in Malaya to the north, had been put on a partial alert until the Japanese intentions in Indo-China were fully understood, it seemed slack after Europe.

In the city lights blazed at all hours, and the shops gleamed with early stocks of gifts and goods for Christmas. The clubs were always full, and Ainslie had been dismayed to discover that there was still a rigid rule about which hotels and places of entertainment could be used by 'other ranks' and which were completely out of bounds to Indian and Malayan troops.

The chief of staff waved them to two comfortable chairs and said, 'Sorry I've not had time to see you before this.'

Critchley said, 'We've been busy too, sir.'

The captain eyed him searchingly as if to seek out some small hint of sarcasm.

He said, 'The big ships have made quite an impression. Good thinking on someone's part. Just the sort of gesture to make friends and enemies sit up and take notice. Pity about the carrier, though.'

Critchley leaned forward. 'Carrier, sir?'

'Yes. The new one, *Indomitable*, should have been in company, but she ran aground off Jamaica while she was working up. She'll be along later, no doubt.' He saw Critchley's uncertainty and said cheerfully, 'God, Critchley, don't look so glum! We have our own air support in fields from here to the Siamese border, y'know.'

Critchley said calmly, 'I know. Wildebeest torpedo bombers which make the Swordfish seem young by comparison.' He watched his shots going home, cracking the other man's confidence. 'There are some old American Hudsons, and for fighter cover I understand there are a few obsolescent Brewster Buffaloes.' He reached out for a desk lighter and held it to the inevitable cigarette. 'Hardly a force to rouse enthusiasm, I'd have thought?'

The chief of staff turned to Ainslie. 'Well, anyhow, that is not the point of this meeting, or your concern, gentlemen.' His smile returned very slowly. 'Your orders are to complete repairs.' He touched the folder on his desk, the one Ainslie had signed just three hours earlier. 'It seems the submarine was not so damaged as you imagined, eh?' He did not wait for a reply. 'You will then take the *Soufrière* to sea for a final check.'

Ainslie watched him. It had been on the tip of his tongue to speak his mind. To tell this officer how hard his men had worked to make the *Soufrière* ready for sea in so short a time.

But he recognized the man's comment as a challenge. It would be just like him to clamp down on local leave until they were ready to sail. His men deserved a whole lot more than that.

He asked quietly, 'What are my orders afterwards, sir?'

'You will be routed round the Cape to England. Then it will be up to Whitehall and Flag Officer Submarines.' He tapped the folder again. 'However, Commander Ainslie, should your report, your *personal* judgement, discover any fault in the submarine after your checks, I am instructed to remove her from any active duty. In which case you and your company will return to England without her.' He could not resist it. 'By *sea* this time, naturally.'

Critchley stood up. 'Still no news from the Japanese, I suppose, sir?'

'Did you expect any?' He was starting to enjoy himself. 'I'm sorry you didn't get the publicity you evidently expected. But we see things somewhat differently out here, you know. There are still standards.'

Critchley smiled wearily. 'I'll bear that in mind.'

Once outside the HQ building with its perfect square of grass surrounded by white-painted stones, Critchley said, 'I prefer the intelligence department to shipboard life, I really do. But if ever their lordships are foolish enough to advance my promotion to captain I will personally pay my own fare to fly back here. Just to punch that pompous, bone-headed twit right on his gin-reddened nose!'

Ainslie smiled, 'Forget him. I'll tell you what we'll do instead. We'll have a party of our own when we've finished our trials. To say thank you to all the characters who *have* done their damndest to help us since we got here.'

Critchley rubbed his hands. 'Fine. No security breach. Just a good, bucolic party!'

As they walked from one patch of shade to the next, Ainslie asked, 'Was that true what you told Captain Armytage? About the old planes?'

Critchley nodded. 'I'm afraid it was. Pity about the carrier being held up. They could do with her here right now.' He shook his head impatiently. 'I see this sort of thing all the time, though not as much as at the start of the war. There are so many people, not all in high appointments either, who still see the line of battle as the answer to everything. They're fighting a modern war with the same ideas we had at Dogger Bank and Jutland.' He shot Ainslie a warm smile. 'It's people like you who spoil everything, by going out and winning battles!'

Ainslie nodded. It was painfully true. And yet without proper air cover you could never win anything for very long.

Critchley said, 'I'm off to see some people.' He touched his gold-leafed cap to a saluting sentry and added, 'Tell you something though. *If* in the unlikely event you do find more faults with the *Soufrière* after your trials, I'll wager a year's pay to a marine's button stick you don't tell friend Armytage!'

Ainslie watched him move away on to the roadway and smiled. Critchley was right. *Soufrière* might never replace the *Tigress*, but she had certainly become very important to him.

For two further days Ainslie's company combed through *Soufrière*'s great hull from bow to rudder, checking, testing, replacing, and finally accepting that if she was not ready to do her test dive she would never be.

Once again an air of secrecy hung over the anchorage as, with a sloop in the lead and a fleet minesweeper bringing up astern, *Soufrière* slipped her moorings and headed eastwards towards open sea.

The spot chosen for the first dive under her new ownership was definitely not submarine territory, with a maximum depth of some thirty fathoms. But it would have to suffice, and as Quinton had dryly commented, 'We can always sit on the bloody mud and think where we went wrong!'

Twenty-four hours after leaving Singapore, Ainslie completed the first series of tests. Flooding and emptying the torpedo tubes, and training the powerful gun turret through ninety degrees while the sloop and the minesweeper watched from a respectful distance.

Once dived they would be on their own. *Not before time*, was the general feeling throughout the boat.

As the hands of the control room clock moved towards the deadline, Ainslie examined his own feelings, wondering how it would be. He had heard of it happening to others, had even seen some of the poor devils who had suffered the sudden shock and realization that their nerves had broken. Round the bend, bomb-happy, they called it. In wartime you had to make jokes about it. But just suppose it happened to you? Ainslie held out his hands in the harsh sunlight and studied them. *To me?*

He tossed the feeling aside, irritated with himself. Then he lowered his head to the gyro repeater, next to the control room voice-pipe.

Quinton was there waiting. 'Two minutes, sir.'

'Here we go again, Number One.'

Quinton chuckled. 'Looks like it, sir.'

Ainslie steadied himself against the voice-pipes, recalling the little French commander, Poulain, his last moments on earth.

'Make to escorts, Yeoman. Am about to dive. Will release smoke-float when satisfied.'

He turned away, shading his eyes to watch the hazy horizon. Nothing in sight. No land. Not even a seabird.

Menzies lowered the lamp. 'From escort commander, sir. *Don't frighten the fish.*'

Lieutenant Forster, who was also on the bridge, murmured, 'Silly sod!'

Ainslie looked at him. It was not like the navigating officer to be so edgy. Another one with too many memories, perhaps.

Quinton again. 'Ready, sir.'

Ainslie nodded and closed the voice-pipe. 'Clear the bridge.'

It felt strange. Like being back in some peaceful Scottish loch, learning it all over again without the harrowing rush and tumble of action to drive you down.

He went last, slamming the hatch behind him, then down the full length of the conning tower to the control room. A seaman reached up to close the lower hatch, his face glowing in the low-powered orange glare.

Ainslie crossed the control room, his eyes taking in and discarding details without effort. Gosling sitting like a white sack at the wheel, the two planesmen nearby, Forster already in his chart space, busy with ruler and dividers.

Quinton stood near the diving panel, with Halliday further aft, leaning over two of his men at their vent controls. Watertight doors were closed, each compartment shut off from the next, and containing its own group of experts.

From right forward where the topedomen waited beside their racks of shining 'fish', down through the hull with all its maze of pipes, wires and dials to the stokers and artificers in the motor and enginerooms.

Ainslie gripped the handles of the forward periscope and turned the greased tube in a full circle. The sea was as before, with the two escorts rolling uncomfortably a cable or so away. How helpless they looked in the periscope's crosswires, as if already caught in the web.

'Turn out the foreplanes.'

He depressed the periscope lens and watched the two hydroplanes turning out from the hull like fins. The after ones were always under water and could not be seen anyway. He studied the dull metal as the planesman moved his controls back and forth.

'Hydroplanes tested and correct, sir.'

'Stand by.'

It was suddenly very silent. Halliday had cut the diesels and switched automatically to the electric motors for submerged running. Just a small humming sound, not even enough to make the massive hull quiver.

A drop of sweat splashed on to his hand as he peered at his watch. Almost angrily he wiped his face with his wrist.

'Group up. Slow ahead together.'

He heard the snap of controls, feet shuffling as Halliday moved in more closely to watch his dials and winking lights.

Ainslie took one more quick glance through the periscope. He could not get used to it, this leisurely drill and careful progress. In the Mediterranean and almost anywhere else it was death to leave the periscope up for more than seconds. The diving bomber, the spectre in the lens. Oblivion. He checked his racing thoughts, feeling the sweat running down his spine, the shirt clinging to his skin.

He steadied himself and said evenly, 'Open main vents. Take her down to fourteen metres.' He slammed the periscope handles into their upright position and a stoker sprang forward to send it hissing down into its great well in the control room deck.

Ainslie looked at the depth gauge as the needle began to creep round. He listened to the surging rasp of water entering the saddle tanks and watched the planesmen, the tell-tales above their heads, gauging the slow dive, the *feel* of the big submarine around him.

Quinton said quietly, 'Easy, Packer.' He, too, was watching the foreplanes' dial, thinking perhaps of the man who had tried to sabotage them.

'Steady at fourteen metres, sir. Periscope depth.' Quinton looked over at him, his lips compressed in a tight smile.

'Up periscope.' Ainslie bent over and gripped the handles, rising to his full height as the lens broke the surface overhead. 'Check all compartments.'

How warm the sea looked, how close, as if he were swimming with just his eyes above water, and yet without feeling or sensation. Around him handsets and voice-pipes chattered back and forth until Quinton reported that every section was functioning as it should.

'Very good, Number One. Down periscope. Steer zero-nine-zero.' He blinked as spray splashed over the periscope as it started to slide down. 'Take her down to twenty metres.' He listened to the smooth purr of the motors, the regular ping of the echo sounder. A glance at Forster at the chart table showed him he did not have to worry. Forster was too watchful even to allow a faulty chart to put them on the bottom.

'Steady on zero-nine-zero, sir. Twenty metres.'

More reports and cross-checks. Like fibres reaching from the ends of the boat to the control room, to Ainslie's mind.

'All checked, sîr. No leaks.'

Ainslie looked round at the silent, intent figures, at the *Soufrière*'s crest, an erupting volcano, above which someone, probably Lucas, had hung a smaller emblem, the Free French Cross of Lorraine. They had done well, all of them.

'Release smoke-float. That'll tell the escorts they can go home again.'

Halliday stood back from his panel, wiping his bony fingers with a piece of waste. 'Just as well, sir. They've probably got an important cocktail party on tonight!' But he said it without malice, and Ainslie knew he was too pleased about his motors and diesels to let anything spoil this moment.

'Open up the boat, Number One.'

As the order was passed and the watertight doors were unclipped throughout the hull, Ainslie picked up the tannoy handset.

'This is the captain. Despite what you may have seen or heard since you took over, this boat is now on a war footing. Vigilance at all times. We shall live longer that way.' He could see them in his mind throughout his command. Smiling at each other, pleased with themselves. Others would be saying, *what's the matter with the skipper, then? Getting cold feet?* And a few, like himself, would be searching their thoughts, wondering how much more of it they could stand. He replaced the handset.

'Fall out diving stations, Number One.' He saw the concern on the Australian's dark features. He would understand all right. They had seen and done too much together. 'I'm going to my cabin to complete my report.'

He saw Lucas come through the after bulkhead and checked himself. It was often like this in the control room. It was a constant reminder to any commander that his eye, his brain, his judgement alone could keep the submarine and crew in one piece.

He walked across to the slightly built French lieutenant and said, 'You have done a fine job.' He saw the dullness leaving the Frenchman's eyes as he added, 'I think I even saw the Chief smiling just then!'

Lucas took the mood and glanced over to Halliday. 'Oh, what a shame, sir! I must have missed it!'

Ainslie turned and walked towards his cabin, seeing the grins and the nudges, essential parts of their special, exclusive world.

In the cabin he closed the curtain and sat down at the desk.

So it looked as if *Soufrière* was going nearer home after all. Just as Poulain had always wanted.

He gave a sigh and picked up his pen.

'Up periscope.'

Ainslie gripped the handles and pressed his forehead against the rubber pad. A cat-nap, a good shower, and a surprisingly good breakfast – considering the cook had barely time to get adjusted to the galley – had worked wonders.

He watched the spray parting around the lens, saw the glitter of small stars on long, undulating curves of dark water. It made him feel like a predator, an intruder.

Around him the *Soufrière* breathed her own special sounds, the echo sounder, the occasional whirr of pumps as Quinton trimmed the boat, a man humming softly to himself as he waited to carry a message, or make some more tea.

'We'll remain at fourteen metres, Number One. Tell the W/T office to make contact and report our ETA at the base.' He glanced at the control room clock. 'We'll stand offshore until dawn. I don't want to barge through a bunch of local fishermen and have to pay for a lot of nets!'

Someone laughed.

Quinton moved nearer, his face in shadow. 'She handled well, I thought. Better than I believed possible with all the top-hamper of guns and the blessed seaplane hangar.'

Ainslie nodded. He felt at home. As if he had been aboard for months instead of days.

'The first real emergency may tell us more.'

Lieutenant Ridgway, the torpedo officer, who was in charge of the watch, said, 'W/T on the phone, sir. PO Vernon requests to speak with you.'

'Not like him at all.'

Ainslie hid a sudden uncertainty from the others. But it was not like Vernon. He was very competent and disliked asking advice. He took the telephone from Ridgway's hand, turning his back to the control room.

'Captain. What's the trouble?'

'Urgent signal, sir.'

Even on the wire Ainslie could sense his anxiety.

'Singapore under bombing attack after RAF report of unidentified aircraft approaching the city. Return to base forthwith and await orders. End of signal.'

Ainslie looked at the submarine's curved side. So it had happened. Just as Critchley had predicted.

He said quietly, 'Acknowledge, Vernon. Then no further transmissions.' He handed the telephone to Ridgway and said, 'Singapore has been attacked. It's my guess that it's just a start, a taste of things to come.'

Quinton breathed out noisily. 'Jesus. Us against the whole world, eh?'

Forster, who was still leaning on his chart table, exclaimed, 'It's hopeless!'

Like a house of cards Ainslie could see his command falling apart. The first optimism and excitement of their capture had been smashed almost before they had got used to it.

He said, 'Lay a course to base, Pilot. We'll surface and proceed at full speed when you're satisfied. Number One, pass the word, we'll go to action stations in ten minutes. I'll speak to the lads on the tannoy before we surface. After that . . .' He shrugged.

Ainslie's words to his company were brief. The small respite was over. They were going back to war.

As the submarine surged to the surface, foam spouting from her saddle tanks like expelled breath, the gun crews, lookouts and the rest of the bridge party hurried to their stations.

Ainslie barely had time to wipe the bloom from his binoculars and jam them to his eyes when the reports were completed. Turret closed up. Lookouts closed up. All tubes loaded.

He said, 'Tell the first lieutenant to increase revs for fifteen knots.'

He shifted the glasses from bow to bow. An air raid on the city, but as yet no follow up. A quick return on the surface might get them past any invasion armada, but he would have to make sure the recognition signals were perfect, otherwise *Soufrière* would be the first target of the day.

Menzies sounded subdued. 'First lieutenant wants to speak, sir.'

Ainslie waited for Forster to take his place on the forward gratings and then bent over the voice-pipe. 'Captain.'

'Another signal, sir. Three Japanese troop landings reported. Pattani and Kota Baharu, both in Malaya, and Singora further north, but no real information yet available.'

'Thank you.'

Ainslie looked at the stars. Just like their pattern in the sky the Japanese command had made each move with precision.

The air attack had been a feint, while the main assault had been high up on the east coast of Malaya. Not towards the great guns of the 'invincible fortress', but behind them. He chilled. No wonder that Japanese submarine commander had made no fuss or protest. As he had sat there watching the *Soufrière* taken from under his nose, he had known all the while that his country was poised for the attack. He must be laughing now.

He thought angrily of the chief of staff's complacency, his thinly veiled contempt for Critchley's ideas. It was to be hoped the defence and counter-attacks would not be left to men like him.

Quinton called, 'Another signal just decoded, sir. Force Z has sailed from Singapore. All patrols are warned to give them complete priority.'

Force Z. Ainslie pictured the two great ships with their escorts steaming at top speed from the base, heading out like angered beasts to smash the enemy before he could do more harm.

He replied, 'Keep a good listening watch. That Jap sub may be about. What a pair of targets for her!'

He turned to Forster. 'Go below, Pilot. I'll need you if I have to dive in the shallows.'

Forster nodded and threw his leg over the hatch coaming. He had just been thinking about Daphne. The letter he would write. Nothing definite or binding. A feeler, to discover how she was managing. Now all of it had been stirred into confusion by the news. Invasion. Attack. What the hell would they do?

But the rest of the night was uneventful, nor were there any more urgent signals from base. A storm in a teacup. A try-on which had gone badly wrong.

As the *Soufrière* reduced speed and pushed her way towards the naval anchorage, Ainslie, like the others of the bridge and casing party, saw the motionless pall of smoke above the city. There must be miles of it, he thought.

A light blinked from the old depot ship, and Menzies read, '*Come alongside when ready*, sir.'

'Acknowledge.' He leaned over the screen and waved to the second coxswain, the 'casing king', who was already directing his men to prepare the springs and breast ropes for coming alongside. 'Port side to, PO!'

'At least the base seems untouched, sir.' Ridgway, tired and strained, stood beside him again, his cap tilted over his eyes.

'Yes.' How bare it looked without the two big capital ships. 'I expect we shall soon get organized.'

The bridge messenger called, 'First lieutenant's here, sir.'

Ainslie crossed to the voice-pipe in a stride. 'Yes, Number One?' He could feel his stomach muscles bunching as if to receive a blow, yet he did not know why.

Quinton said, 'We've just had the news, sir. The Japs attacked the American base at Pearl Harbour and knocked it flat. They say it was just like the Fleet Air Arm's attack on the Italians at Taranto, caught all the battle-waggons napping. Like fish in a barrel.' He sounded stunned.

Ainslie replied, 'At least we'll not be on our own any more.' He forced himself to straighten up, to push the sudden despair away. 'We're going alongside in about ten minutes, port side to. I want the hands fallen in fore and aft. The rest will have to wait.'

He straightened his cap and saw a khaki-coloured car moving along the coast road in a trail of yellow dust. Somebody was up and about.

Lieutenant Farrant bustled through the hatch and paused as Ainslie said, 'A smart turnout, Guns. They'll be feeling a bit worried ashore. So let's give them something to stare at, eh?'

'Yessir.' The hand jerked up and down like a piston. 'If I could have them on the parade ground for just one hour I'd show them a thing or two!' Then, and only then, did it seem to hit him. Singapore, the landings in Malaya, and now Pearl Harbour. He ended lamely, 'I suppose that seems a bit stupid to you, sir.'

Ainslie smiled gravely as he bent over the voice-pipe. 'Port fifteen. Midships. Steady. Steer two-seven-zero.' Then he looked at Farrant's stiff face and said, 'You concentrate on your two big guns. I have a feeling they're going to be needed very shortly.'

Farrant considered it. 'They will be ready, sir.' He clattered down the ladder to the deck and then reappeared on the fore-casing, his voice sharp and metallic as he urged the seamen into lines for entering harbour.

Only then, as silence settled over the submarine for her last half mile to the depot ship, did Ainslie turn aside and allow himself to doubt. Suppose the new enemy could not be held? How could they stop them here, on the island?

He thought of the notice boards. *Out of Bounds. Off Limits.* The smugness and arrogance of people who should have learned from Europe what might happen again here.

As he had half expected, Critchley was waiting to see their return. He climbed down to the submarine as the last line was made fast and lost no time in confronting Ainslie on the bridge.

'How did it go, Bob?' He looked dog-tired.

'She's fine. Everything working as it should.' He touched his friend's arm. 'I've heard most of the news.'

Critchley was looking vaguely at the hurrying seamen with their wires and rope fenders. 'Fine, is she? Good.' He sounded as if he thought the opposite. Almost to himself he added, 'The air raid was made very easy for the Japs. The city authorities neglected to keep the ARP headquarters manned during the night, so nobody was able to switch off the power supply from the street lighting! Can you imagine?' He sounded near to collapse. 'It was a nightmare!' In a brisker tone he said, 'They're sending you out as soon as you've topped up your fuel. I was half hoping . . .' He looked away.

'You were hoping that *Soufrière* would be unable to go, was that it?'

He nodded. 'Yes. She's too big for these waters. Too bloody vulnerable.' He controlled himself with obvious effort. 'The Japs are thrusting inland, Bob. I've been reading the reports. They even landed tanks in the jungle. We've Indian troops up there who've never even seen a bloody tank, let alone had to fight them. God, what an unholy cock-up!'

Ridgway called, 'Boat approaching, sir. Senior officer.'

Critchley said hoarsely, 'May I go to the wardroom, Bob? I can't take much more of it.'

Ainslie watched him go through the hatch. Critchley could always take other people's disbelief or contempt. But being proved right under these circumstances had almost broken him.

Ridgway said, 'Was he right, sir, about these waters being too shallow?'

Ainslie looked at him calmly. 'Tell the Chief to make arrangements for fuelling right away, will you?' He watched the launch slewing round to make for the depot ship's accommodation ladder. 'We'll have to see for ourselves.'

Three hours later, a sheaf of hastily written orders locked in his safe, Ainslie was again on the move, conning *Soufrière* back along the course she had just completed.

The chief of staff had come in person. He had tried to bluster and to maintain his old optimism but, like Singapore's impressive defences, he no longer seemed to count.

5

Found Wanting

THE thirty-six hours following *Soufrière*'s departure from Singapore Island were a test for everyone's nerves. Not because of the prospect of action or immediate danger, but for the lack of it, and the complete sense of isolation. It was even more evident in *Soufrière* than you might have expected in a smaller craft. In the latter, just to move about the hull you usually had to squeeze past someone or duck to cram yourself through a hatch or watertight door. You were in everybody else's pocket, part of the vessel herself.

As hour followed hour, and the big submarine made her way northwards, parallel with the Malayan coast, the tension grew to become something real and personal. Tempers flared, and there were more threats from officers and senior ratings than Ainslie could remember aboard other boats.

At night, when they surfaced to run on the main engines and charge batteries, they listened anxiously for news from the W/T office. There was very little about the enemy in Malaya, other than reports of skirmishes in the jungles, patrol clashes and other meaningless statements. There was more news of Pearl Harbour, however. Five battleships had been sunk, and many other vessels and installations put out of the war for a long while.

An American announcer, his voice almost drowned in static, had been heard to say, 'We will stand by our allies to the end.' That had brought an ironic cheer from the listening submariners.

Ainslie rarely left the control room. He was very aware of the tension in his command, the bitterness at the way they had been treated in Singapore. But a real spark of resentment inside the hull would do far more damage. *Soufrière* might be too large for these coastal waters, but she was the only available submarine. The intelligence department in Whitehall could never have guessed how close their plan to seize the *Soufrière* had been to failure. At this precise moment, under Japanese or German control, she might be stalking the supply routes from the Cape of Good Hope to South America. If there was any justice in the world, Critchley should be returned to Britain and promoted to a position where he could use his talents to real advantage.

On the occasion that Ainslie decided to steal an hour's sleep in his cabin, he had barely laid his head on the pillow when the call came. *'Captain in the control room!'*

It was automatic, done without thinking. One minute he was shutting his eyes and ears to the vibrations of his command, the next he was running along the gleaming passageway and ducking through the watertight door at the forward end of the control room.

Ridgway, the torpedo officer, was in charge of the watch. He was a very withdrawn man, with the impassive features of a thinker, someone who might be lost without a problem to solve.

'Well?'

Ainslie made himself pause by the periscopes, controlling his breathing as he had trained himself to do over the years. It might be anything. Mechanical damage, a leak, a man with some terrible illness with which he would have to deal. *Anything.*

Ridgway said, 'Asdic reports faint hydrophone effect at zero-four-zero, sir. Diesel.'

Ainslie nodded, trying not to bite his lip as he strode to the chart table and leaned over it, snapping on the overhead light. He studied Forster's neat calculations and pencilled fixes. *Soufrière* was steering north-west by north, approximately fifty miles from the Malayan coast. The depth was about average. Thirty to forty fathoms.

He moved across the steel deck and stood behind the leading seaman who was adjusting and readjusting the hydrophone dial, using one hand to press his headset closer to one ear in case he missed something. Ainslie remembered the man's name : Walker. A good and experienced operator. No point in speaking until Walker was ready. Let him decide, not insert ideas into his mind for him.

Walker said slowly, 'Twin diesels, sir. Bearing steady on zero-four-zero. Closing.'

Ridgway rubbed his chin. 'One of ours.'

'Unlikely.'

But Ainslie's thoughts were already working out a pattern. The stranger was probably an enemy support ship. He pressed a spare earphone to his head and listened. That was diesel all right. Regular, confident. Like a heart-beat coming through the sea towards him.

He turned towards the helmsman and saw the gyro repeater ticking slightly this way and that, the depth gauge steady at ninety-six feet. He almost smiled. He was seeing French metres but still thinking in feet and fathoms. Some of Lucas's sticky labels had started to peel from dials and operating controls, but nobody seemed to need them any more. Sailors were very adaptable.

Anyway, it was better than steering into nothing.

He said, 'Klaxon, please.' And as the banshee squawk sounded throughout the pressure hull, and men came running to their stations, he returned to the chart. He felt Forster beside him at the plot and said, 'Alter course. Steer zero-zero-five. We'll take a look at him.'

Quinton was by the coxswain and planesmen, his jaw working on the remains of a sandwich.

'Boat closed up at actions stations, sir.'

'Very well.' He smiled across at him. 'Probably a false alarm, Number One.'

Forster said, 'Starboard ten. Steer zero-zero-five.'

Gosling rumbled, 'Zero-zero-five, sir.'

Walker said, 'HE still closing, sir. Same bearing. I estimate the range to be about four thousand yards.'

'Very good.' Ainslie glanced at his watch. 'Group down. Take her up to periscope depth.' As the stoker PO's hand darted out to a lever he said sharply, 'Nice and easy. Just to be sure.'

He heard Halliday mutter something to his over-eager assistant.

'Fourteen metres, sir.'

'Silence in the boat.' Ainslie checked the bearing and looked at the man by the periscope hoist. 'Very slowly, right?'

The man bobbed and grinned nervously. 'Aye, sir.'

Ainslie bent down and waited as the periscope slid very gently from its well. He snapped down the handles and all but knelt on the deck as he peered through the eyepiece. In his mind he could see the long, greasy bronze tube sliding upwards towards the surface, the clean air. He tensed and jerked his hand to signal the stoker to stop. He was stooping, moving the handles very carefully, watching the picture in the lens changing from distorted blue-green to clusters of tiny bubbles, and then as it broke surface, to an eye-searing glare.

He swung the periscope in a full circle, the motionless figures and ticking mechanism around him already forgotten. His world was out there, resting on the water. A quick look overhead, his wrist arching round the handle to move his 'eye' towards the blue sky. No brief glitter to betray an aircraft or, worse, the terrifying arc of a propeller as a plane dived towards its prey, the roaring engine completely silent in that other world.

But there was nothing.

He said, 'Report target.'

From the Asdic compartment he heard Walker say confidently, 'Bearing zero-five-zero, sir. It's altered course slightly. Revolutions as before. No increase in speed.'

Ainslie nodded to the stoker. 'Full extent.' He trained the periscope on the bearing and rose with it until it stopped.

'Down periscope.' He walked to the chart table and said, 'A small patrol vessel. She's a Jap all right.' He felt his words moving out like a breeze on dried leaves. 'Probably an escort for one of the troopships somewhere.'

He turned away as Quinton said savagely, 'If only we *knew* what was happening! It's like being blind in a minefield!'

Ainslie thought of the brief, blurred picture he had just seen. A high bow, a stubby, raked funnel, and quite a lot of shadows below her bridge, probably guns. At two miles it was not easy to see everything, even with the lens at full power. If the sea had been anything but flat calm he would have discovered nothing at all. This early sighting had given him the edge, a very necessary one if he was to prevent the patrol vessel from pinning *Soufrière* between her and the shore until help could be brought from elsewhere.

Even submerged, a pre-warned aircraft might soon see her whale shape below the surface.

'Start the attack. Tubes one to four.'

He watched Ridgway as he turned the switches on his 'fruit machine' as it was nicknamed, while he waited to feed into it all the bearings, ranges and running depths required for his torpedoes.

'Up periscope.'

He moved it very carefully. There she was, almost end-on now, leaning slightly as she executed a slight alteration of course. He could sense the rating who was Ridgway's assistant peering at the brass ring around the periscope which was marked with the bearings, the degrees of success or failure.

Ainslie concentrated every fibre on the small silhouette. 'The bearing is *that*. The range is – damn!' He stood back. 'Down periscope.' He looked at Quinton. 'The range is less than four thousand yards. But there's another vessel astern of her. On tow. I think. Landing craft most likely.'

'Tubes one to four ready, sir.'

'Up periscope.'

Again the quick search of sea and sky, then round to the target. She was sharper now. More real. So she was not altering course, but swinging to the pull of her unwieldy tow.

'Bow doors open.'

That was Ridgway. Wrestling with his own particular problem. *Soufrière* was years ahead of her time, like some of the most recent U-boats. She could fire a fanlike salvo at her target even though she was turning away. In *Tigress* you had to point the hull at the enemy like a weapon so that you were still heading into danger even as you fired.

Back to the chart table again even before the periscope was down in its well.

Forster's dividers rested on the coastline. 'There's an anchorage here, sir. To the south of Pattani. Could be heading for it.'

Ainslie stared at the chart. If the Japs were that confident and were able to approach the coast without a heavier escort or air support, their advance must be going well. Too well.

He said, 'I'll take another look.' He waited, trying to relax his neck and back mucles as the tube rose from the well.

He watched the high bow edge darkly into the right-hand side of his lens, pushing into the crosswires as if to cut through them.

'Stand by.'

He heard Ridgway's voice, a fierce whisper almost covered by the snick, snick of the 'fruit machine'. 'Ready, sir.'

'Fire One!'

The hull gave a slight jerk, as if it had touched a floating tree, but nothing to betray the menace of the torpedo as it streaked from its tube.

Ainslie slammed the handles against the periscope. 'Down periscope! Carry on firing by stop-watch! Thirty metres, shut off for depth-charging!'

One by one the little red lights glittered on Ridgway's panel, until he said, 'All torpedoes running, sir!'

'Thirty metres, sir.'

'Alter course, Pilot. Steer three-one-zero. Stand by stern tubes, in case we miss him and he comes after us.'

Ainslie gripped a voice-pipe as the hull tilted to the change of course. He could see the four torpedoes as if he were outside in the depths. Fanning out in a lethal salvo while they worked up towards fifty knots.

Ridgway looked at his stop-watch, his face set in a frown. Forster was watching him, and Quinton's fingers were drumming on the back of a planesman's seat as he stared at the curved side.

The explosion, followed by two more at regular intervals, was more like a sharp crack than a bang. The fourth torpedo had missed, but under the circumstances Ainslie was satisfied.

'Periscope depth.'

He saw Ridgway reaching out to pat his assistant on the back and could imagine the sweating torpedomen in the fore-ends, already preparing to reload the empty tubes.

Walker reported, 'HE has stopped, sir.'

When the periscope broke surface Ainslie was just in time to see the patrol vessel's bow as it started to slide down in a great welter of boiling foam, above it the stain of the explosion hung across the sky as if it would never move.

Quinton called, 'Well done, sir. Just like old times.' They were all grinning like schoolboys.

A handset buzzed in its case like a trapped bee, then a messenger said, 'From W/T, sir. Signal.'

Ainslie beckoned Quinton to take his place by the periscopes. He reached for the handset, finding time to marvel at the petty officer telegraphist who had used his radio receiver while the boat was so near to the surface. Despite the grim preparations and then the explosions he had gone on with his own job.

'Captain.'

Vernon sounded tense. 'It was just a garble, sir. Probably a short-range army job.'

'Well?'

'The *Prince of Wales* and the *Repulse*, sir. Both sunk. Just now, while we were doing our attack.'

'Thank you.' He replace the handset and looked at Quinton and the rest. 'Force Z has been wiped out.' He watched their faces freeze, their smiles disappear. Against such a disastrous loss their own small victory was pitiful.

Quinton was the first to speak. 'They could be wrong. Some idiot getting his wires crossed.'

They looked at each other, each knowing in his heart there was no mistake.

'Resume course and depth, Pilot. Fall out diving and action stations.' Ainslie glanced at Halliday. 'Your people did well, Chief. Steady as a rock.' Just words, bloody words. Part of the game. The necessary pretence.

He moved to the centre of the control room, half watching, half listening. The news Vernon had intercepted would soon be across the whole world. In the twinkling of an eye Force Z had been destroyed. Maybe they had run into a more powerful squadron and had gone down fighting. Whatever had happened the result was the same. The whole balance of naval power had shifted in the enemy's favour. The essential shield had been found wanting and had paid the full, awesome price.

Later as he toyed with some food in his cabin he thought of the two great ships. The *Prince of Wales* was a new one with little history to remember, other than she had been witness to the *Hood*'s destruction under the guns of the German *Bismarck*.

But the old battle cruiser *Repulse* he did know, as did almost every sailor in the fleet. She had been part of the tradition and the myth, and with her gone it was one more sign, one further threat to their very existence. He sighed and lay down on his bunk, the food congealing on its plate.

He wondered if he would see any changes when he took the submarine back to Singapore. There might still be time to act, to hold the enemy until the forces in Malaya had been reinforced.

'*Captain in the control room!*'

He threw his legs to the deck, his heart beating faster. *Here we go again.*

The *Soufrière*'s wardroom was unusually quiet. Alongside the depot ship once again, and with most of her company on local leave, she gave the impression of resting.

Lieutenant Farrant, the gunnery officer, was sitting in a corner, utterly engrossed in a month-old copy of *Lilliput*. Lieutenant Forster, who was officer of the day, was re-reading the letter which had awaited *Soufrière*'s return to Singapore. It was from Daphne. A frightening, rambling letter, made worse by the sense of distance and helplessness. She would have to tell her mother about it. And when her husband came home . . . There had been splashes on the ink. He could see her crying as she had penned the last part. *If there's no other way, I shall kill myself.*

Forster looked up desperately. 'God Almighty.' He had read the letter over and over again. It got worse, not better.

Farrant looked over his magazine. 'Trouble?'

Across the other side of the wardroom Lieutenant Christie, the RNVR pilot, glanced at the two men with interest. He could smell the tension, like an animal scenting blood.

'It's nothing.'

Forster dropped his eyes. Angry with himself. He had started to hate Farrant. His smugness, his cock-sure arrogance.

Like their first patrol which had ended this morning. After the attack on the Jap patrol vessel and her tow, which had since been identified as a landing craft filled with men and stores, they had not seen very much. A few fishing vessels, driven to sea out of necessity, one rusty freighter which the skipper had sunk after ordering her crew to abandon, and the big landing craft.

Forster had all but forgotten his personal troubles as he had joined Ainslie and the others in the attack. He had watched Ainslie's face, judged every expression each time the periscope had shot down into its well, listened to the descriptions and reports, checked his plot and marked their progress on his chart. A really big landing craft, Ainslie had said. A fruitless look through a somewhat out-of-date copy of *Jane's Fighting Ships* and a more recent collection of silhouettes suggested it might be a tank landing vessel of considerable value.

She had been moving very slowly, well loaded with vehicles, zigzagging painfully like a giant shoe box on the placid water.

Forster had seen none of it, but looking back, Ainslie had described every detail with his routine reports, so that now it was like remembering a film or a picture.

Ainslie had decided to use the submarine's guns. For one thing it was possible that a full salvo of torpedoes might be necessary, and there was still no certainty of replacing them, the French ones being a different size from the British pattern. Also, the landing craft was very shallow draft, and the salvo might have passed harmlessly beneath her.

Forster looked quickly at Farrant. He was looking at his magazine again. The fact that his eyes were unmoving and fixed made him think he was studying a picture of a nude.

It had been Farrant's perfect opportunity, and to do him justice he had done very well, especially as it was the first shots they had fired from the big turret. With the hull barely trimmed above the surface, the guns had been trained on the landing craft. Inside the hull everybody had been poised, like athletes waiting for the starting pistol. Especially the first lieutenant and the chief engineer. A sharp change of buoyancy, some unknown factor which might throw the submarine out of control, it all had to be watched and prevented. When the guns had fired, one at a time, it had been like nothing Forster had experienced. The crash had been long drawn out, like a great peal of thunder, and the shock of each gun hurling itself back on its springs and cylinders had shaken the hull like some gigantic earth tremor. What it could have been like for the men on the landing craft he could only guess at.

First the sight of the turret and conning tower rising slowly through the clear water, and then the twin guns swinging towards them like a pair of black, pitiless eyes.

They had heard the sounds of the enemy vessel breaking up as it sank to the bottom, its cargo of armoured vehicles adding to the destruction and speeding its end. It was just as well. She must have been carrying high octane fuel, and the agony of her crew and passengers was only saved by the sea.

Dived once more, Ainslie had sent for Farrant. Forster could see him now. Prim, and so pleased with himself it was causing him pain to hide it.

He thought too of the skipper. Ainslie was a good one to have in command. Rarely raised his voice, and was never sarcastic. But Forster felt he did not really know him. Ainslie had asked the gunnery officer to pass his thanks to the men in the turret, as well as the others in the magazine and shell hoist.

Forster glanced at the curved bulkhead at the opposite end of the wardroom. Like the side of a lift shaft, it was the main support for the big turret above, and through which went the ammunition hoists from the magazine to the loaders at each gun. It was like the submarine's core, a symbol of tremendous durability and strength. He turned as Christie remarked, 'I wonder what the skipper's doing?'

Farrant said sharply, 'He's with the admiral and chief of staff. They will be discussing our next patrol.'

Christie smiled lazily. 'He told you, did he?'

Farrant frowned. 'When you've been in the Service a bit longer, or *attached* to it for the duration of this war, you might understand!'

'Oh.'

Christie sat back, enjoying himself. He had done many things in his life, and had flown some of the worst crates imaginable. Even during his naval flying he had had some strange jobs, but this one beat them all. A flyer in a submarine. On the patrol he had been a spectator as much as anything, keeping close to Forster and the navigator's yeoman so that he could study the changing charts, the lay of the area over which he might soon get the chance to fly. At thirty-one, he was one of the oldest men aboard. That also amused him. Some, like Sub-Lieutenant Southby, a slight, pink-faced youth who was Farrant's assistant in the turret, with the additional job of Boarding Officer, whatever that was, were so nervously unsure of everything. Others, a year or so older than Southby, had the confidence of giants but the knowledge of children.

He said, 'The way we're fighting this war, I don't reckon I'll have time to learn much more!'

Farrant stared at him as if he had uttered some terrible oath. 'How *dare* you!' He stood up and moved restlessly across the wardroom like a caged animal. 'Two fine ships sunk, all those men dying bravely, and you – '

Christie's eyes followed the gunnery officer back and forth. 'Balls,' he said calmly. 'The admiral in Force Z was told that Kuantan airfield had been evacuated because everyone was running high-tailed away from the Japs. He bloody well *knew* there was no air cover for his ships!'

Farrant stood stock still in front of Christie's seat, just to one side of his out-thrust legs.

Christie added quietly, 'You talk about those ships and the

brave lads who went down. Why not speak of the bloody fools who put them on the bottom?'

Christie could feel his anger getting a grip. It was all coming back. The carrier he had been in at Crete, the flight deck suddenly bursting wide open in a great mushroom of solid flames. Men on fire, running in circles, aircraft rolling over the side as the old carrier started to capsize.

'Without air cover they were written off from the start. *Before* the start! Stupid, bloody-minded idiots! It's a race for who kills more of our chaps first, the enemy or the high command!'

Farrant had recovered slightly. 'If I ever hear you speak like that again . . .' He swung on his heel and marched out, almost knocking down Torpedoman Sawle who was coming to lay the table for tea.

Forster said, 'I think you upset him, Jack.'

Christie looked at the deck, his eyes blurred. 'Sorry, Pilot. I wasn't getting at you, y'know. Farrant will be an admiral one day. His sort always win.'

Then he stood up and looked at his watch. 'Think I'll get a lift over the Causeway to the club. Have a couple of cold beers.' He winked. 'If they'll let me in the place!'

Alone, Forster took the letter from his pocket and began to read it once more.

Ainslie sat back in a cane chair and drew on his pipe. He and Critchley were in the residence of Rear-Admiral Arnold Granger. He was a sturdy, rounded man, too short for his weight, and his shape was further accentuated by his immaculate white shirt and shorts. Granger was prematurely bald, with just a strip of ginger hair on either side of his head, like feathers.

He said, 'I've asked you here, Commander Ainslie, because I think you've been badly used since you came out from the UK.' He, too, was smoking a pipe, and waved it in the air like a black finger as he added, 'Mind you, you're not the easiest fellow I've met either.' He smiled, changing him to an impish conspirator. 'But we need every experienced brain we can lay hands on. The C in C has assured me that reinforcements are already on the way. But troop convoys take weeks, sometimes months to get here. We require modern fighter aircraft, experienced infantry, and above all the ability to hit at the bastards before they push down south any further.'

He walked to a wall map and let it unroll to its full extent.

In a quieter tone he said, 'See that line, gentlemen?'

Ainslie leaned forward, appalled. There was an undulating strip of yellow tape which showed the extent of the enemy advances inland. It was incredible.

He tried to think back, to recall the length of time since that brief W/T signal about the air raid and then the news of Pearl Harbour. A grand total of ten days. In that small span the Japanese Army had penetrated every coastal defence on the north-east coast of Malaya. From the look of the admiral's yellow tape, which must already be out of date, it appeared there was nothing to stop the enemy from cutting the peninsula in half from the South China Sea to the Malacca Strait. Ten days from now where would they be?

The admiral said, 'So we've not a lot of time. It's not a shortage of troops which is the main problem, but lack of experienced combat soldiers. There are the Indian brigades. Australians, Malay Volunteers, and of course the British regiments.' He dropped his eyes and played with the pipe, making up his mind. Then he said bluntly, 'We probably outnumber the Japanese, and I think you should know that, too.'

Ainslie looked at him, understanding him, and feeling the burden he was carrying. He was the first outspoken and frank senior officer he had met in Singapore since his arrival. Granger had apparently been in charge of coastal patrols and operational training, and had been appointed to this HQ at very short notice. A better mind than his predecessor – or a scapegoat if the worst happened; it was too early to judge.

Critchley turned towards him, his chair creaking. 'The admiral says that civilian morale is important. If it starts to disintegrate, our troops will lose heart. At present the forces in the north are regrouping after making a series of strategic withdrawals.'

Ainslie looked for a hint of bitterness. Retreats had been called withdrawals for long enough. At home, news readers often spoke casually of patrol activity or slight casualties. It made them acceptable.

But Critchley was alert again. Involved. Seeking a way out.

Granger said, 'Reports are bad. The enemy is using terror as a weapon. We've had several accounts of torture, beheading, rape and God knows what else. If we don't hold the buggers

79

back, the retreat will turn into a rout, right down here as far as the Causeway and the Johore Strait.'

Critchley put in, 'And on to the island. They'll not stop at the strait. Anyway, it's only four feet deep at low water, they tell me.'

Granger frowned worriedly. 'Then someone's talking too much. It's true, of course. But you know the British, a strip of water is the English Channel to them. Safety. Separation.'

Ainslie stood up and crossed to the wall map. It was hard to imagine the bitter fighting up there in the jungle, or even the patrol vessel's bows sliding under water, the landing craft flying apart under Farrant's gunfire.

Outside this long, cool room he could hear some shrill bird cries, the sound of a young woman singing in the kitchen, a native policeman's measured tread on the gravel path below the window. Relaxed and secure.

The admiral was filling his pipe with quick stabbing motions. 'Fact is, we can't operate surface units up there to support the army. We've neither the aircraft nor the fields to fly them from. We've lost a few inshore patrols already. I can't risk any heavier units in case' – he looked Ainslie straight in the eyes – 'we have to evacuate.'

Ainslie nodded. Not again, surely? Dunkirk, Norway, Holland, Greece and Crete. Anyway, it was different here. No cliffs of Dover, no narrow seas for the Navy to lift off an exhausted army. What had once been Singapore's true strength had suddenly loomed in his mind as complete vulnerability. And all the while those great guns which were here to protect the island pointed impotently in the wrong direction.

Aloud he asked, 'You want me to go north again, sir?'

'Yes.' The admiral's portly shadow joined his own by the map. 'There is a pocket of resistance on that coast which in a day or so might be reinforced if Army HQ can fathom out how to do it.' He laid his pipe stem on the map. 'Just there. If things go wrong, and the Japs put on more pressure,' the pipe stem moved like a trap door, 'then all those people will be trapped with their backs to the sea.'

Critchley said quietly, 'Could you give artillery support, Bob?'

The admiral watched Ainslie's profile. '*Could* you?'

Farrant's face seemed to appear on the map. How he had enjoyed using the guns. Perhaps he had even found some sort of pleasure in watching the death and destruction through his powerful sights, too.

'I can try, sir.'

It was a dream, or the start of a nightmare. Nobody wanted the *Soufrière* or him. Now there seemed to be no other vessel available, and everyone expected a miracle. Yet he had said, *I can try*. There was no other way.

He asked, 'When?'

Critchley spoke for the admiral. 'Tomorrow morning.'

'You'll get full support from the base, Commander.' The admiral sat down and stared into space. 'Commander Critchley will be coming with you.'

Ainslie looked at his friend. 'Why, for God's sake?'

Critchley smiled. 'Experience. As an extension of higher authority. Or maybe to assist.'

Granger looked at the clock. 'Sun's well over the yard-arm. We'll have a gin, eh?' He pressed a bell switch and then said, 'Commander Critchley may be of greater use than either of us realize, Ainslie.' He smiled. 'Service politics are over my head.'

Ainslie walked to the window and looked across the lush green foliage of a garden.

Critchley was going with him because he felt responsible. It had been his idea to seize the *Soufrière*, just as he had suspected. Now, if things went badly wrong in those shallow waters he had just seen on the map, he wanted to share that, too.

He turned and looked steadily at his friend. 'I'll find a job for you. No passengers in my boat.'

The admiral watched them and felt strangely moved. Perhaps there was still a chance after all.

6

No Second Chance

COMMANDER GREGORY CRITCHLEY stepped gingerly into the control room's orange glow and studied each intent figure in turn. It was very quiet, with just the muted hum of motors and fans and the regular ping of the echo sounder to break the stillness. He could not even hear any of the control room team breathing. In the strange light they looked unreal, like waxworks, not on display but stored for some later exhibition.

In the two days it had taken *Soufrière* to work her way northwards again, keeping well to seaward to avoid enemy ships and aircraft, he had had plenty of time to watch his companions. Critchley had refused Ainslie's offer of the captain's cabin, knowing that Ainslie needed the seclusion, when he could get it, more than anyone. He had enjoyed sharing the wardroom, studying the mixed bunch who lived, slept and worried there.

Quinton, the first lieutenant, was peering over to check the hydroplane tell-tales, one hand on each planesman's back. A good, outspoken and intelligent man. He had a quick temper, too, which when required was a useful foil to Ainslie's calmer approach.

Critchley looked across to the chart space, seeing Ainslie leaning over the vibrating plot table, his face reflecting the light beneath the glass. He may look calm, but Critchley knew what was going on. He had interviewed many submariners, some of whom, like Ainslie, had taken part in hair-raising cloak-and-dagger raids on enemy coasts, fighting at close quarters.

It took guts, and a whole lot of other things to keep going.

Then there was the navigating officer at his side, Forster. A nice young chap with a load on his mind. Probably a woman somewhere.

Halliday, at the diving panel, who looked like the ship's engineer in a dozen sea stories, and the slight French lieutenant close by, Lucas, another man with a well-concealed secret.

Lieutenant Ridgway was lounging by his 'fruit machine', face in shadow. But it usually appeared so even in bright daylight. Like Halliday, he kept to himself.

The others were out of sight, swallowed up within the hull. Sub-Lieutenant Deacon, the assistant engineer. Young Southby, the second gunnery officer, and, of course, the impressive Farrant, who would be somewhere near the turret with his crews, in case he was needed.

The ratings, from the fat coxswain to the messenger by the telephones, were as mixed as their officers. Individuals, who at moments like these became one living body.

Ainslie saw him and smiled. 'Good morning. Sleep well?'

Critchley walked to the chart space. Some of the men nodded to him, then forgot his presence as a light flashed or a dial gave an unexpected quiver to demand their constant attention.

'Sawle got me some tea. He'd make a good butler.'

Ainslie looked at the clock. 'It will be dawn soon. I shall take a look in a minute or two. Number One's checking the trim. It's got to be perfect.' He gestured to the chart. 'We're in fifteen fathoms, no more. Practically crawling along the sea-bed!' He grimaced. 'But Pilot here assures me all will be well.' He looked at Quinton. 'Time to alter course. Steer two-four-zero. Revolutions for six knots.' He turned his head. 'Bosun's mate, pass the word again. Absolute silence throughout the boat.'

· 'Steady on two-four-zero, sir.'

Critchley asked, 'What will you see?' He smiled at himself. He was whispering.

'Not much. Two hills.' Ainslie stooped over the chart again. 'See? Like a cocked hat from seaward. The Japs are all around there, and our troops are pinned down in a fishing village. There was a mission there, too, but I expect it was evacuated when the panic started.'

The messenger called softly, 'Gunnery officer, sir.'

Ainslie took a telephone. 'Captain.'

Farrant sounded impatient. 'Permission to man the turret, sir?'

'After I've had a look, Guns.' He met Quinton's eyes across the control room. 'And don't forget to take the tampions out before you fire the things!'

'Yes, sir.' No hint of a chuckle.

'I don't know why I bother.' To Quinton he said, 'All ready?'

The Australian glanced at Halliday who gave a curt nod. 'Ready, sir.'

'Very well. Periscope depth, please.' He looked at Critchley. 'Say a prayer.'

Critchley moved clear to watch every last detail. The petty officer stoker at the vent controls, the planesmen as they watched for any sign that the boat might rise too abruptly and burst to the surface like a giant dolphin.

'Fourteen metres, sir.' Even Quinton sounded unusually hushed.

Ainslie nodded to the rating with the hoist switch and ducked down to receive the periscope as it hissed smoothly through the deck.

He found he was holding his breath, blinking rapidly as if he could already see above the surface. He watched the lens lightening reluctantly. It was very early in the morning, with a slight swell to sway the hull like an unseen cradle.

'Stop.'

He moved the periscope in a slow circle, his feet and legs moving crablike round the well as he looked for any sign of life. Astern it was pale grey, delicate and giving no hint of the heat and colour to come. He swung the periscope towards the bows. The land was directly across his vision, from side to side like an undulating black reef. In less than an hour there would be green and brown and blue and, if the chart was right, a crescent of silver sand by the village.

He switched to full power and studied the rise of land to the right of his lens. The twin hills.

'Village and hills in sight, Pilot. Dead ahead. Range about three miles.'

He tensed and moved the periscope swiftly to port, just in time to see a bright green light drifting above the land like a drip of molten emerald.

'Flare of some sort. Miles inland.'

He could feel the silence around him, oppressive, concentrated. They were thinking of his brief reports, each man measuring them against a past experience. Somewhere out there, beyond the impartial periscope, were men, probably stalking each other in thick jungle, or lying wounded and alone, waiting to be captured or killed.

Ainslie shivered in spite of his reserve which he kept for such moments. Not for me. Here, we are together. We live or die as one.

'Down periscope.' He straightened his back and looked at Critchley. 'It's like a grave. Everything will depend on the first signal we get from base. After that it's up to us.'

Critchley smiled wryly. *To you, you mean.* Rear-Admiral Granger had allowed for almost everything. If *Soufrière* was unable to reach this point on the chart in time he would make another signal tomorrow at the same time, and so on. Except, of course, his strip of yellow tape had probably moved another few inches by now.

He said, 'If you sight aircraft, what then?'

'I'll head out to sea at a rate of knots.' Ainslie smiled. 'I think we'll have some benefit of surprise though. After their successful attack on Force Z, I should imagine the Japs will be preoccupied with their land advances. They think that the C in C is rushing a million reinforcements to drive 'em into the sea.'

Quinton said softly, 'No fear of that.'

Ainslie wiped his palms on his trousers. 'Tell the gunnery officer to man his turret. When the klaxon sounds he can load with HE. Not before. I don't want the ready-use racks crammed with shells in the middle of a depth-charge attack.'

Gosling gave a throaty chuckle, and the second coxswain remarked, 'Expensive coffin, sir!'

Ainslie heard all and none of it as he checked his mental calculations, whittling and honing, setting his ideas against that unbroken shadow of land. Have to be careful. The sun would be up soon and right astern.

He said, 'Periscope.' He wiped his hands again. They were wet with sweat. 'Stop.'

He peered in every direction, blinking as the shallow swell rose above the periscope, blinding him.

Still quiet. He smiled, thinking of a patriotic film he had seen in London. The officer in a dugout, his voice clipped as he said, '*It's quiet. Too damn quiet.*' They always said that. He blinked as another flare exploded on almost the same bearing. Patrol activity, or an enemy signal for a dawn attack.

Aloud he said, 'We'll surface now. Hold her down on the planes as long as you can, Number One.' He glanced at the ladder beneath the conning tower. They were all assembled. Machine-gunners, lookouts, everyone. They were wearing dark glasses so

85

that the poor light above might seem brighter. In the dull glow they looked like a collection of blind men. He said, 'Open the lower hatch. Tell W/T to stand by.'

He heard his orders murmuring away through the complex of voice-pipes and wires, and pictured the men receiving them in each curved compartment. Torpedo tubes loaded, magazine and shell lifts manned and ready, and aft in the engine and motor rooms the stokers and ERAs would be poised to give power and speed at seconds' notice.

Ainslie slung his glasses round his neck and walked to the ladder. Menzies, the yeoman of signals, followed him up the smooth ladder, waiting to grip Ainslie's legs as he opened the upper hatch. It had been known for a commander to be blown bodily out of a conning tower by upbuilt pressure. It must be a comical sight. A cork from a bottle.

He shouted, 'Surface!' Then he was already swinging the upper locking wheel and knocking off the clips as the klaxon gave a loud squawk and the air began to thunder into the saddle tanks, the immediate buoyancy fighting the planesmen as they held the bows down until the last moment.

Then, as Ainslie thrust through the hatch, his face and shoulders drenched with spray and sluicing water inside the bridge, the *Soufrière* surged up to the surface, the sea parting across her broad spine in two hissing banks of foam.

While Menzies opened the cocks on the voice-pipes, and the seamen panted and cursed to get their heavy machine-guns mounted on either side, Ainslie raised his glasses, astonished at the speed with which they had all moved.

'Tell the control room, all clear.'

A hatch scraped open and Ainslie saw a pale figure leave the gun turret and return almost immediately with the two tampions from the muzzles. The turret gave a slight squeak and moved smoothly to starboard, then back again. Ainslie watched it. It was like something entirely independent from the rest of the boat, from them.

'Another flare, sir. Port bow.' The lookout moved his powerful glasses carefully. 'I think there's a lot of smoke about, too. Too dark for mist.'

Ainslie nodded. 'Thanks. Keep looking.'

He trained his glasses on the two hills. They would soon be plain to see. So will we, he thought.

'Ask Number One what the depth is.'

Menzies came back. 'Twelve fathoms, sir.' He pouted. 'Same for another mile.'

The messenger called, 'First lieutenant for you, sir.'

'Yes?'

'Signal, sir. Right on time. The enemy are still in same position, but our people are down to the last few rounds.'

'I see.'

He turned his head as the turret began to move again. It made a soft whirring sound, and he could see the raised humps at the rear and where Farrant and his sub-lieutenant were searching for the target through their range-finders.

He picked up the small handset which Menzies had just plugged to the side of the bridge.

'This is the captain. Are you ready, Guns?'

He almost expected to see the big turret nod. Instead he heard Farrant say, 'Ready, sir. Loaded with HE. Training on bearing green one-oh. Range oh-four-two. That should deal with the dip between the hills.' He did not elaborate. Like the man or not, he knew his stuff and had memorized every known details of the hills, the narrow road, everything.

Ainslie said, 'They're still holding out, but time's short. So do what you can.'

'Yes, sir.' He sounded indifferent to everything but the target.

Ainslie looked at Menzies. 'Ear-plugs, everybody. Tell the control room to stand by.'

He looked thoughtfully at the distant land. It was getting much easier to see. It was strange to think that the troops in the village could speak with their HQ but not to the submarine.

He stood back from the cold metal and raised his glasses. 'Open fire.'

The turret gave a tiny click, and then as a distorted voice came through the handset, 'Right gun! *Shoot!*', the day seemed to explode in a great searing flash. Seconds later the left gun hurled itself backwards on its springs, and as Ainslie gritted his teeth against the pain of the explosions he saw two vivid flashes erupt from the hillside.

The left gun drooped slightly as Farrant corrected the range. A gong clanged tinnily inside the turret and again the guns roared out, the sound waves tearing across the gently lifting swell like a pair of express trains.

Ainslie watched the fall of shot, both almost together this time. Each shell weighed over two hundred and fifty pounds, and being high explosive would punch holes into hillsides and jungle alike far worse than any military artillery could offer.

Once through his ringing ears he heard Menzies bark, 'Watch your front, man!' He guessed that a lookout's eyes had left their proper sector to watch the bombardment.

When Ainslie lowered his glasses to wipe them free of moisture he saw that the men around him were recognizable again. The sun was breaking over the horizon, opening up the colour chart for another day.

The messenger said shakily, 'Control room say they will have to alter course in six minutes, sir.'

'Very well.'

Ainslie winced as the guns fired, the smoke from one of them rising above the surfaced submarine in a giant ring.

He could see the action plot in his mind, the crude parallelogram around which they could move without fear of grounding, or being caught in too shallow water to dive.

Above his head he could see the two periscopes twisting on the standards as Quinton and Forster made repeated checks to fix their position.

It was bad enough up here. What the gunfire was doing to the men inside the hull was not to be contemplated.

A lookout said, 'Hillside is alight, sir. I can see small-arms fire to the right of the village.'

'Yes.'

Ainslie looked on the same bearing and saw the dense pall of smoke edged with flames, some from the trees, others from automatic weapons. The village was already burned out. Buildings and upended fishing boats scattered about in all directions.

'Tell the gunnery officer that he will cease firing after the next two salvoes.'

It was impossible to gauge the effect of the bombardment on the enemy positions, but the surprise of their attack might have been far more important to the beleaguered troops.

His head was aching badly, and he felt completely drained by the rasping crash of gunfire.

He saw the turret swing round for the last shots as the hull beneath it altered course on the next leg. The air seemed to be full of gritty smoke which drifted downwind like a screen.

Ainslie bent over the voice-pipe. 'Number One?'

'Sir.'

'Secure the turret. We're getting out.'

He turned away as Quinton rapped out a stream of orders. Obediently, the turret swung round to point fore and aft once more, the muzzles still smoking from their unexpected exercise.

There had not been a single shot fired at them in return. Not even a bullet. It was incredible.

'Turret secured for diving, sir.'

Ainslie watched the flames and smoke through his glasses. 'Very well. Tell the first lieutenant to bring her round on course.' They would all be glad to be out of it, he thought. Sailors hated being near land.

'*Sir!*' The lookout's voice made him start. 'Boat on the starboard bow!'

He heard Quinton call, 'Small boat, sir! Green four-five!' He must have seen it through the periscope as he gave the order to alter course.

The bridge machine-guns swung towards it, their muzzles depressed, following the dark shape as it edged nearer and nearer. It appeared to be swinging round the submarine towards the starboard beam, but the illusion was made by the *Soufrière's* own turn.

'Got it!' The starboard machine-gun steadied, the long belts of ammunition shivering as the deck tilted to screws and rudder.

'Hold your fire!' Ainslie held the boat in his glasses. *Dear God. Look at them.* Where were they going? What chance did they think they had? It was an old motor launch. A relic.

He watched the faces in the lenses. Pale, dirty, bandaged and bloody. Soldiers, Malays, even a few children.

He said quietly, 'Muster the second cox'n and his deck party. Fast as you like. Tell the first lieutenant to open the fore-hatch.'

He heard Menzies passing his orders and then the same lookout who had sighted the listing boat say, 'They're stopping, sir. Or turning away.' He sounded confused.

Of course. That was it. 'Yeoman! Run up the ensign!'

And so, as the light strengthened and probed through the drifting layers of smoke the old motor launch came alongside, secured to the saddle tank by a grapnel and heaving line.

It was a dangerous and foolhardy thing to do. On the surface with the big fore-hatch open, unable to dive, and with all hell liable to break loose at any second.

Ainslie watched them being passed or carried along a line of seamen on the casing and through the hatch. Only two soldiers remained in the launch as it was cut free, and they would never know about it.

Petty Officer Voysey crossed his hands above his head and then he, too, vanished through the hatch. The deck was empty again, with only the drifting boat and its two dead soldiers to prove it was not imaginary.

Ainslie stared at the hatch as it clanged shut. He could no more have dived and left them helpless than fly.

'Clear the bridge.' The men rushed to the hatch. 'Dive, dive, dive!' He jabbed the klaxon button twice, looking once more at the drifting boat before he jumped down on to the ladder and slammed the hatch over his head.

He strode to the centre of the control room, knowing they were watching him. 'Periscope depth, Number One.' He looked at Critchley. 'All done.'

Critchley saw the strain, the dullness in his eyes. '*And* a bit more, if you ask me.'

'Fourteen metres, sir. Ship's head zero-seven-zero.'

Ainslie turned the periscope astern and stared at the smoke for several seconds. Then he signalled the stoker to lower it and walked to the chart table.

'Twenty metres. Revolutions for ten knots.'

He stared down at the vibrating chart between his hands. If he did not hold on to something he knew he would start shaking.

'Take over, Number One. I'm going forrard to see our passengers.'

Quinton looked at him. 'I'll go, if you like, sir.' But Ainslie had already left the control room.

Critchley crossed to join him and said quietly, 'I've not seen him like this before.'

Quinton stared past him, straight through the curved side at another sea. 'Oh, I have, sir. Believe me, I have.'

Critchley said nothing, wanting to hear more but afraid to break the spell.

Then Quinton said bluntly. 'Ask the Chief, or the cox'n, any of the lads who've been with him before. They might tell you, sir. What it's like to watch a man doing all he can to stop you getting killed, and killing himself in the process! But please don't ask me. To me it's private. Special.' He turned away, suddenly angry.

'Watch it, Packer, you're all over the bloody place! Like an Aussie barman on a Saturday night, for Chrissake!'

Critchley walked quietly away. It was Quinton's way of ending it.

Unlike conventional submarines, *Soufrière* boasted a sick-bay which was almost as large as a destroyer's.

As Ainslie made his way through the boat he saw the survivors from the motor launch propped in the passageway or lying on blankets waiting to receive attention.

Petty Officer Hunt, the *Soufrière*'s sick-berth attendant, in his clean white coat, stood out against the pain and the despair like some sort of angel.

Some seamen were doing their best to make their unexpected passengers comfortable, and Ainslie heard someone cry out in pain, and a voice say, '*Easy*, mate. Take it easy.'

They fell silent as he stepped carefully amongst them, his eyes moving across their faces, his ears still recording the sounds he had left behind in the control room. He trusted Quinton with his life, but so far from his place of command he felt vulnerable and helpless.

Hunt looked up from bandaging a soldier's head. 'Thirty-five, sir.'

Ainslie nodded. Thirty-five in that small boat. It did not seem possible. The soldier was Australian, his uniform filthy and almost torn from his back. He was about twenty but looked fifty.

Another wounded soldier tried to stand but sank against the steel plating with a grunt of pain. He was a sergeant, and looked as if he had been wounded several times.

He said, 'Thought we was a goner. Bloody boat was crook from the start. Kept breaking down. We were ordered to make a break for it. The Japs was almost on top of us, the bastards!' He fell back, his eyes closed, as Hunt started to cut through a stained dressing on his shoulder. But he went on, 'Then we saw you. Right there. An' I thought, Jesus Christ, they've done for us after all.'

A soldier, lying on his back by Ainslie's feet, said, 'You was goin' to start shootin', right, Sarge?'

The sergeant looked down at him with something like affection. 'Yeh, Tom. Reckon I was at that.'

Ainslie turned, startled, as a woman's voice said quietly, 'Then we saw the flag. A miracle. I still can't believe it.'

Ainslie stared at her. She was dressed in khaki shirt and trousers, her dark hair tied back to the nape of her neck with a piece of bandage. She was as filthy as her companions, but Ainslie could not understand how he had failed to see her.

She saw his confusion and said, 'I should like to meet your captain.'

She reached out and put her arm around someone's shoulders, and Ainslie realized it was another young woman, equally dishevelled and soaked in water, and stained from head to toe with smoke and dirt.

'She's passed out. It was too much for her.' As a seaman took the second girl and began to carry her into the sick-bay she got to her feet and said, 'My name is Natalie Torrance.'

She smiled, and in those brief seconds Ainslie saw what it had cost her to keep up her pretence.

She added, 'What a way to meet someone.'

Ainslie took her hand. 'I'm Robert Ainslie.'

She did not release her grip. 'You are the captain, aren't you? I can tell. It would have to be somebody like you.'

Ainslie said to Hunt, 'I'll send you some more hands.' He saw the SBA give him a short, prissy nod. He was that sort of man, but far better at his job than many a naval surgeon.

She did not resist as he led her to his cabin. It seemed a mile away, and he was conscious of her dazed uncertainty as she swayed against him or groped at a wire cable or some piece of equipment for support.

She said, 'That girl is my sister, Shelly. I had gone up country from Singapore to visit her and her husband. I was alone, and I needed someone to talk to.' She swung round and gripped his arm until her nails broke his skin. 'Oh God, is was terrible. The planes, the buildings all on fire, people in a panic, blood on my dress, screaming.' She stared at her hands around his arm and said huskily, 'I'm sorry. I'm not like this really.' She looked at the cabin as he opened the door for her. 'It's not real. I knew it.'

He replied gently, 'She's French built. Something of a novelty.'

He did not know what to say. He watched her as she sat down in a chair, her fingers gripping the arms as if she expected it to be dragged from under her. She needed rest, to be drugged if necessary to release her mind from what she had endured. But he had to know what was happening, and at once.

Ainslie asked quietly, 'Who put you in the boat?'

'The officer in charge. A nice Australian. A captain, I think. But very young. And Shelly's husband, Michael. He's still there. With the others.'

Ainslie tried to fit the pieces together. The Japs were in the hills, but those flares had been to port, not starboard. They must have been sealing off the last escape route from the village. The unknown Australian officer had crowded some of the wounded, the women and some Malayan children into the only available craft in the faint hope they would be able to bypass the enemy lines and find help.

She was saying in the same dreamy tone, 'They kept shooting all the time, and then at night they brought the people they had captured near enough for us to hear as they tortured them. The women they raped first.' Her head drooped and her shoulders began to shake. 'It was horrible. *Horrible!*'

'How many did you see left behind? Please, I have to know.'

She looked up, her eyes shining very brightly in the dimmed deckhead light.

'About forty, I think. Mostly soldiers. The servants all ran away. I hope they escaped.'

Ainslie unlocked his cabinet and took out a glass and some brandy. It must be happening all over Malaya, he thought. Settlements, plantations, tiny villages, secure in their isolation until a few days ago. The admiral's strip of yellow tape meant nothing up here. It was a complete shambles.

He handed her the glass, watching her as she looked at it in his hand. She was young, in her mid-twenties, and even her filthy clothing could not disguise that she was very attractive. Another part of the wild dream. A submarine, a beleaguered village, a stranded girl.

She said, 'You are very kind.' One hand moved up to her hair. 'I must look like nothing on earth.' But she did not even try to smile. She must have known it would be like opening the gates to hysteria and worse.

Ainslie turned as he heard voices in the passageway, and then

93

saw the other girl framed in the doorway, her arms outstretched as she clung to the sides.

She shouted, 'You're going to kill them, aren't you, Captain?' She was almost screaming, her body shaking with despair. *'Wipe them out!* And I want to watch you do it!'

Behind her, Petty Officer Hunt's white coat bobbed from side to side as he pleaded, 'Please, miss, you must come back with me!'

She did not even hear him. 'Tell him, Natalie! Explain to him what happens to anyone that those yellow bastards get their hands on!'

Her sister made to leave the chair but Ainslie stood firmly between them.

'She's told me. I understand.'

The girl let her arms drop to her sides and she said in a low, muffled voice, 'We've only been married a year. You'll be able to save him, won't you?'

Ainslie looked away. 'It was already too late when we got here. Everything's confused. At HQ they still believe there's a hope of getting the place relieved.'

In the sudden silence he heard the girl behind him, her breathing, and saw her sister standing framed in the passage light, staring at him like a wild animal.

A telephone buzzed and he took it from its hook. It seemed to weigh a ton.

'Captain.' He barely recognized his own voice. In his mind he was watching this girl's husband being butchered.

'First lieutenant, sir.' Quinton sounded calm enough. 'Assuming new course in three minutes.' He cleared his throat. 'W/T received a signal just prior to diving, sir. Most immediate. Japanese troopship and escort believed to be approaching Kota Baharu from Saigon. ETA tomorrow forenoon. Nothing nearer than that, I'm afraid.' When Ainslie remained silent he dropped his voice, 'You all right? Can I come and give some help?'

'No, but thank you, John. Get Pilot working out a possible course and speed to intercept. We'll surface tonight and see if we can pick up any details of the escort, right?' He put down the telephone and said quietly, 'We'll not be going inshore again.' He made himself meet her stare. 'I'm sorry, I really am.'

She would have fallen at his feet but for Hunt and Torpedo-man Sawle. She was shrieking as they half dragged, half carried her back to the sick-bay, her cries echoing around the steel hull like a trapped spirit.

'You bastard! You bloody, cowardly bastard! You're like all the rest! *Run, run, run!*'

Then there was silence, worse in some ways, as Hunt jabbed one of his needles into her arm.

Ainslie looked down as the other girl reached out and gripped his hand.

'You mustn't take any notice. She will understand. One day she will know you can't always do what you want to.'

Ainslie looked at her, at the two pale lines on her cheeks where tears had cut through the grime.

'She'll never understand. I wouldn't in her place.' He saw the brandy bottle quivering gently on the desk. That was what he needed. Oblivion.

She followed his glance and said, 'I watched your face just now. When you were speaking to one of your men on the telephone. I think I know what you were going through.'

Ainslie ran his fingers through his unruly hair. 'Maybe I did you more harm than good by picking you up. I'm not sure any more. In the boat you might have run ashore a few miles further south and been safe.' He waved vaguely around the cabin. 'Here, you might be killed with the rest of us.'

He tried to stop the words but they kept coming. He had never been this way before. Had always been able to control it.

He said bitterly, 'I've been in a war for two years. We've been fighting it with ships and weapons which should have been scrapped ages ago! Now, when the very people who sneered at our efforts are in danger themselves, they expect bloody miracles!' He turned and looked at her steadily. 'But unfortunately we have only ordinary men and women, no miracles at all.'

She watched him as he moved to the door, poised on the edge of the chair.

He turned towards her and added softly, 'Sorry about that. Make yourself as comfortable as you can. I'll not be back until it's over.' He almost said, *one way or the other*.

For a long while after he had left the cabin the girl, Natalie Torrance, sat watching the closed door and the vibrating curtain across it. Suddenly she stood up, walked very erectly to the bunk and then collapsed.

In the control room Ainslie crossed to the chart space and studied Forster's calculations. They must all have heard the girl's screams and accusations. They were looking at him now, he could feel it. Pity, contempt, even surprise that he could turn away and leave men to die.

He was ashamed of himself even as he thought it. These were not ordinary men at all. They had shared a lot together, or with others in different vessels. They knew. Everyone ought to know about such things after the loss of the *Repulse* and *Prince of Wales*. You did not throw away lives to no purpose, and to take *Soufrière* close inshore again, and in broad daylight, would be like committing mass suicide.

But in Singapore they might see it differently. The lure of the big target, and never mind the risks they would yet have to take. The yearning for glory and medals all round. Just as it had shown on the chief of staff's face on that first day.

Quinton asked, 'What d'you think, sir?'

Ainslie looked at him. Quinton's eyes were asking about something quite different. He smiled gravely. 'I think we'd better get into some deeper water as soon as we can. But for now, Number One, would you go forrard and see to the wounded. Most of them are Australians. It might help.' He gave a quick shake of the head. 'Some won't make it, I'm afraid.'

Quinton nodded. 'Right away.'

Ainslie turned to study the chart. 'Send for Lieutenant Christie.'

When the flyer arrived Ainslie said calmly, 'They say you're a good pilot?'

Christie met his gaze and replied, 'The best, sir, in all modesty.'

Ainslie smiled, trying to shut out the girl's stricken face, her grief.

'Good. Provided you can get that plane airborne, I want you to go and look for some ships.'

Christie grinned. 'Piece of cake, sir.'

That night, when *Soufrière* cautiously surfaced to charge her batteries and listen to the radio waves from all parts of the world, three of their passengers were quietly dropped over the side.

One of the dead soldiers came from Melbourne, Quinton's home town. It was fitting and moving to hear Quinton read the burial service over the intercom while Ainslie and the bridge lookouts did the rest.

Later on, as Ainslie stood by the starboard side, an unlit pipe between his teeth, Quinton reported another signal from the W/T office. All resistance had ceased in the little fishing village, and no further news was expected.

Ainslie remained on the bridge for most of the night, following the stars while the watches changed and the lookouts came and went.

Suppose the signal had not been received about the troopship? Perhaps the girl was right after all and he was using duty as an excuse, an escape.

Could he have done something to rescue the last defenders in the village?

Critchley joined him on the bridge after asking permission from the control room.

He said simply, 'I've not bothered you before, you had enough on your plate. But I've kept my eyes on you most of the time. I know what you're thinking.'

Ainslie shook his head. 'Leave it, for God's sake.'

'No. You did the right thing. What you would have expected any captain to do. You would have despised anyone who risked his men for a hopeless gesture.'

Ainslie turned towards him, his hair rippling in the night breeze across the screen.

'But was it *hopeless*?'

'I'm certain of it. The troopship, on the other hand, might be essential to the enemy at this present moment. If they get reinforcements now, we'll never stop them.'

'I know all that.' Ainslie stared up at the stars. 'So why did this matter so much?'

Critchley groped his way to the hatch. 'It's never been easy to let men die. Most of us never have to decide on such things, thank God. But I hope that if I was in that position, I'd have had the sort of courage I saw here yesterday.'

Ainslie smiled wearily as Critchley's head disappeared through the hatch.

'Go to hell!'

7

'It Will Get Harder'

AINSLIE moved his powerful binoculars slowly from bow to bow. It was very dark, although the apparent smallness of the stars showed that dawn was not far off.

The submarine below his feet was moving at a steady eight knots, the occasional rise and fall of her blunt bows revealed by trailing patterns of white foam, but little enough to show where the hull ended and the sea began.

Down in the control room Quinton had completed his final checks, readjusting the trimming tanks against the findings on his slide-rule. The trim, always the first lieutenant's responsibility, was a boring but vital necessity. As the submarine lived off her own fat, consuming fuel and fresh water, losing the weight of torpedoes, stores, food and all the rest, her balance and buoyancy had to be continually watched and altered.

'Control room reports all clear, sir.' Sub-Lieutenant Southby, temporarily released from his duties in the gun turret, spoke carefully, as if aware of his new importance.

'Good.'

Ainslie strained his eyes through the glasses. The *Soufrière* was steering north-east, some seventy miles from the Malayan coast. The sea was empty, but it was always well to check everything. W/T for other vessels' signals, the Asdic and hydrophone equipment for listening through every layer of water. *Soufrière* was a big target, and any undetected patrol vessel would soon pick her up on her radio direction finder.

How crowded the bridge seemed. Extra lookouts, Menzies, the yeoman of signals, Lieutenant Cottier, the Free French electrical officer, and a couple of messengers at voice-pipes and telephones made the prospect of a crash-dive hair-raising, Ainslie thought. Not that it would matter anyway, once they had the hangar open. An early British submarine had once been fitted with a seaplane, but when the boat had dived a fault in the hangar doors had flooded the whole compartment, the sudden weight of top-hamper taking the submarine and all her company to the bottom.

He said, 'Open the hangar.' He heard Cottier on his handset, the sudden grate of metal abaft the conning tower as the doors slid apart. Like imploring arms, the ends of the small catapult made a darker shadow across the casing and, with a whirring sound, like Farrant's turret, the aircraft perched on its release gear swung into view.

Menzies muttered, 'Rather him than me, sir.'

Ainslie craned over the screen to watch the bustling activity below him. If the seaplane failed to get airborne they would have to ditch it. But if *Soufrière* had to dive because of some unforeseen emergency Christie would have no choice but to head for the nearest land and pray it was still in friendly hands.

He had watched the pilot's features as he had outlined his plan. But he had seen little change in Christie's expression, other than relief to be away on his own again. Alone, except for his gangling observer, Sub-Lieutenant Jones. They made a strange pair. Christie, the tough, experienced flyer, and Jones, who had been a bank clerk when the war had started.

'Is everything all right, Cottier?' He knew little of the Frenchman, who was quite unlike Lucas in every way. He laughed a lot, but never with his eyes, and in some odd way Ainslie felt he did not really like the other French lieutenant.

'They are prepared, *Capitaine.*' Cottier showed his teeth in the gloom. 'Shall I make the signal?'

Ainslie nodded. 'Warn the control room.'

He thought suddenly of the passengers. The dark-eyed Malay women and the children clinging to them like ragged pods. The soldiers, those not drugged to ease their pain, seemed to spend their time staring into space, completely separated from their comrades around them. Reliving some of it. Letting parts of the horror ease back into their minds, as a man will feel a wound.

With a coughing roar the seaplane's engine snarled into life, filling the bridge with blue vapour and a chorus of protests and curses from the lookouts.

Cottier waved a white flag over the screen, and like a missile fired from a spring gun the twin-winged plane shot along the short catapult and climbed skyward.

Ainslie felt the shock wave ripping over the submarine, and

felt the excitement around him as they all watched the little seaplane climbing and climbing, dashing across the pale stars like a shadow.

The tannoy droned. 'Secure catapult and hangar. Clear the casing.'

If and when the plane returned, it would land on its floats as near as possible and taxi alongside where it would be winched aboard by its own special derrick.

Ainslie glanced at Southby. 'Well, Sub, what did you think of that?'

'Jolly good, sir.' He sounded as if he had doubted Christie's ability until this moment.

Ainslie forgot about Southby and concentrated on the one short signal they had added to their sparse information about the troopship. She was large, an ex-cargo liner of some twelve thousand tons. There was still no news about the strength of her escort, but two destroyers had been reported leaving Saigon at about the same time. But Ainslie had operated before with far less intelligence at his disposal. Usually his first knowledge of the target had been when it had appeared in his cross-wires.

He was almost certain that the enemy had no idea the *Soufrière* was at sea and operational. They probably imagined she was still in Singapore, or on her way to Britain for safety's sake.

Menzies said, 'Mr Christie's out of sight, sir.' He lowered his glasses. 'I just hope the Japs haven't got a carrier with them.'

Ainslie glanced at him grimly. 'You make Job seem like an optimist, Yeo.'

Menzies turned away grumbling, 'Airmen in submarines. I don't reckon it.'

Ainslie moved to the voice-pipes. 'Depth, please?'

'Thirty-five fathoms, sir.'

'Very well.'

He pictured how it would look. The ship would be zigzagging, leaving the escorts well spread out around her. The Japs did not take chances. They went by the book. Usually.

Torpedoman Sawle asked permission to come to the bridge and appeared carrying a great fanny of cocoa. It was amazing how they could enjoy the thick, glutinous mixture in the humid air. Perhaps because it was familiar. Part of the world they understood.

Ainslie sipped the cocoa slowly, feeling the sweat running down his spine as if to compensate for its penetration.

'All quiet below, Sawle?'

'Few of the kids are playin' up, sir. Lost their mums and dads apparently, poor little bleeders.'

Sawle was a Londoner, and his rough appreciation was somehow more moving because of it.

He added as an afterthought, 'Still, the lads 'ad a whip round for nutty an' tins of milk. Things could be worse.'

Ainslie watched him go below, whistling to himself. How the hell would we manage without the Sawles of this world?

'Captain, sir! Aircraft, starboard bow!'

The machine-guns creaked towards the sound, a faint, throbbing drone, like a tired wasp.

Menzies said, 'It's our flyer, sir.' He peered at his watch. 'Dead on time.'

Ainslie searched the sky, wondering what Christie would say. But he had done well and had arrived back almost to the minute.

'Warn the hangar party.'

The tannoy droned again. 'Stand by to receive aircraft.'

The seaplane passed the starboard side, flashing a brief signal in response to the shaded hand lamp from the conning tower.

Then she was down, curtseying easily across the low swell, the propeller throwing spray over the wings whenever she dipped too steeply.

As the first hint of daylight drew a faint line along the horizon, the hangar clanged shut, Christie and his aircraft sealed inside once more.

'Clear the bridge.' Ainslie watched the orderly bustle around him and then said, 'Twenty metres. Dive, dive, dive. *Negative* klaxon.' He half smiled as he closed the last cock on the voice-pipe. They might be going to die today, and yet he had spared the Malay children and sleeping wounded the additional anxiety of the klaxon. He must be going mad.

As he reached the control-room deck, and the lower hatch was slammed and clipped behind him, he saw Christie and his observer already by the chart table.

'Twenty metres, sir. Revolutions for eight knots. Ship's head zero-four-five.'

'Very good, Number One.' Ainslie nodded to Christie. 'Glad you made it.'

Christie looked very pleased with himself, and had a mask of oil below where his goggles had been, like an air ace from the Great War.

Forster was busy with parallel rulers and dividers, his eyes squinting with concentration.

Ainslie looked at the pencilled lines, then at Christie's grimy finger as he indicated one small cross.

'Here, sir. About twenty miles ahead of us. One big ship, the trooper, and two destroyers. Right astern there were two smaller vessels, but I daren't get any nearer.'

'Did they see you?'

Christie grinned. 'No chance, but I had them pinned down on the first light, right on the horizon. By God, that's a fine little kite, sir. I could win a cup or two with her.'

Ainslie looked at him curiously. They were suddenly face to face with it again. Twenty miles ahead. Even zigzagging, they would be in range within the hour, less if the ships were fairly new. But all Christie could think about was his new toy.

Forster was saying, 'We should pass at this point, sir, if we maintain present course and speed.' His dividers hesitated above some depth figures. Thirty fathoms. It was not much with a pair of destroyers on your back.

'The target's mean course is south-west. She is expected to arrive off Kota Baharu in the forenoon. We'll steer due north for fifteen minutes.'

Ainslie waited as the gyro repeater ticked round above Gosling's massive head. He was thinking aloud. 'Maximum revolutions.' He heard his words being translated into action. 'Group up. Revolutions for eleven knots.'

It was their best chance. To move in now, and fast. When they rose to periscope depth the small convoy should be to starboard, against the sun, while, with luck, *Soufrière* would still have a darker backcloth.

He looked at Ridgway. 'Full salvo. One to eight. As before, keep the two stern tubes as a last resort.'

Forster's pencil rolled over the chart table and fell to the deck, the only hint of the sudden increase in power.

He saw Farrant waiting by the bulkhead door. 'Yes, Guns?'

Farrant eyed the control room with distaste. 'Permission to man turret, sir.'

'Not this time, Guns. But I want you to send some of your

best hands forrard to look after the passengers. Things might get a bit dicey later on.'

'I'd have thought . . .' Farrant shut his mouth tightly. He knew Ainslie well enough now not to argue.

Ainslie dropped his voice and added, 'You may think that it hardly comes under your scheme of things. But believe me, if you'd ever seen panic, you'll know what it could do here!'

Halliday was looking at his diving panel but heard enough to guess what Farrant had started to say.

'Silly bugger.'

Lucas looked at him. 'What did you say?'

'I'm not talking to you, Frenchie.' He jerked his thumb towards where Farrant had been standing. 'God preserve us from numskulls like him!'

Lucas smiled gently. Halliday had said *us*. That was quite a breakthrough for the taciturn engineer.

In his small sick-bay Petty Officer Hunt went about his duties with his usual meticulous care. He was one of the few men in the submarine who cared little for his surroundings. For Hunt the job was everything. Submarine, hospital, or some clapped-out barracks, it was all the same to him.

He paused by one of the four cots. He had moved his worst cases into them after the three men who had died had been buried.

The man was a corporal, a small, wiry Australian whose face was criss-crossed with wrinkles and as tanned as leather. Someone who had lived off the land before he had donned a uniform.

He was dying very slowly, the life draining out of him with the precision of sand in an egg-timer. No hurry, no obvious change, but Hunt had seen enough dying men to recognize the signs.

He looked around his crowded domain. Men lying on the deck in blankets, or sitting on lockers waiting to have their dressings changed. The rest were scattered through the hull like extra provisions. The petty officers' mess, the wardroom, there was even one soldier in the torpedo storage space.

Hunt wondered if he should visit the captain's cabin and see that the two British girls were all right. He had been once, and heard the one whose husband had been left in the village moaning and sobbing, coming out of her drugged respite to go over it all again.

Hunt disliked women, but he had found time to admire the other girl, the one called Natalie, when she had said, 'I'll look after you. We'll be all right. You see.'

All right? Hunt watched the dying man. We'll be bloody lucky to get out of it in one piece.

He looked up, irritated, as a burly leading seaman stepped over the coaming. 'What's wrong with you, then?'

The seaman was a gunlayer, who grinned as he answered, 'Gunnery officer's orders, PO. I'm here to help out.'

Hunt frowned. All this mess to clear up. Women aboard, kids, the lot. And now this intrusion.

He opened his mouth but said nothing as the intercom speaker clicked on.

'This is the captain. We are about to engage an enemy convoy, the main target being a troopship. Our men in Malaya need all the help they can get. We'll try to give some. That is all.'

The dying soldier had opened his eyes and said hoarsely, 'I heard that, mate!' He smiled up at the burly leading hand and reached out to grip the SBA's arm. But his arm froze in mid air, and Hunt folded it gently across the man's chest and then closed his eyes.

The seaman said quietly, 'Poor bastard. And all for nothing.'

Unaware of this and similar dramas throughout his command, Ainslie replaced the microphone on its rack. He did not turn as the first report came through.

'Faint HE at green nine-oh.' The Asdic operator sounded engrossed. 'Too much interference, sir, but more than two ships.'

Ainslie rubbed his palms free of moisture on his trousers. 'Group down. Revs for seven knots. Silent routine.' He listened to the fading purr of electric motors, the hushed voices of a boatswain's mate on the microphone. 'Periscope depth, Number One.'

He thought about Critchley's words under the stars, the Malayan children who had found Sawle's pity.

'Fourteen metres, sir.'

Ainslie glanced at the young stoker who was waiting to press the hoist switch. 'Ready, Tamlyn?'

The stoker was no more than eighteen, but he gave a great grin as he said, 'When you say the word, sir.'

Ainslie stooped down above the periscope well. He's pleased because I remembered his name. God, it should take more than that to make men risk their lives.

He raised his arm slowly. 'Now.'

Every muscle in Ainslie's back and neck seemed to be aching in unison. For no more than seconds at a time he took quick glances through the attack periscope, his eye and brain working like a switch.

Surprisingly, it was all happening as he had expected. Through the spray-dashed lens he had seen the troopship, her side shining in the early sunlight as she completed another zigzag. She was well down, loaded to the hatches with men and weapons.

Behind him Ridgway's 'fruit machine' whirred and clicked as the brief checks through the periscope were transformed into figures and data to be fed into the machine and passed forward to the torpedo tubes.

The troopship's mean course was south-west, her speed about nine knots.

Against the strange yellow glow she made the perfect target, heavy and stark, like a block of flats.

But the escorts were worrying. Each destroyer was slightly ahead of the trooper, one on either bow. They seemed to have no set pattern in their zigzagging courses, or if they did, Ainslie was not getting long enough to understand the key.

'Range six thousand yards.' Ainslie remained crouching beside the well as the greased tube hissed down again. 'Alter course. Steer zero-seven-zero.'

He waited, controlling his breathing, as the gyro ticked round. Further aft, a mechanic was working on the diving panel with a screwdriver, his face completely calm, as if he were doing a job in his own home.

'Tubes one to eight ready, sir.'

Ainslie looked at the young stoker. He no longer had to tell him what to do. Another compact unit.

He gripped the handles, swinging the lens on to the changed bearing. How wet the handles were, in fact his whole body was soaking, as if he were in a downpour. He dared not look at the clock. It felt like hours since that first Asdic report, years since it had all started. But he knew it was a bare twenty minutes.

Ainslie tightened his grip, the sunlight probing his eye as he saw the target rise through the thin mist of spray and moisture.

'Bow doors open.'

Not yet. Not yet. He moved the periscope carefully, hearing the petty officer's breathing as he followed it round to read the bearings. Dear God, where is that destroyer? He could see the furthest one, turning away to show her narrow stern and, further still, one of the other vessels, belching smoke.

This was the testing moment. At any second the submarine might break surface, or the escorts could pick her up on their sonar.

It was no use. It would have to wait. He knelt on the deck as the sea blotted out the daylight again.

He looked at Quinton. 'Bloody destroyer is coming our way. She's big. One of their *Kagero* class, I think.'

He heard Christie leafing through the recognition manual, then the pilot said, 'Thirty-six knots, sir. Six five-inch guns.'

Ridgway was still working his machine. 'Nasty.'

Ainslie did not look up at the curved deckhead. It took effort not to, even though he knew it was pointless. He had heard the sound for himself: *thrum-thrum-thrum*, the destroyer's screws churning the sea above.

The Asdic operator said, 'About a thousand yards, sir.'

Ainslie wiped his mouth with the back of his hand. The passengers would hear it, too. A noise filled with menace, like a reaper in a field.

He looked at Forster. 'It's about the only damned advantage of being in shallow water, Pilot. So many back echoes that their chap probably doesn't believe a thing.' He saw Forster smile, the way his lips were frozen. A mask. Like the rest of them.

He looked at the stoker. 'Last time. Stand by.' He lowered himself to meet the periscope, watching the crystal water, the pale blue above, and then the target, the high bows thrusting across the edge of the lens. Like a door closing.

There was a faint, metallic ping, like someone using a tuning fork against the hull.

Ainslie turned the lens slightly and felt his stomach muscles contract.

The big destroyer was bows on, her stem cutting through the water like a battering ram as she turned towards the hidden submarine.

Ping. The Japanese sonar reached out and found the *Soufrière* again, homing the destroyer towards her like a fox to the kill.

Ainslie said tersely, '*Ready!*' He stared at the troopship's fore-mast, the sudden patch of colour as flags appeared on her yard. The escort must have warned her.

'*Fire One!*' He slammed the handles together and jumped to his feet. 'Carry on firing by stop-watch. Full pattern.' He strode across the deck and peered at the plot. 'Hard aport. Group up, full ahead together.'

He heard the clicks from the firing panel and saw the little red lights coming up as each torpedo leapt from its tube.

'Shut off for depth-charging.'

Seconds before the watertight door was clipped shut he thought he heard a child crying. This was no place for children, no matter what they had gone through already.

'Steady. Steer three-five-zero.'

Ainslie saw Ridgway looking at his watch. The hull was shak-ing more than usual as the motors worked up to full speed.

'Depth here is thirty fathoms, sir.'

'Take her down to forty metres.'

The petty officer stoker at the diving panel moved deftly like a juggler with his vent controls, and Ainslie found himself listening to the controlled inrush of water, watching the hydroplane tell-tales dipping to take *Soufrière* closer to the sea-bed.

'Forty metres, sir.'

Thrum-thrum-thrum. The destroyer was also turning, charging hard round in pursuit.

There was a tremendous explosion, and for a second Ainslie imagined he had been bracketed by depth-charges from another patrol vessel. Then another, the massive shock waves rolling the hull back and forth like a sick whale while the rudder and hydro-planes fought to keep her under command.

Ridgway's face shone with sweat. 'We've hit her!'

Crash. Crash. Crash. As each torpedo found its mark, and the terrible shock waves came bouncing back from the sea-bed, everyone heard and felt other explosions, large and small. It was like being trapped in a cavern filled with exploding dynamite. It went on and on, so that the drone of the destroyer's screws was lost in the din.

Quinton said between his teeth, 'She must have been carrying a whole lot more than soldiers. Enough ammo for a whole bloody army!'

The Asdic operator reported, 'Heavy HE has stopped, sir.'

They heard the last detonation rolling away like thunder, then the grinding sounds of a ship breaking up, machinery and equipment tearing free and plummeting through the shattered bulkheads.

The destroyer's engines took over once more. Nearer and nearer, the sound changing and expanding.

'Hard astarboard. Steady. Steer zero-four-five.'

Forster said, 'Depth twenty fathoms, sir.'

'Bring her up to twenty metres.'

The hull shuddered as two depth-charges exploded off the port beam. But the sudden alteration of course, plus the confusion left by the sinking troopship, had thrown the destroyer's commander off balance.

'Depth twenty-eight fathoms, sir. Constant for five miles.'

'Very well. Take her down to thirty metres. Hard astarboard. Steady.' He winced as another pattern of depth-charges exploded at a more shallow setting. Several lights went out and glass flew from some gauges as if it had been spat out. He said, 'Steer zero-eight-zero.' He peered at the shivering plot table and saw Forster's hands moving across his chart to plan each change of track, seek out every hazard before they hit it.

'HE at red nine-oh. Closing.'

One of the patrol vessels. Slower, less certain, but just as deadly if they could bracket their target.

Forster said grimly, 'They're trying to hem us in, sir.' He pointed with his pencil. 'The big chap here and the other two coming down to port. The other destroyer must have stopped. Either to pick up survivors or to block our escape.'

Ainslie looked at him. 'Good thinking.' To Ridgway he said, 'Stand by nine and ten.'

It was like conning the *Soufrière* into one huge snare. If he could only delay one of the destroyers, the attacking one. Just to give him time to disrupt the pattern. Make them believe *Soufrière* was severely damaged or sinking.

He said quietly, 'You reported that a soldier died in the sick-bay?' He hurried on without looking at Ridgway. 'Tell your torpedo gunner's mate to take the body forrard, along with any blood-stained dressings Hunt can give you. You will fire them from one of the tubes when I give the order.' He turned to Halliday. 'Chief. Get your people to release fifty gallons of diesel at the same time.'

Ridgway swallowed hard. 'Aye, aye, sir.'

The phone crackled, and Ainslie tried not to think of the anonymous soldier being carried forward, to be ejected from a tube like so much rubbish.

'Ready, sir.' Ridgway's voice was hushed.

'*Now!*'

He felt the slight lurch as the tube was emptied, and heard the muffled beat of a pump as oil was sent surging to the surface with the corpse.

'HE lessening, sir. Destroyer reducing speed.'

It had worked. The simplest and the grisliest ruse of all. Ainslie felt sickened by it. Ashamed.

In the Atlantic or the Mediterranean it would not have worked. It had once, but the killing grounds were quick and brutal teachers.

He breathed out very slowly, the bile rising in his throat.

Now for the other destroyer. Waiting no doubt for *Soufrière* to pass beneath or so close to her she would straddle her with a full pattern.

He made himself ignore the tap-tap of the Japanese sonar, the sounds of racing screws – everything but the need to break up the escorts.

'Periscope depth in two minutes.'

He blinked as two charges burst almost within fatal distance, cutting off more lights and bringing down the cork-filled paint from the deckhead like hardened snow.

'Group down. Revs for seven knots.'

'Stern doors open, sir.'

'Periscope depth.' Ainslie knelt down, his heart feeling as if it would split in halves. 'Right, Tamlyn.'

He swung the periscope towards the stern, seeing one of the patrol vessels leaning right over in a tight turn before she made another run-in. There was smoke and wreckage everywhere, the whole scene completely changed. Men floundering in the sea like dying fish, other already floating, gutted or in fragments, blasted apart by their escorts' depth-charges.

He tensed, seeing the second destroyer. 'One thousand yards. Bearing *that*.'

Click, click went Ridgway's machine.

'Fire Nine. Fire Ten.'

'Down 'scope. Group up, full ahead. Thirty metres.'

'Both torpedoes running, sir.'

Ainslie watched the gyro and the depth recorder, and felt a nervous jump in his neck as a torpedo exploded with a violent crash. More tearing sounds. A ship going down.

It went on for another three hours. Twisting and turning, rising and diving deep whenever the depth allowed it. The destroyer attacked again and again, but without her powerful consort, and hampered by the two slower patrol vessels, she was losing ground.

For the submariners, let alone their passengers, it was like an endless bombardment, with the hull rocking and plunging, equipment coming apart, loose gear tearing from racks and hooks while the depth-charges rained down.

But one surface vessel was no match for an experienced submariner. The destroyer lost precious minutes after each attack while she charged past the target, losing the echo on her sonar in the roar of her own screws. With another ship in company it would have been easier. One listening, while the other attacked, so that the echo and the bearing were never lost.

Ridgway mopped his face and exclaimed, 'The buggers knew nothing about a submarine in these waters, sir!'

Quinton said harshly, 'Hell, George, they bloody well know now!'

Ainslie looked at each of them in turn. There had not been a depth-charge for five minutes. The enemy might be calling up other ships, and aircraft, too.

It was time to go.

He said, 'I think we're out of it. Another ten minutes and we'll go up for a quick look round.' They all stared at him. Drained, breathing shakily like old men.

Quinton spoke to the boatswain's mate and then said, 'No serious damage, sir. No casualties.'

Forster said dully, 'Course to steer is one-three-zero, sir. Revolutions for seven knots.'

When they eventually rose to periscope depth the sea was empty once more. Far astern there was still a pall of drifting smoke, merging with heat haze to make the sun waver like reflected fire.

Ainslie turned the periscope slowly, his ears still throbbing from the explosions, his eye picturing the dead soldier floating in the oil. He had probably done more to save them than anybody.

With a start he realized he had held the periscope up too long, and felt the sweat trickling on his skin like ice as he signnalled for it to be lowered.

Vigilance at all times, no matter what. God, he had drummed it into others enough times. Vigilance or sudden death.

He said sharply, 'Forty metres, Number One. We'll surface at dusk. Then we'll return to base.'

A troopship and a destroyer sunk without loss to himself. He should be proud, well satisfied.

He heard Ridgway whispering fiercely on a telephone and knew it was Hunt calling him from the sick-bay. He would want a signature on a form. Just to make the dead soldier's disappearance neat and tidy. That was Hunt all over.

'Open up the boat. Tell the cook to prepare a meal as quickly as possible. Fall out diving stations when you're satisfied, Number One.'

Quinton watched him, hiding his anxiety. One more like that and the skipper would be over the top.

Not if I can help it.

He said, 'You did a great job, sir. I was a bit bothered back there, once or twice.'

Ainslie took the offering like a lifeline. 'It will get harder. It always does.'

8

Drink Up, and Forget

REAR-ADMIRAL GRANGER rested his hands, palms down, on his big desk and regarded Ainslie gravely.

'You look done in, Commander. It can't have been a picnic for any of you.'

Ainslie felt his resistance going, his eyelids drooping. He had barely brought the submarine alongside the same old depot ship when he had been called to Granger's office.

He had waited to see the wounded put ashore into the waiting ambulances, but when he went to ask the two British women if he could be of any help, he discovered that Rear-Admiral Granger's flag-lieutenant had already whisked them away.

The soldiers, ragged and silent, had looked smaller on the jetty, and the scene had been made worse by a sudden downpour of heavy, persistent rain. He could hear it now, flogging the neat lawn into a bog, battering the corrugated roofs like ball bearings.

It made the air heavier, not cooler, and the slowly revolving fans overhead seemed to have no effect.

'I've told the C in C about your success with the troopship. You did very well.' He tried to smile. 'As I knew you would.'

Ainslie looked past him at the wall map. The yellow tape was almost taut now, and ran diagonally across the whole peninsula, cutting the west coast at Penang.

Granger followed his glance and said heavily, 'Yes. They've split the country in two. Occupied Penang yesterday.'

So it was all wasted. The troopship, the destroyer, the dead soldier, everything.

Ainslie said at length, 'It seems that nothing can hold them, sir.'

'I know what you're thinking. You're wrong. The enemy *need* every man, just as we do. Your risks were not in vain.'

'I wasn't thinking of the risks.' The incessant rain was making his head ache. 'I was remembering all the bluff and bluster I got when I arrived here. I'd laugh if I wasn't so sick and tired of it.'

Granger watched him worriedly. 'I'm not laughing either. Believe me, you and your *Soufrière* are needed now, and I don't think anyone would disagree.'

There was a tap at the door and the flag-lieutenant peered into the office.

'Sorry to butt in, sir.'

Granger frowned. 'It's nothing new, Flags.'

'I thought you should know that I put the two young women into the Royal Hotel, as you suggested.' He glanced at Ainslie and withdrew.

Ainslie watched the admiral's stubby fingers ramming tobacco into his pipe.

'You know them, sir?'

'Yes. I had them taken off your boat without waiting to pay respects, so to speak. I guessed there might be some tension. Better to let things cool down. I knew all of them quite well. Michael Holmes was a mining engineer employed by the government. Bright young chap. Lots of prospects. His wife Shelly used to be full of life.' He shook his head. 'Rotten business.'

Ainslie asked quietly. 'The other one, Natalie, her sister, what about her?'

'Very nice girl. I didn't see her before she went up country. I expect she'll tell me when she feels like it.'

Ainslie could hear her voice as if she were here, now. Granger's remarks had brought it all back. *I was alone, and I needed someone to talk to.*

Granger was saying, 'I read your report. Damned clear and concise, though God knows how you found the time to write it.' He lowered his eyes. 'Brings me to another matter.' '

Ainslie tried to stay calm. Here we go. The next mission.

Granger looked up suddenly. 'You were unable to take off the rest of the soldiers from that village because of the shallows, and the fact the Japs were closing in on two sides, not one as we believed?'

'Yes, sir.' He knew he sounded defensive and it angered him. 'It would have been suicide.'

'I know.'

Granger stood up and walked to his map. From the back, in his gleaming shirt and shorts, he looked like a white egg.

'Fact is, Ainslie, we need to get supplies to another coastal strongpoint. It's not in immediate danger of being outflanked, but it's virtually impossible for us to get the supplies overland at present.'

His finger rested on a small inlet.

'How deep, sir?'

'Nothing much, even at high water. You'd have to go in on the surface. Even then you'd need to keep your eyes peeled.' He hesitated, watching Ainslie's face. 'You would do it at night, of course. The Japs have two airfields now, and there was word of a carrier in the Gulf of Siam two days ago.' He shrugged. 'Well, what do you think?'

'What would I be carrying, sir?'

'Ammunition mostly, but rations and medical supplies as well for the troops.'

Ainslie joined him by the map. A proper chart would show the margin of safety. Or the lack of it. But on the surface *Soufrière* had already shown what she could do, twenty knots and a couple more to spare. In and out overnight, find deep water before daylight when the planes came looking for them.

Ammunition mostly. If *Soufrière* became stranded on a sandbar she would herself be a giant bomb.

'I think it *could* be done, sir.'

The admiral frowned as the door opened a few inches and the chief of staff glanced through the gap.

'Oh, thought you were finished, sir.'

'Come in, Philip, no sense in hanging about.'

Captain Armytage entered the room and asked, 'What does Commander Ainslie think, sir?' He did not look at him.

'He agrees in principle.' Granger glared. 'But there may be snags. Tides, that kind of thing.'

Then, Armytage did look at Ainslie. 'Oh, yes. Like the fishing village. Rotten luck about that. Still, I suppose you knew what to expect.'

Ainslie eyed him calmly. 'I knew.'

The captain gave a wry smile. 'Still, you did rescue those poor soldiers, and some civilians, about thirty all told, wasn't it?'

Granger snapped, 'That's quite enough, Philip! Commander Ainslie used his experience and his discretion. The troopship had to come first anyway.'

Ainslie looked at each man in turn. They simply did not under stand. They probably believed that war was made up of dashing, miraculous incidents, all linked together under some godlike authority.

He said abruptly, 'It was hopeless. If you ask me, I believe the army should fall right back and try to re-group right now. Shorten the line. Double the strength.'

Armytage snapped, 'I went to staff college, too, you know.'

'Yes, sir.' Ainslie stood up, feeling the floor rise to meet him like a ship's deck. 'I am just saying what I think.'

Granger looked at his pipe. It had gone out again. 'Go and get some rest. My people will see to your supplies and fuel. The maintenance commander will make arrangements for the cargo.'

'How long, sir?'

Granger looked uncomfortable. 'Day after tomorrow. At the latest. Things are moving pretty fast.' As Ainslie picked up his cap and started for the door he added, 'I would suggest you land all your torpedoes. Lessen the load. You're not going to fight this time.'

It made good sense, but Ainslie felt a twinge of uneasiness at the prospect of losing his attacking power, if only for a short while.

In the outer office, where a writer was hammering away on a typewriter, Ainslie paused as he heard Granger say, 'Why the hell do you have to criticize everything, Philip?'

Ainslie saw the writer staring at him over his typing paper and knew he ought not to stay and listen. Then he heard Army-tage reply stubbornly, 'I can't stand his sort, sir. Have a bit of luck and glory, win a few medals, they forget the rest of us who have to do the work!'

Ainslie was surprised that it did not anger him. He felt almost relieved.

With a nod to the typist he walked out into the rain and was soaked to the skin in two strides.

He found Quinton waiting for him in *Soufrière*'s control room. He had showered and changed and looked his old self once more.

'Cabin, Number One.'

As they walked through the narrow passageway Ainslie mar-velled at the speed with which things could appear normal again. Where the wounded had waited to be treated and the dead to be buried, it was spick and span, the steel and brass shining like new. The control room looked strange without the tense, un-shaven men at the controls, and felt at peace.

He busied himself with bottle and glasses while Quinton lounged in a chair watching him.

'Day after tomorrow, John. We're to run ammunition and supplies to another outpost. Surface job. In and out under cover of darkness.' He held out a glass. 'Suit you?'

'The drink or the job?'

'Both.'

Quinton drank very slowly, without even his customary warn-ing to his stomach.

'No option, I suppose. They'll keep up some sort of pretence to the end.'

'Pretence?' Ainslie refilled the glasses.

Overhead he heard Petty Officer Voysey's muffled voice as he called the hands out of shelter to get on with cleaning up the submarine. The rain must have stopped.

'Yeh. I've been talking with the blokes in the base while I was waiting for you to come back. There are refugees by the bloody thousand streaming down from Malaya. The military police say some of 'em may be Indian deserters. Went completely nuts when the Japs arrived. Poor sods had never seen anything like it. Armour and artillery, planes and support ships. Must have seemed like a bit of H. G. Wells!'

Feet scraped in the passageway and Commander Critchley pushed the curtain aside. He was carrying a small grip.

'I shall be coming with you again, gentlemen. If you can stand it.' He smiled sadly as Ainslie reached for a third glass. 'After that I'm ordered home. Back to dear old London, bless it.' He took the whisky. 'I'll miss you, though.'

Ainslie asked, 'What are they up to?'

'You mean, the brass?' Critchley swilled the drink round the glass. 'They want a report from me, that's all I know.'

Quinton gave a short laugh. 'So that they'll know what to do when it happens again!'

'You sound bitter, Number One.'

'I am.' Quinton stared at the curved side. 'I hated it. All those poor Aussie bastards getting killed for nothing. I'll not forget.'

There was a discreet tap on the door, and Sub-Lieutenant Southby, wearing a heavy revolver on his hip, said, 'The cox'n wishes to know about leave, sir?'

'Out of the question, Sub. Libertymen will be allowed only inside the perimeter, the fleet canteen and so forth. We're under orders.'

'I see, sir.' It was obvious he did not.

When Southby had gone Quinton asked, 'What about us, sir?' He spread his hands. 'I seem to recall there was talk of a party?'

Critchley smiled. 'The yacht *Lady Jane* is still officially at your disposal, Bob. What about it? A forget-it-all party!'

Ainslie said, 'Good idea. See to it, Number One. Get Lieutenant Christie to help you. He seems a bit of a goer.'

'He'll want to bring his bloody seaplane.'

'What about guests?' Critchley spoke casually but was watching Ainslie's face very carefully.

'Oh, you know. Nurses, the people from the dockyard who helped us, but not too many. The yacht's a bit ancient and might capsize.'

Critchley asked, 'How about the two sisters?'

'This is the last place they'll want to come, man.'

He looked away. But the one called Natalie might. If only to get away from her sister's grief. It could not have been easy for either of them. He remembered the other girl screaming at him, cursing him, labelling him a coward. *Run, run, run.*

Quinton said, 'David Forster's got to go ashore for some charts. He could sound things out. We might all pretend it's peacetime. The people round here seem to do that quite well!'

Ainslie made a sudden decision. 'No, I'll go myself. I've things to do anyway.' He smiled awkwardly. 'Skipper's privilege.'

As the door closed behind them he looked round the cabin, wondering if he was doing the right thing. If he stayed here he would either sleep or be pestered by questions and demands which Quinton could handle just as easily.

Ainslie studied himself in the mirror, at the lines of strain around his eyes and mouth. He was being dishonest with himself. He *wanted* to see her again, needed to explain, or just to talk.

Then back through the control room, wondering what he was going to say. Perhaps she had already left the hotel. Or would refuse to see him.

Quinton, and Southby as OOD, waited on the casing to see him over the side.

The sun was very bright and the rain-water was changing to steam, as if the hull was about to explode.

He would miss Critchley. He paused to look along his command. Pipes and power lines trailing like snakes, fuel hoses being winched down from the depot ship. Bare-backed sailors everywhere, faces he now knew better than when they had all started on the plan to capture the 'largest submarine in the world'.

Some men were scraping the saddle tanks before applying fresh paint to cover the scars left by one of the depth-charges. It had been as close as that.

The hangar was open, and he saw Christie, naked but for a pair of filthy shorts, busy with a spanner under the engine of the seaplane.

Soufrière had become real, personal.

Then he touched his cap to the saluting side party and stepped ashore from the brow.

Ainslie took a taxi only part of the way to the hotel. He was not quite sure why. Perhaps it was to give him time to change his mind if his nerve failed. The Sikh taxi-driver shot him a curious stare as he got out. The Royal Navy officer who had paid to be dropped nowhere.

As he walked through the drifting groups of servicemen, civilians and native traders, Ainslie kept his eye open for signs of military preparedness. Apart from a few of the more expensive shops and bazaars where sticky paper had been pasted across windows in case of bomb-blast, there was little out of the ordinary. By a government office he saw two sandbagged sentry posts, an armoured car parked in the shade of some palm trees. Perhaps Quinton was right. It was all a great pretence, a bluff to keep up morale.

He paused and glanced up at the Royal Hotel. It was much the same style as Raffles, which was close by, but smaller and more intimate.

He walked through the white-walled entrance and stood looking at the rectangles of lawn, the bright flowers and gently moving trees. The hotel was only two stories high, with a stuccoed veranda running right round the upper floor, on to which the suites and rooms opened. Beneath the veranda was an arcade, shadowed and cool, with blue and yellow blinds reaching out towards the gardens, where there were little chairs and tables dotted about for the guests.

A very tall Indian porter, in khaki suit and old-style topee bowed politely.

'Yes, Commander–sahib. May I help?'

He had been at the old Royal for years and knew every rank of all three services better than some people did in Britain.

'I am not expected. I want to see if one of the guests is in her room.'

The man beamed. 'But of course, Commander–sahib. I will be honoured to enquire.'

Waving aside any protests he ushered Ainslie through the doors and into the hotel foyer. After the bright sunlight Ainslie could barely see and almost fell over a cane chair.

It was all getting out of hand, rushed.

Another face appeared at the desk, and a voice asked smoothly, 'What can I do for you, sir?'

Ainslie sighed. Now there were two hands to be crossed with silver.

'I am looking for a Miss Torrance. She arrived today.'

He cursed himself. She was probably in bed. Trying to rest and forget.

The clerk made a great show of examining the book. 'I am very sorry, sir. We do not seem to have – '

'Why, Commander Ainslie!'

Ainslie swung round, confused by the turn of events.

He could barely recognize her. She was wearing a simple white dress with a small green scarf knotted around her throat. Her hair was pulled back into a coil at the nape of her neck, but instead of appearing severe it accentuated the oval line of her face from forehead to chin.

'The clerk said that . . . I thought you . . .' He broke off as she held out her left hand. It was small and well shaped, but all Ainslie saw was the wedding ring.

She said quietly, 'He was right. You asked for *Miss* Torrance, you see?'

'Yes, I did.' He looked away. 'I'm sorry.'

She led the way to one of the small tables.

'I wanted to thank you before we left your ship. For saving

our lives.' She shrugged. 'For everything. But you heard what happened. The admiral sent his aide to collect us.'

A waiter hovered by the table and she asked, 'Would you like some tea, Commander?' She watched his uncertainty. 'Or something stronger?'

Ainslie smiled, fascinated. She was incredible. Not merely lovely to look at, but she showed no sign of her ordeal. He should have thought of it himself. No girl who looked like her would stay single for long out here.

He said, 'Something very long and cold, that is, if you will join me.'

She nodded to the waiter and said, 'Is everything all right for you now?'

He looked at his hands, remembering them slipping on the periscope grips.

'Getting better.' He laughed. 'I was going to ask you to a party. I seem to have made a bit of an ass of myself.'

The waiter returned and presented a tall glass misted with ice.

The girl said gravely, 'The Royal special sling. Ninety-nine per cent iced gin!' She picked up her own drink and put the glass to her lips. 'Your very good health.'

Ainslie felt the cold gin running through him like ice-water. There was Benedictine and Cherry Brandy in it, too.

She said, 'It was very considerate of you to come.' Just for an instant her expression altered and her eyes seemed to cloud over. 'My sister had no right to speak to you like that. I was ashamed.'

Ainslie wanted to reach out, to touch her hand. It was impossible to think of it as the same hand which had dug into his arm, breaking the skin, after she had been brought from the motor launch.

'She could not understand. I didn't enjoy it. I hated leaving those men behind.'

He looked down, avoiding her eyes.

'It keeps coming back, all the time.'

She said gently, 'You saved my life. I owe you my honesty at least. I went to see Shelly and her husband Mike because I needed advice, escape, if you like. But it was all sham. They were rowing most of the time, fighting like cat and dog. Mike was a good engineer, but he knew nothing about women, even less about a girl like Shelly. She craves excitement, and has the ability to tease men until they don't know what they're doing.' She put her hand flat on the table beside her glass. 'Then the attack began. We couldn't believe it, that the enemy would get through the defences so easily.' Her lips trembled as she added, 'It was so bad that I can't really accept that it happened. Perhaps when I do it will get worse.'

Ainslie knew it was time to leave. He knew, too, that he could not.

'We shall be off to sea again soon.'

She looked at him, her eyes startled. 'But I thought . . . after what you had to do . . .'

He smiled. 'It doesn't work like that, I'm afraid. My command is the odd one out here. Like having my own navy.'

'I mustn't ask.' She suddenly put her hand on his. It was very smooth and surprisingly cool. 'But will you be coming back to Singapore?'

'I mustn't answer.' He watched her hand. 'But yes, I believe so.'

'Well, I expect . . .' She suddenly withdrew her hand and exclaimed, 'It must be later than I thought.'

A woman in nurse's uniform was crossing the foyer. She was leading a small girl by the hand, and when she saw the table, led the child towards it.

Ainslie stood up. The child was aged about six, and he did not need to be told she was Natalie Torrance's daughter. The same gleaming black hair, the same eyes.

The nurse said, 'I'll take her up to the suite, Mrs Torrance. She can rest before luncheon.'

The child was staring fixedly at Ainslie. Then she saw his cap on the chair and picked it up with her free hand.

'Please, Frances, put it back.'

Ainslie smiled. 'It's quite all right, I . . .' Then he saw the pain on her face and knelt down in front of the child. She was holding the cap very carefully, her eyes fixed on the oak leaves around the peak. But there was not a single spark of understanding or recognition on her face. It was like a small mask, or a dead replica of her mother's.

The nurse took the cap and handed it to him without a word.

As they walked towards the stairs Ainslie said, 'I am very sorry. I didn't understand.'

She was still staring after the nurse and the child. 'There was an accident. Her brain was damaged. I keep hoping.' She looked past Ainslie, her eyes misty. 'But I don't know any more.'

Ainslie's original feelings of foolishness and disappointment had gone. Instead he felt only warmth for this sad, beautiful girl. But it was a helpless feeling.

He noticed she had not referred to her husband at all.

'I had better get back to the base.'

Some of the people at nearby tables were looking at him with flat, curious stares. Like the framed photographs on the wall, showing various important guests and dinner parties from many years ago. Thick dinner jackets, unsmiling, moustached faces. Rubber planters down from Malaya, government officials and district officers. Another era.

She said quietly, 'Frances needs a lot of care. My husband has money.' She turned to look at him again. 'I would do anything for Frances.'

And I would for you.

He said, 'If ever I can help . . .'

She nodded, studying his face. 'I shall not forget.' She picked up her bag. 'But please don't ask us to your party.' She touched his arm with the same impetuous motion. 'It would be quite impossible. But I hope we meet again.'

He watched her go. 'I should like that.'

The hall porter touched his topee with a flourish. 'All fixed, Commander–sahib?'

Ainslie thrust some coins into his hand. 'No.'

Then he walked out into the jostling spectators on the street. A taxi passed him and swung into the gates. He could not be certain, but the pair inside looked like the girl's sister, Shelly, and Lieutenant David Forster.

The saloon of the yacht *Lady Jane* was like an oven. Because of the new regulations about air raid precautions, every scuttle was sealed and covered, and the vessel's fans were totally inadequate for the packed mass of figures. As was usually the case with naval parties, there were more guests than had been allowed for.

Ainslie stood crammed in a corner, wondering what all the previous owners of the old yacht would think of this hullabaloo.

Officers of every rank and age from the base and dockyard workshops. A few officials with their wives. Some girls from government house all talking at the tops of their voices, their faces shining with sweat.

Quinton said, 'Good party.They're having a great time.' He tensed. 'God, look at this.'

This was the navigating officer, David Forster, with a radiant-looking girl on his arm. She was wearing a flame-coloured dress which hid very little, and left even less to the imagination.

Quinton added, 'Hell, it's the girl we picked up. Shelly some-thing-or-other. She doesn't look much like a grieving widow just now!' He downed his glass. 'Here we go.'

Forster managed to push through the crowd, taking two glasses from the tray of a perspiring steward en route.

'You've met, of course.' He beamed at Ainslie. 'We ran into each other ashore, sir.'

The girl regarded him calmly. She was a year or two younger than her sister, and very attractive. She knew it too.

Ainslie held out his hand, half expecting her to ignore it. She was a far cry from the ragged, screaming girl in *Soufrière's* passageway.

She said, 'Good of you to have me.' She squeezed his hand. 'I shall call you Bob. I'm not one of your crew, am I?'

Quinton grinned. 'Hardly.'

Ainslie said, 'You're looking well.'

She had not taken her eyes off him. They were shining, laugh-ing. At him perhaps? Why had she come?

A boat bumped alongside, and Quinton said, 'I'd better get on deck to meet the guests. Just a few more and I'll start worrying about the trim here, too!'

The girl watched him push his way towards the after doors. 'He must be Australian.'

Forster said, 'Let's get some drinks.' He took her elbow but she shook his hand away. Ainslie saw the way she was staring at the doors at the far end of the saloon, the quick rise and fall of her barely covered breasts. She was excited, like a wild animal.

The doors opened and the new arrivals started to climb down from the upper deck.

Natalie Torrance stared at him across the heads of all the others until she reached the deck and was momentarily lost from view. In those tiny seconds Ainslie saw the paleness of her face, the look of someone trapped. Behind her came a man in a white dinner jacket, very tanned, with a clipped, military-looking moustache. It must be her husband.

Forster stared entranced as the newcomers appeared through the crush.

'This is my husband, Commander Ainslie.' She looked up at the man beside her, her eyes pleading.

The man had a firm handshake. 'My friends call me Guy.' He grinned. 'Amongst other things.' He had a thick, resonant voice of an older man, and yet looked about thirty.

A steward brought a tray, and he seized a glass and said, 'You did a fine job, Commander. About time somebody showed a bit of spunk round here.' He shook his head. 'Pity we couldn't get aboard your sub. Maybe later, eh? God, when I think of it. What it must have been like. What you must have thought.'

Another drink rose and fell, the glass replaced empty.

Ainslie darted a glance at her. Despite her obvious discomfort, she was even more beautiful. She was dressed in black, a dress which left her arms quite bare and accentuated the perfect lines of her body.

Torrance said brightly, 'Like picking up a couple of mermaids, eh?'

She said, 'It wasn't like that.'

'Oh, well.' He searched through his thoughts. 'But when I heard from young Shelly about the party, I invited us along, d'you see?'

Ainslie glanced at Shelly. So that was it. It was her doing. To provoke something or somebody.

Lieutenant Ridgway, who was officer of the day aboard the submarine, appeared through the noisy visitors. He saw Ainslie and said, 'Just thought you should know, sir. Signal from HQ. Loading ammunition will begin tomorrow at 0730.'

Ainslie digested the information slowly, to give himself time. Guy Torrance had only been aboard ten minutes and had consumed at least seven drinks, and they were not small ones. No wonder she had not wanted to come. She had known what would happen. How could she stay with him? He was an alcoholic of the worst kind. The hard one, who goes on and on, barely showing any signs, until the explosion.

He suddenly remembered her face at the hotel. Her words.

I would do anything for Frances. That was why she stayed with him.

Ridgway gratefully took a drink from Forster. 'Any reply, sir?'

Ainslie shook his head. 'Tell the cox'n, and just acknowledge it. All quiet?'

Ridgway looked at the two girls. It was obvious he had not recognized either of them.

'Patrol activity in the north, sir. Not much change.'

He turned back to the others as Torrance exclaimed loudly, 'Now then, my young friend!' He was grinning fiercely at Forster. 'I saw you looking down the front of my wife's dress! Worth looking at, very true, but not for you!' He threw back his head and laughed. 'God, this is splendid!'

Forster looked at Ainslie, flushing with embarrassment. 'I didn't – I mean – I wasn't – '

'It's all right, Pilot. Just listen carefully. Fetch our flyer, Christie, and Deacon. I want them over here double quick, and get them to pour as much drink into Guy Torrance as they can.' He knew that both Christie and Deacon had reputations of being able to hold their drink.

He touched the girl's arm and felt her start. 'I'd like you to meet my chief engineer.' He saw Christie's face looming through the crowd, shining and determined.

Christie probably imagined Ainslie wanted him to get the man drunk just so that he could make a play for his wife. It was not unknown at shipboard parties.

Torrance boomed, 'Good show!' He swung round, knocking over some empty glasses as Christie introduced himself by saying, 'Now, you are an English gentlemen, sir. This half-baked engineer insists that we are no match for his ability to drink. He dares to say that he will take on the pair of us!'

Torrance grinned. *'Does* he?' He snapped his fingers. 'Steward! Here, boy! Brandy, and I mean a bottle!'

Deacon looked at Christie and winked.

Ainslie glanced round just once. He saw Torrance's head going back, the pink film spreading across his eyes as he swallowed the brandy in a gulp.

He felt her trembling and knew some of the guests had stopped talking to watch the contest.

He said, 'We can go on deck if you like?'

Outside it seemed almost cold, but the air was fresh and there was no cloud about. It must seem strange to the people who lived nearby to see no lights from the anchored ships. Ainslie had become used to it. Resigned.

He said quietly, 'I am certain my navigator didn't know about this.'

'It was Shelly. She creates chaos, then triumphs over the survivors. I think she hates me sometimes.'

Ainslie guided her past the galley where the Chinese messboys were frantically washing and polishing glasses. A woman and an anonymous officer were entwined against the motor dinghy, and even in the stars' dim glow Ainslie could see that the woman was half naked.

'Quite a party,' he said awkwardly.

She paused by the guardrail and looked down at the water alongside.

'Guy has been like this since Frances had her accident. But he gets worse.'

She did not look at Ainslie, and it was difficult to hear everything she said.

'We came out from the UK to take over Guy's father's business in Rangoon. Coastal shipping, lighterage and that sort of thing. He had been helping to open up more business here, which is why we are at the hotel. Now it looks as if our world is falling apart. Even Rangoon may be in danger.'

She pointed. 'What was that?'

Ainslie saw a line of white foam passing slowly between the darker shadows of anchored ships.

'The guardboat. Probably hoping to get a drink from us.'

She had turned towards him, and he could sense her watching him.

She said, 'What about you? I've been unloading all my troubles, but you've told me nothing.'

He smiled. 'There's not much to tell, really. I'm the son of a sailor, and he was the son of another. I was born in Dundee, but have lived mostly in England.'

'Are you married?'

'No.'

She hesitated. 'I'm surprised.'

He said, 'It was a near thing. But I was away from England too long. She married a nice, sensible farmer instead.'

She began to walk along the deck towards the bows. He took her arm to steer her away from the hazards of ring bolts and coils of mooring ropes.

'I shall see your husband is taken ashore safely.' Ainslie did not know why he had brought it up. 'My first lieutenant is a good hand at this sort of thing.' He felt her arm stiffen. 'That was stupid of me. I didn't mean it to come out like that.'

She turned to face him, her arms at her sides. 'I saw what you did. It's terrible to watch him destroying himself.'

Ainslie said, 'I know this sounds crazy, but I want you to like me so much that I'll do anything.'

He put his hands on her shoulders, his mind reeling. One wrong word and everything would disappear. *Smash.*

He felt her skin under his palms. Very smooth. He moved closer until her head was against his shoulder.

'I'm not going to spoil everything. I just want to be near you.'

She looked up, her eyes filling her face in the darkness. But still she said nothing.

Very, very gently he held her against him, feeling her supple body beneath the dress, the pressure of her breasts on his ribs.

Then she moved away. One second she was moulded to him, the next she was by the rail, as if he had imagined all of it.

He heard himself say, 'I'm apologizing again, but I'm not just another man after your favours. Perhaps I've been a sailor too long, have hardened myself too much to know how to behave any more.' He watched her despairingly. 'But I meant what I said. Every last bit of it.'

She said, 'I had better be leaving, if you could arrange it.' She brushed past him and then just as swiftly turned her face upwards and kissed him on the mouth. 'Don't hold me. I'm not made of stone, any more than you are.' Then she was gone.

Quinton appeared on deck and said, 'Mr Torrance has passed out, sir. He won, by the way. Christie and Arthur Deacon are on their backs. Phew, what a drinker!'

'Call away the boat, Number One. We'll get them off to their hotel. She'll be worried about her little girl. There might be an air raid.'

A door banged open and laughing shapes spilled over the deck, bathed in light from the deckhouse.

From across the water the guardboat's loud-hailer roared, 'Darken ship there! What the hell are you doing?'

Quinton said, 'She's got a child, then?'

'Yes.' He looked away. 'Better get these characters over the side and away before something embarrassing happens.'

Halliday came out of the darkness as Ainslie walked aft to the accommodation ladder.

Quinton nodded. 'Good party, Chief?'

Halliday sighed. 'If you like that kind of thing. One or two folk will have sore heads in the morning, I'm thinking.'

Quinton watched Ainslie's pale figure shaking hands here and there, helping Forster and some seamen prevent the guests from falling into the water.

Halliday asked, 'Skipper okay?'

'Not sure.' Quinton looked at the engineer thoughtfully. He was one of the very few men he would confide in. 'I think that last job had a crook effect on him. He's been at it too long without a break.' He thought of the girl in the long black dress who had walked past him. Just what Ainslie needed. But she was bloody well spliced already, and to that drunk.

A girl shrieked with laughter, and Quinton saw the flame-coloured dress moving amongst the people in the boat like a spirit. Forster had made his claim with that one. Quinton smiled bleakly. She would have him for breakfast.

Ainslie stood back from the rail, his hand in the air as the boat swerved away into the darkness. The party was over, and when he searched his mind for regrets he discovered only a kind of elation.

Forster lurched along the deck and groaned, 'There's one of them still aboard, sir. He was sitting flaked-out in the heads. We'll have to recall the boat.'

But Ainslie walked past him without hearing a word.

9

Victim

'SURFACE!'

After hours of altering course and depth on their tortuous approach towards the coast, the sudden activity of breaking surface seemed all the louder. Ainslie heaved open the upper hatch, shutting his eyes against the splatter of salt water while he groped for handholds and tried to keep his binoculars dry at the same time.

As usual after being submerged, the air seemed headier, the smells more pronounced. He ran to the fore part of the bridge, just in time to see an arrowhead of white foam as the bows surged above water.

Some fleecy clouds moving across the stars, a sliver of moon like a piece of shell, even less impressive than it had looked in the periscope. As his eyesight grew accustomed to the darkness he saw the water close alongside, molten glass, breaking occasionally along the saddle tanks, or leaving fiery tendrils of phosphorescence to mark their slow approach.

With practised ease the lookouts and machine-gunners took up their positions, with only an occasional grunt or clink of steel to show that anything was happening.

Ainslie moved his glasses slowly across the screen, breathing deeply to steady his nerves.

He heard the yeoman of signals checking that the voice-pipes were open, and that the bridge was again in contact with the control room.

Lieutenant Ridgway clambered on to the bridge and waited for Ainslie to notice him.

'Asdic reports all quiet, sir. Nothing about.' He concealed his feeling about losing his torpedoes very well.

'Good. Tell the Chief to switch to main engines and begin charging batteries.'

He returned to the screen, the thick glass still dripping with salt water.

Halliday must have been waiting for the order. The diesels were connected now, drumming throatily through the water, shaking the conning tower in a regular vibration.

An hour should do it. The last run-in, the hard bit. It was best not to contemplate the hull below his feet, crammed with every sort of ammunition you could think of.

He wondered momentarily what his mixed company thought about it, of their rapidly changing role. Cottier, the French officer, was asking to come to the bridge, as he always did when surfaced, to check the communications systems. It was strange to think of him and Lucas and their handful of Free French sailors ending up in *Soufrière* like this. There were no longer any clear margins to the war. They were vague and obscure, like the invisible coastline they were heading for.

According to the best information available, the enemy were still advancing, but at a slower pace. Whether this was due to stiffening resistance or to lack of support, it was hard to say, but the Japanese advanced units were within three hundred miles of Singapore itself. It still sounded a lot when you thought of England and the Channel. But there were no white cliffs of Dover across the Johore Strait.

'Steady on two-seven-zero, sir.'

'Very well.'

Ainslie stared into the darkness, feeling the lazy rise and roll of the bows. He could just discern the two long guns pointing forward as they cut across the bow wave like tusks.

Farrant and his crews were in their turret. The gunnery officer would be even more full of himself now, knowing he was the submarine's only defence.

'Time to turn, sir.'

Ainslie peered at the luminous dial of his watch, feeling the drifting spray plastering his hair across his forehead.

'Carry on.'

Quinton and Forster were in charge down there. They were more than capable.

The alteration was so slight it barely registered. But that was how it had to be, this way and that, a whole series of dog's legs all the way to the inlet. If it were daylight the sea would appear placid and friendly, but the charts said otherwise. Sudden shallows and spits of hard sand, little islets no bigger than rocks which ran off in either direction below the surface in long barriers of craggy teeth.

Forster, leaning over his gently vibrating table, a pencil gripped between his teeth, was thinking much on those lines as he rechecked his calculations and made another neat cross on the chart.

Stooping, or leaning forward in their steel seats, the other members of the control room team were apart from Forster's domain, and his sense of isolation was made stronger by that other unwinding world on his chart and plot.

It was one of the reasons he liked his work. It gave him responsibility for the whole boat, probably even more than the first lieutenant, who was after all an extension of the skipper's ultimate command.

'Seven fathoms, sir.'

Forster glanced at Quinton who was in his customary place between the helmsman and the raised periscope. He shared the latter with Christie, the seaplane pilot, who had been told by the skipper to understudy just about everybody but the chief engineer.

He thought suddenly of the girl in his arms when he had visited her just prior to sailing. Another advantage of being the navigating officer, he could usually drum up an excuse for getting ashore when others could not.

God, widow she might be, and he had been unable to put it completely from his thoughts, but she had left him in little doubt of her willingness to –

Forster looked up, startled, his head cracking against a deckhead pipe.

'What? Repeat that!'

He was not usually so abrupt, and it brought an edge of resentment to the rating's voice as he repeated, 'Seven fathoms, sir.'

Forster snatched his parallel rulers and ran them across the chart. It could not be. It showed ten fathoms on the chart. A drop of sweat splashed across his wrist as he worked to clear his racing thoughts.

The course to steer was two-eight-five exactly.

Quinton's shadow moved over the chart space and he asked calmly, 'Trouble, Pilot?'

'No. Not really. The bottom round here must have changed since this chart was corrected, although . . .'

Quinton stared from the calculations to the gyro repeater above the coxswain's head.

'What the bloody hell!' Quinton spoke in a fierce whisper. 'Look, man! We're five degrees off course!'

Forster looked from the chart to Quinton's angry face and stammered, 'He must have misunderstood, Number One.'

Quinton strode to the opposite side. 'Misunderstood, my flaming arse! I heard the order myself. You said to steer two-eight-zero.' He stood by the coxswain and added, 'Alter course, Swain. Steer two-eight-five.' He returned to the chart space, his dark features working dangerously. 'Will that do it?'

Forster peered at the chart. 'It should. But the bottom is so confused hereabouts.' He broke off, his mind refusing to accept his mistake. He heard Quinton speaking to the bridge, his voice clipped.

'Captain, sir. First lieutenant speaking. We were five degrees off course. I reckon about four minutes.' There was a pause and he added, 'Yes, It was my fault.' He half turned to glance at Forster. 'I should have watched.'

'Slow ahead both engines.' The repeated order broke some of the tension.

By his panel Halliday watched the flickering lights and dials, but he was thinking of Quinton's words and of the words Ainslie must have left unsaid.

Dead slow. He could picture the beast. Like a great whale, a blind one now if Forster had made a cock-up of it. Halliday saw his petty officer tapping a gauge with an oily finger, sensed his satisfaction that all was well.

It must have been the party, he thought. Forster must have been thinking about that girl. Halliday felt his anger rising. The bloody young fool.

From his vantage point above the conning tower Ainslie shut Quinton's voice from his thoughts as Menzies called, 'Light flashing, sir! Starboard bow!'

Ainslie nodded, lowering his head again to check the time. Perfect, in spite of everything.

He asked, 'Is it the correct signal, Yeo?'

'Aye, sir.' Menzies' Scots accent became more pronounced when he was excited. 'Just like the wee man said.'

Ainslie wiped his face. Spray or sweat he was not certain. 'Acknowledge. Then ask Commander Critchley to come up, will you?'

Critchley's ability to relax was almost unnerving. He could sleep, curtained off in one of the bunks, as if he were in a country inn. He had explained that he would only be in the way if he hung about the control room, and 'if the boat sinks I don't even know which way to run!' He would be missed by almost everyone aboard when he returned to Britain.

The seaman at the voice-pipes reported, 'Four fathoms, sir.'

Ainslie replied, 'Just right.'

It was stupid, of course. In daylight the submarine would loom above her reflection, impossible to miss. But he had to watch every word as it left his mouth. The man at the voice-pipes, should he even sense doubt or anxiety, might be just the one to panic, to jam the hatch as the boat dived. Not that she could dive here. If they were bombed, they could stand on the tower and periscope standards and not even get their feet wet!

The messenger said, 'Commander Critchley coming up, sir.'

Ainslie trained his glasses towards the shore. He thought he could see it. A black barrier beneath the stars. The inlet must be in direct line ahead.

He tried to imagine the sort of men who had been waiting and watching for *Soufrière*'s arrival. They would have been told by radio, but hardly anyone in the armed services ever took much notice of assurances from higher up.

He heard Critchley's voice, echoing strangely in the conning tower.

Then, as his head appeared over the rim of the hatch he felt himself losing his balance, as if he was being sucked forward by some invisible force.

Ainslie half fell the rest of the way to the voice-pipes, hearing the startled voices below, Quinton's curt orders to restore control.

Ainslie said, 'Stop engines!'

Critchley asked quietly, 'What's happened?'

Ainslie waited for Quinton to come to the voice-pipes. 'We're aground.'

'Yes, sir. Asdic has just reported a sudden shelving. Another few yards and we'd have passed clean and away.' Even he could not disguise his bitterness. 'It was that fault earlier.'

'Never mind that now. Clear the fore-ends. Get all hands aft. I'm going to try and work her free with the main engines.'

In his mind he could see it all, as if the words were painted a mile high. The falling tide. The sudden, stark reality of being aground. But errors happened all the time. Just one flaw, a small mistake, and . . .

'Control room to captain. All spare hands aft, sir, excluding turret crews.'

'Those, too. I'm not planning a war at the moment.'

Menzies muttered, 'They need a few more Scots down there, sir. We canna manage it all.'

Ainslie stared at him and then said, 'Thanks, Yeo. That was just right.'

Critchley touched the yeoman's arm. 'Well done.' He had sensed Ainslie's sudden anxiety and felt it as clearly as a change of direction.

'Slow astern together.'

Ainslie climbed up to the starboard side and peered aft at the sudden commotion of thrashing foam. If the enemy had but one patrol boat and its commander was half blind he could not fail to detect *Soufrière* now.

'Full astern port.'

He pictured Halliday's taciturn face at his panel. The violent wrench of one engine against another was not the best way to treat machinery. But it was that or something much worse.

Someone gave a muffled cheer.

'She's coming off, sir.'

Ainslie brushed past the other vague figures as he ran to the gyro repeater. 'Stop both engines!' His mind was throbbing with effort. 'Yeoman. Call up the soldiers again.' He heard Menzies suck his teeth. 'I must get a fix. We could be any-where.'

He felt the submarine sliding noiselessly astern on her momen-tum, the water lapping and gurgling along the saddle tanks.

The clack-clack-clack of Menzies' signal lamp sounded like guns firing in the stillness. Fortunately, the army must have been expecting trouble and they replied at once, the small light low down near the water like a faint yellow eye.

Got it. But if there was another sand-bar. . . . Ainslie groped for the voice-pipe. 'Slow ahead together. Steer two-seven-six.'

The hull had swung right round to the reverse thrust. Without the signal light from the shore it would be like heading blind into a brick wall.

He waited for his breathing to steady. But his lips and throat were like dust.

'Tell the first lieutenant to have the turret manned again. Same routine as before.'

Twenty minutes later *Soufrière* made fast to the remains of a rickety pier, having been led the last few yards by two soldiers in a rubber dinghy.

Ainslie watched the shadowy figures emerging from the deeper darkness, reaching out to receive heaving lines, or leaping bodily on to the saddle tank nearest the pier to lend a hand.

'Ring off main engines. Open the forward hatch. Turn the hands to.'

Ainslie heard Petty Officer Voysey shouting instructions to the men on the pier, and was thankful to see some of his sailors leaping ashore to make the springs and breast ropes fast to whatever was available. A gruff voice was answering from the pier, and Ainslie thought for an instant it was Torpedoman Sawle. It was so Cockney he could have stepped straight out of Whitechapel market.

Quinton came on to the bridge. 'All secure, sir. Chief's checking his valves and pumps to make sure nothing got silted up when we grounded.' He stood aside as more hurrying figures came through the hatch and scrambled down the outside of the conning tower to join those from the forward hatch.

Ridgway said, 'Army type coming up, sir.'

It was a young captain, who seemed rather at a loss now that the submarine had actually arrived.

Ainslie shook his hand and said, 'We've brought everything but the kitchen sink. Just get your lighter alongside and we'll get started.'

The soldier stared with disbelief at the seamen, who with their petty officers looked in danger of falling from the crowded casing into the water.

He said, 'That's just it, sir. We were shot up yesterday by fighter-bombers. We lost most of the pier and all the available boats. My CO has had to put half our strength six miles up the coast road to reinforce the battalion there.' He spread his hands and added apologetically, 'I've got two platoons standing to, and the HQ platoon resting.'

Ainslie said quietly, 'Do you still want these supplies?'

Just for an instant the young army officer showed the strain he was under. He took off his cap and ran his fingers through his hair as he said, 'The battalion on our left withdrew yesterday. They're all to hell. They were no match for this in the first place. Clerks and cooks, all the odds and sods left over from the first assault.' He seemed to realize what Ainslie had asked and said grimly, 'With them it's a matter of time. Without them we might as well chuck it in right now.'

Quinton whispered, 'We'll never do it before daylight, sir. We need derricks, even sheer-legs would be better than nothing. And we need the men to get the stuff unloaded and hidden ashore.'

Ainslie looked past him. Quinton was right. In just a few hours it was impossible to unload such a tightly stowed cargo.

He said to the soldier, 'Get every man you can spare.' He turned to Quinton. 'Tell Farrant to rig tackles on his two eight-inch guns. We'll use the power on the turret so that it acts as a double derrick.'

He saw a red glow flicker across the sky and die almost as quickly. The war was going on somewhere.

Quinton rubbed his chin. 'Even so, we'll never make it on time.'

Ainslie leaned on the screen and watched the men bustling along two makeshift brows. One ingoing, one already loaded with staggering figures making their way ashore, bowed almost double with the first packs of supplies.

'I know. We'll just have to stay here for the day and sweat it out.'

He twisted round as a soldier ran along the pier and shouted, 'See, Jim? I *told* you th' bloody Navy wouldn't let us down!'

Ainslie said quietly, 'And nor will I.'

Ainslie made his way through the control room and saw Halliday speaking with his assistant, Sub-Lieutenant Deacon, and the Chief ERA.

He automatically straightened his back as he approached, but even that effort was like an extra pain.

'All well, Chief?'

God, how weary they all looked. It was morning, and they had been hard at it all through the night. Only the control room retained an appearance of watchfulness and order. Throughout the rest of the boat every area, large and small, was littered with cases and abandoned crates, torn wrapping paper and smaller items waiting to be carried bodily ashore. They were like ants. Up ladders, down ladders, pausing only to snatch another load and be sent away again by a petty officer at one end or a sergeant at the other.

Halliday watched him warily. 'Aye, sir. Nothing we can't manage.'

Ainslie walked on. 'Fine. There'll be some tea and sandwiches coming round shortly.'

'Look, sir, don't you think you should take a rest a while?'

Lucas took out a cigarette and shook his head. 'He does not hear you.'

Halliday sighed. 'I should know him by now. But he still amazes me.'

Ainslie climbed up the gleaming ladder, seeing the oval of blue sky broken at the edges by green fronds which Sub-Lieutenant Southby's landing party had gathered ashore and fashioned into a crude camouflage.

On the bridge it was searing hot, and after the cooler darkness the sights were also brutally obvious. Great black patches where fires had raged after an air attack. Crude graves along the top of the beach, marked by steel helmets or plain wooden crosses. Like something from the Somme or Passchendaele.

Of the strongpoint there was little sign, and Ainslie guessed it was dug deeply into the jungle by the remaining coast road. He could hear the rumble of mortar and artillery fire, rising and receding, like a great beast dragging itself, complaining, through the jungle.

How thick the trees looked. In there it must be barely possbile to see the sky, he thought, even more difficult to hear an enemy's stealthy approach.

Ridgway was standing on the gratings watching the unloading, his stubbled face streaming in the heat. He saw Ainslie and saluted.

Ainslie joined him and said, 'I'm going ashore for a moment. Tell Number One to take over.' He watched the sluggish wavelets lapping along the saddle tanks. *Soufrière* was considerably higher in the water after losing so much of her deadly cargo.

He climbed down to the dock and waited until he could join the shuffling line of figures going ashore.

On the pier a weary-looking corporal held out his fist. ''Ere mate, where're we off to then? Bleedin' Southend?'

Petty Officer Voysey shouted, 'That's our captain, you twit!'

Ainslie nodded to the corporal. He had come ashore without his cap and was in the same stained shirt he had worn since Singapore.

'At ease, Corporal. And you were right. I *should* have carried something, too.'

He left the astonished corporal behind and strode gratefully beneath the nearest line of trees. After men and steel, diesel oil and sweat, the heavier scents of jungle and rotting undergrowth made him feel slightly unsteady.

A sentry guided him towards a sandbagged door which appeared to be cut straight through a mound of earth and rock, and seconds later he was confronting the commanding officer.

The young captain said, 'This is the submarine's commander, Colonel.'

The colonel shook Ainslie's hand and gestured to a brightly coloured deck-chair. Before he sat down Ainslie noticed there was a dark stain on the back of it. Dried blood.

'Bit early, old chap.' The colonel waited for the other soldier to leave and then poured some whisky into two enamel mugs. He was a small man, very neat despite his torn uniform and stained boots. 'But I reckon we both need one. Cheers.' He sat down slowly and grimaced. 'Getting old for this sort of caper.'

Ainslie felt the spirit in his empty stomach and all the sense of relaxation which went with it. He thought of her face as she had watched her husband drinking glass after glass at the party, and again when he had remarked so crudely about Forster looking down her dress.

The colonel said, 'You're a bloody godsend, I can tell you. We're pretty strong here now that we've got supplies, but I'm not too happy about our left flank.' He swallowed some more whisky. 'Glad to see you,' he added absently. 'Used to go to Portsmouth as a lad to see the warships. But my father had me cut out for a soldier, so there it was.' He became very serious. 'I don't know how much you've heard, but things are getting damn bad. The Japs control the air completely. We can't move a thing on the roads without getting strafed and bombed. I've had fifty casualties in two days.' He pushed the bottle across the table. 'Help yourself. The bloody Japs will have it otherwise.'

'Bad as that?'

'Worse, if that's possible. Refugees are pouring down through the lines with terrible stories of atrocities. The Japs are seemingly trying to break up the people into separate factions, the Chinese against the Indians, the Malays against the rest, and so forth. I'll wager they've sent saboteurs through the lines, too.' He rubbed his eyes fiercely. 'I tell you, Commander, if the high command at Singapore don't get their finger out they'll have fighting on the island by Christmas!'

A telephone hanging in a webbing case buzzed impatiently and the colonel put it to his ear, his eyes drooping with exhaustion. He listened for a full minute and then replaced it carefully.

'The left flank has collapsed, I'm afraid. Brigade are sending reinforcements, and I'm to hold the road and about a mile to the west of here. A miracle would come in handy, too.'

He looked up as a sergeant peered in at him. 'Yes, Roach?'

'Message from the submarine, sir.' His eyes moved to Ainslie. 'Recce aircraft sighted just to the south of us. It's bin 'ere before, sir, but it may spot your ship. I've told the men to get some more camouflage nets spread, sir.' The eyes were back on the colonel. 'Any orders, sir?'

'No, everything's fine, Sergeant.' The man withdrew and he added vehemently, 'It makes me weep to keep up this stupid pretence! My men are pure gold, and I'm expected, no, *commanded* to hold them here at all costs.'

The telephone buzzed again and the colonel smiled apologetically. 'I'll rustle up some food in a minute.' He picked up the phone. 'Colonel.'

Ainslie leaned back in the stained deck-chair. Whose had it been? A planter up country perhaps? A poor, simple soul who still believed it could not happen?

The colonel replaced the telephone and said quietly, 'That was my MO. There has been another casualty, I'm afraid.' He was looking at Ainslie as he added, 'Your naval officer from intelligence. A sniper got him.'

Ainslie lurched to his feet, seeing Critchley's face in the first light this very morning. Hearing his chat with some of the seamen as he had gone ashore.

'Is he dead?'

The colonel nodded. 'That sniper's done for several of my men already. Never misses, never loses a chance. My adjutant should have taken more care to warn him.' He looked at his hands. 'But he's had no sleep for days. He probably thought your man would know.' He stood up. 'They're bringing him in now.'

Later, as an invisible reconnaissance plane droned somewhere to the south of the little inlet, and gunfire crashed and echoed threateningly along a hundred miles of jungle, Ainslie turned back the blanket from the stretcher while the two helmeted bearers stood like work horses, their eyes glazed with fatigue.

Critchley looked very calm, with no sign of the shock of that quick, final agony.

Ainslie could almost hear him speaking. *Back to dear old London. Bless it.*

The MO asked, 'Shall I have my chaps put him under?'

Put him under. Like so much rubbish.

'No. I'll take him back.' He looked at the sky, searching for the persistent drone. *If we catch it, he'll still be with us.*

He turned on his heel and walked back towards the pier, looking neither right nor left.

Quinton saw his face as he climbed aboard, and even though he had guessed what had happened he was shocked by what he saw.

Ainslie said, 'Keep the hands at it, Number One. I want every last ounce ashore before we get under way.'

Quinton said quietly, 'Leave it to me.'

Ainslie swung on him, his blue eyes blazing with hurt and bitter anger. But he steadied himself and said, 'No. We'll do it together.' He tried to smile. 'Like you said. The old firm. Remember?' Then he lowered himself through the hatch.

Quinton raised his glasses and peered up through the netting and fronds towards the persistent drone.

To Ridgway he said, 'Tell Sawle to take some food and drink to the skipper's quarters. He won't touch it, but if he sits still long enough he might fall asleep.'

He swung his glasses, but the shadow had only been a solitary sea bird.

Ainslie had been about to go for him. And why not, after Forster's mistake, and his own failure to notice it.

But instead, he had made another effort to hold them all together, as he always had in the past.

A heavy shell exploded in the jungle, shaking the hull like a piledriver hitting a roadway.

He saw a covered stretcher approaching the pier, the bare-backed troops and sailors parting to let it through.

Poor old Critch, Quinton thought. Then with a sigh he said, 'Man the side. Commander Critchley coming aboard.'

10

Nobody Lives Forever

AINSLIE awoke with a violent shudder, his mind reluctant to accept he had been asleep, or that he had given in to his exhaustion. As he gripped the sides of his bunk he saw Quinton peering down at him, with another figure, Sub-Lieutenant Southby, hovering in the rectangle of light from the passageway.

'What is it?' Ainslie fumbled with his watch, seeing his untouched food by the bunk, realizing he must have fallen asleep even as he had rejected it.

'Sorry to bother you, sir.' Quinton stepped back as Ainslie lurched from the bunk. 'Just had a shout from the Army. The Japs are attacking in depth. It doesn't sound too bright.'

Ainslie stared at himself in the bulkhead mirror, seeing the wildness in his eyes, remembering with startling clarity that he had been dreaming when Quinton had touched his shoulder. Of a beach, of the girl, dressed in that same long dress, her bare feet on the hard, wet sand. There had been danger. Terrible but unseen. He had tried to reach her, to warn her, but the words had been choked, his mouth filled with sand.

He steadied his racing thoughts and asked, 'Are our people on board?' How could he have fallen asleep? Tiredness, despair made suddenly sharper by the memory of Critchley's death put an edge to his voice. 'For God's sake, you should have called me!'

Quinton stood his ground. 'We need you to be rested, sir. Any fool can run cargo.' He watched Ainslie's mixed emotions. 'I've finished unloading. The Army are bringing their wounded aboard now. It's about all we can do.'

Quinton's quiet resignation helped more than anything. Ainslie was suddenly aware of the sounds, muffled by the hull, but still filled with menace. The unbroken rumble of gunfire, the decks quivering occasionally as a shell fell close to the inlet.

It was noon. Incredibly, Ainslie had slept for four hours. He said, 'We should stick it out until dusk. After that . . .' He did not finish.

He tucked his shirt into his trousers again and pushed the hair from his forehead. For a few moments he looked at his cap, lying on the desk. He thought of the little girl's face in Singapore. The nurse, wary and hostile, ready to rush in and protect her charge from comment.

'I'll go ashore. Tell the Chief to be prepared to get under way. He knows already, but tell him anyway.'

Ainslie looked at Southby. In the dim lighting he was a boy, determined but unable to conceal his anxiety.

'Come with me, Sub. We'll see the colonel.'

After the false shade on the conning tower with its camouflage netting and layers of palm fronds, the heat on the steel casing was almost unbearable.

The humid air was heavy with other smells, too. Burning, charred wood and cordite.

He stepped ashore, where Petty Officer Voysey and some seamen crouched or lay by the small brow, ready to cast off, to run, to to die if things went wrong.

Ainslie strode past them, Southby walking in his shadow. To Voysey he called, 'You did a good job. The boat feels lighter without all that cargo!'

Voysey chuckled, his face grimy and tired. 'Be glad to get out of 'ere, sir. Even Chatham is better than this lot!'

He jumped up as the first group of wounded soldiers appeared amongst the trees. 'Ready, lads. Lend a 'and.'

The soldiers passed Ainslie without a glance, supported by their comrades, limping or being carried; they were like living dead, their faces moulded into a pattern of misery and defeat.

Southby said between his teeth, 'They look done in, sir.'

A cloud of brightly coloured birds rose shrieking from the trees as a single whiplash crack echoed across the inlet.

Ainslie watched the way one of the soldiers cringed. The sniper was out there still. Probably marking down another kill. Like Critchley, and some of these dazed, stumbling survivors.

The attack was mounting and spreading. Even as a sailor Ainslie had heard its like before. The impartial chatter of machine-guns, further off, like woodpeckers on a sunny afternoon in England. The deeper thud and bang of mortar bombs, the crack of rifles.

He found the colonel in his command post, as if he had never moved. But he noticed that he had found time to shave and put on a clean, if patched, shirt.

'I was about to send for you.' The colonel waved to the deck-chair with its bloodstain. 'Take a pew.' He spoke rapidly into his field telephone. 'Yes, yes, dammit, I know that, Simpson! Tell the sappers to put some mines down, and try to reopen the line to Brigade.'

He dropped the handset and said in a flat voice, 'The Japs are coming down the road right now. They've got light tanks with 'em, and their artillery has made a real hole in our defences.'

Ainslie waited, hearing Southby's rapid breathing beside him. The colonel looked round the bunker. 'I can't contact Brigade at all, and the whole flank is on the turn.'

'What will you do?' Ainslie's voice seemed louder than usual.

'Do? What I've just been told. Hold on here until Brigade HQ says otherwise, or Division can re-group.' He looked up from his litter of maps, his eyes ringed with fatigue. 'I can't give the Navy orders, but I suggest you get out, daylight or not. The Japs will probably try to land more troops to the south of here. That's what their spotter plane was searching for. A good landing place.' He sighed as the telephone buzzed again. 'But thanks for the help. We'll need all that ammo now, I'm thinking.' He turned back to the telephone, Ainslie and the *Soufrière* no longer his concern.

Ainslie walked back to the smoky sunlight, his mind grappling with the sudden threat. To put to sea in broad daylight would seem like madness. To stay and be cut off was no better.

He saw a soldier with a red cross armband bending over a sprawled body beside the track. He was removing an identity disc and the dead soldier's wallet. There was a sudden crack and a sharp, metallic clang. The medical orderly fell across the body without a sound, bright blood running down from beneath his steel helmet, in which the sniper's bullet had punched a hole big enough for a man's finger.

Southby made to run, but Ainslie said sharply, 'Still! He's not far away.'

Two soldiers charged round the corpses firing sub-machine-guns wildly into the trees. Something fell through the branches but did not reach the ground.

144

Ainslie walked slowly to where the two soldiers were standing and saw a body swinging slowly like a pendulum, back and forth from a kind of harness.

One of the soldiers said dully, 'The bastards do that, so if they get hit they won't fall and show their position.' He had a round West Country voice like Petty Officer Vernon.

Southby said in a husky tone, 'He's moving!'

The rasping clatter of the tommy-gun made the birds scream once more. The soldier who had fired said, 'Not now, he ain't.'

Ainslie nodded to the soldiers and continued down the slope towards the water. He had seen the sniper. Dressed from head to foot in green rags to conceal his position, like a figure in a nightmare. Even his powerful rifle had been tied to his body.

It was quite likely the same sniper who had killed Critchley. What had he thought as he had seen his face through the telescopic sight? Ainslie released a deep sigh. Probably no more than he felt when he saw a target edging into the cross-wires of a periscope.

The same old reasons. It's him or me. The war, survival. Everything and nothing.

'When will they do something to stop them, sir?'

Ainslie could feel Southby watching him, his concern, his sinking faith.

'It will have to be soon. Maybe reinforcements are already landing at Singapore. There was a troop convoy due by way of Ceylon.'

He looked up as an aircraft roared overhead, guns clattering before it zoomed low over the tree-tops and vanished. He thought of Critchley's anger when they had first arrived, his insistence on air cover above all else. It had been too late even then.

The gunfire was continuous, although Ainslie could not tell one side from the other.

He saw Lieutenant Ridgway mopping his face as he spoke with some soldiers at the waterside, saw his relief as he looked up and called, 'These men want to come with us, sir!'

The wounded seemed to have disappeared into the submarine, and as far as he could tell the handful of soldiers with the torpedo officer were unmarked.

One of them, a corporal, said gruffly, 'It's no use us stayin' 'ere, sir.' He looked at his companions and added desperately,

'I know what you're thinkin', sir, but it's not like that. What's the point of it all?' He waved his hands in the air. 'We can't get out of this, no chance! Bloody HQ's on the run, and they expect us to stay an' be killed!'

Southby exclaimed, 'It's desertion, it's – .' He closed his mouth as he saw Ainslie's eyes.

Ainslie said quietly, 'Back there, your colonel is doing his best for the rest of us.' He watched his words go home, like nails in a coffin. 'I know how you feel, but my officer is right. It would be desertion, and worse.'

Another of the soldiers slung his rifle across his shoulder and said, 'Forget it, Corp. Anyway, nobody lives forever.'

In a slow, sad file the soldiers walked back towards the trees and the mounting crescendo of gunfire.

Ridgway said, 'I almost let 'em aboard, sir.'

Ainslie was still staring after the little group of khaki figures.

'*Almost* is the word which always gets in the way. But for it, the war would have ended at Dunkirk.'

A mortar bomb exploded amongst the trees with a violent bang. Before the dust settled again Ainslie heard a man cry out, imagined him lying there amongst the trees, dying, written off.

He said, 'Take a party of men and see if there are any more wounded. If so, get them inboard double-quick.' He glanced at his watch. 'We're getting out.' He saw their quick exchange of glances. 'If we can.'

Quinton was waiting below the conning tower, his holster unbuttoned as if to emphasize the closeness of danger.

Ainslie said, 'Get the dinghy, and take the yeoman with you. I want you to paddle to the end of the inlet, but keep under cover. The Army don't care much what the Jap Navy is doing, they've got problems enough.' He saw Quinton's quick understanding and added, 'But we do care!'

He was amazed how clear his mind had become, the weariness gone from his body like the end of a drug.

For a brief moment he looked along his command, realizing with a start how short a time it had been since Poulain had killed himself in his cabin.

Now they were like one, and he knew that most of the company felt much as he did. No wonder Poulain had been determined to hold on to her, no matter whether his reasons were right or wrong. He had seen his world crumble, just as the corporal had recognized the approach of a crushing defeat back there on the jungle track.

Farrant was in the control room, straight-backed and without any sign of strain on his narrow features.

He reported crisply, 'Wounded are all inboard, sir. Hunt says that a couple may die if they can't get to hospital soon.'

He followed Ainslie to the chart space where Forster was rubbing out pencilled calculations, his face tight with concentration.

'By the way, sir. W/T decoded a signal just after you left the boat.' Farrant flicked open his notebook, the one he used to write down comments and criticisms on his gun crews. 'Petty Officer Vernon thought you would be interested, sir.' His eyes fixed on the right page. 'The submarine *Psyche* has been reported sunk in the Mediterranean. No survivors.' His cold eyes rose and settled on Ainslie, seeking a reaction.

Ainslie nodded slowly. All that was going on here, and just a mile or so up the road, and yet there was still that other world far away, the one he had so recently left behind.

Petty Officer Telegraphist Vernon used his receiver like a lifeline perhaps. Shut in his steel box with his assistants he listened while the rest of them waited.

He replied slowly, 'I did my first dive in the *Psyche*, when I was a subbie at *Dolphin*.'

Now she has gone, like *Seamist* and *Tigress*, and all the others which littered the bottom of the sea. Trust Vernon to remember. He had been a green telegraphist aboard her with him.

Forster could scarcely breathe. It was just like being crushed beneath a great weight, or stifled by a massive blanket. *Psyche* had gone down, taking Daphne's husband with her. God, he had never considered that might happen, even though the odds mounted each time a submarine put to sea.

He had been thinking of Daphne, and more so of himself. Now she was alone, praying for a letter, for some strand of hope.

Ainslie leaned over the chart. 'We'll go out surfaced, but by a more northerly course.' He glanced at Forster. 'Are you all right?' Maybe he was still worrying about his mistake on the inward passage, brooding how it might affect his chances of promotion.

147

Forster swallowed hard. 'The *Psyche*, sir. I met her CO once. Nice chap.'

Ainslie knew it was a lie, but not the reason for it.

He said, 'Well, let's get on with this, Pilot, or we'll be next in line!'

Thirty feet away in the *Soufrière*'s wardroom some of the officers were drinking tea and munching the remainder of Sawle's sandwiches.

Halliday sat with his elbows on the table, a cup in his hands, as he listened to the muffled gunfire. One mortar bomb, let alone an artillery shell, was all it would take to cripple the submarine. He heard the murmur of a generator and knew his men were still checking everything.

Across the table Sub-Lieutenant (E) Arthur Deacon, his assistant, sat like an untidy sack, his face streaked with oil as he stared unseeingly at the opposite bulkhead. A good engineer, but no imagination. He was probably thinking about his wife in Gosport, the house they were trying to buy.

Halliday glanced at the two Frenchmen, Cottier and Lucas. Halliday had previously thought of all Frenchmen as being the same. Foreign. But whereas he had grown to like the slightly built Lucas, and had even been made to admit that he was a first-class engineer, Cottier was something else. He was always so pleased with himself, confident in a superior way which was equalled only by Farrant. The odd thing was that the two Frenchmen did not seem to like one another much either. Halliday had heard it was because Cottier was a Parisian, and in his eyes Lucas, a lowly Breton, was not worth bothering about.

He wondered what had happened to all the Free French sailors who had helped to train and prepare them for the *Soufrière*'s capture. In other ships probably. Not sitting in a ruddy puddle waiting for a ton of HE to fall on them.

Southby came in and said wearily, 'I just saw the troops kill a sniper.' He picked up the teapot but it was empty. 'The captain says we're pulling out.'

Lieutenant Christie looked at Jones, his observer. 'Good thing. If I'm to die, I want it from five thousand feet!'

Cottier removed a cigarette from his lips and smiled. 'It might have been better to have left *Soufrière* under her old flag, eh?' He spread his hands, enjoying their frowns. 'Then we would have been safe in England, whereas . . .'

Lucas said quietly, 'He does not mean it. He is like all his kind. More mouth than mind.'

Cottier sprang to his feet, his good humour gone, but Halliday said, 'When I was an ERA aboard an old H-boat we had a bloke go off his rocker.' He made a movement with his finger across his forehead, leaving a greasy smear. 'That means crazy, see?'

Cottier regarded him coldly. 'I am well aware of the English lack of respect for language!'

Halliday did not smile. 'Scottish, if you don't mind. Anyway, I had to lay the bloke out with a wrench, and I'll do it to you if you start a brawl, see?'

Christie grinned. 'Quite right, Chief. This is time for OLQs just now.' He looked at Lucas's mystified expression. 'Officer-like-qualities, *that* means!' His grin broadened. 'I don't have any myself, as it happens.'

Cottier sat down again, arranging himself like a bird smoothing its feathers.

He said, 'I would never have guessed.'

Ridgway stood in the doorway, his shirt black with sweat.

'Captain's compliments, my friends, and we are getting under way in an hour.' He looked at Southby. 'You're to mount an extra machine-gun up there.'

'But how . . .?'

Ridgway shrugged. 'Your problem, not mine.'

Forster pushed past him and walked to his locker at the far end of the wardroom. They all watched him, testing his reactions against their own apprehension.

Cottier asked mildly, 'Are you ready to steer us all to safety?'

Forster looked at him searchingly. 'What did you mean by that? I admit I made a mistake, but I don't need you to tell me!'

Cottier examined the tip of his cigarette. 'But of course. I would be the same after I had been with a girl like that.'

Forster seemed to explode. 'Damn your bloody eyes! When we get ashore again, just you watch your step!'

Cottier stood up and left the wardroom. As the curtain fell across the door he said, '*If* we get ashore again.'

Forster sat down, his chest heaving. 'Sorry, everyone.' He tried to smile. 'He got to me then.'

Halliday leaned across and shook Deacon from his torpor. 'Come on, Arthur, time to move.' He looked at Lucas. 'You too, my lad.'

One by one the others left the wardroom to prepare themselves and their departments for the moment when they threw their camouflage aside.

When only Christie and Forster were left, the flyer asked, 'Anything I can do?' He watched the signs, the resentment changing to something softer.

Forster nodded. 'Thanks. But I don't know. There's a girl in England. I had a letter.'

Christie said bluntly, 'In the family way, is she?' He saw Forster nod, felt his anguish like something physical. 'How d'you feel about her?'

Forster shrugged helplessly. 'That's just it. I'm not sure now. Before, all I wanted was to get out of it.'

'Before what?'

'*Psyche*'s been sunk in the Med. Her husband was the skipper.'

Christie winced. 'Hell!'

Forster walked slowly towards the door. 'Anyway, keep it to yourself, Jack. I've got enough on my plate at the moment.'

'Sure thing, Dave.'

Christie stared around the empty wardroom. Just to be up in the clouds again, even taking those trippers for short flips over the sea and back, anything but here. Never mind, after the war he would start again. His own plane. There would be millions of them when this lot was over. He'd go somewhere away from it all. Tahiti, that was it.

His observer peered in at him. 'Just had a thought, Jack. Suppose we could scrounge an old Lewis gun or something? There's a ring mounting of sorts on the plane.' He grinned. 'We'd be able to protect ourselves then.'

Christie stood up and yawned. 'With a bloody Lewis?' But he nodded. Anything was better than brooding.

Ainslie stood in the centre of the wardroom and looked at the faces around him. He could feel the submarine trembling slightly as the artificers tested and rechecked each section. There was an air of expectancy, of tension. It was all he could do to control his own feelings as he said, 'Number One has come back with some bad news. He spotted two enemy patrol vessels outside this place, and the fact they are not being fired on shows that our local artillery must have been pulled out or been overrun.'

He sensed their anxiety, the same he had felt when Quinton had told him.

'But we're leaving just the same. The Japs obviously don't know about our presence here yet. Otherwise we'd have had half of their air force on our heads a long time ago. So we have surprise, speed and good armament.'

He saw Farrant nod approvingly, as he had when he had explained what he intended.

Ridgway said, 'And the two patrol vessels are just sitting out there waiting, sir?'

'Yes.' He knew what Ridgway meant. The enemy were so sure of themselves they were prepared to bide their time. He said, 'Just think how much worse it must be for the soldiers who are being left here to cover the retreat.'

There were several nods, and Halliday asked, 'How long will it take us, sir?'

The question was the only one which counted.

Ainslie replied, 'An hour. If we can cripple one of those ships and reach deep water, we stand a good chance.'

He looked at Christie. He of all people would know that it would take half that time for the enemy aircraft to reach them.

'That's it, gentlemen. We're on our own again.'

Twenty minutes later Petty Officer Voysey and his line-handling party charged along the pier, ducking whenever an explosion hurled earth and timber into the air, or something metal whined dangerously overhead.

The brows were dragged hastily aside, one falling into the water as Halliday's men revved up the big diesels in readiness for getting under way.

On the bridge, Ainslie, his cap tilted over his eyes, trained his binoculars above the jungle, searching for aircraft, but finding only dense clouds of drifting smoke, lit regularly by vivid red flashes.

'All clear aft, sir!'

'Stand by.'

Ainslie saw some soldiers running, bent double, between the trees, their rifles catching in bushes as they vanished into the smoke. The din of automatic weapons was getting heavier, and he guessed the little colonel was engaging the attackers on the road now.

'Let go forrard!'

'Slow astern starboard.'

The headrope splashed into the water and was hauled rapidly aboard, but as the remaining seaman on the pier made to leap on to the casing a mortar bomb exploded on the beach, and with a scream he fell headlong.

Menzies muttered, 'He's still alive, poor devil.'

Ainslie tore his eyes from the solitary white figure as the man tried to drag himself along the pier towards the slow-moving submarine.

But the effort was too much and he rolled over on to his face, revealing the great red stain across his spine.

'Slow astern port.'

The acknowledgement echoed up a voice-pipe. 'Both engines slow astern, sir. Wheel amidships.'

Ainslie pushed past the machine-gunners and Southby to peer over the rear of the bridge as the *Soufrière* edged slowly into the shallows on the other side of the inlet.

Far enough. 'Stop both.' Still he waited, listening to the boom of explosions, thinking of the dwindling defenders. The corporal who had said, *What's the point of it all?*

'Slow ahead port. Starboard engine half astern.' He recrossed the bridge. 'Hard astarboard.'

He watched the dark jungle passing across the bows as *Soufrière* continued to revolve in the small space. Smoke, explosions, a terrible sense of helplessness. It was a wonder that every man-jack of those troops had not broken and run to demand to be taken aboard.

The sea showed itself for the first time. Straight, hard blue like solid glass between the elbows of land.

'Stop together.'

His eyes watered as he scanned the sea through his glasses. A glance at the gyro repeater, and a quick search through his mind.

'Slow ahead together. Steer zero-six-zero.'

Something clattered against the hull, a spent bullet, a piece of shell splinter, he had no idea. It was like a last contact, a rebuke from those who were about to perish.

A sand-bar slid abeam, an abandoned fishing boat with half its bows burned away pulled up with great care and then left. When he looked astern he could barely see the pier, or the track which led to the command post and the place where Critchley had died.

'Half speed ahead together.'

He felt the instant response and saw the bow waves rolling back to wash the little fishing boat aside like a piece of driftwood.

He said, 'Connect me with the turret, Yeo.'

Menzies tested the little handset and handed it to him.

'We'll be passing the headland in about five minutes, Guns.' He pictured Farrant at the other end of the line. He was probably glad to release Southby to control the bridge machine-guns. In his own kingdom, all their lives in his hands.

'Very well, sir.'

Ainslie gave the instrument back to Menzies. Farrant was probably right. There was nothing more to say.

Ainslie watched the land falling back from the port beam as *Soufrière* thrust her way towards the open sea.

He lowered his eye to the gyro compass and took two rapid bearings before saying, 'Alter course now. Steer zero-seven-zero.'

He felt the sun beating through his shirt, rasping at his skin. The heat seemed to be contained inside the bridge, making it shimmer.

If the two Japanese warships were still in the same area as Quinton had described, they should soon be in view. He heard the turret squeak on its mounting and saw it begin to train round very slowly. He knew Southby was staring at it, probably thinking how much safer it was behind that thick shell than up here, exposed to everything.

The acknowledgement came up the voice-pipe. 'Ship's head is zero-seven-zero, sir.'

Southby said, 'There are a lot more fires at the top of the inlet, sir.'

Ainslie did not lower his glasses, and said quietly, 'Forget them, Sub. That's behind us now. Watch the sea.' He raised his voice for the lookouts' benefit. 'Keep to your sectors. Never mind the rest.'

How blue the sea looked, empty and pure, safe enough for anything. It was hard to believe it was so shallow, so littered with treacherous sand-bars and worse.

'Ship! Starboard bow!' The lookout's cry made them start.

Ainslie snapped, 'Increase to full revolutions!'

The deck began to tremble as the engineroom responded to the order.

Ainslie had to stop himself from wondering how she would look to the patrol vessel as she surged from cover like an enraged sea monster.

'Open fire!'

The right gun fired immediately, as if Farrant's finger had been on the trigger before the order. The whole conning tower shook violently, and before it could recover the left gun recoiled on its springs, the crash of the shot echoing across the water like a thunder-clap.

A tall column of water shot up alongside the small warship, another far beyond it. Both eight-inch guns whirred softly in their turret as Farrant adjusted the range to allow for the fall of shot. He was good, all right. It had been a perfect straddle with the first salvo.

Ainslie watched the warship, blurred in haze and distance, as realization reached her commander. There was a flurry of foam at her stern, and with sudden urgency she began to turn, her shape shortening.

'Right gun, shoot!' He heard Farrant's disembodied voice through the turret speaker, and then ducked as the bang exploded across the bow and long trailers of smoke drifted into the bridge in a choking cloud.

But he saw the brilliant flash as the shell hit the side of the Japanese vessel, a violent explosion amidships as the second shell burst dead on the target.

A machine-gunner yelled, 'Second ship, sir! Starboard beam!'

As the submarine swept from the inlet's last protection, Ainslie saw the other ship, the warning flash of her guns, his mind recording everything even as two shells screamed overhead and exploded in the shallows.

The second vessel was larger than Quinton had been able to distinguish, and he realized she was anchored, her hull lined with several smaller craft, while another was already speeding towards the shore.

Ainslie snatched up the handset as the turret started to shift target. 'They're landing troops, Guns! I'm going to close with her!'

He peered at the gyro again, his mind blank to everything but the cluster of landing craft.

'Starboard fifteen. Steer one-four-zero.' That would give Forster something to think about.

The machine-guns' belts of ammunition clattered against the steel sides as the hull tilted over to the sudden change of direction.

He heard two more shells tear over the conning tower, nearer this time, before they vanished in a great welter of bursting spray.

Then both of Farrant's guns fired, the shock so bad that it felt as if the turrret would hurl itself over the side.

Ainslie gritted his teeth as two lines of bright tracer lifted from the vessel's decks and then came plunging down towards him.

He touched Southby's arm. 'Open fire!'

The heavy machine-guns on either wing of the conning tower clattered into life, the red tracer floating with deceptive grace towards the enemy before ripping across the hull and landing craft like a steel whip.

'A hit!'

A mushroom of fierce flame burst upwards from the vessel's after part, wreckage splashing amongst the released landing craft like missiles.

Ainslie peered round the port machine-gun, seeing the seaman's bared teeth, his eyes half blinded by sun and sweat as he poured another long burst into the enemy. He saw the first warship settling down by the bows, her deck slightly towards him as she began to capsize. About the size of a corvette, and no match for Farrant's big shells. Had *Soufrière* been submerged, and the little warship on the surface above her, the roles would be very different.

Steel slashed and clanged against the conning tower and struck bright sparks from the casing, and Ainslie knew that some of the troops in the landing craft, realizing their own sudden danger, were joining in the fight.

Farrant continued to fire on the major warship, until with another tremendous explosion she broke free of her anchor and spewed flames and dense smoke from everywhere but the bridge.

Ainslie felt blood splash on his cheek and turned as a seaman fell choking to the gratings. There was blood everywhere and he saw Southby staring at the writhing man as if he was stricken.

Menzies took charge. 'Get this man below. You, Dyke, take his place!' With a beefy fist he thrust the other seaman against the smoking gun and added, 'Hit those buggers, man!'

And here was a landing craft right alongside. It was like a nightmare, upturned faces, inhuman beneath those small helmets as they fired rifles and pistols. Some of the troops fought their way from the side as the craft hit the saddle tank and heaved over like an overloaded crate.

A machine-gunner was yelling like a maniac as he swung his gun back and forth across the water, whipping the sea into froth, changing it from blue to pink.

The warship had ceased firing altogether, and was apparently surrounded by blazing fuel, amongst which soldiers and sailors alike thrashed and screamed until the flames silenced them forever.

'Cease firing.' Ainslie wiped his mouth with his wrist. 'Control room, this is the captain. Resume course and check all departments for damage.'

Still at maximum revolutions, the *Soufrière* headed out and away from the land, the inlet and all but some hills hidden by drifting smoke.

The first warship had already disappeared beneath the surface, but the other one was still afloat and burning fiercely. On the bridge they heard the explosions within her hull, the crackle of ammunition caught in the fires, and Ainslie hoped the little colonel and his men would hear them also.

Two shells fell without exploding somewhere between the submarine and the wrecked landing craft. Fired by the enemy or the remaining British artillery it was not possible to know.

Forty-five minutes after Farrant had secured his scorched guns the lookouts sighted an aircraft, far away on the port beam, tiny and remote, like a chip of glass in the sky.

Ainslie followed it with his binoculars, watching each change of direction. It was making for the smoke which covered the horizon in a brown veil.

He held his breath, counting seconds, waiting for it to turn and fly straight towards the lens.

'Control room to bridge. The depth is now twenty fathoms, sir.'

Ainslie looked at Southby. He too was splashed with blood, his fair hair stained by smoke.

'Take your gun crews below, Sub.' He watched the slow realization on his face. 'I think we've made it.'

Then he looked at the yeoman of signals, unbreakable, like a rock.

'Clear the bridge, Yeo.' He pressed the diving button twice. 'And thanks.'

Ten minutes later the sea was unruffled once more, with nothing to show that *Soufrière* had ever been there.

11

Time to Go

REAR-ADMIRAL GRANGER removed the pipe from his mouth and said, 'I'm very sorry to hear about Commander Critchley. I didn't know him well, but what I heard of his intelligence work was good. Very good.' The pipe smoke hung motionless above him, the fan unmoving.

Ainslie looked past the admiral at the wall map. The yellow tape had moved still further south, and there were some new arrows across the water to the east, probing through Sarawak towards Borneo.

The admiral nodded. 'Full-scale amphibious attack. The Australians are putting in some more troops, but they're not having much luck.'

Captain Armytage, who had been standing by the window, said, 'That Japanese submarine you met up with when you went after the *Soufrière* was probably smelling out the land for all this.' For once he sounded very low. 'The Japanese are pushing through the islands like ants. It will take years to drive them out again.'

'Anyway.' The admiral seemed eager to finish the meeting. 'I'm glad you got back safely. And with two more sinkings to your credit.'

Armytage said, 'There have been no signals today from that sector, so it looks as if the enemy have overrun that position after all.'

Ainslie looked down at his hands, very tanned against his fresh drill uniform.

He had berthed the *Soufrière* that afternoon, not alongside the old depot ship, for she had been moved to a southern anchorage at Keppel Harbour. In fact the base had appeared very deserted, with only a few harbour craft and some old river gunboats to keep them company.

The streets, on the other hand, were full of people, the air tense with rumour and speculation. There had been several hit and run air attacks, but the damage had been slight compared with the devastating effect on morale.

There was talk of looting and deserters robbing abandoned houses. Of spies and saboteurs, although much of the damage was probably caused by lack of maintenance, the people employed having gone elsewhere. If the admiral's fan was out of order, it did not say a lot for the rest of the island.

The admiral said, 'Captain Armytage is taking over here as acting commodore. You will await your orders through him, although God knows when that will be.'

Armytage said smoothly, 'I am sure we will get along.'

Ainslie looked at the admiral. 'May I ask where you are going, sir?'

His smile was without warmth. 'Oh, I shall be around. Not too far away.'

Armytage said, 'The admiral is taking charge of commercial shipping movements.'

Ainslie thought of the dead medical orderly, the seaman falling on the pier, the man bleeding on the conning tower.

He said quietly, 'Preparing to evacuate, you mean, sir?'

'I said no such thing, dammit!' Armytage's anger was back again. 'You take too much on yourself, too much by half!'

The admiral said wearily, 'We're taking no chances, Ainslie, that's all. We have to prepare, just in case.'

Armytage said irritably, 'When the reinforcements get here we shall see a change all round. The Japs can't go on over-reaching their supply lines like this. We'll show them a thing or two.'

Ainslie said, 'Commander Critchley implied that *Soufrière* would be going to England soon, sir. She would be very useful either as a long-range patrol submarine or even running supplies to Malta.'

Armytage glanced at his watch. 'Well, Critchley's no longer with us. I shall see what Whitehall has to say.' His eyes hardened. 'In due course.'

There was a commotion in the passageway and Ainslie heard a voice, vaguely familiar, exclaiming angrily, 'Don't tell me what I can and can't do, you pompous idiot! I'm not asking. I'm *telling* you, see?'

The door burst open and Guy Torrance strode into the room.

His well-cut, light-weight suit was patchy with sweat, and his face was flushed, dangerously so.

The flag-lieutenant hovered behind him saying, 'I could not stop him, sir!'

The admiral asked grimly, 'Well, sir? To what do we owe this noisy intrusion?'

Torrance glared at him. 'I have two boats building here, under contract. Launches for my lighterage business in Rangoon.'

Granger nodded. 'They've been commandeered for the emergency. Those and a lot more.'

Torrance shouted 'Emergency is it? God damn it man it was of no bloody importance last week! What the hell are you talking about?'

Armytage snapped, 'Now look here, whatever your name is – '

But the admiral shook his head abruptly and said, 'I will look into it. Leave it with me.'

Ainslie had seen the admiral's signal to his subordinate. Either Torrance held a lot of influence or he was afraid he might spread fuel on the fire of rumour.

Torrance seemed partly satisfied. 'Well, then.'

He turned and saw Ainslie for the first time. His eyes sharpened, focusing like gunsights.

'Robert Ainslie, right? The chap who dragged the girls from the sea.' He grinned. 'Never thought to find you in this dump!'

'Commander Ainslie is about to leave this, er, dump.' Granger shot Ainslie a warning glance. 'He can see you to your car.'

Outside the room and past the busy typist, Torrance murmured, 'Bloody fools. Wouldn't know an emergency if it kicked them up the arse!'

Ainslie fell in step beside him. The sun was getting low and the water looked strangely hostile.

There were a lot more troops about, and some sandbagged emplacements around the base.

Torrance stopped beside an expensive-looking car and asked, 'Where are you going now? Spot of leave?' He did not wait for an answer but added, 'I was joking just now. I knew you'd been away in that ruddy submarine of yours. I've friends in high places, y'know. You look worn out. The smart uniform doesn't fool me. Christ, if I wasn't doing essential work I'd be in uniform myself. I could show them a thing or two.' He paused and asked, '*Well?*'

'No leave, I'm afraid. Not yet, anyway.' He watched a ragged Malay in handcuffs being marched past by some grim-faced military police.

Torrance followed his glance. 'He'll get the chop, that one. Looter, I expect.'

He opened the door of his car, the wretched prisoner forgotten. 'Hop in. Come and have a tot at the hotel. The service is going to hell, but the drink's okay.'

Ainslie felt all his refusals falling away. 'I could telephone the base from there.' He watched Torrance's face for some hint of guile or suspicion. But his mind seemed to blunder from one thing to the next, each disconnected from the other.

'Course you can.' He pressed the starter impatiently. 'Play golf, do you?'

The car swerved away, almost running down a man who was approaching them with a tray of celluloid Father Christmases. With a start Ainslie realized Christmas was only two days away.

Torrance drove faster than he should, the horn going vehemently whenever somebody got in his way.

He said, 'My sister-in-law's husband is alive, by the way. Prisoner of the Japs somewhere. An estate worker came through the lines with the news.'

Ainslie thought of the girl screaming at him, calling him a coward. Then again aboard the yacht, so full of sexual excitement. Of how her sister had described the marriage. What would she think of the news? Her husband alive, but unlikely to get back to her for years, if at all. His question answered itself.

The car stopped and Torrance said, 'Just a quick nip before we go in.' He reached under the seat and took out a heavy silver flask and shook it. 'Good.'

He did not offer it to Ainslie, and held it to his lips for a full minute, his eyes unblinking, lost to some inner thought.

'There now. All done.' He wiped his mouth and set the car in motion again, humming cheerfully to himself.

'Will you be going back to Rangoon when you've finished your business here?' He saw the error too late.

Torrance said brightly, 'Told you, did she? Not like her. Doesn't mix very well. Not like her sister, what?'

They swept past Raffles, avoiding the beggars and traders who waited hopefully for unwary servicemen, and Torrance said, 'No, UK probably. She wants to see a top man in Harley Street.'

He swung the wheel, his voice suddenly changed and angry. 'God knows why. Keeping on about it. It's best forgotten.'

The Indian porter hurried forward to open the door, saluting as he did so. He saw Ainslie and bobbed. 'Ah, Commander-sahib, splendid to see you again.'

Ainslie darted a glance at Torrance but he had apparently not heard.

He said, 'Thank you,' and thrust some loose change into his ready palm.

She was seated at one of the small tables, and was even wearing the same white dress.

As they approached she sat very still, her eyes on her husband, and yet somehow looking at Ainslie.

'Brought your friend along. Thought he might need a drink.' He snapped his fingers at a waiter. 'Christ, I'm parched.'

Ainslie took her hand. Then she did look at him openly, her lips slightly parted as if she was seeing him for the first time.

'I'm glad you came. Sit down. It's so hot, isn't it?'

Torrance was speaking with the waiter, his hands moving to describe the size and quality of the drinks he required.

Ainslie said softly, 'We met at the base. I'd just got in.'

She nodded, a pulse moving in her throat. 'I know. I've thought a lot about you lately.' She spoke in an unnatural, matter-of-fact tone, but her eyes told a lot more.

A messenger came from the desk and said to Torrance, 'Telephone call for you, sir.'

Torrance stood up violently. 'Hold my drinks for me.' He winked at Ainslie. 'Keep both hands where I can see them, eh?' He went off laughing.

Ainslie looked at her, but she showed no concern over his comment, and he guessed she was used to it.

He said quickly, 'May I just say something?' He watched her tense, the sudden alarm in her eyes. 'You look absolutely lovely. I shouldn't be saying this to someone else's wife, but I can't help myself.'

She smiled, pleased or embarrassed he could not tell.

Then she said, 'I thought you'd forgotten about us.' She glanced round, but Torrance had his back to them on the other side of the room, his head nodding as he spoke on the telephone. 'You look so tired, but I shan't ask you what you've been doing.'

Impetuously she touched his arm. 'I'm glad you said it. Just don't laugh at me, will you? I mean, later on, when – '

She leaned back, breaking the contact, as Torrance came back from the desk.

'That was your admiral. He's had second thoughts about my boats.' He beamed at them. 'Thought he might.'

The nurse came through the entrance leading the little girl by the hand. 'Here's your daddy, Frances.'

But the child walked past him and stood gazing at Ainslie's cap on a chair.

The nurse said, 'We've been finishing our Christmas shopping, Mrs Torrance.'

Torrance glanced at the child and asked. 'All right, Frances?' She ignored him, but he added, 'That's a good girl. Just you trot along, eh?'

He stood up, downing his drink with one swallow, and exclaimed, 'Damn! I've left some important papers in the car. I'll get 'em before some light-fingered chap gets his hands on 'em!'

With that he was gone, taking long strides, like a man hurrying for a train.

She said, 'He's gone for a drink.' She spoke without bitterness or emotion.

Ainslie held out his hand to the child, feeling the nurse watching him like a protective hawk.

'Hello, Frances.'

The child regarded him for a few seconds and then turned away towards the stairs.

Ainslie said gently, 'He said you may be going to England?'

Once, the thought of a long sea passage from Singapore to the U-boat-infested waters of the Atlantic would have seemed extremely hazardous. But now, after what he had seen on the peninsula, he was not sure of anything.

'If it can be arranged. She had to be a certain age before there was any possibility of treatment. Even then . . .' She shrugged, the movement painful to see.

Then she said brightly, 'Anyway, you don't want my troubles.' The brightness got no further than her voice, and she added quietly, 'But thank you, all the same. I don't feel so alone any more. Ridiculous, isn't it? You saved my life, and that should be enough.'

Ainslie dropped his eyes. 'But it's not, is it?'

Torrance came back noisily. 'Must have left them at the ship-yard. God, the crowds out there. Like a bloody festival!'

Ainslie stood up slowly. He felt as if he were standing on thin glass.

'Be off, must you?' Torrance looked at him dully. 'See you again, I s'pect.'

Ainslie gripped her hand. 'I have to go. But maybe we can all have a drink together. For Christmas?'

She did not release her fingers. 'That would be nice.'

Ainslie walked out into the hot evening air, his mind hanging on her words. What was he doing? He must be raving mad to get involved. She had tried to let him down gently, make light of it. Had even warned him that she needed her husband if only for the child's sake.

It was no use. Just to see her again, to feel her nearness, it would have to suffice.

He recalled suddenly how he had answered her question about not being married. *She married a nice sensible farmer instead.* It had not been like that at all. He had been in love with Penny, or thought he had. She had been unable to put up with it. It was as simple as that. Every time he went to sea she would suffer, be helpless to prevent herself from showing it when he got back safely.

Perhaps the war really did change a man. Maybe only others saw it in you, while the one concerned remained in ignorance until he cracked wide open. He had seen the anxiety in Quinton's eyes, Halliday's, too. Was he that bad?

The hotel porter was standing in the shadows, his old topee in his hands. He was quite bald, and the realization that he was much older than Ainslie had believed seemed unsettling.

He replaced his hat carefully and saluted. 'A taxi, Commander-sahib?'

'No. But thank you.'

The man followed him to the gates. 'Be watchful for thieves, sir.' He lowered his voice. 'It will be all right, will it not, Commander-sahib?' When Ainslie looked at him he added un-certainly, 'The war, the Royal Hotel, everything.'

That about sums up his whole life, Ainslie thought, suddenly moved.

'In the end. I am sure it will.'

The man seemed satisfied. 'They dare not invade. We will drive them into the sea.'

Ainslie walked out on to the crowded pavement. With so many people around him it certainly felt safe enough. Then a long way off he heard the crash of breaking glass and the shrill of police whistles.

He turned into a small bar he had visited once before. There were several army officers, and one naval lieutenant who was about to leave. The lieutenant did a surprising thing. He walked across to a Chinese hostess and put his hands on her shoulders.

'So long, Anna. Take care.' Then he kissed her and turned on his heel.

Ainslie saw that the girl was crying, the tears running down her face and on to her silk dress.

The lieutenant saw Ainslie and stiffened automatically.

Then Ainslie said, 'John Welsh, right?'

The lieutenant thrust out his hand. 'Right.' He looked at Ainslie's shoulder straps. 'I heard you'd done well.' He grinned. 'Sir.'

'Stay for a drink?'

The lieutenant lowered his voice. 'I've been too long in here as it is. We're sailing in three hours. The whole flotilla.'

'Where to?'

'Australia, UK, nobody's saying. Away from Singapore, that's all we know. Don't worry, sir, you'll soon be following, I've no doubt.' He gestured to the girl. 'Be nice to her if you like. She's pretty good.'

Ainslie stared after him, a man he had once known, now a slightly tipsy lieutenant. Getting out. Surely it was untrue? Not the Navy already?

He left the bar without thinking of a drink. He passed a shop and saw the owner about to lower his shutters. Just inside the door was a large yellow elephant.

'How much?'

The man eyed him doubtfully, measuring up the chances of cheating.

'For you, sir, very cheap.' He wilted slightly under Ainslie's level stare. 'But as it is Christmas, even cheaper.'

Ainslie picked up the toy elephant and handed the man some notes.

'This about right? For Christmas, I mean?'

The man ignored the sarcasm. 'It is *exactly* right.'

Ainslie walked out clasping the stuffed elephant, seeing the grins on the faces of passing servicemen who deliberately saluted him to see how he would manage to return the compliment.

Somehow he got a taxi and ordered the driver to take him to the base. The driver said nothing, did not even try to bargain for the return fare which he would miss by taking a passenger so far.

He was worried, too. Like all the rest of them. It was bad enough for *Soufrière*'s company, they had seen some of it, and knew they could still get away if need be.

What must it be like for these simple people? Rumour and threat. The impossible image of some terrible force coming south towards them, engulfing and destroying everything in its way.

He found the base blacked out, armed sentries everywhere, but when he made his way aboard the submarine Quinton said, 'No orders for us yet, sir.'

He followed Ainslie below, and grinned when he saw the toy elephant.

'Mascot?'

'For the little girl I was telling you about.'

Quinton nodded. 'Good thought. I'll bet my folks are getting ready at home, too. A great fat turkey and all the trimmings, in ninety degrees of sunshine!'

Ainslie glanced through the deck log. Men ashore, tomorrow's routine, a stoker to be charged with drunken assault. The usual.

Quinton said, 'I'm waiting up to see the libertymen aboard. After a few schooners in the fleet canteen they'll be ready for a brawl!'

In his quarters Ainslie sat down and poured himself a drink. Across the cabin the elephant regarded him with a fixed stare.

Then he stripped off his clothing and laid down on the bunk, his hands beneath his head.

What would she be doing at this moment? he wondered. Getting ready for bed, with perhaps her drunken husband watching her as she undressed?

He turned his face to the pillow and tried to be rational. But it only got worse, and the thirteen miles from the bunk to the hotel seemed to grow longer and longer.

Captain Armytage looked grimly at Ainslie over his desk. 'I

will be sending your new orders across to you tomorrow. My writer's not here.'

Critchley would have said, 'But it *is* Christmas Day, sir.' Ainslie merely looked at the wall map. It was beyond belief. The Japanese advanced units were right down in the south-west corner of the peninsula. He felt a chill on his spine in spite of the heavy air. Another hundred and fifty miles and they'd be up to the Johore Strait and the Causeway. It was like a mad dream, a fantasy.

And yet in the past two days he had sensed the sudden change. More air raids on the island, with the amassed anti-aircraft batteries turning the sky into a vivid pattern of shell-bursts and tracer.

It was as if the retreat had quickened its pace and the army units still fighting to stem the enemy advance could only think of that strip of water at their backs, the promised security which awaited them on the island.

Granger had been busy, and Ainslie had seen in his daily orders that several large merchant ships had left the port loaded with the families of British residents and civil servants. The retreat was becoming a rout with each hour.

Ainslie said, 'You'll want me to move round to Keppel Harbour.'

'Well, the admiral does. Personally, I'd order you to destroy the *Soufrière's* engines and use her guns for covering the Causeway from her present mooring.'

Ainslie was surprised it did not anger him. Armytage was completely out of his depth and using his usual bluster to conceal the fact.

'Is that all, sir?'

'For the present.' He moved two files and replaced them in exactly the same position. 'Carry on.'

As Ainslie made to leave Armytage said abruptly, 'Keep it to yourself for the present, but Hong Kong is due to surrender tomorrow.' It was as if the enormity of his knowledge was too terrible to keep to himself. The final blow, the end of delusion. He added, 'Borneo looks like going next. It's the same everywhere.'

Ainslie closed the door behind him and looked at the abandoned typewriter, recalling the typist's face when he had stopped to listen to Armytage's scathing attack through the door.

He telephoned straight through to the submarine to make sure everything was all right and that Quinton was having as good a Christmas as could be expected.

Over the telephone his voice sounded more Australian than usual. 'We're having a great time. God help us if we have to slip and put to sea!'

'I'm going to the city, John. I'll be back in an hour or so. Phone me at the Royal if you need me.'

There was a long pause and then Quinton said, 'I hope she likes the elephant.'

A naval patrol van drove Ainslie to the city, and the leading seaman in charge said he could be available to drive him back again when required. He did not elaborate, but he obviously thought an unescorted officer might be in some danger.

The fact that it was Christmas Day only made things worse, Ainslie thought. As he hurried into the hotel he saw the paper decorations, a Union Jack flying above a portrait of the King. Across the street a house had been hit by a bomb, while inside the hotel lobby he saw the steps to the cellar had been supported by timbers, with sandbags above and a board labelled 'Air Raid Shelter, Guests Only'.

There was also a lot of drinking going on. At one table an elderly couple sat facing each other, wearing paper hats and sipping champagne, their faces incredibly sad.

Some were quite drunk, sleeping where they sat or peering round for the busy waiters.

Nobody asked Ainslie who he wanted, like that first time. He climbed the stairs and stopped outside the suite. Then he pressed the bell.

The door opened instantly and the nurse said, 'Happy Christmas, Commander Ainslie.'

Ainslie smiled and walked inside. An hotel servant was clearing away the Christmas dinner, and the little girl sat on a rug surrounded by presents and bright wrapping paper.

There was even a tree in one corner, decorated with chocolate figures and reindeer.

Surprisingly, Rear-Admiral Granger was sitting in a deep chair, a drink in his fist, his pipe puffing as usual.

He grinned. 'Come in, Robert. Don't mind me. Friend of the family.'

Ainslie saw her watching him from another doorway opposite

him. She wore a long dress in pale yellow with a red flower pinned at the point of her shoulder. He saw that her hair was no longer in a coil but hung down her back untied.

He held out the elephant. 'For Frances.'

She moved towards him, her eyes never leaving his. 'That was nice of you. It matches my dress. What do you say, Frances?'

But the child did not look up from her collection of presents.

'I can't stay. I just thought I'd like to wish you – ' He stopped, feeling the hopelessness sweeping over him.

She took his hands in hers and said, 'You *will* stay. Please. My husband has gone to visit some friends with Shelly. You just missed them.'

Granger said, 'You sit down, like Natalie says, Robert.' He became serious. 'I'm here for another reason. I'm putting them in a ship tomorrow. One of the last big ones to leave.'

Ainslie looked at her, glad for her safety, hating the sudden ending of it. Of what, he wondered?

He said, 'That's good news.' He smiled at her. 'I'll sleep better now.'

Granger looked at his watch. 'Must dash. Got to drop in on some of the ships. Wet the baby's head, so to speak.' He watched her as she went to collect his cap and then murmured, 'It's bad. We're not getting the reinforcements. If we can't hold them at the Johore Strait, it will be weeks, not months.'

He gave a broad smile as she re-entered the room. 'Fine, then. I'll be off.'

She kissed Granger on the cheek and said, 'It was good of you to come.'

The servant went out with the admiral, and the room was suddenly quiet.

Ainslie sipped his drink and watched her as she tidied the child's presents and then stood the elephant beside her on the floor.

What sort of a man was her husband? To go off on some pretext or other with her sister? The thought made him angry for her.

She crossed the room and looked into his glass. 'Another?'

'In a minute.'

She sat on the arm of his chair and watched the child. 'She'll love the elephant.'

He said very quietly, 'I'm going to miss you. Very much.'

For a moment he thought she had not heard, then she reached behind her and seized his hand, squeezing it so tightly it hurt.

He said, 'I've no right, no right at all. But being here with you like this, it means everything.'

She turned, her hair touching his shoulder as she looked down at him.

'It means a lot to me, too. Really. I'm not saying it just because I'm leaving. I'm not like that.'

The nurse was busying herself in the other room, but she could have been on a different planet.

Ainslie put his hand gently on her hip, feeling her warmth under the dress. She did not move away but watched him, her eyes very bright.

She said huskily, 'You had better stop.' Then she stood up, her hand still holding his.

He got up, his mind dazed.

She said, 'You should leave before he comes back.' She met his gaze, and he saw her chin lift as she added, 'I don't want him to spoil it.'

Together they walked to the door. Once through it and it would all be finished. It was hard to accept, harder still to believe.

He had his hand on the door when she said, 'Kiss me, please.'

She stood quite still as he put his arms around her, her eyes closed as he kissed her on the mouth, feeling her against him, the urgent heartbeats matching his own.

'Mrs Torrance!' The nurse's voice made them move apart with something like guilt.

But the nurse seemed oblivious to their embrace and what it meant. She was pointing at the child, who was walking very slowly towards the door.

When she reached them she looked up at Ainslie, her face still devoid of any recognizable expression. Then with equal gravity she reached up to him, opening her hand as she did so.

Ainslie stared at the paper flower in the child's hand.

The nurse said quietly, 'It may be nothing, Mrs Torrance. Don't get your hopes too high now!'

But Natalie Torrance was on her knees, holding the child and saying, 'Oh, Frances, darling! You want to give him a present, too!'

The child released herself and walked back to her elephant without another glance.

Ainslie helped her to her feet and held her against him, sharing the small moment of hope.

She exclaimed, 'She knew you, Robert, she *really* did! She's not done anything like that before!'

He raised her chin with his fingers and studied her face. 'I really am leaving, Natalie. I'll drop an address where I can be contacted when I'm in England. If you want to see me, that is.' He stepped back, feeling her slipping away. 'Take care.'

She nodded, unable to speak properly. 'You, too.'

The door closed, It was over.

Just out of sight from the hotel he found Rear-Admiral Granger waiting for him in a Humber staff car.

'I'll drive you.' He waited for Ainslie to settle himself before saying, 'I guessed the score. Thought you might be good for each other.'

The car glided through the drifting people and the admiral added, 'Something's happened, hasn't it?'

'The child. They think she recognized me.' He took the paper flower from his pocket. 'She gave me this.'

'That's really something.' The admiral shook his head. 'Her husband, Guy, got much worse after the accident. The driver of the car was drunk, it turned out, and I suspect Guy'd had a few, too, but he was thrown clear. The child was hurled against a tree. Rotten business.'

Ainslie thought about it. Until now he had imagined that Guy Torrance had been the direct cause of the accident.

'You'll get them aboard that ship tomorrow, sir?'

'Yes. It will have a good escort. Just as well. The Japs have already sunk a few of our transports outside the port.'

They drove past saluting sentries and into the base. Then the admiral said, 'Watch your step if you meet up with the Torrances again. He may be a drunk, but he has power, and would use it against you at the drop of a hat.' He grinned. 'But

I'm wasting my time telling you that, aren't I?' He drove away, the pipe jutting from his jaw like a gun.

Ainslie walked through the deserted buildings and on to the jetty. Try as he might he could not forget how she had looked as she had closed the door on him.

Nor did he wish to. Ever.

12

Obligations

Quinton shaded his eyes with one hand as he stared across at the busy waterfront. It was like bedlam. Every class and size of harbour craft, fishing boats and stately junks crowded the anchorage from end to end.

In the midst of the chaos some large merchant ships, elderly cargo liners, were hastily completing loading, their derricks diving and probing towards the lighters alongside like gaunt prehistoric monsters devouring their prey.

Petty Officer Voysey shouted from the fore-casing, 'All secure, sir!'

Ainslie waved to him. 'Ring off main engines.'

It had been a strange passage from the Johore Strait, around Changi Point and down here to the main harbour in the south. A feeling of escape, of loss.

And now what? Wait for more orders. To head for England. To stay and evacuate the top brass. To scuttle the submarine and get away by other means.

Quinton said, 'Like a bloody madhouse. Look at 'em!'

When people realized there were no more big ships, no further hope for the masses of frightened refugees, it would get far worse. All the old pent-up hatreds and grievances, the rigid barriers between white and coloured residents would explode into a separate war altogether.

A siren hooted mournfully, and the yeoman of signals said, 'The biggest of the transports has weighed, sir. *Bengal Princess*. She used to be on the run to Japan before this lot. Seems like a bad joke now.'

Ainslie trained his glasses on the dull-painted transport as it began to glide clear of the other shipping. She would be somewhere on board, she might even see the rounded grey hull of the *Soufrière* before the ship cleared the harbour and joined the waiting escorts.

Quinton was watching him thoughtfully. 'Any orders, sir?'

Ainslie looked down at the seamen who were taking away the unwanted wires, while Voysey, under the cold eye of Farrant, the gunnery officer, checked the lashings on the moorings and prepared to run out the brow.

Peace or war, a commanding officer still had his routine to follow.

'Find out from the hospital how our AB is getting on.'

It was incredible that the man who had been wounded, right here on *Soufrière's* bridge, was still alive. The PMO had said he had a hole in his side you could put your hand in. Hunt, the SBA, could take the credit for his survival.

With the inlet overrun and captured by the enemy there was no way of knowing whether the other seaman who had been cut down by the mortar bomb on the pier was alive or dead. It would mean a letter to his parents. *Missing*. That must be even worse. Not knowing. Losing hope every day.

He said heavily, 'Tell the Chief to go over all the machinery. If he needs spares we shall have to get them fast. I think we're a bit isolated in all this muddle.'

Quinton turned to leave. Then he asked, 'Was everything all right? With the elephant and things?'

Ainslie nodded. 'Yes. But they're well out of it now.'

The coxswain heaved his massive frame through the hatch and saluted, his eyes watering in the sunlight.

'What about leave, sir?'

Ainslie shrugged. 'I'm waiting to hear. But it will be confined locally, I expect.'

Gosling considered it. 'We staying, sir?'

'Doubt it. As the air raids increase it'll be too dangerous to stop here.'

He looked towards the colourful waterfront. Now everyone would know about the *Soufrière*. That would mean the Japs knew, too.

He lowered himself through the hatch and made his way to his cabin.

Forster was waiting for him, his face grim.

'If it's about the muck-up you made, Pilot, you can forget it. I imagine it will not occur again.'

But Forster showed no sign of relief. He said, 'Well, thanks a lot, sir. But I was thinking of something else. I – I was wondering if I could make a special signal from here. I want to tell someone not to worry.' He ended lamely, 'To wait until I get back.'

Ainslie sat down and stared at him. 'A woman, no doubt.'

'The wife of *Psyche*'s skipper, sir.'

Ainslie nodded. 'Widow.'

'Well, yes, that is . . .' He clenched his fists. 'I want to marry her.'

'There's a child involved?'

'There will be, sir.'

'I see.' He wanted to have a shower, to be alone for a while, but Forster's anxiety pushed it aside. Perhaps he was growing up after all. It was to be hoped he did not regret it later on. 'You're certain about this?'

'Quite, sir.'

'Very well. I'll get it sent off today if you let me have the details. It will make a refreshing change from most of the signals from Singapore, I should think.'

Forster went out, looking like a condemned man who has confessed at the last minute.

Petty Officer Vernon tapped on the door. 'Shore telephone line connected, sir.' He grinned through his beard. 'Makes a change.'

Ainslie leaned back and ruffled his hair as the door closed. He knew what Vernon meant. In other times a submarine, even the big *Soufrière*, would have been well down the list for telephones. There were few other vessels of any size flying the white ensign here now.

He started as the telephone buzzed, remembering those other occasions, like the little colonel when he had received news of Critchley's death.

He picked it up. It was Rear-Admiral Granger.

'Good, you're alongside then.' He sounded very near and as if he was worried. 'I'm sorry I've got to drag you ashore so soon. Something's come up. Rather urgent. The FOIC wants you in his office right away.'

Ainslie said, 'I'll be ashore in fifteen minutes, sir.' He waited, thinking of all the staff officers with no ships to supervise.

Granger added, 'Are you ready for sea?'

Ainslie moved to the edge of his chair, his old instincts flashing a warning.

175

'Yes. Fuel, torpedoes recovered, all but some machine-gun ammunition.'

'I'll get on to the commodore's office about it.' The admiral seemed relieved.

Ainslie put down the telephone. Another job. He had been expecting it, so what was the matter with him? He stood up, searching for his cap.

By the time he got through the army pickets and barbed wire barriers a staff car had arrived for him. It carried him to a newly commandeered building on the city outskirts, again heavily protected by anti-aircraft batteries and armoured scout cars.

Ainslie had only met the admiral once before. A tall, austere man, with neat grey sideburns and a Victorian face.

There was a senior RAF officer present, too, and a foreign-featured man in a cream, light-weight suit.

Granger was also there, looking tired, even dispirited.

The admiral said, 'This is Air Vice-Marshal Thomas, my opposite number, and Major Zahl, American Intelligence.'

They all shook hands, checking what they saw, assessing viewpoints without words.

A lieutenant brought Ainslie a chair, and the admiral said briskly, 'You will know the present position better than most. I'll not go over it all again. What might have been done, what should have been prevented, and so forth. It's water under the bridge now. What we have to do is to stop a disaster from becoming a disgrace as well.' He nodded to the American.

Major Zahl had an easy voice, totally at odds with what he had to say.

'The fact is, Commander, the United States' commitment in the Pacific is still reeling from Pearl Harbour. Next year, things may be different, who can say? But right now we cannot help the Commander in Chief here.' He gave a small shrug. 'Except by sharing what we know.'

The Air Force officer interrupted, 'Major Zahl has brought news of another Japanese aircraft carrier. She's the *Sudsuya*, one of their newest, and best.'

Ainslie watched him, seeing his despair. It could not be easy for him. With his airfields and planes in ruins.

The admiral said, 'She's in Indo-China, at Cam-Ranh. The Americans scored a hit on her last week, but the damage is not too serious. She is reported to be sailing in a few days.'

Zahl nodded. 'Our agents have made it perfectly clear. The flat-top is to reinforce the Nip Navy, but more to the point, to destroy any chance of further evacuation from Singapore. Without air cover you – '

Ainslie gave a tight smile. 'I *know*, Major. I've seen it all before.'

'I've brought you here, Ainslie,' the admiral seemed able to exclude everyone else present, 'to put it plainly to you. I am sending *Soufrière* to attack the *Sudsuya* as I have nothing else. There *is* nothing else.'

The silence was oppressive, like the approach of a tropical storm.

Ainslie said, 'I understand, sir.' Did he really? Even if he managed to sink the carrier it would delay but not prevent the inevitable.

The admiral and the air vice-marshal looked at each other, and then Granger asked, 'Is there anything I can get for you?'

Ainslie shook his head. 'A crystal ball, sir. That's about the only thing which might help.'

The admiral said, 'If you'd like me to speak to your people, Commander? To tell them how important this mission may be to all of us?'

Ainslie stood up. 'Thank you, but no, sir. I know them pretty well, some of them over a long period.'

'Well, I suggest we get it started.' The air vice-marshal looked at his watch.

Ainslie left the room without realizing it, Granger beside him, already groping for his pipe.

Granger muttered, 'Pompous bugger.' He did not explain what he meant.

At the entrance Granger said suddenly, 'The Torrances didn't get aboard the *Bengal Princess*, by the way. There was some argument, I'm not yet certain of the real reasons.' He eyed Ainslie steadily. 'I didn't tell you earlier because I knew you'd take on this assignment for *her* sake, am I right?'

Ainslie nodded, his heart heavy. 'Probably, sir. What will they do now?'

'Oh, I'll manage something. I've got a reserve of vessels laid on. Leave it to me.'

They shook hands, and then Granger said, 'It's asking a lot of you.'

Ainslie replied, 'The enemy will know about us this time. It'll not be easy.'

But he was really thinking of her. She was still here, in the city. It did not seem real. Nothing did.

He said, 'You will get Natalie Torrance and Frances into a ship of some sort?'

'I said, you can leave it to me.' Granger smiled sadly. 'Of *course* I will.'

The staff car was waiting to carry him back to the harbour. He was tempted to ask the driver to take another route, by way of the Royal Hotel. But it would not help either of them. Especially now.

The air vice-marshal hurried down the steps as the car drove away in a cloud of sandy dust.

'All buttoned up?'

Granger eyed him coldly. The air vice-marshal was leaving the island on the next available vessel.

'Yes. That was a brave man I just shook hands with.'

'Of course.'

'Too bloody good to throw away!'

Granger strode away, flushed and unusually angry.

As dusk moved in across the harbour the *Soufrière* slipped her moorings and without fuss turned her bows seaward.

That afternoon, after an argument with the local military police and then a terse telephone call to Granger, Ainslie had been able to take over a large transit shed on the dockside. It was the only place large enough for him to address his whole company at once.

It had been a moving occasion in many ways. Ainslie had stood upon a packing case while his officers and ratings had broken ranks and gathered round him.

He tried not to mince words, because he had never known lies to help when lives were at risk.

Ainslie had explained where they were going, and why. As his voice had echoed around the big shed he had watched their faces, remembering all the incidents, the moments of tension and humour which had somehow welded them together.

Gosling, looking shabby and old beside his friend Menzies. Sawle, who knew the officers better than anyone. Hunt in his white jacket, his lips pursed and vaguely disapproving. Young

Southby beside Halliday in his boiler suit. Farrant, Christie, the flyer, and all the others.

There had been one incident which he had not planned for.

As he had made to leave, Quinton had climbed on to the packing case and had called, 'Now listen to me, all of you. Some of you probably believe this is a crook deal and not what we came out to do. Well, maybe it is at that. But it's the same bloody war, and the same reasons for getting on with the job, *our* job.' Then he had turned to look across the breadth of the shed to where Ainslie stood by the entrance. 'And if we can get through this without being chopped, then I know one skipper who can fix it.' He had thrown up a salute. 'And that's a fact!'

Now, as Ainslie stood beside Forster's chart table listening to the reports and instructions being passed through his command, he could still hear the burst of wild cheering which had followed him through the doors of the shed.

Quinton had timed it well. A few seconds earlier and they might all have seen their captain break down.

Eight hundred miles to go, with orders to ignore any other targets.

He crossed to the voice-pipe. 'Captain to bridge.'

Farrant was up there, holding the fort as they slipped past the last small vessels and patrols.

'Sir?'

'Clear the bridge. We're diving.'

The klaxon shrilled raucously, and then Ainslie looked from Quinton to Halliday.

'Here we go.' He heard the hatches clanging shut, the usual commotion as the lookouts' feet thudded down to the deck. 'Ready?'

Halliday gave a crooked smile. 'Aye, sir.'

Ainslie listened to the softer purr of electric motors, the awakening ping of the echo sounder. But he saw her face, felt her heart beating against his body, as if she were somehow here beside him.

He said sharply, 'Group up. Slow ahead together. Open main vents. Take her down to fourteen metres.'

As the water roared into the saddle tanks and the deck gave a deliberate tilt, Ainslie went to the periscope, searching for the land but finding only the early stars.

'Down periscope.' He stood back as it hissed into its well. They were on their way.

One day and eight hours after clearing the harbour limits the submarine *Soufrière* was crossing the sixth parallel and heading north approximately midway between the Malayan peninsula and the coast of Indo-China.

At any other time it would have seemed like a leisurely passage. The weather had been kind, and they had neither sighted nor detected another vessel of any sort.

Surfaced, her diesels growling steadily while Halliday completed another battery charge, the submarine thrust through the unruffled waters with barely any motion at all.

Ainslie stood on the high bridge, watching the stars as they began to fade. It would soon be dawn. Time to dive again.

Around him the lookouts, very aware of his presence, scanned their different sectors, while Ridgway, who was OOW on deck, kept his own binoculars levelled towards where the horizon would soon appear.

'I'm going below.' Ainslie paused and took a deeep breath. Another old habit. Then he slid down to the control room, to that other world, separate yet connected to the one he had just left.

Quinton was checking the trim again, while Halliday was in a deep conversation with his panel watchkeeper. The French lieutenant, Cottier, was studying a wiring plan as he tried to discover what was going wrong with the lights above the pump gauges.

Forster said, 'Signal for you, sir.' He held out the pad. 'Nothing new about the carrier, except that she's still at anchor.'

Ainslie eyed him calmly. 'Then what is new?'

'That evacuee convoy was attacked, sir, several of the ships were sunk near Banka Island, including the *Bengal Princess*.' He watched as Ainslie leaned over the table. 'And the Japs are still advancing.'

Ainslie studied the chart, giving his mind time to relate the brief, stark signal. Had she been aboard the transport she would be dead, or trying to keep afloat until the Japs captured the survivors.

He felt a sense of panic. Suppose nobody else would be able to get away and were forced to wait for the Japanese Army to smash its way on to the island? He gripped his hands into tight fists until the pain contained his new anxiety.

Granger had given his word. She would get away. There would be a better chance in a smaller, faster vessel, one which could slip through the many islands, or hide during the day from searching aircraft and warships.

Forster asked, 'Something wrong?'

He answered, 'Your message was sent off, Pilot. I hope it does some good.'

'Thanks, sir.' Forster did not seem to notice how his question had been parried.

The smell of frying bacon floated through the boat, making the watchkeepers rub their tired eyes and lick their lips. From the W/T office came the stammer of morse, the overriding surf-noise of static. There was music too, strange and distorted, probably from some Japanese station.

Ainslie moved restlessly around the control room. He kept thinking about his orders. The feeling that someone very high up in Whitehall had got things moving so quickly. It was quite unlike what he had found earlier out here. Maybe it was Winston Churchill who had said the right words after hearing the news from Washington and Singapore. Preparing for the day when the story of another disaster would fall on the world, but mostly on the long-suffering people in Britain. The destruction of one of Japan's largest warships might be some compensation for the loss of *Prince of Wales* and *Repulse*, might even help to smooth over the brutal fact of this defeat, for a while anyway.

'Trim completed, sir. Diving stations in five minutes.' Quinton waited, watching his mood.

'Very well. By this evening we shall be in enemy patrol area Item Fox. We'll have to keep our wits about us.' He smiled. 'A good breakfast might help.'

Quinton moved away from the helmsman. 'I heard the news about the convoy, sir.'

'They weren't aboard, John.' He saw the relief on Quinton's dark features and added, 'So that's something to be thankful for. God, she doesn't deserve all this!'

Quinton turned to watch a messenger carrying more tea to the watchkeepers, his face as intent as any professor.

He said, 'Well, if I know you, Skipper, you'll change all that if you get half a chance, eh?'

Ainslie slapped his shoulder and walked towards his cabin, knowing Quinton was still staring after him.

Tonight they would rise once more to periscope depth and contact base. After that, all their lives would be in his hands.

He was still considering the fact when the klaxon tore the air apart and the tannoy blared, 'Diving stations! Diving stations!'

As he strode aft to the control room he heard Sawle say, 'Two eggs, sir! Be ready in a jiff!'

It must be marvellous to be like Sawle or the messenger with his fanny of tea.

'Revolutions for six knots. Silent routine.' Ainslie glanced at the panel clock. It would be pretty dark up top. He half listened to the whispered commands, the fading whirr of the motors.

It had been a bad day, submerged for most of the time, rising just when necessary for a quick look round.

Ainslie was very conscious that they were getting closer to the enemy-occupied coastline. Several times *Soufrière*'s 'ears' had reported fast-moving vessels in the vicinity, anti-submarine patrols most likely. Once, during one of his brief searches of the sea and sky Ainslie had seen an aircraft, a flying boat of some kind, circling abeam, as if it had already seen them. They had dived as deep as possible, waiting for depth-charges or the sounds of fast-moving screws as a destroyer was homed in for a kill.

Soufrière would not be hard to see from directly overhead, he thought. Even below periscope depth she might be visible. A harder shadow. The beast. Maybe the Japs knew already and were waiting until she was in such a position where there was no escape.

If only the wind would get up to make the surface choppier, alive with broken wavelets to hide the periscope's eye.

Forster's quiet voice broke through his thoughts. 'Time to alter course, sir. Course to steer is zero-three-zero.'

Ainslie nodded. 'Very well.'

He allowed Quinton and the burly coxswain to swing the submarine just those few extra degrees, and tried to picture the location, translate the lines and landmarks from the chart into rock and earth, trees and rivers. Before midnight they would be nearing the Mekong River Delta, but standing well out to sea to stay in deep water and avoid the inshore currents.

Quinton said, 'No HE, sir. All clear.'

'Very well. Periscope depth, please.'

The same young stoker was waiting to work the switch, his face shining with sweat, as Ainslie crouched by the periscope well.

Quinton watched the hydroplane tell-tales and the depth gauge, while Halliday and his men checked the sudden change of buoyancy as they pumped compressed air into the tanks.

'Fourteen metres, sir.'

Ainslie rubbed his palms on his hips. 'Tell the W/T office to stand by.'

He looked at the stoker and realized he must have been staring at him. He forced a grin, the effort bruising his mouth. 'All ready, Tamlyn?'

The youth nodded. 'Aye, sir.'

Ainslie controlled the impulse to yawn, knowing what it would mean to the others near him. Fear, uncertainty, gripping at his guts like claws.

He raised his hand slowly. 'Now, Tamlyn. Nice and easy.'

He slithered like a crab around the well, ignoring the scratches to his knees and ankles as he studied the confined perimeter of his vision.

Dark and misty, but still no wind.

Without taking his eyes from the small, misty picture he asked, 'Still quiet?'

'Yes, sir. Asdic is making a full sweep. Nothing, unless – .' Quinton checked himself.

Ainslie twisted one of the grips, watching the faint stars, a feather of cloud as the lens probed upwards. *Unless.* Unless there was a patrol vessel up there, her engines stopped, waiting for the off-chance of a victim.

He snapped the handles inwards and stood up fully. 'Stand by to surface.' He signalled to the lookouts below the conning tower. 'Be ready.'

Five minutes later he was on the streaming bridge, his body shaking with unexpected chill as he searched through the shadows for a possible enemy.

The big carrier was probably heading down towards him right now, her escorts making a lethal arrowhead of steel in her path.

It would need every skill he had seen in others and had learned in each command since. A full fan of torpedoes, there would be no second go.

He thought suddenly of Natalie Torrance and wondered what she was doing. Going to bed, or reading to the child who never spoke? Perhaps Granger had put her aboard a ship already.

'Control room to bridge.' It was Quinton. 'Signal. Most immediate.'

'Read it, please.'

He kept his glasses to his eyes as he listened to Quinton's words. 'Aircraft carrier *Sudsuya* is still in harbour. Will be further delayed. Imperative that she is destroyed. Situation critical. End of signal, sir.'

'Thank you.'

Ainslie lowered the glasses and straightened his back. They had been wrong about the carrier's damage. A few more days and she would be at sea again. But he could not keep *Soufrière* patrolling up and down, waiting for tit-bits of intelligence, deaf and blind to the real facts.

Situation critical. It said it better than any emotional encouragement.

Soufrière must engage at all costs. Even though it would mean entering a heavily defended area, with little or no chance of survival.

He lowered his face to the voice-pipe. 'Tell Pilot to open the intelligence pack on the Cam-Ranh Approaches.' He thought he heard Quinton's quick intake of breath. 'This will have to be done damn carefully.'

Cam-Ranh Bay was described as one of the finest harbours on the coast, with a good anchorage for every sort of ship all year round. Also it was likely to be one of the best protected.

'Asdic reports faint HE at red nine-oh, sir.'

Quinton's voice brought him down to earth with a jerk. They might not even reach Cam-Ranh Bay.

'Clear the bridge. Dive, dive, dive! Take her down to thirty metres!'

As the lookouts scuttled below and he groped for the locking wheel of the upper hatch, Ainslie looked at the stars, feeling the urge to stand where he was until the sea roared over the screen and plunged him into oblivion.

Then with a gasp he jumped down two rungs and slammed the hatch above his head.

He did not have the choice. Only obligations.

13

Target

ALL through the final night before *Soufrière* reached her intended destination Ainslie was forced to keep his command submerged. The Asdic compartment reported one vessel after another, and although it was more than likely that most of them were coasters or fishermen, it only needed one to be a warship.

The air throughout the boat was heavy and stale. They had been on silent routine for most of the time, with fans and unnecessary ducts switched off. The rounded sides were wet with condensation which poured across the paintwork and misted the dials, while the watchkeepers and unemployed men sweated in much the same fashion.

Ainslie had gone over his proposed attack twice with Quinton and his other key officers. Observation. Method. Conclusions. But that was all on paper. Course and speed, depth and current, sunrise and angle of light. All parts of an intricate pattern to be settled before Ridgway had a single item to feed into his fruit machine.

It was difficult for most of the company to tell night from day. Watchkeepers from the engine and motor rooms came and went, crossing the paths of the control-room staff and the torpedo crews, an ever-changing complex, like creatures in a steel burrow. It made tempers brittle and nerves edgy. If you tried to snatch an hour's sleep behind the damp curtain of your bunk, some idiot would need to squeeze past or below you to get his tea before going on watch.

And all the while they were conscious of the motors' muted hum as the boat carried them through the unseen water towards their objective.

It was almost a relief to get started, or to believe that you were actually beginning to complete the job.

As the order was relayed through every compartment the officers and ratings went quietly to their stations.

In the control room Ainslie handed his empty cup to Sawle and glanced at his watch. He could sense the boat gaining strength as her company took their positions.

Quinton looked at him. 'All closed up at action stations, sir.' He tested his mood again and then said, 'Happy New Year, sir.'

The fat coxswain turned in his steel seat and muttered, 'Gawd, is it, sir?'

They all stared at one another, the realization that it was the first day of another year moving through the boat like a rumour.

Ainslie smiled gravely. 'I'd forgotten.'

Halliday looked up from his panel. 'A Scot, too! That's best kept a secret, sir!'

Walker, the senior Asdic operator, because of his headphone unaware of the brief humour, reported stolidly, 'All quiet, sir.'

Ainslie tugged his shirt away from his chest. It was like a wet rag.

'Let's take a look, Number One. Periscope depth, please.'

Using all his skill, Halliday brought the great submarine close to the surface with barely a vibration to show any difference.

Ainslie dropped to his knees by the periscope. How many times had he done it before? Amongst ice-floes, off the North African coast. In the bitter Atlantic. Always the stomach-wrenching fear. The expectation of death.

'What bearing, Pilot?'

Forster was peering at the chart, his hair flopping over his forehead.

'Should be at about red four-five, sir. Three miles.'

Just like that. It was like a small miracle if you had time to think about it. Altering course and depth, back-tracking to avoid some threatening hydrophone effect, feeling their way by instruments and constant calculations.

And a whole lot of luck.

He nodded to the young stoker. 'Ready when you are, my lad.'

The periscope rose with the same caution as the boat. Ainslie squinted at the brass ring above his head and turned the periscope on the estimated bearing. Easy now. Nice and smooth. He held his breath as the light in the lens strengthened and filled with tiny bubbles, like steel bearings, or those silver balls they used to decorate cakes. Then came the sky, bright and clear, as the lens broke surface with barely a ripple.

He clicked the periscope to full power, seeing the nearest

headland loom larger in response, as if the boat had leapt bodily through the water.

Between his teeth he said, 'Southern headland on the port bow. Well done, Pilot.'

He moved the periscope very slowly in a full circle. The sea was very bright, like thin silver foil, moving, breathing in the slight swell.

It was very still. Seven o'clock in the morning. He turned his attention back to the headland, trying to count the seconds, the lengthening risk.

The only sign of life were a few tiny sailing craft near the headland, like moths on the water in the harsh light.

He moved the grips very carefully. Then he said, 'There's a ship of some kind just around the point. Seems to be anchored. Could be a boom vessel or blockship.' He stood up fully. 'Down 'scope.'

He walked to the table and rubbed his chin. The *Sudsuya* must be hidden by the headland. According to the American intelligence pack, the carrier had been hit by at least one bomb from a force of five aircraft. All but one of the American planes had been shot down in the attack, and the survivor had not been close enough to determine the exact damage, other than it was right aft.

The fact that the Japanese captain had brought his ship this far without tugs pointed to some very localized damage, most likely the steering mechanism or rudders.

It had to be something he and his company could repair without going into dock. Otherwise he would have struggled up one of the tortuous river channels to Saigon further south.

Aloud he said, 'She'll probably be well moored, with a stream anchor out aft to stop her swinging too much. It would make her easier to protect with anti-torpedo nets and steadier in the tides for the work to be carried on without interruption.'

In his mind's eye he could see her exactly, all twenty-seven thousand tons of her. She was known to carry sixty strike air-craft and probably more on a war footing. She could decimate Granger's refugee convoys like a man swatting a fly.

'We must get closer. I want another look. Alter course to close with the northern headland. Revs for six knots.'

He listened to the responding clicks and rattles, Gosling's acknowledgement of the new course to steer.

Ainslie was still thinking, his mind alert now that it had a problem to cope with. The entrance to Cam-Ranh Bay was extremely wide, marred here and there by some small islands and reefs. Once through the headlands the bay narrowed before opening up again to its full extent, a large, safe anchorage where the depth was rarely less than forty feet. It had saved many a ship from storm and attacker alike.

He said, 'I think the carrier will stay in the outer anchorage.'

Forster was watching his plot, gauging their movement through every foot of the way. 'Maybe the brute's put to sea already, sir, and we've missed her in the night?'

Quinton said, 'Wishful thinking. A ship that size, to say nothing of the bloody escorts, Christ, you'd hear 'em all the way to Darwin!'

Ainslie studied the chart as Forster's pencil made another small cross.

'Another look.'

He moved to the periscope. This was so important he would have liked to raise the second periscope so that Quinton could confirm what he saw. He dismissed it instantly. There might be some powerful glasses trained on this patch of water right now. The small, barely raised periscope would be hard to spot, but two, with the additional feathers of spray to betray them, were not worth the risk.

He nodded to the stoker. 'Now.'

Even in the minutes which had passed it looked different. He could see the hill on the northern headland, shivering from side to side in some haze, like a giant jelly on a plate.

The little sailing boats were nearer now, creeping out from the land and more scattered. Probably fishing, he thought.

He turned again towards the motionless vessel. There was a power boat crossing her bows, her progress marked by a great moustache of white foam.

He lost more time as he searched around and above for other vessels or aircraft, but the place looked dead. Although it was still early morning it was probably like an oven up there, he thought. He brought the periscope back again, blinking as spray spattered playfully over the glass.

Ainslie said, 'There's another ship inside, coming this way, I think. Freighter, one funnel, 'bout a thousand tons.'

Ainslie heard Ridgway's yeoman writing these brief notes in his log.

Walker said, 'Nothing yet, sir.'

Quinton murmured quietly, 'No. The freighter's probably masked by the headland.'

'Right.'

Ainslie was about to signal for the periscope to be lowered when he saw something in the corner of his picture, like an error in a painting. He twisted the grip to full power again and trained it on the first, unmoving vessel. Around her was a lot of trapped mist and haze, with a green hillside beyond that. But right on the limit of his vision was a rigid grey line. It was either the bow or the stern of the biggest carrier he had ever laid eyes on.

'Down 'scope.' He looked at Quinton. 'Thirty metres.'

To Forster he said, 'Lay off a course to take us six miles south-east of this point.' To Ridgway he added, 'I saw the *Sudsuya*, or her bloody twin sister.'

Forster said formally, 'Course to steer is one-five-zero, sir.'

'Got that, Number One?' He waited as the deck settled again at the new depth. 'Bring her about, will you?' To the control room at large he added, 'I think I saw a patrol vessel coming out astern of the freighter. We won't be able to get nearer at this stage.'

With *Soufrière* set on her fresh course away from the coast Ainslie brought Quinton and Forster together at the chart table while Ridgway took over the watch.

He said quietly, 'This will go on all day. Regular patrols, but nothing special until it's time for the carrier to leave with her escorts. Then, you may be sure they'll have the whole area covered, aircraft as well, I would imagine.'

Quinton looked dully at the chart. He was probably thinking the same as Forster. Six miles out meant the same back again, and every cable covered either by patrol vessels or listening devices from the shore.

The carrier would not be left at risk for a minute. Any navy which could sink two British capital ships within an hour would have learned the all-important lesson of vigilance.

'She'll have booms, nets, the lot,' said Quinton gloomily. 'It'd take us too long. We shall *have* to wait.'

'And wait for her escorts, Number One?' Ainslie watched him, trying to conceal his sense of finality, or total commitment.

'What else?'

'We had planned for an early daylight attack, today or dawn tomorrow.' He could feel his limbs trembling, the sudden rawness in his throat. 'It would take too long, you're right about that. We're too large a target for a normal approach.'

A trickle of condensation ran across the table's edge and quivered in the small vibration.

Quinton stood back, his hands on his hips. 'God damn it, sir, you're going in *surfaced*!'

Ainslie looked from him to Forster, the latter suddenly pale.

'Can you suggest anything else, apart from getting the hell out of here altogether?' He watched them considering it. 'Surfaced we have speed, with some element of surprise to back it up. If we go in at dusk, we stand an even better chance.' He ticked off the points on his fingers. 'We'd lose most of our tin fish in their nets, even if we got that far, with a normal approach. This way we can cut the booms, illuminate the target with star-shell and throw in some eight-inch bricks for good measure. What d'you think?' He looked at Quinton.

Quinton licked his lips. 'If you weren't my commanding officer I'd say you were losing your marbles.' He nodded very slowly. 'It's worth a go.'

Forster said huskily, 'Peter Farrant will be pleased, anyway.'

Quinton grinned. '*Peter?* That his name? I always thought it was Jesus Christ.'

Ainslie watched them, stunned at his decision and their acceptance. It was like a madness, an uncontrollable urge to destroy, and be destroyed.

'All we have to do is keep out of trouble.' He saw Halliday and Lucas looking over at him. 'Until this evening.'

'Ship's head is three-zero-zero, sir.' Gosling sounded totally absorbed, his thick fingers moving the brass wheel very slightly this way and that.

Ainslie looked at the bulkhead clock by the *Soufrière*'s crest with the builder's plate above it. Built in Cherbourg 1934. She had sailed many miles since then, but none as hazardous as these last few would be.

'Well, Pilot, what about daylight?'

Forster tapped his lower lip with his pencil. 'Early dusk, sir. Visibility still fairly good.'

Ainslie crossed to the chart. Two miles to go. The bows were pointing straight for the entrance to the bay. There was no turning back now. It was amazing that he could feel so cool, so remote. Like a spectator.

Through the open watertight door he saw some of Farrant's gun crews bustling about, like members of some strange order of monks in their hoods and anti-flash gear.

While they had idled back and forth in a narrow rectangle of open sea during the day, Ainslie had spoken with Quinton alone. If the bridge received a direct hit during the run in, it would be the first lieutenant's job to complete the attack, worthless or not.

Quinton had not said much, but each of them had been very conscious of the past, the strong links which had always held them together.

What lay inside the bay presented the real problem. The enemy were apparently content to boom off the narrows further inside the bay, that being the most valuable anchorage for naval vessels. For the carrier there would be other arrangements but, with luck, no mines like there were said to be outside Saigon.

The mood in the boat seemed different, he thought. The men near him had shaved during the day and were dressed in clean clothing. They had managed to enjoy a good meal, too, the best which Noake, the cook, could produce from his array of tins and packets.

Perhaps they all expected to die? Clean and tidy, as the men aboard Nelson's ships had been at Trafalgar while they had waited for the fleets to reach one another.

He jerked round as Walker called suddenly, 'HE on green one-seven-oh, sir.'

Quinton was already there, peering over Walker's shoulder as he manipulated the pointer around the dial of his set with patient concentration.

'HE increasing. Moving slightly left.'

Quinton looked at Ainslie. 'Some bastard's following us in!'

Ainslie nodded. 'Inform the gunnery officer. He'll need to know.'

A communications rating connected the gunnery officer's

speaker to the Asdic compartment as Quinton said, 'If he over-hauls us he'll pick us up.'

To confirm his words Walker said, 'Fast HE, sir. Patrol vessel, most likely.'

Ainslie took a few paces from side to side. Of all the bad luck. Perhaps he had been too eager to get it started. Had he left it a few minutes longer he might have been able to turn away and then follow the other vessel straight up to the entrance.

He said, 'Check that the machine-gunners are briefed on our new companion.' He made his lips smile and saw the messenger by the rack of telephones wink quickly at one of the stokers. He could almost hear the man's mind working. *The skipper's not bothered, so why should we be?*

'Increase revolutions for eight knots.'

Ainslie folded his arms, they seemed to be in the way what-ever he did. He must risk the increase of speed, weigh the chances of detection from the bay against the very real risk of being attacked from astern.

He looked at the two periscopes, glistening dully in the dim-med action lights. At times like these, all you wanted to do was see, to know what was going on above the surface.

Walker said, 'No increase in HE, sir.'

Ainslie pictured the other vessel as best he could. A visitor, or one of the local patrols returning to base for the night? God, they would soon get a shock when they discovered they were right behind a submarine.

Forster was looking at the pad by his elbow. 'Time to alter course, sir. Three-zero-five.'

'Very good. Bring her round, Cox'n.'

Ainslie was watching the gently ticking gyro repeater. Like a merciless clock, marking off their remaining time.

Then Forster said, 'Five minutes, sir.'

Ainslie stood beside him and examined the neat lines and calculations. The nearest headland would be on the port bow now, reaching out to embrace them as they headed inshore. Maybe those same sailing craft were directly above; if so, they would lose their nets or lines at any second.

'Close all watertight doors. Shut off for depth-charging.' Ainslie glanced meaningly at Ridgway and his yeoman. 'Ready?'

The lieutenant licked his lips. 'Aye, sir. We've just got to open the bow doors, then – '

Walker's voice cut him off. 'HE increasing, sir. Bearing green one-seven-five.'

Damn. Aloud Ainslie said, 'Bridge party take stations.' He tightened the strap of his binoculars around his neck, his eyes on the control room clock and its red second hand. Tick . . . tick . . . tick.

He said, 'Open the lower hatch.' Some droplets of water left from the last dive spattered across the seamen below like pellets.

'HE closing rapidly, sir.'

Ainslie tried to keep his mind clear and under control. He could hear the other vessel now, the beat of her screws scraping at his brain like a scalpel.

'Stand by to surface.' He did not need to look at Halliday or Quinton now. They were professionals, dedicated to this one, desperate moment.

Ainslie looked up the dark shaft of the conning tower and then started to climb, the lookouts and machine-gunners crowding up under his buttocks, fitting themselves into a tight wad of arms and legs, wasting no space, cutting down the seconds it took to reach the bridge. They did not have to be told either.

He tested the locking wheel and then began to turn it to ease the stiffness.

'*Surface!*'

He heard the roar of compressed air, the immediate change of pressure in his ears as the big submarine started to glide towards the surface.

He heard Quinton blow his whistle and threw his weight and shoulder against the hatch.

A man cursed as someone stamped on his fingers in the frantic eagerness to get through the oval hatch, the clang and clatter of metal as the guns were hauled up to the sides, the seamen slipping and gasping in spray.

Ainslie ran to the fore-gratings, shutting out the confusion as he sought out the bay, the anchored ship, all suddenly so close and stark.

The top of Farrant's turret glistening with salt and spray changed colour as bright balls of tracer floated above the periscope standards. The patrol vessel was dead astern now, a dark grey wedge above a creaming bow wave as she charged in pursuit.

'*Open fire!*'

The heavy machine-guns on the bridge started their insane clatter, the long ammunition belts writhing through the hatch, the red tracer flashing astern in twin arcs, knitting with the enemy's before plunging down towards the target.

Through the turret speaker Ainslie heard Farrant's crisp voice, saw the two guns begin to swing to port; the seaman who had darted through the tiny hatch in the turret to remove the water-tight tampions and drop them in their rack was halfway down to safety again when bullets hammered the thick steel, beat across the curved top and tore him almost in half. The man was dead instantly, cut to ribbons, his blood pouring down the turret and mingling with the spray on either side.

Hands plucked the corpse out of sight and the hatch clanged shut. Over the speaker Farrant was heard to say, 'Get that thing out of the way, man! Don't just stand there like a mindless idiot!'

Ainslie groped for the handset. 'Guns. Open fire.'

The right gun fired first, then the left one seconds later. Ainslie trained his glasses, keeping his head down as much as he could as metal cracked against the conning tower and ricocheted over the sea.

The two star-shells burst beyond the headland, changing the dull light to blinding, arctic brightness.

And it was all there, to the left side of the bay, the great carrier, some moored boats and platforms around her stern, and a hard black line reaching across the glittering water towards the anchored merchantman. A boom, just as Ainslie had expected.

He ignored the activity behind him and snapped down the voice-pipe. '*All tubes ready!*' He heard the periscope squeaking round above his head, pictured the tense figures right forward in the bows, the eight loaded tubes, their doors open, Ridgway's men waiting to reload. If they got the chance.

A shell exploded between the *Soufrière*'s port side and the land, hurling a waterspout high in the air. In the searing light from the flares it looked like solid ice.

More metal against the hull and turret, but so far no one on the bridge had been hurt.

Ainslie pressed his forehead against the bridge sights, watching the carrier in the wires. God, she was big all right. Like a great ugly flat-iron. She had no visible funnels, they were built like long trunks half the length of the ship, tailing off outboard at the after end. The bridge too was cut as low as the flight deck. In the fading glare he could see some assembled aircraft, glistening in the eerie light like brightly painted toys.

'Tell the gunnery officer to continue firing with semi-armour-piercing!'

He dared not take his eyes from the sighting bar now. A seaman ran to the gunnery handset, but was hurled against the side as something punched through the steel plating and flung him down. Another took his place, retching and gasping through his message as the wounded seaman thrashed around on the gratings, the life draining out of him.

It should have been me. Ainslie swallowed hard. *Another second and I would be lying there.*

He felt the hull shake as the thin boom parted across the *Soufrière*'s bows, heard the nets scraping along the saddle tanks as they sank rapidly out of sight.

He blinked rapidly to clear his vision. *Now.* 'Fire One!' He felt the small jerk as the torpedo flashed from its tube. 'Carry on firing by stop-watch!'

Ainslie ducked as more tracer licked from the boom vessel. 'Guns! Shift target!'

The twin barrels purred round smoothly, settled and fired, the shells both hitting the elderly vessel amidships, throwing up a wall of sparks and flames. The range was so short that pieces of the ship splashed down alongside the submarine.

Satisfied with their work, the guns swivelled back towards the carrier, with only the hoarse cries of the layers and trainers to betray the control of humans.

But before Farrant could fire the first torpedo struck home, the column of water shooting up the carrier's side, blasting the air apart with the crash of its explosion. And another, then another, seven in all along the great hull, the eighth, which passed across her bows, burst eventually amongst some rocks.

A searchlight licked out from further along the bay, swung over the submarine in a long pale arm and then came back again, holding the conning tower, blinding them with its sudden intensity.

The guns recoiled, and two more explosions made vivid flashes on the carrier's side. There was an internal one, too, and some of the aircraft bounced into the air before falling drunkenly amongst the rest.

Two waterspouts shot up close abeam, the spray cascading across the bridge in a choking flood, tinged with smoke and cordite.

One of the escorts had risen to the occasion. Too late for the *Sudsuya*, but not for her attacker.

Tracers ripped above the bridge and more shells exploded in the water. The smoke was growing and spreading low over the water, and then it rippled with a dull red glow as fires probed through the carrier's hull and reflected on the bobbing craft around her.

'Hard astarboard!' Ainslie did not have to be told of Halliday's efforts. Every rivet seemed to be shaking loose as the big diesels mounted to their maximum revolutions.

'Midships.'

Ainslie made to wipe the spray from the gyro compass and felt the bile rise in his throat. In the flashing lights his hand looked black, but he knew it was the dying seaman's blood.

'Steer one-three-zero!'

He heard Quinton call, 'I've got her, sir!'

Ainslie wiped his face with his wrist, seeing the land swinging across the bows and the way the guns pivoted on their mounting, still tracking their target.

Then he saw the patrol vessel properly for the first time, swinging away, her role changing from hunter to hunted as the surfaced submarine turned to meet her.

'Shift target! Patrol vessel at red one-five!'

An enemy shell exploded just beyond *Soufrière*'s stem, like a giant hammer blow, deluging the casing and turret with water and smoke. What it had done to the fore-ends and the torpedo-men there was impossible to tell.

Ainslie's head throbbed as the guns recoiled again, straddling the patrol vessel in white columns, making her turn more violently, revealing her full length when the fire gong rang once more. One over, the next a hit, the creaming bow wave dropping away as her engineroom exploded in lethal steam and splinters.

Ainslie ran to the rear of the bridge, realizing that another man had fallen to his knees, clasping his stomach and gasping in agony as Menzies tried to pull him to the hatch.

The whole bay seemed to be filled with fire and smoke, and when he managed to jam the binoculars to his eyes he realized that the *Sudsuya* was beginning to turn turtle, her aircraft spilling over the side, one catching fire like a moth in the flames as it fell.

He shouted wildly into the smoke and din, '*We did it!*'

Two further shells burst near the submarine. One warship at least was in pursuit. To catch the carrier's executioner or to pick up her company, which would her commander decide? Another pair of shells exploded slightly to starboard, an answer to his unspoken question.

Ainslie yelled down the voice-pipe, 'Stand by stern tubes! We might get this one as we clear the headland!'

He did not hear any acknowledgement for at that moment something struck him violently in the shoulder. For an instant he thought that a piece of one of the periscopes had been cut down by gunfire and had fallen on him. Then as the searing pain exploded through his body he started to fall, his arm shining with blood in the drifting tracers.

Menzies was kneeling beside him, cradling him away from the side where two holes had suddenly appeared.

Ainslie gasped, 'Tell Number One, Yeo! Tell him to – '

Then the pain tightened its grip, and he found himself spiralling down into darkness.

14

Survival

AINSLIE became aware that someone was wiping his face and throat with something cool, but when he opened his eyes it felt as if the lids were glued together.

Everything was blurred and indistinct, shapeless and somehow disconnected from his dulled mind.

A face loomed in front of him, Petty Officer SBA Hunt, his eyes screwed up with concentration as he examined his patient.

'You all right, sir?'

Ainslie felt his mind cringing and knew something was about to happen. Then he heard it, the threatening roar of screws, the sudden shock of explosions against the hull. The deck swayed up and down, forward and back, and as some kind of realization came back to him he knew he was in a cot, a webbing strap over his chest to hold him secure. He felt numbed, his limbs like his mind, without proper function.

He heard glass and other objects clattering across the deck, and when he craned his head over the edge of the cot he saw mess everywhere. Broken bottles and tubes, torn bandages and a bowl full of blood-stained dressings.

The noise was coming back again, sawing away at his brain, then two more crashes as depth-charges burst overhead.

So they had got out and were submerged. He groaned and tried to move, but Hunt seized him and forced him back. His hands were smooth and soft like a woman's but his grip was like steel.

He said, 'You've been hurt, sir. My orders are to make you rest.'

Ainslie stared at the cot above him. 'How long?'

Hunt shrugged. 'Two hours, sir. Maybe more.' He winced as the submarine bucked wildly and swayed to one side for several seconds. 'God, I'm scared to death.'

Ainslie looked at him, seeing his terror and able to admire his determination not show it.

Someone groaned, and when Ainslie peered over the other side of the cot he saw the seaman who had fallen at the rear of the bridge. He was propped in a sitting position, tied with bandages and straps, in one corner of the sick-bay.

Hunt said wearily, 'I've drugged him best I can, sir.'

Ainslie watched the wounded seaman. His face was ashen, and there was a lot of blood on his dressings.

Hunt added softly, 'I can't let him lie down and die in peace, sir. He's hit in the lungs. Nothing more I can do for him. He'll drown in his own blood if he lies down, you see?'

Ainslie reached up and touched his injured shoulder, feeling the bandages, the way his arm tingled with the mere effort of movement.

Hunt said, 'Splinter, sir. Bad one, but nothing broken, as far as I can tell.'

Crash . . . crash . . . crash! Triple charges exploded nearby, and more racing screws thundered overhead. A bottle rolled across the deck, and Ainslie knew the boat was turning and changing depth at the same time.

And it had been going on for over two hours. The realization was like a spur, and he gasped, 'Get me up. I've got to go.'

Hunt tried to grin. 'Well, sir, it's more than my life's worth.'

Feet crunched on glass and Sub-Lieutenant Jones, the sea-plane's observer, staggered through the door.

'Number One sent me, sir. To see how you are.' He almost fell as the hull tilted right over again and every light flickered dangerously.

'Fine.' The pain was returning. Hunt's drugs must be wearing off. 'What's happening?'

Jones crouched by the cot and held on to it with both hands.

'Three destroyers from the Jap base, sir. They've been after us all night. But we bagged another with the stern tubes just after we left the place. Like you were telling us when you were hit.'

His face was dripping with sweat, and Ainslie could almost smell his fear. Up in the sky in some flimsy seaplane with his rough-and-ready pilot he would do anything. Down here was something different. Quinton had probably sent him to give him something to do, to keep his mind off it.

'What depth?'

Jones shook his head. 'I forget, sir.'

'Tell Number One I'm all right.' His eyes focused on Hunt. 'How many did we lose?'

He shrugged. 'Two killed.' He did not look at the propped-up figure in the corner. 'Another to go soon. And four injured, mostly by being thrown about.'

Hunt crouched down as the drumming screws came towards them again. 'Oh God,' he whispered, 'I can't take much more!'

Ainslie tensed, holding his breath until his head swam, as the destroyer's engines thundered louder and louder and then quite suddenly began to fade away.

He looked at Hunt and was shocked to see the tears running down his face. He had bunched his hands together as he waited for the final pattern of depth-charges to split the submarine's hull wide open.

Ainslie wanted to comfort him, to thank him for all he had done for the wounded and the dying. But nothing would come out, and he felt his mind going away once more down the spiralling tunnel.

Then Quinton was leaning over him, his forehead cut by flying glass, his face lined and weary with strain.

Ainslie tried to speak lucidly. 'I heard that last one, John. Has it gone?'

Quinton smiled down at him. 'That was two hours ago, Skipper. You dropped off again.'

It was not possible. Perhaps he was dying and they were trying to make it easy for him. How could it be two hours? He looked over the cot and saw that the man had gone from the corner and a body lay covered by a sheet beside the door.

Quinton said quietly, 'We are out of it, Skipper. A bit battered here and there, but we made it. Thanks to you.'

The tannoy said, 'First lieutenant in the control room!'

Quinton ran his fingers through his hair, dislodging paint flakes and grit. 'I'll be back, Skipper.'

He darted a meaning glance at the SBA, and as Ainslie turned his head he saw another needle going into his arm.

He tried to protest, but it was already too late.

In the control room they stood around like dazed survivors, their feet amongst the litter of broken gauges and equipment blasted from their fittings by the endless bombardment.

Some of the men were still looking at the deckhead, listening for the destroyers, the hunters after their kill. Others stared at nothing, eyes dulled by fatigue, spent to a point of collapse.

Forster had his head in his hands, elbows propped on the vibrating plot table.

Once more, he had survived.

Halliday finished tying a bandage around a stoker's arm and said gruffly, 'We'd better get to it, lads. You never know. They might come after us again.'

Lucas nodded, his mind still reeling from the noise, from the feeling of being crushed in a vice of pain and violence. All through it he had thought of Ainslie being brought down, bleeding, from the bridge. Of Halliday's grim determination through each mind-bending crisis. Of Quinton, riding the boat, legs astride, shouting orders and abuse, encouragement and curses, holding them all together.

Quinton said, 'You're right, Chief. We'll get some food and drink laid on, too.' He smiled painfully. 'Skipper's going to be all right.'

As they began to put themselves together again, Gosling handed over the helm to Voysey, the second coxswain. When he stood up he felt his bones creak, his fingers sore from gripping the wheel.

He looked at the yeoman of signals and winked. 'Reckon you were right, Jock. After we get clear o' this little lot, I'm putting in for a nice cushy billet ashore!'

They both knew it was unlikely. But a few hours earlier so too had been their very survival.

Ainslie remembered very little of the passage back to Singapore. Drugged into a state of half understanding what was happening, he lost count of time and distance completely.

In moments of awareness, as the searing pain of his wound made him sweat and writhe in the cot, he heard many feet passing the sick-bay, the sounds of repairs being carried out seemingly everywhere.

Only Quinton and Halliday ever visited him, and then rarely and for short periods. Ainslie guessed it was by careful agreement between them and Hunt to keep him quiet, to prevent his joining in the boat's affairs as she headed very slowly back to harbour.

Hunt took good care to see that when he left the submarine on a stretcher his journey to the hospital was as painless as possible.

It was like being in a nightmare, or helplessly drunk. Ainslie dimly recalled the sunlight, the tall conning tower looming above him as he was carried towards the brow. Faces looking down at him as he passed, some smiling, others just watching, remembering perhaps how they had shared all of it with him.

The events which followed his departure from *Soufrière* were equally confused. Gliding along an endless corridor, his drugged mind trying to count the lights as they passed overhead.

Then cool stillness, more faces bobbing above him, scissors cutting away at the dressings, eyes without faces above their masks, giving nothing away.

And then a bed somewhere, a small white room without windows which he guessed was underground.

His wound, the great loss of blood, added to his fatigue, were enough to keep him unconscious for much of the time.

Once or twice he awoke, struggling with his sheets as he heard distant explosions. But they were bombs falling, not depth-charges. As a patient nursing orderly explained to him, 'It takes time, sir. You've got to realize that you're out of it. For now, anyway.'

Ainslie thought a lot about that. The *Soufrière*, and the Japanese carrier capsizing in flames. With the tired dignity that most ships seemed to show when they died. As the days passed and he felt his strength returning he was able to put his thoughts in order, to remember the sequence of that last terrible attack. It was not so easy as the nursing orderly imagined, to let go, to forget.

Eventually Rear-Admiral Granger came to see him, a doctor close at hand to make sure Ainslie was not worn down by questions.

Granger sat on the only chair in the room, his plump legs crossed, somehow incomplete without the pipe.

He said, 'I would have come earlier, but they thought it best this way.' He glanced around the room. 'Looking after you all right?'

Ainslie tried to push himself up on one elbow, but it was hopeless. He fell back again and said between his teeth, 'I'd like to know what's happening, sir, if you don't mind.'

Granger nodded slowly. 'Of course. Your exploits in Area Item Fox made tremendous reading. Your first lieutenant put in a good report, and with what I knew already it seems you did the impossible. If we'd known just how many Jap warships there were in the bay, I don't think we'd have let you go at all. But it's done, and the *Sudsuya*'s on the bottom for good.'

Ainslie closed his eyes, feeling the prick of emotion, the nearness of collapse and shock.

He said, 'What about me, sir?'

Granger replied cheerfully, 'Oh, they'll be getting you away from here, I expect. I'm like everyone else. Waiting for orders.'

Ainslie opened his eyes and looked at him. It was no use. Granger had told him nothing.

He asked, 'Are we holding the enemy back, sir?'

Granger came to a decision. 'No. In my view, the Japs will be down to the Johore Strait in a couple of weeks. After that, it's anyone's guess. I could lie to you, but you've done too much, seen too much to deserve that kind of deceit. It's bad, all the way. I'm organizing another convoy to evacuate some more of the women and dependants. It's a race against time, nothing else.'

Ainslie lay very still, aware of the steady throb beneath his bandages, the unnatural quiet of the underground room.

'The Torrances, sir? What happened?'

Granger looked at his shoes. 'Still here. Guy Torrance has been a bit difficult about the boats he was having built. We need them now, but he's being bloody awkward, to put it mildly. Trouble is, and this is just between us, there are lots of people like him. Heard of a case the other day. The poor bloody Army wanted to dig slit trenches across the golf course, but the club secretary wouldn't hear of it. Anywhere else, the Army would have kicked his backside out of it. But this is different.' He added with sudden bitterness, '*Good old Singers*, it will never fall to a bunch of Japs!'

Ainslie felt his strength dropping away in spite of his efforts. 'I should like to return to my command as soon as I can, sir.'

'No doubt you would.' Granger saw the doctor frowning at

him. 'You'll be moved from here pretty soon. Beyond that I can't say.' He stood up and gave a great sigh. 'I wish to God I was at sea. That I *do* know.'

Ainslie saw the door close and realized that the rest was missing. Granger and the white-coated doctor had vanished, like the dying seaman in the sick-bay.

He felt something like terror sweep over him. He would never get a ship again if his mind had broken under the shock. Not even a clapped-out escort, never mind a submarine.

He had to get back. *Must.* He felt tears running down his cheeks. Despair, self-pity, even anger at his inability to find the power to reason made him groan aloud.

An orderly was at the bedside in seconds.

Ainslie said weakly, 'Keep your bloody needles away from me!'

The man grinned down at him. 'Not this time, sir. This time it's a visitor.'

Ainslie turned his head and stared at the door. She was standing just outside in the passageway, wearing a pale dress, her hair hanging loose as it had at Christmas.

The orderly beamed. 'When Rear-Admiral Granger came yesterday, sir, he said it was all right.'

Ainslie swallowed hard. *Yesterday?* Was it possible?

She crossed the room and sat on the chair, her mouth smiling but her eyes filled with concern and pity.

She said softly, 'They wouldn't let me come sooner. Your Lieutenant Quinton came to the hotel and told me about it. I think he left a lot out, but the rest was awful enough.'

Ainslie was almost afraid to speak in case he broke down again.

He said, 'You look lovely. God, I think that but for you I'd have gone under completely.'

Her eyes widened. 'You meant that!' She rested her fingers lightly on his bare shoulder. 'Don't excite yourself. I heard about your wound.' Despite her care she was unable to prevent her lip from quivering or her fingers from gripping his skin. 'But you're back now. That's all that matters.'

'You should have gone. When I heard about the *Bengal Princess* being sunk I realized how dangerous it's all become.' Ainslie tried to move closer to her. 'You must get away. I couldn't bear it if you were still here when they – '

She put her hand on his mouth. 'Shhh. We'll manage something. You'll see.'

Ainslie smiled. He could smell her skin, feel her softness. It was like another dress.

She saw his sudden anxiety and said, 'No. It's real this time, Robert. I shouldn't be here like this. You know it, and I know it.' She withdrew her hand and pushed some hair from her forehead. 'But I don't want it to stop.'

Somewhere, a hundred miles away, a bell rang, and she said, 'Why is it that when you want to stay it's time to go? When you hate something it lasts forever.'

Ainslie watched her as she stood up and smoothed her dress.

'When can I see you again?'

'Soon.' She watched him gravely, as if she wanted to remember everything, to share his pain. 'Arnold Granger will try to help. He's a dear.'

The door opened and the orderly said, 'Time's up, sir.'

She bent over the bed and kissed him slowly on the mouth, her hair falling across his shoulders like warm silk.

He said, 'Take care.'

She moved to the door. 'You, too.' Then she was gone.

The next visitor was Quinton, strangely alien in clean whites after his battle-torn appearance in the submarine.

He said, '*Soufrière*'s almost back to rights again. We've done most of the welding and patching ourselves. The dockyard mateys are too scared to risk getting their heads blown off. But we're fairly well protected, plenty of ack-ack and heavy flak around the harbour.'

'I've not thanked you yet, John.' Here it was again, the emotion, the inability to find the right words. 'I don't know how you did it, but thanks.'

Quinton smiled. 'You got us in and out. The rest was a case of thinking ahead of the Jap skippers up top. Fortunately, we've been at it a helluva lot longer than they have.' He became serious. 'Things look pretty ropey. I've heard that the line is falling right back to the island, double-quick. Then they'll blow up the Causeway and dig in. Operations think the Japs will try another naval attack now that they've got Malaya in the bag. But I intend to make it my business to get you out, no matter what.' He grinned. 'I found the lady for you. Okay?'

Ainslie reached out and gripped his wrist. 'Okay.' It was all he could say.

Quinton looked at his watch. 'Must get back. I'm restricting our lads to the harbour. Things are a bit ugly in town. Everyone's so busy blaming somebody else they can't see the danger coming smack at them!' He was unwilling to break the contact. 'Don't worry, Skipper. I'll take good care of the boat until you get back.' He jammed on his cap. 'So long.'

Three more days of uncertainty were to pass before Ainslie was told that he was leaving the hospital.

He had taken his first steps around the little room, aided by the same patient orderly, and had even been allowed to see the savage-looking scar on his shoulder where they had probed to make certain there were no more fragments of shell splinters.

Feeling like a new boy at school, carefully dressed in a loose white shirt and shorts, the orderly following him with his cap, Ainslie was guided to a field ambulance.

The doctor said cheerfully, 'Take a few days to get the feel of things, old chap. After that, well, we shall see, eh?'

Sitting propped in the slow-moving ambulance, Ainslie got his first glimpse of Singapore for over three weeks. Bombed buildings were everywhere, upturned carts and other vehicles had been dragged into side streets and abandoned like piled rubbish. The police were very much in evidence, and scores of soldiers roamed the streets like a lost army.

The orderly remarked, 'Now that the RAF has regrouped on the island we're getting better air cover, sir. Bit too late if you ask me.'

The ambulance jolted over some scattered bricks and turned into a familiar road.

Raffles, apparently unscathed, passed the line of Ainslie's vision, and he felt his heart beginning to thump wildly.

What had she said? *Granger will try to help.*

He struggled round in his seat and peered at the Royal Hotel. One wing had been sheered right off, leaving a blackened tangle of charred frames and fallen masonry. It was like a disfigurement to the old place. An insult.

There were armed soldiers at the gates, and a corporal waved the ambulance inside with barely a glance.

There was a large notice on the wall. *Off Limits To All Personnel.*

The orderly made ready to help Ainslie to the ground. He said, 'We took over part of the hotel for walking wounded, sir. There are still some civvies here, but not many now.'

Ainslie looked at him. He did not know. It was like a precious secret.

He saw the old Indian porter coming to meet him, and was shocked to see how he had aged. His coat was stained and patched, and there was a burn mark on his topee.

'Greetings, Commander-sahib!'

Ainslie smiled. 'Thank you. It takes more than a few bombs to scare you, I see.'

The old man dabbed his eyes and sniffed. 'We will show them, sahib.' He shuffled away, his world already gone.

A sergeant was sitting at the reception desk, and he jumped to attention as Ainslie walked stiffly into the cool shade.

' 'Mornin', sir.' He waved to some bearers. 'I'll have you taken up to your quarters. In the event of an air raid, we are supposed to go down to the cellars.' He did not smile as he added in the same clipped voice, 'Fact is, I'd as soon die in bed meself as go down there!'

The orderly was giving some papers and Ainslie's bag to the sergeant, while two Chinese servants waited for their instructions nearby. Ainslie examined the big room, feeling its shabby defiance all around him. A crack in the far wall, zigzagging and widening, some plaster hanging from the ceiling, the clock face broken, as were some of the pictures.

But a few civilians were sitting at the little tables, neatly dressed, their faces giving nothing away.

The orderly said, 'Now, sir, if you'll go with these chaps?'

Ainslie turned stiffly and saw her coming down the stairs.'

She said quietly, 'I will show the commander his room.' She was watching his face, linking them together with her eyes, excluding everyone else.

'Very well, miss.' The soldier winked at the sergeant behind the desk. 'I'll be back tomorrow.'

The sergeant watched the girl's legs up the stairs and saw her slip her hand through the commander's arm. Her husband had been in the hotel yesterday, but would not be back for several days.

The sergeant looked down at his desk. *It's all right for some.*

Ainslie opened his eyes and stared straight up at the ceiling while his mind grappled with the unfamiliar surroundings. It was very dark in the room, although through some slits in the shutters he saw moonlight.

His mouth felt parched, like dust, and he groaned aloud with sudden anger. They must have given him something to put him under again. It was night-time and very quiet. He could vaguely recall getting undressed, taking some tea which another orderly had brought him. Then nothing, until now.

Something like muffled thunder moved against the shutters. It was gunfire, artillery, and a long way off. Like a threat.

A shadow moved across the small slivers of moonlight, and for a moment he thought it was an orderly.

Then he felt her hand on his forehead, the clink of glass as she poured some water from a jug.

She said softly, 'Here. This will help.' She put her hand under his head, tilting it so that the ice-cold water could trickle down his throat.

'How long have you been here?' He felt ashamed that she should find him like this. He was sweating badly, the sheet clinging to him.

'I came after I had put Frances to bed.' He sensed her turning away to look at the opposite wall, beyond which the child was sleeping. 'You were tossing and turning. I thought it might be useful if I stayed.'

He felt her sit carefully on the side of the bed, her presence, her warmth close against him.

'How is she?'

She sounded nervous and unsure. 'Better, I think. I am full of hope since that day. Frances never leaves your elephant out of her sight.'

'Is it all right your being here like this? I wouldn't want to cause trouble for you. After all you've done.'

She shook slightly, with a laugh or sob he could not tell.

'Done? What have I done except involve you?' She tossed her head in the way he remembered so clearly. 'Anyway, Guy's away. He's off on one of his trips to see what's happening about his precious boats. But I'm glad he made a fuss.' She touched Ainslie's shoulder very gently. 'Otherwise we'd not be together like this.'

He took her hand and held it to his face. 'I know. I'm grateful.'

'Would you like me to leave now? Will you be all right? You ought to try and get some proper sleep.'

He reached up and gripped her arm through her robe. He felt useless, clumsy and unable to think clearly. The touch of her beneath his fingers, the pounding of his heart, it was all making his mind reel.

He replied unsteadily, 'I'm selfish, but I'm telling you the truth. I want you here. Now and always.'

She stood up lightly, and for an instant he thought he had spoiled everything and driven her away. Then he saw the shutters swing open, so that she stood out in silhouette against the pale moonlight. Then very deliberately she dropped the robe from her shoulders and turned towards him.

Her skin held the reflected light, making her shine like a statue, and then she was near him once more, her hand pressing against his chest, holding him down as she slid into the bed beside him.

'No. You're not well. I'll not have you hurt yourself.'

She silenced his protests with a kiss, and then another, her hair tumbling around them, making their embrace even more secret.

She drew away very slowly, and he could sense her looking at him, her back and shoulders curved above him in the moonlight.

Then, equally slowly, she came down, until her breasts were touching him, exciting him further until he thought he would cry out.

Ainslie said huskily, 'I love you. You know that now.'

Her hair was touching him everywhere, and as her body arched over him, embracing him, holding him like a captive, he heard her whisper, 'I know. And I will show you *how* I know.' Then she enfolded him completely, gripping and receiving him until they were joined as one.

It seemed as if the torment of their passion and love would never stop, until with a gasp she lay limp across him, her lips murmuring in his ear, her fingers caressing him to bring back the fire yet again.

She remained with him until he eventually fell into a deep sleep and the moon had exchanged its light with the dawn. Then, very carefully, she stood up beside the bed and for a long moment stayed looking down at him before covering him with a sheet.

Booted feet clattered in the yard outside, and she slipped into her robe before moving to the window to stare out at the city.

In the grey light it looked almost beautiful. She thrust her hand through her robe, touching her breast as he had done, speaking his name to herself.

Then she closed the shutters and left the room to a new peace.

15

The Secret

CAPTAIN PHILIP ARMYTAGE, acting commodore, tapped the wall map with a pointer and said bleakly, 'This is a sad moment, gentlemen, but nevertheless I believe it makes our position less perilous.'

Ainslie glanced around the small, airless room at his companions. A handful of naval officers and two army majors. And yet Armytage spoke as if he was addressing a multitude.

The temporary HQ to which Armytage had moved his staff was little more than a cellar, situated between the city and Kallang airfield. The map on the wall was the one which Rear-Admiral Granger had used, but the yellow tape had been removed, as if out of consideration for the final collapse of all resistance on the Malayan mainland.

What did Armytage *really* believe, he wondered? The Causeway had been blown up, the last rear-guard from the jungles, Australian infantry and men of the Argyll and Sutherland Highlanders, had crossed on to the island. The final battle for the fortress was set.

The harbour was littered with wrecks as the Japanese kept up their daily air raids and brought home the close reality of war. It seemed as if the enemy's juggernaut was increasing speed rather than the opposite, and each day brought news of fresh advances and landings from Borneo to Celebes. Against them, seemingly in another world, was arrayed an assorted bag of Dutch, Australian, British and American warships, their overall command as mixed as their methods. And yet Armytage had just been speaking of 'backs to the wall' and 'tempered by battle', as if it was just a matter of time before roles were reversed.

Ainslie leaned back in his chair, letting Armytage's words wash over him. All this had been inevitable, and yet in the past days he had discovered more happiness than he could ever have hoped for.

As soon as he had been able to return to duty, he had taken every opportunity to visit Natalie Torrance. With the worsening news, and the air of tension filtering through the city like poison gas, they had drawn joy from one another, stealing each precious moment, hoarding every memory like a defence.

Her husband had been away for most of the time. Always he left the battered hotel angrily, and when he came back he was usually too drunk to make himself understood.

Ainslie had been lying beside her, holding her smooth body while she slept, feeling her heartbeats, wondering what they should do, when the telephone had rung on the bedside table. He had waited for her to awake and pick it up, had felt her spine stiffen as she had said, 'Very well. I'll tell him.' Then she had turned on to her back, her face outlined by her hair. 'That was Lieutenant Quinton. The Japanese are at the Johore Strait. The island's cut off.'

He could not remember how long they had lain together. Just holding each other without words, picturing the crude events of war, how they would affect them.

Ainslie looked up as Armytage said, 'We will continue with Rear-Admiral Granger's evacuation, with every sort of vessel we can get hold of. Lists have been made by my staff, and all those to be put aboard the convoys will be shifted to the harbour vicinity forthwith.' He glanced at Ainslie, his eyes wary. 'I will need working parties from every vessel under my control, and as the next senior officer, Commander Ainslie, you will assist in this plan.'

Ainslie nodded, feeling the others looking at him. Reservists mostly, young and with little experience. What a way to learn about war.

He thought suddenly of his first visit to the *Soufrière* after he had been given a clean bill of health by the MO. Quinton had worked wonders, but the scars of the battle and withdrawal from the Japanese-held bay told the story better than any words.

There were still no final orders for the submarine. She would probably be used to evacuate more personnel when the time came. It was unnerving, but he never considered any other possibility but eventual defeat. When the high command had convinced themselves that the enemy had no intention of being content with local advances, it had already been decided. Now, the Japanese were swinging out and around the South China

Sea, sealing off the whole vast area like pulling the strings of a sack.

This had to be a definite, crushing victory, to be seen by the whole world as a threat, a promise of what would happen to anyone who resisted or tried to interfere.

Armytage concluded, 'That's about it, gentlemen. I will keep you informed in daily orders.' He looked at Ainslie and added, 'A word, please.' As the others moved gratefully outside to the fresh air he said, 'I think I've thought of everything.' When Ainslie made no comment he snapped, '*Well?*'

'I believe that the C in C should ask, *demand* more ships, sir, and a carrier with some aircraft which are a match for the enemy's. The Army can't be expected to hold the island without full air cover, and if Rear-Admiral Granger is not supported with ships and planes he hasn't a hope in hell of getting the troops away if so ordered.' He waited, breathing hard, feeling his wound throbbing in time with his heart. 'It will be no Dunkirk this time.'

Armytage looked at the floor. 'Still harping on that, are you? Well, we're better suited now for all-round defence.' His voice unexpectedly trailed away. 'And that sort of thing.'

Ainslie stared at him, shocked at his sudden collapse, appalled with what it must mean. The high command had no intention of taking off the troops if the island fell under attack. All those men, dropped like lepers, abandoned to the mercy of the Japanese Army.

At any other moment he could have found understanding, even pity for a man like Armytage. In all the years of peace he had never trained himself to prepare, to change with the times.

But the cost was going to be terrible, and the fate of the many left behind too ghastly to contemplate. All the envy and hatred of Britain's colonial influence would be sealed up here, with no hope of escape for anyone.

Ainslie said bitterly, 'I shall return to my command, sir.' He had to get away, to detach himself from the air of despair and shame.

'Oh, one thing more.' Armytage tried to reassert himself but failed. 'There's a signal waiting for you on board. I'll tell you the rough context now.' He frowned, his eyes vanishing into wrinkles as he pulled his thoughts together.

'The signal is from the Admiralty. The Free French admiral in London has received a full report about your exploits. He's worried. Not what he had in mind when his people gave their assistance for your original task of capturing the submarine.'

Ainslie clenched his fists. 'We didn't know about Malaya and Pearl Harbour then, did we, sir?' It was all he could do to control his voice.

'Well, there it is. Nothing's settled yet. The emergency here takes priority. But *Soufrière* was to have been the largest vessel in the Free French forces once you had got her back to Britain, that I do know. You can see their point.'

'Frankly, no.' Ainslie jammed on his cap. 'But I suppose it doesn't matter a damn any more what I think.'

He went out of the room, his mind filled with faces. *Capitaine* Poulain, lying shot beside his desk. Lucas's eyes when the tricolour had come down from the conning tower. The sailor who had died in a corner of the sick-bay, propped up to avoid drowning in his own blood. Every one of them, even Poulain, had done what he imagined was best. Now, even in the face of tragedy, they were arguing and bargaining about it in London.

A sentry saluted and said, 'Air-raid warnin', sir.' He squinted at the evening skyline. 'Shame, annit?'

Ainslie could barely look at the man. An ordinary soldier, with the sort of homely face you saw on the newsreels. Norway and Crete. Dunkirk. And now here.

In the past there had always been a miracle, even at the final moment. The warships, the defiant 'thumbs-up', the tired faces watching the vapour trails in the sky, wondering if the miracle was going to be snatched back.

Then he saw Quinton waiting for him, sitting behind the wheel of a sports car.

He called, 'Thought I might catch you, Skipper. I've just been in HQ for the list of people to be moved to the port area. And I've got a signal for you, too.'

Ainslie climbed in beside him. 'About *Soufrière* and the French in London?'

'Yeh.' Quinton gunned the engine. 'They're bloody nuts, if you ask me.'

Ainslie looked at him searchingly. Quinton was as near to being drunk as he had ever seen him. Angry drunk.

'Where did you get the car?'

Quinton swerved round some people with handcarts. 'You can get any damn thing for a promise of a berth out of Singapore!'

Then he said, 'I keep thinking about all our blokes. They're going to be left in the lurch. I knew it from the start. The lousy, rotten bastards!'

Quinton steadied himself and said in a calmer voice, 'Shall we go back via the hotel, Skipper? I think you should do something for that girl, and pretty damn quick.'

'I was going to ask you to drive there.'

Ainslie put out his hands to prevent himself from going through the glass as Quinton jammed on the brakes.

A tall Sikh policeman loomed over the side and called excitedly, 'Air-raid warning! You get off the road, sir, very quick!'

Quinton dropped his voice so that the man had to put his head inside the car to hear him.

'If you don't get away from this car, I will personally stuff you down the nearest drain, right?'

He drove on, the policeman calling threats after him.

Quinton muttered, 'Bastard! I'll bet he and his cobbers will all be wearing the rising sun when the little yellow men march in!'

They slowed to pass through the gates of the Royal Hotel. There were some army vehicles loading an assortment of luggage, soldiers standing around chatting and smoking, listening to the occasional bark of anti-aircraft guns.

Guy Torrance's big car was slewed through one of the lush flower beds, a door hanging open.

Quinton said grimly, 'Christ, and I thought *I* was a lousy driver!'

Ainslie slid from the car. 'You are. But never mind that. Come on.'

As they reached the foot of the stairway he heard Torrance's voice. He was shouting wildly, the sound filling the upper floor like the fury of a madman.

The orderly sergeant, who was watching the hotel clerk emptying his safe, said, 'Bin like that since 'e come in, sir. Your lot 'ave commandeered 'is precious boats. 'E didn't go much on it!'

215

They reached the door of the suite and stood looking at each other.

Torrance was yelling, 'They're bloody thieves! Think they can tell *me* what to do!'

There was a clatter of breaking glass, and Ainslie heard her say, '*Please!* Not in front of Frances!'

'You and that kid! That's all you ever bloody well think about!' Another crash. 'Well, I'll show the damn lot of you!'

Ainslie opened the door, his eyes taking in everything as they all froze in their various attitudes of anger and fear.

Drawers pulled out, contents strewn across the floor. Broken dishes and scattered food. Torrance must have dragged the cloth from the table and hurled the laid-out meal amongst the rest.

The nurse was standing by the far door, obviously terrified, her bony hands on the child's shoulders as she too cowered away from her drink-crazed father.

Natalie Torrance was sitting on the arm of a chair. Her dress was torn from one shoulder and her cheek was red, as if she had been slapped hard, even punched.

Torrance swung round and stared at the two naval officers, baring his teeth as if he were about to attack them.

'Well, well, well! What are you here for?'

His tie was stained with drink and his white suit badly soiled. He must have fallen down several times. That he had managed to drive the car was hard to believe.

Ainslie looked at her, shutting out Torrance for fear of what he might do to him.

'All right?' He kept his voice level, seeing her terror give way to desperate hope.

'Oh, yes! She's all right *now*!' Torrance's angry red eyes loomed across his vision. 'Have you come to *protect* her, eh?'

He gave a wild laugh, and Ainslie saw the child shrink even further into the corner. He noticed she had jammed the yellow elephant there, too, as if to protect it from hurt.

Quinton drawled, 'Why the hell don't you stow it? We've got troubles enough.'

Torrance ignored him, and Ainslie saw the maggot in his mind, spreading and expanding as he bellowed, 'Or to put your hand up her skirt, that's more bloody like it!'

Ainslie said evenly, 'You are to go to the harbour. There will be transport – '

Torrance lurched towards him, his face suddenly deathly pale. 'Jesus, *it's true*!' He seized his arm and staggered helplessly. 'I can see it on your damn face, man!'

She called, 'Oh, Guy, stop it *now*!'

Torrance released his hold and retreated, nodding the whole time, his eyes fixed on Ainslie's as he continued in the same slurred voice, 'All this time. Wouldn't let me lay a finger on her precious body, oh no, not her! But you, with your medals and death-or-bloody-glory, she couldn't get enough of it from you, I'll wager!'

Quinton exclaimed harshly, 'Shall I belt him, sir?'

Torrance turned towards the motionless figure on the chair. 'You'll see, my girl. You'll see who wears the trousers around here!' His shadow loomed over her, but she sat quite still as he added thickly, 'That slap was nothing, believe me!' He looked at the nurse. 'It's all my money, remember?' He nodded again, spittle running down his chin. 'Oh, yes, my little puritans, you'll do some paying now.'

Ainslie stepped amongst the scattered china. 'If you make any attempt to hit anyone again, I'll – '

'*You'll what?*' Torrance swayed back on his heels and rebounded from the wall. 'Sue me for trying to tame my own wife?'

He was grinning wildly, enjoying all of it in some distorted way. Later it would be different.

Torrance wagged his finger. 'You'd better start looking for another job. When I've done with you, you'll be lucky to command a bloody rubber duck!'

Ainslie walked past him, expecting an attack at any second. He knew that if Torrance touched him he would probably kill him.

He said quietly, 'My first lieutenant will drive you and Frances to the port office now.' He looked at the nurse. 'Pack some things.'

Natalie stood up and tried to pull the torn dress across her shoulder.

'I'm sorry I got you into this.' She looked up at him, and once again they were their own island, as if the danger and fury were somewhere else.

Ainslie replied, 'I want it this way.' He guided her towards the door. 'You can come back later if you forget something.'

There was a thin, abbreviated whistle, and then Ainslie felt himself smashed down by an explosion. As his mind struggled to grasp what had happened, he imagined for a few seconds that Torrance had shot him.

Then, coughing and gasping he levered himself to his feet, jarring his wounded shoulder on what he suddenly realized was part of the roof.

There was swirling smoke and dust everywhere, and as he staggered through it he heard whistles blowing and somebody screaming shrilly like a tortured animal.

He found her sprawling in the passageway, her hair covered in dust, her clothes almost blasted from her body.

He knelt down, lifting her against him, gasping her name. When he brushed the hair from her face she opened her eyes and stared at him. He waited, hardly daring to breathe or hope, seeing the understanding and fear returning as he held her even closer.

Her mouth formed the name. 'Frances!'

Ainslie turned his head, seeing the fallen beams and stone-work, the smoke, sensing the danger, the stench of burning.

He could see the evening sky above the dust-haze, and realized the hotel had taken a direct hit.

If only that thing would stop screaming. It was probing his eardrums, making the girl shake in his arms as he pressed her against him.

Feet stumbled and kicked through the debris, and he heard Quinton say huskily, 'Thank God! I thought they'd done for you!'

He was carrying the child, who in turn had somehow managed to keep hold of her yellow elephant.

Like survivors on a raft they huddled together as Quinton ran his fingers through his tangled hair.

He said, 'The bloody roof caved in, and I think half the build-ing has gone, too.' He glanced meaningly at Ainslie. 'Better get them out of it. The nurse is cut to ribbons back there. Her body took most of the blast.'

'What about him?'

Quinton shrugged. 'Alive, but pinned under the main beam.' He looked down at the child and added, 'Not long, I'd say.'

Ainslie helped the girl to her feet, watching for the first hint of injury or collapse.

They looked at the shattered door as Guy Torrance groaned loudly.

Then she said, 'I'll go to him.'

Shouts came from outside the building, the sounds of men running. But the screaming continued, as if it would never end.

Ainslie said, 'I'll come with you.' To Quinton he added, 'Stay with the child, John.'

Torrance was pinioned by the beam. He must be in agony, his back smashed under the great weight.

He saw them and whispered, 'Come to gloat?'

She looked away. 'Don't, Guy. Please.'

He closed his eyes and gasped. 'For Christ's sake stop Frances screaming!'

Ainslie glanced back at the door and saw the child standing as before, silent and unmoving, one hand in Quinton's.

'It's not Frances. She's safe.'

But Torrance did not seem to hear. He said vaguely, 'Just like that day. She was screaming then. All her bloody fault. But for her, Dicky would be alive, and I . . .' His voice faded slightly, then he muttered, 'Poor old Dicky. Said he should drive, so that I could sit with the kid an' keep her quiet.' He shook his head, smiling as he relived the moment. 'To hell with that, I said!' Plaster fell on his mouth but he did not notice it. 'I turned to slap her, and the damn car went off the road.'

Ainslie turned and looked at the girl beside him. All this time she had believed her husband to be innocent. Instead he must have been thrown clear, but had returned to the wrecked car to put his dead friend behind the wheel.

The great beam moved very slightly, bringing down more rubble into the room. As a faint breeze pushed through the wreckage and cleared some of the dust, Ainslie saw the hideous bloodstains on the opposite wall where the nurse had been cut down.

He said, 'Help is coming.'

Torrance stared at him. 'Oh, it's you. Never forget a face.' The beam dropped again and Torrance gave one last, terrible gasp.

Ainslie realized the screaming had stopped, too. He said, 'Come now, Natalie. It's over.' He led her out into the passageway where some soldiers were groping their way into the various rooms with axes and ropes.

Quinton said to a lance-corporal, 'Two dead back there, chum.'

Down the stairway, treacherous with rubble and broken glass. The whole place was a ruin.

Outside the main doors the army vehicles were on their sides, one blazing fiercely. The soldiers Ainslie had seen chatting were lying nearby, or what was left of them.

He made himself ask, 'Your sister, where is she?'

'In town. Not here.' She was clutching his arm while he tried to shield her from the sights and sounds around them.

Quinton said, 'The car seems all right. Shielded by the wall.' He opened the door. 'Better get away now. In case they come back for another go.'

Ainslie said quietly, 'Just a moment.'

He helped her into the car with the child and then retraced his steps to the hotel. It was on fire now, somewhere at the back, probably the kitchens. It was doubtful if anyone would try to put out the blaze. The old Royal was finished.

Ainslie paused only to retrieve a piece of one of the striped sun-blinds. Then he stopped to look down at the old Indian hall porter. He was dead, killed outright by the blast as he had hurried to do his duty.

Ainslie covered him with the sun-blind and said quietly, 'Poor old devil. You're best out of it.'

Then he returned to the car and put his arm around her shoulders.

'All right, John.'

They drove in silence for most of the way, too stunned by what had happened, too shocked to accept that they had survived.

At the last check-point before the harbour Quinton stopped the car and said, 'I'll ask the army where we've got to sign in. I lost my list when the bomb went off.'

Alone in the car, Ainslie said, 'I don't know how we're going to get out of all this mess, Natalie, but when we do, will you marry me?'

When she did not answer he added desperately, 'I've not much money, but we can manage, and in England we can take Frances to that expert, just as you wanted in the first place.'

She looked at him then, her eyes brimming with tears. 'You know the answer. I'd go anywhere with you, married or not.'

They both stared at the child with disbelief as she stood

against the driver's seat and put her arms round her mother's neck.

'Oh, darling Robert!' She could barely contain herself any more. 'Frances spoke to me! *She really did.* She tried to say something!' She hugged the three of them together. 'Now I *know* we're going to be all right!'

Ainslie let his mind drift, wondering how any man on earth could feel happiness in the middle of hell.

Quinton came back and took the wheel again. 'Got it.' He drove through the check-point and realized something tremendous had happened during his absence.

But being Quinton he said dryly, 'By the way, that policeman has reported me for dangerous driving!'

Ainslie put his hand over the girl's torn dress, as if by doing so he could eliminate the memory of that final hurt and Torrance's terrible secret.

It was terrifying when you thought about it. If they had obeyed the policeman's order to stay off the road during the air raid, the bomb would have fallen anyway. But she would have been in the room with her husband. She had been sitting directly beneath the beam which had killed him.

Ainslie squeezed her shoulder and felt her move against him, lost in her own thoughts.

She might even be thinking of this latest irony of war. That Japanese pilot would never know that the bomb which had killed the old hall porter, and God knows how many others, had provided some sort of shock which had given the child another chance. True or not, it was a first real hope, and that was more than they had dreamed of.

The car halted outside a plain white building where some nurses and official-looking civilians were checking arrivals.

They all stopped doing their work to turn and stare at the two dirty and dishevelled sailors, the black-haired girl with the dress torn from her shoulders, and the small child who was carrying a dusty but intact elephant.

Quinton watched Ainslie as he guided them through the door and then very slowly lit a cigarette.

'I'll bet that made their day.' He blew out a stream of smoke. 'It did mine!'

Ainslie sat at his desk and stared at the piles of stapled signals. Despite the danger and threat of invasion, nothing seemed to slow down the tide of signals.

Opposite him, in the other chair, Lieutenant (E) Halliday watched him gravely. Halliday seemed to symbolize all that was happening to their own special world. Waiting and worrying, wondering what the next day or hour might bring.

Outside the hull it was halfway through the forenoon, the harbour bathed in smoky sunlight. Smoke from another air raid, although this time a fighter had managed to shoot down the enemy bomber. Some of the smoke was the Jap's funeral pyre.

But it could not go on. Sooner or later *Soufrière* was going to get hit, or be so damaged by a near miss she would have to be abandoned. The signals from London and the French admiral were nothing to do with it any more. Ainslie knew that most, if not all, of his company felt the same. They had got this far, and they *needed* the submarine now. Not just as a weapon, but as a kind of symbol.

He leafed through Halliday's list of repairs and wondered how the engineer officer had managed it.

'Good, Chief. You and your chaps have done well.'

Halliday watched him, seeing the quick, nervous movements of Ainslie's hands. But if half he had heard was true, things would be far worse but for the Torrance girl. He thought of his own wife in their little house near Tower Bridge, and hoped fervently she was safe. Women could be a curse, or they could be stronger anchors than anything man-made.

Ainslie said, 'The enemy are keeping very quiet on the mainland, or so HQ informs me. The occasional artillery duel, but not much more.' He looked up as someone tapped his door. 'Come in.'

He heard the door open, and as the curtain slid aside he saw the two French lieutenants. Very smart in their white uniforms, yet so different from one another in every way.

Ainslie said, 'I'll discuss the fuel with you later, Chief.' He and Halliday looked at each other. Just a glance, but it was enough.

As the curtain swished across the door again Ainslie said, 'You've probably guessed why I've sent for you.' He picked up the top folder of signals. 'As you are well aware, your part in this whole operation was to assist my company if some problem arose with the mechanical and electrical equipment. Something which the instructors in England might have forgotten. You did all that, and more. But things have changed. Your naval staff in London have requested through the Admiralty that I should put all Free French naval personnel in the next convoy out of Singapore. Number One is dealing with that now, and I will speak with the men myself before they leave.'

The only Frenchmen still aboard were six petty officers and the two lieutenants.

Ainslie looked at each in turn. Lucas, slight, even delicate. Cottier, tall and outwardly confident.

Then he added quietly, 'As officers you are entitled to go with the others, or remain on board. If you choose the latter, I can promise you nothing, for I know nothing. You must decide. When the convoy leaves it will be too late. After that, any available vessel will be for dependants and priority cases.'

Lucas looked around the cabin, remembering when he had stepped aboard with Ainslie, the mad rush to get the submarine under way without a last-minute disaster. On the face of it, why should he stay? This was not part of his war, the one where he could hit at the Germans and use his skills against those who brutally occupied his country. To die out here, or to rot in some Japanese prison camp would keep him even further away from his family in Nantes, his parents and young sister.

He felt the sweat running down his spine, the urgency made worse by the knowledge that the petty officers he had controlled were already preparing to leave.

Lucas felt he would never really understand the British, but he had come to like them very much. And he would have only the Channel between him and France, whereas here. . . .

Cottier stared at a point above Ainslie's shoulder. He was more surprised at his feelings than he had imagined possible. His beloved Paris was under the jackboot, but he had accepted that. Sooner or later it would re-emerge as the finest city on earth, and until that time he had his own life to consider.

He thought, too, of the French command in London. They were the same in every way. Full of advice when the hard work was done by someone else.

And *Soufrière* was French. No amount of tea and those terrible corned-beef sandwiches which the British seemed to thrive on would change that.

Cottier made up his mind. 'I will remain, *Capitaine*.'

Lucas glanced at him, amazed. He disliked Cottier's suave superiority, his perfect manners, his obvious charm. He had fully expected him to leave with the rest.

Ainslie nodded and looked at Lucas. 'What about you?'

It was on the tip of his tongue to repeat what Halliday had told him about Lucas. Of his long hours, working like a demon to get the submarine's machinery in perfect order again. Ainslie knew a lot about Lucas's situation, of his family in France. How would he have felt? How would he still feel if Natalie was left behind, trapped by the enemy if Singapore fell without warning?

Lucas said softly, 'I, too.' He looked at the deck. 'It is better I stay.'

When they had left, and after he had said good-bye to the French petty officers, Ainslie sat for a long time in his cabin, thinking about them, and all the others around the world who were trying to win a war. Boys for the most part, led by other boys. It took the steel of the Hallidays and the Quintons to give them a hope in hell.

That night, as he lay on his bunk fully dressed, staring up into the humid darkness, he listened to the boat's sounds all around him. The noises which gave every sort of vessel personality, life, if you wished to call it so. Landsmen laughed about it. But it was there all the same.

He closed hs eyes, thinking of Natalie, how she had been when he had last seen her. To get her to safety, no matter where, was all that counted now.

Ainslie awoke, breathless, as the telephone buzzed in his ear. He struggled with the light switch above the bunk, his ears probing beyond the hull, searching for bombs or gunfire.

'Captain?' There was an unnatural edge to his voice.

'SDO here, sir. I'll put you through.'

Ainslie sat up, peering at his watch. *Put you through*. What was the man talking about, and why couldn't it go by way of the switchboard?'

'Hello? Granger speaking.'

Ainslie relaxed his body piece by piece as he pictured the round little admiral and his pipe.

'Sir?'

'The enemy have landed on the island. They're attacking in full strength, landing craft, pontoons, the lot.' A pause. 'Are you there?'

'Yes, sir.'

So it had happened. He had expected it, waited for it, but it was a shock all the same. And an incredible feat, too. Two months to the day since those first Japanese troops had smashed ashore in the north of Malaya, and now they were here. The sudden realization made him chill all over.

Granger sounded very calm. 'My next convoy will have to be brought forward.' He gave a short laugh. 'So I thought you might like to know at once.'

The line went dead, and Ainslie sat back, wondering how the admiral had found the time to think of his problems.

There was a rap on the door and Quinton came into the cabin. He was fully dressed and wearing a revolver.

'Signal, sir. They're invading. First-degree readiness for everyone. Be prepared for anything from riots to Acts of God!' He seemed stunned by the news. 'What do you reckon the bastards will try and do now?'

Ainslie walked to the hand-basin and slopped some lukewarm water over his face. It tasted faintly of diesel.

'Try and split the defences like they did in Malaya. Then they'll go all out for the reservoirs. When they capture those, it's all over.'

Quinton smiled briefly. 'Well, at least we know. I'll go and rouse the hands, though most of them have been standing-to half the night.'

Ainslie remained staring at the door. One thing was certain, he would be getting new orders now.

Then he left the cabin and made his way through the boat, as he had done so many times. Silent figures stood near their stations, drinking tea, heads cocked as if to detect something alien.

He nodded to Lucas and Halliday at their switchboard and then began to climb the long polished ladder to the bridge. There the heavy machine-guns were already manned and ready, the long barrels black against the stars.

Forster and Ridgway were on the bridge, watching the darkened city, the pin-pricks of bright lights beyond, flak or artillery fire, it was too far off to determine.

Forster said, 'We heard rifle fire just now, sir. More looting, I expect.'

He did not know if he cared or not. The dramatic news of Daphne's husband being lost at sea, his own change of heart, all had moulded together in new uncertainty. No signals, no messages. Was she all right? Or had she carried out her threat to kill herself? She might have done it without even knowing she was a widow.

Ridgway said, 'If we have to move, sir, I'll not be able to get any more torpedoes for us. We'll have to make do with what we've got left.'

Ainslie barely heard him. He was watching the spreading glow in the sky and remembering all those who were not here to see it. And he thought, too, of Natalie and the child, somewhere over there in the shadows, waiting for the order to embark. He had even seen the old yacht *Lady Jane* standing ready to make her most dangerous voyage ever. And ironically, almost alongside, Torrance's brand-new launches.

He must see her again before she left. It might be the last time. He tried to shut it from his mind, the effort making his head throb. To be parted, after all this, was worse than dying. She had given him a purpose, the one thing he had not realized he had lacked.

Ainslie thought of the boat resting beneath his feet. He would have to watch and examine every move he made. He had heard of captains being caught off guard when their skill and vigilance were at a premium. A home bombed, an unfaithful wife, a sick child. The pitfalls which could blunt a man's ability. Could kill all who relied on it.

Menzies crossed the gratings, his binoculars hanging around his neck.

'Proper Brock's Benefit, isn't it, sir? I'll no be sorry to leave here.'

Ainslie looked at the yeoman's sturdy profile. So confident. No note of doubt.

Below the conning tower, sealed in their tiny hangar, Christie and his observer, Sub-Lieutenant Jones, crawled under and around the little seaplane. In spite of the battering which *Soufrière* had received, nothing on the aircraft had been damaged which they had been unable to repair. By bribery, theft and

Christie's hard-won ability to make do they had got the seaplane in full running order.

Jones stared at the stripped Lewis gun which he had fixed to
his cockpit and said, 'Now we'll be able to look after ourselves,
eh, Jack?'

Christie grinned. Jones was a simple soul, and if he still believed in miracles it could do no harm.

He said, 'I just want to get out of here.' He drew a great
breath and stared at the riveted steel around the folded wings.
'To breathe again.'

Jones was not sure if he meant the hangar or Singapore. They
had survived this far. He could see no reason why they should
not go all the way.

Lieutenant Farrant was also busy. In a crisp white boiler suit
and carrying a hand-lamp, he was exploring his turret with slow,
infinite care, followed at a discreet distance by Sub-Lieutenant
Southby and his senior gunnery rating. Farrant did not really
need the lamp, for the whole turret was ablaze with light, the
white painted top and sides adding to an appearance of precision and sterility. The two big guns, elevated slightly so that
their shining breeches glittered like gold, the loading trays, the
snaking cables and wires, the protective guard above the ammunition hoist, it was Farrant's world.

Farrant looked aft, at the two seats where he and Southby
would control and fire the guns. He bent over and picked up a
scrap of cotton waste and handed it to the gunlayer. Then he
wrote a few notes in his little book and continued on his way.

Southby followed, sweating. Another one for the high jump.
How dare he soil Farrant's turret? He felt the urge to laugh, or
burst out crying. He had been ashore in charge of a working
party and had seen the tragedy of Singapore at close quarters.
After an air attack, the bodies smouldering where they had
fallen, people scurrying past with barely a glance. The stench
and the flies. People weeping, others too drunk to know or care
what was happening.

He collided with Farrant before he realized the lieutenant had
stopped and was peering at him.

Farrant rasped, 'We are going to *fight*, Sub. Have no doubt
about that.' His face thrust forward until it was almost touching
his. 'So get a grip on yourself! It's what you trained to do,
right?'

'Yes. I – I mean, yes, sir.'

Southby saw the gunlayer watching sympathetically, but was more aware of Farrant's mood. He was looking forward to it. The new paint had been his idea, too. The seaman who had been disembowelled right here on the upper ladders of the turret had turned the place into a bloody nightmare.

All Farrant had said afterwards was, 'They had far worse to put up with at the Nile and Trafalgar, I should imagine! So let's get it cleaned up!'

He was mad, or nearly so. Perhaps that was why he was so good at it. You could never fault Farrant on anything.

Outside on the casing Quinton stooped to peer at the water lapping along the saddle tank. He was checking the moorings, stretching his legs, breaking the tension in his own way.

He had heard the click of machinery from within the turret. The way he went on about his guns, it was a wonder Farrant didn't request to have his bunk in there as well.

A louder bang than usual echoed across the water, and he guessed that the sappers were demolishing a bombed building for some reason. He saw a red glow spread momentarily over the harbour, revealing the scattered wrecks and the vessels which still waited for sailing orders.

He thought of the explosion at the hotel, and could still feel it ringing in his eardrums whenever he bent over. The picture of the enraged drunkard swaying about the room, the girl's face, beautiful in defiance, the child taking his hand after they had staggered from the collapsed room.

Another explosion rolled out of the darkness. The poor devils out there must be terrified.

And after this, what then? Would the Japs reach Australia? He clenched his jaw, making himself face the possibility.

Right in the bows the sentry was leaning on the safety rail, his hands in his pockets as he watched the city.

Quinton stood beside him.

'All quiet, Evans?'

'Aye, sir.' As Quinton turned to go he asked, 'We goin' to be all right, sir?'

Quinton looked at the conning tower's silhouette. The skipper was up there, hoping and praying like the rest of them. *Just one more time*, they always said in the past.

'I bloody hope so. I can't take much more Pommie beer!' He

strolled aft, knowing the seaman was grinning, relieved. It was that easy.

A mile or so from the submarine, Rear-Admiral Granger sat in his office, smoking his pipe and drinking coffee with barely a break. Typewriters clattered busily in the adjoining room and dust filtered down occasionally from the ceiling. Distant gunfire, bombs or the Royal Engineers and their detonations, he neither knew nor cared. He looked at the watch on his fat wrist.

Half past four in the morning. He smiled grimly towards the typewriters. A few weeks back and you'd not get anyone to work in the afternoon, let alone at this ungodly hour.

Doors banged and feet shuffled in the corridor, then the admiral strode into Granger's office and said, ' 'Morning, Arnold. Sorry to burst in like this. How's the convoy coming along?'

Granger removed the pipe from his mouth. He had been biting it so hard his jaw ached.

'Fair, sir. A few days yet.'

The admiral, as neat and tidy as if he had just come from divisions, said, 'You'll have to get them to sea tomorrow, Arnold. The enemy is breaking through already.' He shrugged. 'So you had better get started now. I've instructed the maintenance commander to give you all the aid he can.' He hesitated. 'Sorry, but there it is.'

Granger stared at him, unable to grasp it. 'We're pulling out, sir?'

The admiral's austere features did not alter. 'There is talk of a parley with Yamashita, the Japanese field commander.'

Granger sat down heavily. Surrender already. It was incredible. Overwhelming.

'However, Arnold, you'll do what you must. The point is, we've received an intelligence report about another naval force heading down from Cam-Ranh Bay. It's under the command of Vice-Admiral Ozawa, a very efficient officer. I met him once at a review. This force is destined for Sumatra, I'm told, so you see why I'm concerned.'

'Yes, sir.' Granger needed no map or chart now. The enemy warships would be passing through the same area as his convoy. 'I understand.'

'Good.' The admiral turned to go. 'So I'm sending the *Soufrière*.'

Granger stared at the closed door. *I'm glad I didn't have to make that decision*. Then he thought of the crowded buildings along the waterfront, the fleet of small and unsuitable vessels he had under his command and the people who were depending on him to get them away.

He picked up the telephone. 'Get me the duty signals officer.'

16

Now or Never

'WARN the motor room to obey telegraphs.'

Ainslie pulled his oilskin more tightly about his throat and craned over the side of the bridge. The rain squall would be short but was without any kind of relief. Beneath the oilskin his body felt as wet as if he were naked.

It was as if the rain had come as a curtain for their final departure, and to hide the island's own misery from outsiders.

'Standing by, sir.' Ridgway and Southby were with him on the bridge, subdued like the rest of the men who were preparing to get under way.

He saw Southby's wet face shine suddenly in another explosion from the shore. It had been like this all day. Rumours, bombings, gunfire, sudden death.

Under his shoes he felt the big submarine quivering, the beast scenting the prey, getting excited. He checked himself. It was like a madness, an end of everything. Just when you thought there was hope. A chance.

Ainslie recalled the faces of his officers when he had told them of their orders. To attack and delay an enemy naval force. Not a couple of ships, but a whole bloody squadron. He could feel for them now as he had then when he had listened to his own voice, unreal in the confined space of the wardroom.

If the Frenchmen had second thoughts about their decisions to remain with him they had concealed them well.

He could have suggested that the intelligence reports might be wrong, they often were. But if they were all going to die, they should be told the reason. Ainslie had shown them on the chart the huge span of the South China Sea, the enemy's destination, sweeping beneath Singapore and on to Sumatra. The final seal on the trap.

Quinton had said softly, 'At least we know the Nips don't

have a carrier! We saw to that!' But nobody had been able to smile.

If only there was some hope. The orders had touched on the other naval forces in this vast area. Even the old cruiser *Exeter*, the darling of the River Plate battle with the German *Graf Spee*, was somewhere out here. Had some high authority put in more ships and planes earlier things would have been very different.

Ainslie thought about it again while he watched Voysey's shaded torch moving along the casing as he checked the last mooring wires. But would they have been so different? The Japanese seemed to have planned every move to the last bullet.

He had seen his men lining the *Soufrière*'s casing and upper deck that same afternoon as Granger's convoy had got under way. If they felt resentment and dismay at their orders, they must have understood the desperate need for them. Vessel after vessel had headed out from the harbour, most of them too small even to send a wash as far as the moored submarine.

Along the waterfront a crowd had also watched. Husbands, friends, or merely those who had hung on to a hope of getting away. Now the other fighting would begin, the bribery and the spent morals of betrayal, that was the only description for it.

Guided by a small patrol boat, like a sheepdog with its flock, the convoy had wended its way amongst the wrecks and shoals, until the craft were strung out for several miles. Some fighters had circled overhead, and to seaward three destroyers had waited to act as escort. Ainslie had never seen anything like it in his life, not anywhere. It was pathetic, and moving, hopeless, but as brave a sight as ever painted on canvas.

'Out starboard engine clutch.'

It took real effort to concentrate, to ensure that each order was repeated and executed. He would have to go astern from the quay before making his exit. There was a wrecked freighter leaning against the piles, and an upturned hull of some kind right behind. It was a wonder *Soufrière* had not joined them.

The starboard engine stopped to be replaced instantly by the electric motor. The diesels were not fitted with reversing gear and the electric motors were used for all complicated manoeuvring. He would need to be quick about it. To drain the batteries would earn him little praise from Halliday and his men.

'Let go.'

'All gone aft! All gone forrard, sir!'

'Half astern starboard. Port thirty.'

Ainslie felt the responding quiver of the screw, the sudden surge of foam sweeping along the saddle tank as the boat began to go astern.

The quay was already fading into the gloom, and he thought he saw someone running along the top of it, waving, but he could not be certain.

'Stop starboard. Group up. Half ahead port.'

He felt *Soufrière* slowing down, the sudden rustle of noise as the watch on deck removed their oilskins. No more rain. Just a big, oily swell. Dull and unbroken.

Ainslie walked to the rear of the bridge, brushing past lookouts and gun crews. Men. Flesh and blood like himself. He ground his teeth together. *Stop it.*

Far enough now. 'In starboard engine clutch.'

A quick look round again. There was the little boat to lead them through the wrecks, a tiny blue sternlight rocking on the swell.

'Starboard thirty. Half ahead both engines.'

He stripped off the oilskin and took the towel from around his neck, rubbing his face and throat until it stung.

'Midships. Steady.' Ainslie peered at the gyro, seeing the blue sternlight over the screen like a moth. 'Steer one-three-zero.'

Again and again he heard the sullen boom of artillery, the deeper thuds of exploding shells. Ainslie thought of the convoy, pushing along through the darkness now at an average speed of seven knots. If Granger had had more time he could have split the craft into groups, but with so little left, and not enough escorts at his disposal, he had been forced to revert to the old rule. The speed of the convoy shall be that of the slowest ship in it.

The yacht *Lady Jane* had not been so unusual after all, Ainslie thought. He had seen every sort of vessel, including a coal-fired river gunboat which must have been launched before the Great War.

Ridgway lowered his night glasses. 'Coming to starboard, sir.'

'Very well. Starboard ten. Steady.'

The strangest coincidence had been the destroyer in charge of the escort. She had been the *Arielle*, the same ship which had taken from on the first leg of their attempt to seize the *Soufrière* from her French owners.

Quinton had been watching the destroyer wheeling round to count and check the line of escorted vessels and had said, 'Well, her skipper knows what it's all about now, right enough.'

'Ship's head one-three-five, sir.'

Farrant's head and shoulders appeared above the side of the bridge. 'All wires stowed and secured, sir. Permission to dismiss the casing party?'

'Carry on, Guns.'

They were clear of the worst part now, unless the lookouts sighted an unreported wreck across their path.

'Take over the con.'

He saw Ridgway step up into his place and then moved to the port side to watch the flickering fires on the land, the brilliant diamonds of drifting flares.

The convoy and its small escort was not much, but it was better than remaining in Singapore.

He wiped his face again, remembering her eyes, her struggle to appear unafraid.

If she had known about *Soufrière*'s orders . . .

A sixth sense jarred through his thoughts. 'Watch that piece to starboard. The swell seems to be breaking just there. Probably a submerged wreck or remains of one.' He waited until Ridgway had brought the submarine out and then back on course again.

Natalie. Up there somewhere, heading for the shelter of the islands.

Southby said, 'Sawle wants permission to come up with some cocoa, sir.' He sounded nervous.

Ainslie nodded. Trust Sawle. First things first. He would be making sandwiches at the gates of hell if asked.

'Launch is signalling, sir!' Menzies read the stabbing light slowly. 'Must be squaddies to send so badly!' Then he said, 'They say, *give them one for us*, sir.'

Ainslie took a mug of cocoa and stared at it blindly. *For us.* That was every mother's son being left behind.

'Make, *it will be an honour*, Yeo.'

He watched the little blue light begin to fall away as the boat curved round to allow *Soufrière* to pass.

Soon it was gone altogether, and drifting smoke had merged the distant fires and explosions into one angry glare.

To Ridgway he said, 'Have you got the feel of her?'

Ridgway bared his teeth. 'Aye, sir.'

'Then I'm going below to look at the plot. Call me instantly if . . .' He let it drop. The torpedo officer knew. They all did now.

Southby stepped up beside the lieutenant as Ainslie vanished through the hatch.

'I'll *never* forget it. I don't expect I'll ever see Singapore again.'

Ridgway trained his glasses above the screen. You probably won't see any land again, he thought sadly.

Aloud he snapped, 'Smart look out all round, lads. We'll be in open water soon.'

At the foot of the conning tower ladder Ainslie paused, his fingers still locked around the rungs like claws. He controlled his breathing and swallowed hard. When he turned and strode under the deckhead lights there was nothing on his face to betray his ache, his despair. He was the captain again.

'Periscope depth, sir.'

Ainslie nodded to the stoker and crouched down to seize the grips.

It was noon. All the previous night and this morning they had worked their way south-east, altering course occasionally to investigate a sound, an echo, or a patch of smoke on the horizon. Somewhere to the west of their position Granger's convoy would be crawling southwards, keeping close to or amongst the many islands off the Malacca Strait, ready to disperse and hide if they were sighted and attacked. A snail's pace.

Ainslie blinked rapidly as the periscope gingerly broke surface. The sea's face had changed yet again. Greener now, with a dull blue edge to the horizon. A very pale sky, almost colourless, and the same unending swell. It was hard to prevent the lens from being covered and then laid bare with alarming suddenness.

Nothing. Not a bloody thing. He lifted the lens and searched around the sky, wincing as the sun probed into his eye. Where the hell were the Japs?

'Down periscope.' He straightened his back and glanced at Quinton. 'Thirty metres. Continue patrol routine.'

He crossed to the chart table as the pumps hissed into life and the hydrophone tell-tales began to move again.

Suppose the admiral's information was wrong? The Japanese ships might be anywhere. But it certainly looked promising enough. Some two hundred miles south-east of Singapore was Banka Island, an obvious stepping-stone on to the coast of Sumatra. Harbours, airfields, oil, it would be a prize indeed.

They had not missed them, anyway. Even the intelligence department would have known about another invasion.

'Thirty metres, sir.'

'Very good. Tell the cook to rustle up some food.'

Quinton joined him by the table. 'Nothing yet, eh?'

Ainslie shook his head. Every hour gave the convoy another breathing space, a few more miles.

He said, 'The Jap admiral will know all about us. He might think we've left the area, but just in case we've not, he'll be taking no chances this time.'

Quinton sighed, his eyes on the planesmen. 'The Jap pilots probably took pictures of us in harbour. If not, there'll be plenty ready to sell them some when the white flag goes up.'

He spoke without bitterness, and Ainslie guessed he was thinking of the brief but heart-rending signal they had picked up during the night.

All hostilities were to cease on Singapore Island on fifteenth February when resistance would end and the British troops would lay down their arms. Lieutenant-General Percival would put the fate of his army and every living soul there into the enemy's hands from that moment.

'If only we knew how many ships there are, and what class. But by the time we're close enough to know that, they'll be on us like a ton of bricks.'

It was easy to share it with Quinton. It had always been like that.

'If they're coming, it will be this way.' Quinton rasped his hand across his chin. 'I'll bet they send some ships nearer to Singapore to pick off any escapees and slam the gate on the rest of them.' He leaned on the table, his armpits and spine making dark stains on his shirt. 'We need six boats for this job, not just us!'

'Could I suggest something, sir.'

Ainslie turned and saw Christie looking at him. 'Shoot.'

'If you're prepared to risk surfacing in broad daylight, I'll have a go at spotting for you.' He grinned. 'It's not so daft as it sounds, sir.'

Quinton nodded. 'Too damn right. It makes sense.'

'Hold on, you two.' Ainslie took time to examine the chart. Through the next group of islands. The water was deep enough, and the cover should be good. He felt the edge of excitement moving inside him, and said, 'Grasping at straws. D'you realize what you're asking?'

Christie shuffled his feet. 'I do, sir. She's a big submarine, and on the surface you'd be a sitting duck.'

'It's *you* I'm talking about.' Ainslie watched him gravely. 'If I have to leave you, you'll be all on your own. You will have to ditch, or land in the islands. Or you could go looking for the convoy until your petrol runs out.'

Christie nodded. 'I've thought about it. It's worth a go, sir.'

Forster said helpfully, 'I'll get you some good charts. Just in case, Jack.'

'Thanks.' Christie sounded so relieved that the others stared at him. 'I'll fetch my mate.' He hesitated by the watertight door. 'One thing, sir. I'll not let the bloody Nips take me, alive that is.'

Another hour passed while they moved closer to the next huddle of islands. Using both periscopes, they examined every angle and bearing without sighting even a gull.

Ainslie had the feeling it would be now or never. He compared his notes with Forster's calculations and checked the estimated position of the enemy force on the chart.

Repeatedly he broke off to try and plot the convoy's progress. Allowing for perfect conditions and no breakdowns they had still covered very little distance. He kept thinking of her face as he had held her against him. The thrusting, jostling throng by the jetty stairs had been a blurred background, somehow meaningless.

As the minutes had passed the din had grown louder and more threatening. Several times the police and soldiers guarding the waterfront had been forced to drive the crowds back to avoid swamping the boats below.

He had seen Natalie's sister walking with some other women down the heavily guarded stairs to the boat which would take them out to an old freighter.

She had paused and looked at them, seemingly oblivious to the crowds and the danger still ahead.

'We're still running, Commander Ainslie.' She had nodded to her sister. 'I hope it works out this time.'

Then it had been time to go. A quick hug, a brief kiss, and he had seen her moving away from the jetty, almost hidden by waving arms as the refugees made a last contact with those being left behind.

He could remember the child, too. Exactly. Like a photograph. Her eyes had seemed too large for her face as he had stooped on his knees and kissed her.

'Take care,' he had said. What empty words when he had needed to say so much to both of them.

Ainslie took a towel and wiped his face again. Then he un-buttoned his shirt and did the same to his chest. As if he had to be clean, to be fresh.

'Periscope depth again.'

Ainslie glanced at the Asdic compartment, but there was no warning from the operators.

He peered at the sea, the nearest island misty-green with a low necklace of surf on one side.

'Sir!' It was Forster on the other periscope. 'Boat at red four-five!'

Ainslie clenched his jaw and swung the periscope smoothly on the bearing, clicking it to full power as the boat edged across his sights.

It was rolling heavily on the swell, tipping this way and that, as if trying to rid itself of its lolling passengers.

He hear Forster whisper, 'Oh, my God.'

There were about a dozen in the boat, and but for their blist-ered faces and staring eyes could have been alive as they jerked and nodded to the motion.

Tall splinters stood like quills from the hull, and he could see that the plane must have crossed and re-crossed the boat with its machine-guns until the pilot was satisfied.

Two had been women, no more than girls. The rest were soldiers. God alone knew where they had been escaping from or to, but it had ended here.

'Down periscope.' He glanced at Quinton. 'Diving stations. We're going to get Christie airborne.'

The klaxon squawked loudly, and Halliday stood over his

panel and switchboard, hands on his hips like a schoolmaster.

Ainslie thought of Christie, how they had gone over the plan, what there was of it. If he sighted nothing, it might mean it was really a false alarm. If he saw the enemy, it would give *Soufrière* room to manoeuvre.

But he kept thinking of the drifting boat. The guilty people who had allowed it to happen should be made to see it, to take off the identity tags, to meet those staring, terrified eyes. One of the girls had been wearing an Australian bush hat. Someone had been trying to shade her from the glare when hell had burst in on them.

It could have been Natalie.

'Standing by, sir.'

Ainslie tightened the strap of his binoculars and ran quickly up the ladder to loosen the upper locking wheel.

'*Surface!*'

The unchanging pattern. Grim faces, water sluicing out of the bridge, the scrabble of fingers and feet to reach the right place in a minimum of seconds.

Strange how you expected the air to be cool. It was like an oven.

The binoculars swung over the water, ignoring the distant boat, searching for danger.

'Open the hangar. Stand by to fly off aircraft.'

Surfaced, hangar wide open. This was the most vulnerable moment.

He heard the hiss of compressed air, the squeak of metal, and knew the catapult was being guided from the hangar.

He had thought it before. A million times. *Now or never.*

'Affirmative.'

He wished he had said good luck to Christie. *For us.*

With a snarling roar the little seaplane hurtled along the catapult, and after a hesitant dip towards the clear water lifted steeply and headed for the sun.

'Secure hangar.' Quick look at his watch. 'Dive when ready, Number One.'

As the seamen, followed by the yeoman of signals, scurried from the bridge, Ainslie took another slow look at the drifting boat. Like silent spectators. With all the time in the world.

'Dive, dive, dive!'

He slammed the hatch over his head.

239

Christie peered through his goggles at the altimeter and then thumped it with his fist. It was jammed. But what the hell anyway? That was the trouble with this aircraft. Sealed in a damp hangar, thrown about diving and surfacing, shaken by depth-charges. The men who built it had known a thing or two.

At least the compass was working. He settled more comfortably in his cockpit and pointed the propeller boss towards the nearest island.

He had known that the others had thought him mad. Never volunteer for anything. That's what they always said. But to get out, free of the constricting steel, had seemed like a reward.

Christie twisted round to look at his observer. He was the same, he thought, glad to be in the air.

He switched on his intercom. 'More like it, eh Jonesy?'

Jones bobbed his head and swung the stripped Lewis from side to side, like something from the Royal Flying Corps patrolling above the trenches.

The island seemed to rise to meet them, and Christie saw the seaplane's shadow flitting above the green scrub like a crucifix. He thought of the drifting boat, all the other dead and half-demented souls between here and Singapore.

Jones said, 'Two more islands up front, Jack. After them we might see something.'

Christie nodded and groped for his binoculars. There were a few canoes, or prahus, lying on one tiny beach, and he wondered if they were being used by escaping troops, or natives too frightened to show themselves. He turned round in his cockpit, searching for the *Soufrière*, but she had dived, and was probably heading towards the channel between the islands.

He smiled to himself, hearing Jones singing softly into the intercom. He always sang the same one, to the tune of *Tipperary*. 'That's the wrong way to tickle Mary, that's the wrong way I know. . . .'

He eased back the stick and pulled the nose up over a ridge-backed hill, the propeller blades making a silver circle in the glare.

Jonesy was probably right. Over the next island and we'll see for bloody miles. After that, we'll be spectators. Nothing worse.

The little seaplane growled through a patch of haze, and there below the wing was the sea again.

Christie gasped as Jones punched his shoulder and yelled, 'Bloody hell! Look at them!'

It had all happened so suddenly. Nothing was ever as you expected it.

Christie tilted the aircraft over, kicking the rudder hard round as he stared at the ships directly beneath him. He tried to keep his mind clear, to control the plane and to count those grey shapes.

He swore to himself, twisting the seaplane from side to side. *Here comes the bloody flak.*

Puff-balls of brown smoke drifted past, lazily, harmlessly, but the plane rocked and plunged, and Christie saw two jagged holes appear in the port wing.

'I'm going down, Jonesy!'

He put the plane into a steep dive, shutting his mind to bursting flak and the jarring slam of splinters. He had to get a closer look. So that *Soufrière* would know. Be ready.

He heard Jones whooping like a lunatic, then the sharp stutter from his Lewis gun as he poured a burst towards the nearest warship, a destroyer, with her guns already tracking round to follow them.

'That's the stuff, Jonesy!' He had caught the madness, too.

A shoulder of hillside jutted out to shield him from the ships. As if they had never been. Christie thought frantically. Remembering, putting the pieces together.

A big cruiser, and least three destroyers. And what looked like two camouflaged troopers, too. They must have paused to put men ashore to search the islands. He thought of the drifting boat and all the others he had seen.

Another vessel swam across his vision, a smaller one, but firing without pause as the seaplane rose above the land again. Shells, tracer, the whole bloody shooting match this time.

Christie continued to weave from side to side. A torpedo bomber, even an old 'Stringbag', would be better than this. Just to lob a tin-fish into that bastard. He heard Jones cursing as the gun jammed, then the click as he slammed on another magazine and opened fire once more.

The submarine was probably in mid-channel now, and the Japanese ships would be right there, waiting for her, or anything else which had been set to delay them.

He saw a pale crescent of beach on the next island, two hills he could fly between and then . . . The plane gave a tremendous jerk, and he felt a pain stab through his flying boot like a white-hot iron.

'Christ, Jonesy! That was a bit close!'

He looked round and saw the observer hanging half out of the cockpit, his arms spread and bouncing in the wind. He had been hit in the head and his goggles were filled with blood.

Christie turned back towards the enemy, gasping as the pain lanced through him.

'I'm sorry, Jonesy! I really am!'

What was he saying? He felt a sort of terror and peered down at his leg. There was blood everywhere, and he saw the sea speeding beneath him through the splinter holes, and realized that the starboard float had also been blasted away.

He laughed weakly. 'A plane with one bloody leg!'

More bangs, and a smoke cloud which seemed to cling to the cockpit like gas.

Christie croaked, 'No good, Jonesy. We're going into the drink. The skipper will never know in time. Not now, chum.'

As if in agreement, the dead observer bobbed and swayed across his useless machine-gun.

'Oh, God, the pain!' The agony seemed to clear his mind like a scalpel. If he got through the hills and did a sharp turn to starboard to gain height, he might still be able to let Ainslie know. He opened the throttle wide. 'Come on, old girl. I bloody taught you to understand English, didn't I?'

Shells exploded above and below him, for as the seaplane regained height and headed for the next island, it presented itself to every ship like a pheasant at a shoot.

Pieces flew from the fuselage, and Christie gave a great cry as a splinter smashed into his side like an axe, numbing him, driving away his breath.

Oh, dear God, help me. The words unspoken or yelled aloud went unheard as Christie nursed the controls and headed past the nearest hill. Up, come on, bit more. Oh, God, *help me.*

More flak, bright balls of tracer, ripping at the battered air-craft, closing in like fiery claws.

There was the sea again. Bright and clear-green.

Christie leaned forward to look at it, his head touching the perspex shield. He saw oil spurting around the cowling, the first tails of smoke from the engine.

The sea looked beautiful. Decent.

A few shells pursued the seaplane, but most of the ships were once more hidden by the islands.

'Just like Tahiti, Jonesy! You an' I'll set up there after this bloody lot's over. I'll teach you to fly . . . you see . . . *Jonesy*!'

He tried to turn but the pain gripped him like a vice.

The seaplane hit the sea and exploded, burning debris splashing down in a wide circle. Eventually there was nothing.

17

A Symbol

EVERYONE heard the roar as Christie's seaplane exploded in the channel. It was more of a sensation than a sound, and it murmured around in the *Soufrière*'s hull long after the remains had been scattered across the bottom.

Ainslie stood back from the periscope as it hissed into its well. He did not see it or the pale-faced stoker with his switch, only that last lingering picture, made more terrible by the lens's impartial silence.

He had watched the seaplane lift desperately above the island, weaving and falling away like a stricken bird. Pursued all the while by shellbursts and tracer, its own smoke trail marking each painful yard of the way.

When it had dived into the water and burst apart in one vivid flash, the sudden sound against the hull had seemed far worse. Like an intrusion.

Even with their backs turned, the men in the control room were looking at him.

Quinton asked, 'Did he manage to make any signal, sir?'

Ainslie nodded, hardly daring to speak. 'Yes. The bravest signal I ever saw.'

Almost to himself he added, 'He could have flown off, hidden, saved himself and Jones. He might have done anything. But he didn't. We don't know how many of the enemy there are, but by God, we know *where* they are now!'

He picked up the microphone of the submarine's intercom.

'This is the captain. That explosion was our seaplane.' He swallowed hard. 'They've given us a chance to get one in first. Let me just say this. When things hot up, remember all those helpless people in the convoy. When the tubes are empty I want them reloaded and set quicker than ever before. And if it falls to a gun action, I shall expect the best.' He felt his eyes sting like needles. 'The best you can give. That's all.'

A murmur of approval ran around the control room, and Halliday said quietly to Lucas, 'Quite a man, eh? I'm glad it's him and not me.'

Forster gripped the chart table to control his emotions. All the worries he had created and tried to disperse meant nothing now. He was going to be killed, but it didn't seem to matter.

The fat coxswain adjusted his buttocks on his steel seat and said gruffly, 'I reckon we'll stand a good chance, sir.' He chuckled. 'I'm all set for a shore job, y'see.'

Menzies, the yeoman, shook his head. 'Silly old sod. You? Never in a thousand bloody years, man!'

Ainslie was at the chart table, his mind clearing reluctantly as he tried to forget what he had witnessed. His own words had been totally inadequate, trite. He had wanted to say so much. To tell them what their trust and courage meant to him, and all those people who would never know about their sacrifice.

The enemy was beyond those islands. Probably steering towards Sumatra as reported. They had no carrier, but more to the point, had no catapult aircraft either. Otherwise someone would have chased after the little seaplane. To shoot it down before it could signal the danger, to discover where it had come from. So there could be no battleships in the Japanese force. They always carried aircraft.

He made up his mind. 'Revolutions for eight knots. Course zero-one-zero.'

He walked three paces back and forth and rested his hand on the vibrating plot table. Unless the enemy sent a ship through the channel to search for the wrecked seaplane, there was little immediate danger. He pictured the islands in his mind, overlapping, the deep water between them made treacherous by sudden twists and a swift undertow.

'Ship's head zero-one-zero, sir.'

Yet another look at the chart. He could feel Forster beside him, sense his despair and, strangely, a sort of elation.

'All right, Pilot?' Ainslie glanced at him gravely. 'You're very quiet.'

Forster licked his lips. 'I'll manage, sir.' He forced a grin. 'Thanks.'

For what? He said, 'Just here, Pilot. See this outcrop of rock on the chart.' He jabbed it with his brass dividers. 'That's a hell of a place to alter course in a hurry.' He watched the understanding on Forster's strained features. 'For them, not us.'

Ainslie reached over for a stop-watch and pressed it to begin, the red needle seeming to symbolize their remaining time better than any sand-glass.

'Up periscope.' It had better be right, or else it would all end now.

Ainslie swung the periscope in a slow arc. There was no longer any point in looking astern.

He checked his irregular breathing as he found the island he had just studied on the chart.

There was the high ridge and hill where Christie had appeared bracketed by shellbursts. Then the island sloped gently towards the sea, to a vague white ripple of surf which appeared to reach the shore of another island. But it was deceptive. The channel turned there to port. Wide, and if the survey was correct, deep enough for a submarine. Even the beast.

He could sense Ridgway watching him, his yeoman poised to begin feeding ranges and bearings into his precious machine.

'Bring tubes One to Eight to the ready.' Ainslie raised the lens slightly, but the sky was empty, the stains gone.

He watched the horizon's edge between the islands until his eye ached with strain.

'Port ten.'

He listened to the wheel, Gosling's deep breathing, and saw the opposite headland move slightly into the left side of his sights.

'Steady. Meet her, Swain.'

'Steady, sir. Course three-four-zero.'

Forster said quietly, 'Adjust to three-four-six degrees.' His voice was hushed, as if he was afraid to intrude between the submarine and her commander.

'Tubes standing by, sir, bow doors open.'

Another minute, maybe less. He could not recall keeping a periscope raised for so long. In any other ocean it would be suicide.

He tried not to think of Forster's little crosses on the chart where he had plotted the convoy's approximate position. If they could not delay the enemy, the convoy was finished. The Japanese admiral would be in too much of a hurry to complete his part of the overall operation to waste time. He would shell the brittle convoy to pieces, holding the agony and slaughter at arm's length.

Ainslie thought, too, of her face. Happy, wistful, loving. Their brief time together, and what it had meant, could have become, given the chance.

He said, 'Reduce to six knots.'

The motors' purr faded again as like a whale the *Soufrière* continued slowly through the channel.

The last vessel to fire on the seaplane had been close inshore, the tracer going almost straight up into the sky. That meant she was small, probably an anti-submarine escort or the like. No sense in giving her hydrophone operators a free gift.

He jammed his forehead hard against the rubber pad, his eye widening as if to consume every section of the picture.

He said, 'Ship, small destroyer, moving from right to left, bearing *that*. Range four thousand yards.' He wanted to swallow, to lick his lips, to shut out the flat tones of Ridgway's yeoman, the click of the machine. 'Here comes the next. Fleet destroyer.' He watched the second ship, further to seaward, on the smaller destroyer's quarter, making them look like one long silhouette.

'Tubes One to Four, *stand by*!'

The deck quivered very slightly under his feet. Probably the undertow, but it felt as if *Soufrière* was yearning for the killing to begin.

'Fire One!' He felt the sensitive jerk run through his fingers. 'Fire Two! Carry on by stop-watch!'

He was already turning the periscope to starboard as, like an armoured giant, the cruiser moved slowly into his lens. Bridge upon bridge, it was hard to tear his eyes away and seek out the rest of the force. Two destroyers, standing well out from the land, and then a pair of tall-sided merchantmen, their hulls garish with dazzle paint, troop transports for the invasion of Sumatra.

He swung the periscope back again and fastened on to the cruiser.

'Heavy cruiser, bearing *that*.'

The hull gave a great lurch as if they had hit a wreck, and Ridgway said tightly, 'One hit.' Another violent explosion echoed through the water, made more persistent by the confines of the channel.

Ainslie saw the small destroyer erupting smoke and flames,

while beyond her the larger one was slowing down as if to offer assistance. But she, too, was wreathed in smoke and falling spray, and as another explosion threw a sheet of flame high above her mast Ainslie realized that a torpedo had ignited her quarterdeck depth-charges.

'One to Four, reload!'

Ridgway said, 'That will be the last, sir.'

Ainslie watched the cruiser, scarcely able to believe it. Quinton had been right. The Jap admiral, Ozawa, had sent part of his force to share the honour of Singapore's humiliation and capture.

He saw the other destroyers shortening and heeling over in the fierceness of their turns, tearing back towards the islands from whence danger had suddenly emerged.

The cruiser was partly hidden now by the next island, increasing speed until her powerful escorts could reach her.

'Tubes Five to Eight, stand by!'

The men glanced at the deckhead as the sounds of a vessel breaking up grated against the hull. Dull explosions meant ammunition, fuel, heavy machinery tearing adrift. A ship dying.

Ainslie concentrated on the destroyers. 'Increase to eight knots again.'

Shellbursts made livid marks on the sea. The ships were firing at some wreckage, imagining it to be a periscope.

Forster said hoarsely, 'Time to alter course, sir. Steer three-zero-zero.'

'Down periscope.' Ainslie stood up and looked at Quinton. 'We'll give them two minutes.' He watched the gyro repeater ticking round on to the new course. 'Those destroyers will be on to us soon! We've got to cripple the big chap before then.' After that it would end. He knew it. They all knew it.

Ridgway reported, 'All tubes loaded, sir.' He almost smiled. 'Half their usual time, too.'

'Good.'

Ainslie clutched an overhead valve for support as something shuddered against the hull, rebounded away and then scraped along the port saddle tank like a giant saw.

'What the hell!'

Voysey, the second coxswain, shouted, 'Forrard hydroplane is jammed, sir!'

Ainslie looked at Quinton, knowing he was staring wildly, but unable to contain his disappointment, his anxiety.

It must have been part of the first destroyer, blasted clean away from the main hull to float barely buoyant across their path.

'*Emergency! Stand by to surface! Stand by . . . gun action!*'

Halliday looked away from his sweating assistants and muttered to Lucas, 'The bloody hydroplane was fractured when we repaired it! That last thump won't have done any good either!'

Ainslie felt strangely calm, removed from the hurrying figures, the bark of orders around him.

In spite of everything, he had failed. His men and the convoy. Natalie most of all.

'Blow all main ballast!'

Awkwardly, clumsily, *Soufrière* broke to the surface, and as the water parted across her streaming bows Ainslie saw the hydroplane buckled and snared by a piece of twisted metal. Part of the wreck, the destroyed striking back at her killer.

The first shell fell near the submarine even as the main engines roared into full throttle and Farrant's big turret purred smoothly towards the onrushing ships.

Ainslie had his glasses jammed against his eyes as he watched the nearest destroyer. But the cruiser was the real target. Neither the troopships nor the destroyers could harm the convoy, even though they were more than enough for a damaged submarine, unable to dive.

At his back he heard a lookout gasp incredulously, 'What the hell, Yeo? Why are you hoistin' the flag now, for Christ's sake? There's nobody to see!'

The halliards creaked, and Ainslie knew Menzies had hoisted the ensign to the periscope standards.

Menzies replied calmly, 'They will, laddie. And so will we.'

Ainslie swallowed hard. 'All tubes to the ready. Full salvo. Cruiser at green one-five, one thousand yards!' He adjusted the sighting bar, his fingers slippery with falling spray from the last shell. '*Commence firing!*'

Sitting rigidly on his steel chair at the rear of the turret, Lieutenant Farrant felt the torpedoes leaving their tubes, each one making the hull give a small shudder as it sped away towards the target.

Farrant thought no more about them than that. Through his

powerful sights he could watch the oncoming destroyer with something like detachment, more concerned with the complete silence below him where the two gun crews stood staring at the sealed breeches.

To his left, Sub-Lieutenant Southby was on a similiar seat, eyes pressed to his sights as he waited to report the fall of shot, to compensate for it, to do whatever Farrant dictated.

Just over two thousand yards across the submarine's starboard bow. Farrant tightened his grip on the brass trigger, hardly daring to breathe as he gauged the exact moment.

'Right gun . . . *shoot*!'

The gun hurled itself inboard, an empty shell case clattering away into a net even as the crew dashed forward to reload.

'Left gun . . . *shoot*!'

Farrant licked his lips, seeing the two white columns burst skywards just beyond the nearest ship.

'Down two hundred!'

The hull shivered violently as shells exploded nearby, and then gave a sudden convulsion which Farrant knew was at least one torpedo striking a target.

The crews were moving like robots, the breech workers and loaders thrusting in the gleaming projectiles, then stepping aside as the guns lifted for the next shoot.

They fired again, and Farrant saw the destroyer reel away from the exploding shells. Neither had scored a direct hit, but they burst so close to the vessel's bows they must have riddled her like a pepper-pot.

He grinned, tasting the acrid cordite, the grease and oil of his own trade.

It was almost worth being here just to imagine the enemy's surprise. To be mauled by a surface submarine would be hard to take. *Loss of face*.

Southby tore his eyes from the smoke-wreathed destroyer with the flashing guns to peer momentarily at Farrant. He was grinning, loving it, devoid of fear, of anything.

'Both guns ready, sir!'

'*Shoot!*'

A gunlayer was hurled from his seat, his head smashing against the steel turret like an egg, as a shell exploded right alongside. Splinters scraped and rattled against the steel, and Southby retched helplessly as the gunlayer continued to slide down below the mounting, his skull leaving a red smear on the paintwork.

'Turret refuses to train, sir! Mechanism is jammed!'

'Check, check, check!' Farrant yelled into the drifting smoke. 'Will they elevate? *Answer*, you dolt!'

The leading seaman nodded, his face ashen.

Farrant said almost offhandedly, 'That last shell must have sheared off one of the rollers.' He picked up his red handset. 'Captain, sir? We cannot train. Will you take over?'

Another tremendous explosion rocked the hull, and Farrant heard water cascading over the turret like a tidal wave.

High on the conning tower, Ainslie seized the handset and replied, 'Yes, Guns. Do what you can.' He crouched over the voice-pipe and yelled, 'Take over the con, Number One. The turret is trained on green four-five. Use the attack periscope to hold the boat on the same bearing.'

It was sheer lunacy, a wild instinct to hit back, which held all of them helpless.

On one side, the cruiser was still moving away, running before further torpedoes were sent after her. Her captain was not to know that the submarine which had probed between his ship and the escorts was without any more torpedoes, and now that the turret had jammed *Soufrière* herself had become the target.

That last shell had buckled the casing and killed two seamen on the bridge. Below his feet Ainslie could picture the others working like fiends, running the engines, searching for and plugging leaks, waiting for death to blast in upon them. They had not even had the satisfaction of seeing two torpedoes hit the cruiser below her after turrets. Not enough to sink her, but sufficient to make her head for safety, the quarterdeck barely feet above the water.

The turret shimmered in smoke as the two guns fired again, ripping the air apart as the shells screamed towards the destroyer. The second ship was heading away to port, to divide Farrant's fire, like hounds after a stag. When the turret failed to respond they would guess what had happened and speed round to *Soufrière*'s disengaged side. There were probably other ships already racing to their assistance, with ample time for destroying the convoy after they had put *Soufrière* on the sea-bed.

Figures bustled through the hatch and up over the side of the conning tower.

Ainslie seized Halliday's arm and yelled, 'Where the *hell* are you going, Chief?'

Halliday cringed down as another shell burst in the water within yards of the side. It made the hull boom like a drum and sent splinters cutting through the air above the bridge searching for victims.

He shouted, 'That forrard plane, Skipper! It's our only chance!' When Ainslie made to protest he added firmly, 'You can say what you will, court-martial me later if you like, but I'm going down there!'

He hauled himself after his small party of men, one of whom Ainslie saw was the Frenchman Cottier, an electric cutter over his shoulder like a broadsword.

The deck bucked to the twin detonations from Farrant's guns, and Ainslie had to duck as an enemy shell exploded almost simultaneously.

Forster had come up to the bridge to help con the submarine in conjunction with helm and guns.

He shouted wildly, 'God, one of them's down already!'

A stoker had dropped to his knees, fingers interlaced across his stomach, staring intently at the racing water along the saddle tank until he pitched forward and was swept away and down into the screws.

Deafened by gunfire, blinded by smoke and spray which burst over the bows as if they were diving, Halliday reached the hydroplane, his men searching for handholds while Cottier connected the cutter to the casing.

Halliday winced as several explosions flung water over the deck in solid waves.

'Be ready with jacks, lads!' He slapped Cottier's arm. 'Easy with that thing now!'

He peered into the frothing water below him. One slip and you were done for. Halliday found time to remember Ainslie's face as he had defied him on the bridge. After what he did for me, did he imagine I was going to let him lose his boat?

A fluke shell exploded in the air high above the submarine, raking her with splinters and whipping the sea around her into bursting spray.

Ainslie fell against the side, his ears ringing and every muscle tensed to withstand pain. In those few seconds he saw it all. Two tiny holes punched into a voice-pipe within inches of his mouth. A neat slit in his shirt and yet the splinter had not even bruised his skin. But just a few feet away a machine-gunner had been killed outright, hurled to the rear of the bridge by the savage impact.

Then he saw Menzies, the yeoman, lying on his back, his eyes fixed on the flag he had hoisted as his own gesture of defiance. He, too, was dead.

Forster limped through the drifting smoke, his face white with pain as he gripped his thigh, his trousers bunched into a red rag as he tried to stop the bleeding.

Ainslie seized him and pulled him against the vibrating steel, supporting him while he groped for a dressing.

Between his teeth Forster gasped, 'Oh, Christ!' He was trying to stay conscious, but the shock of his wound was sapping away his strength.

The bridge shook to another tremendous explosion from somewhere forward of the turret. Splinters rained across the conning tower like metal hail, and Ainslie realized that but for Forster leaning back for him to dress his wound they would both have been killed.

Forster was delirious, his head lolling from side to side as he murmured, 'I wanted to marry her, you know. I really did.'

Ainslie lowered him to the gratings and jammed his cap under his head as a pillow.

He said quietly, 'You will, Pilot. Believe me, you must.' He did not know why he had said it, or how he could find time to care. But it mattered, and he did care.

The last shell which had been fired by the other destroyer had exploded close to the turret. Splinters ripped through Southby's observation slit, killing him before he could cry out or know what had happened. Three of the men at the port gun had also dropped dead or were badly wounded, and one of the loaders was crawling below the breech, blinded and whimpering for help.

Farrant realized what had happened just as his mind recorded that the port gun was useless. Even if it could still fire, the risk of an internal explosion or a flash-back to the magazine outweighed any other value.

He also accepted that because of the damage the turret would have to be sealed by its lower hatches if or when the submarine

253

ever managed to dive. Anyone left inside would be drowned when the turret was flooded.

And yet in some strange way all of these things seemed unimportant when compared with one overriding fact. That last shell had cleared the turret's training mechanism. Maybe it had not been damaged by splinters as he had believed, but merely jammed by some metal blown from the casing.

He watched the destroyer move into his sights. It was perfect. Exact.

'Shoot!'

This time there was no error. A mushrooming orange flame burst through the destroyer's bridge, while funnels, boats and masts exploded in all directions around her.

Farrant sat back in his chair, almost relaxed as he began to train the turret towards the other destroyer. He felt satisfied, but strangely drowsy.

A gunlayer clambered up towards him, and after a brief glance at Southby's slumped body exclaimed, ' 'Ere, sir! You've bin 'it!'

Farrant regarded him glassily. 'I know that, you fool!' He steeled himself to look down at his legs. He was amazed he had lived this long, let alone feel no pain.

The gunlayer eyed him sadly. 'I'll stay an' give you a 'and, sir.'

And with the man holding him upright in his chair, Farrant continued to train the turret towards the enemy.

As the shadow of the two guns passed over the punctured casing, Halliday saw the buckled piece of metal fall away from the hydroplane and vanish into the submarine's bow wave.

His remaining helpers, an artificer, took his arm, and like two drunks they lurched aft towards the conning tower. The others lay dead where they had fallen, except for Cottier, who had died even as his cutter had released the last of the obstruction and had pitched overboard.

Halliday was in great pain, for he, too, had taken a splinter in his back. And yet he had kept going, with a sort of wildness mixed with a sense of pride as he had endeavoured to complete the work. Shock and loss of blood made the last steps to the conning tower blurred and meaningless. Halliday remembered little until he opened his eyes and discovered he was being carried through the control room towards the sick-bay. Somehow he cocked his head as he had done a million times to gauge the beat of the engines, *his* engines.

Through the mist of pain he saw Lucas staring after him and shouted, 'Can you take her, laddie? I'll not be much help. . . .'

Lucas saw the needle going into Halliday's arm and sighed. For an instant he had imagined Halliday was going to die, and he had realized just how much it meant to him that he should stay alive.

He looked at his men at the panel, the valves and dials which were the *Soufrière*'s means of life.

Halliday trusted him. And that was everything.

Quinton strode to the voice-pipe, his feet crunching on shattered glass and brushing against dazed and wounded men. There was even a stench of death down here, he thought.

'First lieutenant speaking, sir. Fore-planes tested and correct.' He could picture him above, gripping the bridge for support as the submarine maintained her charge towards the enemy. 'Are you all right?'

Ainslie answered, 'Yes. Thank you, John.'

He hesitated, and Quinton thought he had after all been hit. Then he added slowly, 'I'm just watching a miracle. The second destroyer is turning away from us. *They're all running,* John. Probably think we're after the troopers.' He gave a short laugh which sounded like a sob. 'With *what,* for God's sake?'

Quinton looked at Ridgway. 'Take over. I'm going up. Tell Hunt to clear the turret of anyone who is still alive.' As he made for the ladder he called, 'And then lay off a course to intercept the convoy.'

When he reached the bridge Quinton stood quite still for several seconds, scarcely able to believe that anyone could stay alive. Could all this have happened up here and there were some still able to see it, to speak of it?

Sprawled bodies, riddled plating, the fury of a battle.

Something touched his leg as he stepped carefully towards Ainslie, and when he looked down he saw Forster staring up at him. He was trying to grin, to show that he knew what was happening, what they had done together.

Quinton patted his shoulder then stood up to stare at the smoke on the water. A screen laid by the last warship or the damage from Farrant's shells, he neither knew nor cared.

Ainslie wiped his face with his forearm and said quietly, 'I used not to expect too much of miracles, John.' He shook his head. 'But after this, I don't know.'

'Any orders, sir? I've told Torps to lay off a course for the convoy. After that –'

Ainslie reached out and gripped his arm. Then he smiled, the shadows of battle dropping away completely as he said, 'After that, we're going home.'

Quinton understood and shared his feelings for what had happened. Against the fall of Malaya and Singapore their victory might not even register. But a convoy had survived and an impossible sacrifice had been made into a triumph, a symbol.

Soufrière had carried them all. Soon she would go to sea again, in other hands, and perhaps for different roles. But they would all remember her, and what they had achieved in one interlude of war.

A pale-faced lookout reported shakily, 'Torpedoman Sawle requests permission to come to the bridge, sir. Something to drink.'

Quinton grinned. 'Perfect timing.'

Moments later, with her two guns still pointing stiffly towards the horizon, *Soufrière*, the largest submarine in the world, altered course, leaving the smoke further and further astern.